PRAISE FOR
K

National Reader's Choice Award Finalist
Daphne du Maurier Award Finalist

"If you like your books sexy, but with a fabulous whodunit story line following a crime, then this is the book for you. It's much more than just a romance and I 100% recommend it." *-Buried Under Romance*

"Violet and Richard have been added to my favorite characters list. He felt very Darcy-ish to me and that is definitely a good thing. I loved their banter and the use of period expressions. As always with GC, the chemistry and heat were there in spades as well." -Ltlmer, *Goodreads*

"As always, Callaway delivers such steamyyy scenes...I loved the couple in this one! Violet's a total tomboy and is usually labeled "hoyden," while Carlisle is all propriety and sticks to the rules. Egads, I love the opposites attract trope."-Aila, *Goodreads*

"I couldn't have asked for a better book. Violet was perfect, the kind of girl you root for, not conventional, and Richard is a dream and her perfect match...funny and super hot." -Donna, *Goodreads*

"Pride & Prejudice with a murder mystery thrown into the mix and possibly the WORST proposal in history! I was entertained." -Skye, *Goodreads*

"This was so much fun!!! I absolutely love love/hate relationships. There was so much tension and chemistry between Violet and Richard...yet they were very much a fun couple. They were always bickering and with each interaction, the tension and heat rose higher and higher.... Their relationship was actually very Pride and Prejudice-like....The whole murder-at-a-house-party mystery made things so much fun for me. It felt like I was reading a romance novel and a cozy mystery novel at the same time." -*Romance Library*

"What a fun and fantastic read this was!....Violet was a hoot with her hoydenish ways and outrageous exploits. Richard was just perfect for her and it was so enjoyable to see how their relationship developed. I loved how Richard's insecurities from past rejections made him vulnerable. Then the murder mystery just added more entertainment to the plot. Did I mention how scorching hot the love scenes were? They were off the charts hot and steamy. This novel had me riveted and turning the e-pages as fast as I could." -Lily, *Goodreads*

"I read the first half of this book until 1 o'clock this morning then woke up at 6:30am to finish it so this should tell you how much I loved this book...I am never disappointed by anything I have read by Grace Callaway. She is an amazing historical romance author." - Michelle, *Goodreads*

"For me, this is the best book of the series so far. It is so exciting, with hot sexy scenes, and an unexpected murder mystery. I especially enjoyed how the relationship between Richard and Violet developed. This is a thrilling and delightful read - PERFECT!" -Elaine, *Goodreads*

ALSO BY GRACE CALLAWAY

LADY CHARLOTTE'S SOCIETY OF ANGELS

Olivia and the Masked Duke

Pippa and the Prince of Secrets

Fiona and the Enigmatic Ea

GAME OF DUKES

The Duke Identity

Enter the Duke

Regarding the Duke

The Duke Redemption

The Return of the Duke

HEART OF ENQUIRY (The Kents)

The Widow Vanishes (Prequel Novella)

The Duke Who Knew Too Much

M is for Marquess

The Lady Who Came in from the Cold

The Viscount Always Knocks Twice

Never Say Never to an Earl

The Gentleman Who Loved Me

MAYHEM IN MAYFAIR

Her Husband's Harlot

Her Wanton Wager

Her Protector's Pleasure

Her Prodigal Passion

THE *Viscount*

ALWAYS KNOCKS TWICE

HEART *of* ENQUIRY

GRACE CALLAWAY

USA *Today* Bestselling Author

Cover Design Credit: Erin Dameron-Hill/ EDH Graphics

Cover Image Credit: Period Images

At the Yuletide ball, Violet Kent was having the time of her life. She adored dancing, and her favorite partner was her friend Wickham Murray. Nobody spun her like Wick. His turns were so outrageous that, twice so far during the waltz, they'd veered within a hair's breadth of neighboring dancers before twirling away at the last possible second. Once, they'd actually crashed into a plaster column, laughing uproariously when it teetered.

Dancing was *tip-top*—as much fun as galloping through an open field or playing cricket with the lads back in Chudleigh Crest, the village where she'd lived most of her life. After her beloved papa's death three years ago, she and her four siblings had moved to London to be near their eldest brother Ambrose. For Vi, the transition to Town had been rocky, but she'd kept her chin up and eventually found a band of merry cronies much like the ones she'd had back home.

The number ended all too soon, and Wick escorted Vi off the dance floor. The fete was a crush, the *crème de la crème* herding into the festively decorated ballroom and grazing on the abundant food and drink. Wick steered her to one of the niches lining the room's perimeter. From an archway festooned with ivy and holly, she cast a furtive glance around the room; seeing no sign of her chaperoning family members, she expelled a sigh of relief and sank onto the red velvet bench, her butter-yellow skirts settling in a silken swish.

A bit more freedom before the watch comes looking, she thought.

Wick sat beside her and stretched out his long legs. "Fancy some lemonade or punch?"

"What I'd truly like is another dance," Vi said wistfully.

As always after physical activity, she felt at home in her own skin. Her heart pumped pleasantly; her mind—which her exasperated papa had compared to a frog leaping about on hot coals—was calm and clear. "But Emma will have my head if you and I dance for a third time. Of late, my sister has become an authority on proprieties."

"I suppose that's part and parcel of being a duchess?" Wick's hazel eyes twinkled.

Vi didn't bother to stifle a snort. "Seeing as Emma wed the most notorious rake in all of London, I fail to see how she's suddenly an expert on proper behavior."

At present, Violet resided with her eldest sister Emma and brother-in-law, the Duke of Strathaven, and she loved them both. Yet ever since Em had given birth to Olivia, she'd become even more of a mother hen—and she'd always been broody, having raised her younger siblings after their mama's death almost a dozen years ago. At present, Em fussed over Vi as if she were the same age as Olivia rather than the mature age of two-and-twenty.

"You're no longer in Chudleigh Crest," Emma would lecture. "Here in London, your tomboyish antics will land you in the suds. I'm not saying you need to change completely... but can't you curb your instincts a little, Vi? For your own good?"

Easier said than done, Vi thought ruefully. She tried, she really did, but curbing her instincts was like stopping the flow of the Thames. An impossible task.

There was no denying that she was the eccentric one in her family... which was saying *a lot*. As unconventional as her siblings might be, however, none of them had Violet's history of getting into scrapes. She didn't *mean* to fall from high perches (trees, fences, horses, et cetera), hit unintentional targets during slingshot practice (Tabitha, Em's cat, still held a grudge), or blurt out inappropriate things, yet trouble had a way of finding her.

Vi had learned to live with her own shortcomings. Whenever she did something mortifying without thinking, she'd learned to laugh and shrug the whole thing off. She simply kept her chin up and carried on. The last thing she wanted was for others—especially her family—to witness her embarrassment or hurt.

She'd never been a watering pot or one to wear her feelings on her sleeve. Pulling herself up by the slipper laces was her preferred strategy and one that she'd had to employ frequently since her three eldest siblings had all married titles, plopping the middling class Kents in the midst of the *ton*. In Society, one was expected to follow rules—a skill Vi could not claim as her forte. At times, she fancied herself an explorer in an exotic jungle, hopping from foot to foot to avoid the steaming pits of Scandal and Ruin.

"All older siblings are experts. Or, rather," Wick said with a touch of aspersion, "they *think* they are. My brother Carlisle being a case in point."

At the mention of Viscount Carlisle, anger ignited in Violet's chest, her gloved fingers curling in her lap. Typically, she didn't take offense easily and let bygones be bygones. But Wick's older brother had earned her hostility fair and square.

At a ball last month, the high and mighty viscount had been overheard making disparaging remarks about her, his callous words becoming fodder for gossip. Being fair-minded, Violet could understand if she'd actually done him wrong, but she and Carlisle had met only once before and briefly at that. She'd done *nothing* to deserve his scorn.

"I still haven't forgiven Carlisle for what he said about you." Wick ran a hand through his windswept brown locks, his ornate signet ring burnished by the light of the chandeliers. "Will you accept my apology on his behalf?"

Although Vi had no intention of forgiving Carlisle, she didn't want to place her friend in an awkward position. Wick complained frequently about Carlisle... but family was family, after all, and she didn't want to add to the tension between the brothers. Being a Kent, she understood loyalty and the impor-tance of kin.

Sighing, she said, "You don't have to apologize, Wick. *You* didn't say anything."

"But I feel responsible for my brother's rudeness. Ever since he lost the family fortune, he's been an ill-tempered tyrant." Wick's mouth took on a sullen edge. "If he had his way, I'd spend every waking moment heiress hunting. Can you believe he wants me to court the likes of Miss Turbett?"

"What's wrong with Miss Turbett?"

"Her name sounds like a fish. And she looks like one, too."

"That's unkind, Wick. She's quite nice." Vi had a passing acquaintance with the heiress, who seemed reserved but pleasant. "But the point is your brother isn't your keeper. You shouldn't have to marry someone unless you want to."

"Carlisle threatened to cut off my allowance if I don't do what he says," Wick said bitterly. "He wields the purse strings like a master puppeteer, and I'm but a hapless toy at his command."

"How *horrid* of him." Indignant on Wick's behalf, she said, "Must you rely on Carlisle's beneficence? Couldn't you make your own living somehow... find some sort of employment?"

"Egad, Violet, I'm a gentleman." Wick sounded aghast. "A gentleman doesn't *work*."

Vi frowned, thinking of her brother Ambrose. He'd wed one of the *ton*'s wealthiest widows, yet he continued to run a private enquiry business for the satisfaction of putting in a good day's work and delivering justice to those who most needed it. To Vi, this made Ambrose the epitome of a true gentleman, even if he didn't quite fit with Society's definition.

Mulling it over, Vi said, "If you can't work, perhaps you could economize?"

In the past, her family had known lean times, and she could recall many a meal where a loaf of bread and some cheese had been stretched to feed them all. Her belly rumbled at the memories.

"It wouldn't be sufficient." Color crept up Wick's jaw; his gaze slid away. "I suppose I'll have to pursue Miss Turbett and her twenty thousand after all."

"I'm sorry, Wick." Vi didn't know what else to say.

"There's no need for pity. An advantageous marriage will help not only me, but my family." He drew his shoulders back, the gold buttons of his blue waistcoat gleaming like miniature medals. "I'm willing to make the sacrifice for the good of all."

"That's awfully noble of you," Vi said admiringly. "You're a jolly fine chap."

She wished with all her being that she could help her friend, to whom she owed so much. Before Wick, the *ton* had been a lonely and hostile place. Subtlety wasn't her strong point, but even she couldn't miss the snubs of the other debutantes, the way their circles closed when she came near. Coy, overly loud voices had oft drifted in her direction.

... her gown is fashionable enough, but her manner—so unrefined! She's a veritable hoyden...

... I vow I've never seen a lady laugh with her mouth open so wide. She'll catch flies if she's not careful. And the way she eats, like a horse...

... that hurly-burly will never land a husband—unless one of her brothers-in-law can purchase one for her...

Violet had soldiered through those first months. Not wanting to worry her family (or give them further ammunition for lectures), she'd kept things to herself, silently repeating her motto:

pull yourself up by your slipper laces. She told herself that it didn't matter what others thought. But the snide glances and whispers had gradually doused her excitement at being in London, and she'd begun to dread social events... until Wick had come along.

Dear Wick—he'd changed everything. The two of them had hit it off from the start. He'd introduced her to his friends, and the jovial bunch had welcomed her into their fold.

With Wick and his cronies, she'd found a place of belonging. Being with him was as easy as being with her older brother Harry, who'd been her closest companion growing up. Wick was a ripping chum, and she was never bored in his presence. Best of all, be it a game of cards or a bet to see who could tolerate the most spins during a dance, he never let her win just because she was a female. He treated her as an equal, took her seriously. He didn't try to control or change her.

He accepted her; for that, he'd have her gratitude and friendship forever.

Now he gave a doleful shake of his head. "Enough palavering about my let pockets. You're so easy to talk to that sometimes I forget that you're a female—no, scratch that. What I mean is you're like one of the fellows... bloody hell." His mouth had a sheepish curve. "By the time this conversation is finished, I'll have dug a hole all the way to China."

"Bring back some tea, will you?" she quipped. "I'm particularly fond of the Souchong."

"Wretch." Wick's smile deepened. "Never mind my future prospects—what about yours? See anything of interest on the Marriage Mart tonight?"

Violet wrinkled her nose. To her, the prospect of marriage wasn't the least bit appealing. It would mean having one more person telling her what to do. Her family was overprotective as it was, and the last thing she needed was the added supervision of a husband.

Moreover, romantic attraction remained a mystery to her. It

was, she thought with a smidgen of worry, one more way in which she was different. One by one, her older siblings had fallen passionately in love—and she couldn't even figure out how to carry on a flirtation. Or *why* to.

Growing up, she'd found boys to be excellent co-conspirators in adventures, yet the notion of forming a *tendre* for one of them was... puzzling. She'd witnessed her companions engage in spitting contests, brawl in the mud, and scratch their unmentionable areas in the manner of flea-infested canines. They cussed in colorful terms (usually referencing the same unmentionable body parts) and seemed to find anything pertaining to chamber pots hysterically funny.

Then, as the lads had gotten older, the discovery of the opposite sex had turned them either into moonstruck greenlings or dedicated skirt-chasers. Wick was an excellent example of the latter. He was a charming rake through and through and thrived off female attention.

None of these male tendencies bothered Violet. They didn't make her want to *marry* one of the dolts, however. Freedom held far more appeal.

Rolling her eyes, she said, "You know I'm not shopping, Wick."

"How lucky you are," he said with such heartfelt emotion that she laughed. "Well, I'd best go troll the waters. Shall I return you to the loving bosom of your family?"

She cast a furtive glance around. Seeing that the coast remained clear, she decided she wasn't yet ready to surrender to the shackles of chaperonage. "I think I'll explore a little first."

"Suit yourself. But stay out of trouble, you hear?"

"Did the pot just call the kettle black?" she returned.

Exchanging grins, they went their separate ways.

Keeping to the potted palms and other concealing foliage, Vi trotted along, idly observing the revelry around her. Already she could sense the return of the restlessness that had bedeviled her since she was a child. She'd frustrated her scholarly papa to no end with her fidgeting and inability to focus on books and lessons. Unlike her brother Harry, who could work on mathematics problems forever, she felt ready to burst from her skin just moments after her bottom came into contact with a chair.

Luckily, one of her favorite forms of distraction caught her attention. She followed the tantalizing smells to the queue at the heavily laden buffet table. When it came to her turn, she happily inspected the offerings and took one of everything. She was finishing the last bit of a tasty mince tart when her gaze caught on a gleaming golden spire peeping above a row of potted ferns.

She headed over to investigate. Entering the ferny grove, she discovered that the spire was in fact the top of a champagne fountain that rose some twelve feet tall. A red-tinted beverage frothed from its three gold-plated tiers, and the bottom reservoir was wide enough to take a bath in.

Impressed, she went to the side table, exchanging her empty plate for a champagne flute. She was approaching the fountain to fill her glass when a deep masculine voice caused the hairs to prickle on her nape.

"Miss Kent, I'd like a word."

She pivoted, her eyes narrowing when she saw who'd joined her. As usual, Viscount Carlisle emanated an aura of arrogant authority, his booted stance quietly aggressive. Not for the first time, she was struck by the differences between the Murray brothers.

Whereas Wick resembled a gleaming young Apollo, Carlisle wore his coal-black hair short and possessed a swarthy and rugged mien. Topping six feet, the viscount was far taller than his younger brother and at least three stone heavier, all of it heaped on in uncompromising muscle. And while Wick had a charismatic smile, entertaining all with his rapier wit, Carlisle was more apt to hammer one down with a glowering look.

He bent at the waist; she returned the courtesy, matching her brusque motion to his.

"Lord Carlisle." The syllables rolled off her tongue like an epithet. "Hasn't anyone told you it isn't polite to sneak up on others?"

"Being neither a thief nor a highwayman, Miss Kent, I do not make a practice of sneaking up on anyone. I cannot be blamed if the other is simply not paying attention."

Her cheeks heated. It was just like Carlisle to make note of one of her lifelong faults.

To cover up her embarrassment, she said coldly, "I was about to get something to drink."

"I wouldn't get it there if I were you."

Her teeth ground together. She didn't like being told what to do—and least of all by some pompous *prig*. Turning her back to him, she marched to the fountain. Just as she held the flute out toward a stream of liquid, a loud belch rumbled from the fountain's depths. She looked up... and saw a red wave spewing directly over her head. Before she could react, a muscled arm hooked her around the waist, hauling her backward. Champagne splattered on the parqueted floor where she'd been standing but an instant earlier.

Shock sizzled through her. From the near escape, yes, but more so from the intimate contact with a man's physique. Although she'd done her fair share of dancing, none of her partners had ever touched her this way before. With her back molded against Carlisle's front, she felt every inch of his disciplined form: it was like being trapped against a wall of ridged iron.

She became aware of the warm brush of his breath against her ear, the heat of his surrounding strength. His scent entered her nose, clean and ineffably masculine. Simultaneously, she registered his steely thigh wedged against her bottom. Despite the layers between them, she shivered, a strange hot pulsing at her core. Even though she'd just eaten, pangs gnawed at her lower belly.

"Let me go," she managed.

He released her so quickly that she tottered before catching her balance.

"Gladly." His derisive tone wiped any gratitude for the rescue from her mind. He snatched the glass she'd forgotten she was holding and strode to the side table, taking undue time setting it down. When he returned, he said with a scowl, "I wish to speak to you."

"About what?" *Why do I sound so breathless?*

"About the fact that you are monopolizing Wickham's time."

It took a moment for the words to sink in. When they did, she glared at him and said, "I'm doing no such thing."

"I saw you dancing with him. Flirting with him." Carlisle's lips flattened into a hard line. "Leave him be, Miss Kent, for he has bigger fish to fry."

He thought she was *flirting*... and with *Wick*?

She said incredulously, "He's like a brother to me."

"Well, he *is* my brother, and I'm telling you to leave him alone. He needs his focus."

"You mean he has to clean up the mess *you* made," she retorted without thinking.

"I beg your pardon?"

His blistering tone would have incinerated a lesser miss on the spot. For some reason, it just angered her more. "You're not being fair to Wick." She crossed her arms. "He has the right to make his own decisions."

Hostility smoldered in Carlisle's eyes. They were the color of scorched earth: black with glints of bronze ore. His hands fisted at his sides, muscles bunching beneath the sleek skin of his jacket as if he were struggling to hold onto his self-control.

"My family is my business," he stated with grim finality. "Stay away from my brother."

"Wick is my friend, and I'll spend time with him if I wish. What do you have against me, anyway?" Her resentment broke free. "Why did you spread such vile rumors about me?"

The crest of his broad cheekbones reddened, but he said emotionlessly, "I spread no rumors, Miss Kent. Some old hens eavesdropped on a private conversation."

"You called me a hoyden. Said I'm *barely respectable*."

"That is not what I said."

"So you *did* say something." She pounced on the admission. "At least be man enough to repeat it to my face."

A muscle ticked along his jaw. "You're a female. You can't handle the truth."

She didn't know what irked her more, his misogynistic assumption or his dismissive tone. Steam gathered in her head, threatening to pop it off altogether. "Dash it all, I *can*."

"Fine. What I said was that my brother requires a wife who can keep him in line, and you're not suited for the job. I said that you can't spell propriety let alone put it into practice," he said succinctly.

For an instant, she was speechless.

"You uppity *blighter*." She could barely think over the roar in her ears. "You don't know me! You have no right to sit in judgment."

"I call it as I see it, Miss Kent. Once I form an opinion, I rarely have cause to alter it."

His calm superiority enraged her past the point of rationality. "Well, you're *wrong*. I can spell propriety, you condescending bastard! *P-R-O-P-R-E-I-T-Y*."

For pulsing moments, she glared at him: she'd be damned if she was the one to look away first. But the oddest thing happened. Lines suddenly fanned from the corners of Carlisle's eyes. Flecks of copper glinted in the dark depths. The stern line of his mouth quirked.

He was... *laughing* at her? Why on earth...?

She reviewed what she'd said—and her face flamed. Butter and jam, Papa had always said that her terrible spelling would prove her downfall. The realization of her stupidity was followed by a swift and forceful undertow of humiliation. All at once, her armor of indifference crumpled, and she felt the blow of each and every insult she'd ever been subjected to.

Hurly-burly... hoyden... never land a husband... The smirking glances of the other debutantes, her family's worried expressions...

A muffled sound escaped Carlisle. The past faded, everything narrowing to the incendiary present: the cad was *laughing* at her. Mortification met fury and combusted.

"Don't you dare make fun of me," she said through clenched teeth.

His wide shoulders shook.

She took a step closer, jabbed a finger at him. "I'm warning you. *Stop laughing.*"

He held his big hands up in defense. "Or what, Miss Kent?" Mockery glinted in his eyes. "You'll spell me into submission?"

Red saturated her vision. Her hands acted of their own volition, shooting upward, planting on his chest. They gave a shove—and time suddenly slowed. She had the sensation of watching from the outside as Carlisle stumbled, surprise rippling across his face as he lost his footing in a puddle of champagne, his large body falling backward like a felled tree...

The thudding splash brought her to her senses. In stupefied horror, she took in Carlisle sitting on his behind in the fountain. Blood-red champagne rained merrily over his head and shoulders.

Gadzooks, what have I done?

She took a halting step toward him... stopped at the hellfire raging in his eyes.

He growled, "Get out of here. *Now.*"

Panic made her obey. She dashed out the back of the grove, slipping between two potted ferns, walk-running until she reached the safety of the crowd. Like a criminal, she continued to sneak glances behind her, her heart thumping and mind whirling with the latest calamity she'd caused.

Richard Murray, Viscount Carlisle, jolted awake. Angry voices sounded... some fracas in the street. As Cheapside's thoroughfare was just a few blocks away, such disturbances were not unusual, but it didn't make them any less annoying. Richard stared through the dimness at a crack in the ceiling, his mood darkening further when he realized that he sported, at present, a raging morning cockstand.

With an aggrieved sigh, he sat up. The bedclothes slipped down his bare torso, bunching at his waist and catching on his erection. Shoving his hands through his hair, he raised his knees, resting his elbows there and willing the insistent throbbing of his groin to subside.

"Insolent little baggage," he muttered. "This is all her fault."

He had no doubt that Miss Violet Kent was responsible for the state of his mind and body. Regarding the former, what man wouldn't be furious at being assaulted—*pushed* into a bloody fountain and by a mere chit at that? Under normal circumstances, her little tap wouldn't have budged him, but she'd taken him by surprise and then he'd slipped in that goddamned puddle...

Embarrassment scalded his gut. In all honesty, the fact that a close encounter with a female had resulted in him emerging a fool should come as no surprise. In his dictionary, women were synonymous with trouble. Miss Lucinda Belton and Lady Audrey Keane had taught him that lesson long ago. In fact, they'd schooled him so well that he'd avoided entanglements with respectable ladies altogether.

Whenever he required female companionship, he purchased it. A simple exchange and one in which both parties left satisfied. In bed, he dealt with women just fine.

Outside of bed, however, they were a damned nuisance. All he'd wanted was for Violet Kent to leave his brother alone: was that too much to ask? Instead, she'd made him the laughingstock of the party.

Well, he'd refused to give the *ton* the blood they wanted, the satisfaction of seeing his humiliation. He'd exited the gilded arena as if he weren't dripping with champagne. As if his bloody boots weren't squishing with every step. He'd walked out of there as if nothing had been out of the ordinary, and he'd managed that by focusing on varied and creative ways of retribution.

Bending Violet Kent over his knee, for instance.

Unfortunately, that led to his second—and persistently throb-bing—problem.

He ought to have let her get doused by the fountain, he thought savagely. That would have served the little romp right. But, oh no, he'd had to obey his instinct to pull her out of harm's way. The resulting jolt of lust had been his own damned fault.

He chalked it up to animal urges. What red-blooded man wouldn't respond to the wriggling of a pertly rounded derriere against his groin? It was only primal instinct that had caused the lurid image to blaze in his head: of bending Miss Kent over the nearest surface, tossing up her cheerful yellow skirts, spreading her sleek thighs and...

He glanced down; to his disgust, his shaft now tented the sheet.

Just bloody perfect.

Throwing off the bedcovers, he stalked over to the table holding the basin and ewer, grimacing as his aroused flesh bobbed heavily with every step. He splashed icy water onto his face and, gripping the edges of the rickety washstand, waited for the room's drafty chill to cool his blood. Although there was a more appealing way of discharging the problem, he refused to yield to the primitive impulse.

Self-discipline and rationality were his ruling principles. From experience, he'd learned to distrust his emotional reactions when it came to the opposite sex and relied instead on his intellect to guide his decisions. Despite his body's inexplicable reaction to Miss Kent, he told himself he had only one objective pertaining to the chit: to keep her out of his brother's life.

The thought of Wickham smothered the remnants of his arousal. Knots tightened in Richard's gut as he yanked on a tattered robe. His younger brother knew nothing of restraint and was infinitely susceptible to the dangers of the opposite sex. And Wick was up to his ears in hot water already.

For Wick was in debt—and this time, Richard hadn't the coin to pay it off. Wick's only hope of staying afloat was marrying an heiress. To that end, Richard had spent no small effort in securing a lifeboat for his brother. He'd paved the way with Alfred Turbett, a wealthy merchant. All Wick had to do was take that last step and propose to the man's daughter.

Which Wick wouldn't do if he remained mesmerized by Violet Kent.

Richard was intimately acquainted with Miss Kent's type, all right. She was a shallow flirt who waltzed her way through life with no care for consequences. She thrived on male attention, gave no damn about anything but herself and her own pleasure. The brazen minx would have Wick wrapped around her little finger—and then, when her fun was done, she'd toss him away like last season's slippers.

Over my dead body, Richard thought fiercely.

He rang for Bartlett; the valet was one of the few servants he retained in this small house he rented. Reduced circumstances had made such economies necessary. He was not a man to live beyond his means; if only he could say the same of his brother.

He had just sat down for breakfast in the small and shabby parlor when Wickham sauntered in. The latter was still dressed in last evening's clothing—typical, seeing as the young rakehell never went to bed before dawn. Also typical was the fact that despite whatever debauchery Wick had been engaged in, he still managed to emerge looking like a Greek god.

Shadows accented Wick's long-lashed hazel eyes, the hollows beneath his sculpted cheekbones. His golden brown curls were fashionably rumpled. Their mama had been a famous beauty in her day, and Wick took after her in looks and temperament—the opposite of Richard, who resembled their father and all the viscounts before him.

A stroll through the family gallery showed a line of dark, swarthy men with the hulking bodies of peasants and the glowering disposition of Hephaestus. Unfortunately, like that humble god of the smithy, they were also attracted to their natural opposites—dazzling, vibrant Aphrodites—which had led to a family legacy of disastrous unions.

Staid and vivacious never made for a good match.

"No need to get up on my account, old boy," Wick said. "Thought I'd stop by and join you for a spot of breakfast. Though I had the devil's time getting here. Don't know what you were thinking leasing this hellhole."

"It's Cheapside, not the Ninth Circle—" A pungent odor tickled Richard's nostrils, and he sneezed. Twice. "Holy hell, what is that smell?"

"What smell?"

Eyes watering, Richard said, "The noxious odor that suggests you rolled in a field of lily of the valley before diving into a vat of musk."

Wick sniffed at his jacket. "Ah, that. Must have rubbed off on me. It's French," he added in lofty tones, "and expensive."

Seeing the smudges of rouge on his brother's collar, Richard said dourly, "Are you referring to the perfume or the tart who wore it?"

"Both," Wick said with a smirk.

Given the strain between him and Wick of late, Richard refrained from pointing out that costly trollops, French or not, were well beyond Wick's means. A lecture on fiscal responsibility would only alienate his brother further. Besides, he remained wary of his brother's purpose in calling.

Wick left before the mishap, he told himself. *It's possible that he doesn't know what happened.*

Going to the sideboard, Wick let out an aggrieved sigh. "Kippers and eggs *again*? How're such meager offerings supposed to fuel a fellow for the day?"

"If you don't like it, don't eat it." Richard forked up eggs.

Setting down a plate piled high, Wick took an adjacent seat at the table. "So you don't look any worse for the wear."

Damnation. He decided to bluff his way through. "And why should I?"

Wick gave him an innocent look. "Because of the *splash* you made last night?"

Heat crawled up Richard's jaw. "It was an accident."

"Accidentally got tap-hackled, did you?"

"I wasn't drunk."

"Then how the bloody hell did you take a tumble into a *fountain*?" his sibling chortled.

Devil take Violet Kent. Richard's face burned. Yet he couldn't reveal the truth of what had happened. First of all, he'd slit his own throat before admitting that he'd been downed by a female— and a slip of a miss at that. Second, his sense of honor precluded him from incriminating a lady, which was precisely why he'd instructed her to flee the scene of the crime.

Beneath his seething anger, he also felt an uneasy flicker of... guilt. In a way, he supposed he owed it to her to protect her reputation after the gossip he'd inadvertently started about her. He regretted that his private conversation with his friend Blackwood had been overheard and circulated by the wags. His worry over Wickham had prompted him to speak brashly, causing Miss Kent unintentional harm.

Her face rose in his imagination: the high, creamy slope of her cheeks and her tip-tilted eyes, which were the rich, tawny shade of his favorite whiskey. Her bee-stung mouth was too generous for her face, the bottom lip particularly full. A retroussé nose added to her air of feminine mischief and merriment.

In and of themselves, her features were not beautiful, but together they exuded an undeniable appeal, a vividness that made it difficult for one to look away. She wasn't Aphrodite, but Aglaea, one of the Three Graces, the embodiment of glowing good health and vitality. Grudgingly, Richard had to admit that Violet Kent's attractions went beyond skin deep, stirring a dangerous, primal response in him. And if her charms were not lost on him—a sensible, level-headed man—then what untold peril did she pose to his hapless brother?

"Never mind the bloody fountain," Richard said abruptly. "There are more important matters to discuss. How did things go with Miss Turbett last eve?"

In a blink, Wick's merriment turned to sullenness. Richard bit back a sigh. He ought to be used to his brother's lightning shifts in mood by now, but somehow he wasn't. Somehow in his mind Wickham was still the tow-headed boy who'd followed him everywhere and took his word as gospel. The younger brother who'd worshipped him—and whom he'd protected in turn.

But ever since their papa's death six years ago, things had changed. Wickham had transformed from a fun-loving lad to a wild and reckless rake. The worst of it was that any advice or solutions Richard had given had only made Wick surly and resentful... until all possibility of rational discourse was gone.

Thus, Richard had resorted to leveraging the last means available to him. He'd threatened to cut off Wick's quarterly stipend—and only source of income—if Wick didn't take gainful steps toward discharging his debt of ten thousand pounds. Owed to a *moneylender*, for God's sake.

Richard's temples throbbed. If only he hadn't been preoccupied by the financial quagmire left by their father, he could have kept a better eye on Wick. Stopped the whelp from frittering away an astronomical sum and jeopardizing his future in the process—

"I danced with Miss Turbett once. She had all the charm of a dead fish," Wick said, his chin lifting belligerently, "and the conversation of one, too."

"It's not her charm or conversation you're after: it's her twenty thousand pounds. Devil take it, you agreed to this." Richard's jaw clenched in frustration. "I met with Turbett and cleared your path to courting his daughter. You should count yourself fortunate that he's willing to take you on for the connection to our family. Miss Turbett's fortune is your only hope for salvation."

"I don't want to marry that antidote of a female, and you can't make me."

"By Jove, stop acting like a child." Richard's grip on his temper slipped. "Don't you comprehend the danger you're in? Your moneylender isn't some merchant who will wait patiently at the tradesmen's entrance to get paid. Garrity is a *cutthroat*: if you don't make good on your debt, you'll be parting with more than your good name. He'll take his pound of flesh—literally."

Wick paled but recovered quickly.

"This is all your fault," he shot back, angrily swiping jam onto his bread. "If you'd gone into the canal venture with me, we'd both be rich as Croesus. I could pay off my debts, and the family estate wouldn't be teetering on the brink of ruin. But you refused, and I hadn't the coin to go at it alone. Therefore, *you* brought this situation upon our heads." He pointed his knife at Richard, the initials of his gold signet ring flashing with accusation. "And Mama agrees with me."

Of course she does. Guilt churned, which only heightened Richard's frustration. He'd done the best he could, yet he knew full well that their mother hadn't forgiven him for putting limits on her expenditures. She'd made her displeasure quite clear in her scathing correspondence.

Your papa would turn over in his grave if he knew how you were treating me. He'd never forgive you... and neither will I. I can only regret giving birth to such an ungrateful child.

As was her wont, Mama had glossed over the truth: Papa had paupered himself and the estate trying to keep her in her accustomed style, and, in the end, the stress of it had killed him. He'd died, face-down in a ledger book, his heart collapsing from the weight of his debts.

And he'd left Richard to clean up the mess.

Over the past year, Richard had sold his own personal possessions, including his hunting lodge and stables to clear the debts. With severe budgetary measures and estate reform, he was managing, just barely, to keep the family seat afloat. He'd had no choice but to curtail his mama's spending—not that she'd listened to his explanations. Her preference was to shoot the messenger.

"The accord between you and Mama doesn't make either of you right," Richard said wearily. "I couldn't risk the estate on a canal scheme, and you know it. My man of business and I researched the proposition thoroughly. The chance of such a venture yielding profits was extremely low."

"But this one *did*. And because you didn't listen to me, I'm bloody doomed! Why should I have to marry some nitwit because *you* didn't do the right thing?" Wick's high cheekbones reddened. "Why am I the one who must suffer in all of this?"

Richard could scarce credit his brother's twisted reasoning. Nor the fact that Wick believed that he was the only one to face unpleasant consequences. Richard had dismantled his stables, the breeding program he'd spent years building. All that remained, that he could not bring himself to auction off at Tattersall's with the rest, was his personal mount Aiolos.

He was not a sentimental man, but he hadn't been able to part with the Thoroughbred. Guilt panged. Now the old boy was trapped in stables as dilapidated as Richard's own lodgings, their exhilarating gallops through the countryside curtailed to sedate trots in Hyde Park.

"Your debt is your own failing—not mine," Richard said quietly. "You had choices other than marriage. Years ago, I offered to purchase you a commission or set you up in a respectable profession." With Wick's easy charm, good looks, and ready wit, he could have been anything he wanted. "But you refused."

"Can you honestly see me marching to the drum? Or preaching some sermon or mucking about in the courts? I'm a *gentleman*."

"You'll be a dead gentleman if you don't pay Garrity off soon. And this time, brother," Richard said flatly, "I cannot help you."

Wick said nothing, his expression mulish, yet his hand trembled as he reached for his teacup. Fear stiffened his normally indolent posture. Richard pressed his advantage home.

"There's still time to remedy the situation. Turbett and his daughter will be at a house party in Hertfordshire two weeks hence. He's secured us invitations as well. He's willing to give you a final chance to come up to scratch."

"Secured *us* invitations?" Sarcasm dripped from Wick's words. "He's in trade, for Christ's sake. I sincerely doubt we'd aspire to attend an event thrown by one of his mercantile cronies."

"Nonetheless, we will be going." As much as Richard detested house parties, he would go to secure Wickham's future. And, he thought with resignation, to deal with his own. He might have staved off disaster, but the estate would need more income to ensure its long-term health.

"The host of the party, Billings, is a wealthy banker. He has a daughter," he said.

Wick's expression lost its surly cast, and for an instant, he resembled the younger brother Richard had always known.

"Never say *you* are considering matrimony?" Wick's brows shot toward his hairline. "You, whose portrait currently appears next to the word 'bachelorhood' in the dictionary? You, who once said you'd rather clean all the stables in the kingdom than be leg-shackled to a female?"

After the fiascoes with Miss Belton and Lady Keane, Richard had sworn off respectable females. That business had taken place years ago, however. He was no longer a greenling who expected a lady to want to marry him for any reason other than his title. Marriage for him would be a bloodless exchange: her money for his status. He'd lead by example and teach Wick that courtship could be a pragmatic endeavor free of sentimental complications.

"One does what one needs must," he said severely.

"God's blood, I do believe you are serious," Wick breathed.

"I am. So you see, brother, we're in this together."

Wickham shrugged, but at least he offered no further argument. Richard took the other's acquiescence as a good sign, and it renewed his resolve to see Wick settled. He would personally deal with any obstacles to his sibling's future contentment—which meant that a certain troublesome miss had better stay out of his way.

✣ 3 ✣

Guilt, Violet discovered to her dismay, had a way of disrupting one's concentration. God knew that she didn't need further intrusions upon her focus, yet thoughts of Carlisle assailed her in the week following the Yuletide ball. Never a sound sleeper, she tossed and turned more than usual at night. Her appetite was diminished. During her daily activities—lessons, shopping expeditions, even rides through the park—she found herself wrestling with her conscience.

Was what happened my fault... when he was being such a boor?

Her sense of fair play invariably won out. For no matter how arrogant and condescending Carlisle had been, he didn't deserve the ridicule he now faced.

Every gossip and tattle rag in Town seemed obsessed with his downfall. He'd become the butt of jokes—in fact "The Butt of a Joke" was the caption used over a caricature of the viscount sitting on his derriere in a fountain, knees splayed, being drenched by a torrent of champagne. Other similar cartoons included *How to Make a Splash in Society* and *Pride Goeth Before a Fall*. Worse yet, the lampoons depicted Carlisle as a scowling giant, his rough-hewn features viciously exaggerated.

Every time Violet encountered the consequences of her impulsivity, her insides twisted. *Act in haste, repent in leisure* as Mama had been wont to say. She was ten when her mother died, and at times like this she missed the other more than ever. For Mama had been the one person who'd truly understood Vi's nature; she'd never lost her patience or gotten exasperated with her middle child's antics.

Heavens, my girl, you're like a pot about to boil over, Marjorie Kent would say with a warm twinkle in her eyes. *Let's put that steam to work, shall we?*

Then she'd send Violet off to do some chore. After weeding the garden or milking the family cow, Vi would always feel better.

But Mama wasn't here now, and Violet was so ashamed of what she'd done that she couldn't bring herself to confide in her other family members. The thought of their reaction—the *I-told-you-so* looks and lectures, not to mention the increased chaperonage—bolstered her motivation to keep the matter under wraps. Which made her feel even guiltier.

When Emma had asked about the telltale red champagne splattered on Vi's skirts, Vi had mumbled some shoddy excuse, saying that she'd walked by the scene of the accident. Even though Em let the matter drop, Vi's distress manifested itself in worse than usual distraction, which her sister and the others, not knowing the true cause, remarked upon with growing annoyance.

Never a favored pupil amongst her tutors, she was even less focused than usual during her weekly lessons. She made poor Monsieur Le Roche tear at his wispy hair, and she feared he'd be bald before she learned to conjugate a French verb. She fared no better at her music lesson: Master Fromm had stormed out, declaring that he would have better luck teaching a pig to play the pianoforte.

He was probably right... although she would have liked to have seen him attempt the latter. Just for novelty's sake. With a private snicker, she'd wondered who would be more annoyed at the undertaking: Master Fromm or the swine?

By week's end, Violet's natural equilibrium returned. Bit by bit, her guilt had eased; the gossip about Carlisle had begun to die down, replaced by some newer, juicier tidbit, and she told herself that what was done was done. She couldn't undo her actions, and, thus, there was but one solution. She would offer Carlisle her most sincere apologies whenever they next met.

And that, she concluded with a mental dusting of her hands, would be that.

Her spirits were further lifted by a visit. She and her youngest sister Polly raced down the stairwell to greet their sister-in-law Marianne, niece Primrose, and Miss Billings, a family friend. Emma had refreshments served in the main salon, a room with a soaring ceiling and lush green furnishings. They all took seats around the coffee table and accepted cups of fragrant tea from Emma. Vi also helped herself to a plate of iced cakes from Gunter's, her favorite confectionary.

"Lud, Violet, how can you eat like that and never gain an ounce?" Marianne said. A stunning silver blonde, Ambrose's wife patted a hand over her own willowy form, impeccably displayed in a promenade dress of dove grey silk. "I daresay I would resemble one of those hot-air balloons they launch at Vauxhall if I had your appetite."

"I'm hungry," Violet said around a mouthful of marzipan-covered sponge.

"You're always hungry." Perched next to Marianne on the settee, Em shook her head, her brunette curls gleaming. "When it comes to food, your stomach brings to mind the Pit of Tartarus from Greek lore."

Vi had never been good at the classics. "What's the Pit of Tartarus?"

"A bottomless abyss," Marianne said dryly, and everyone laughed.

Violet gave a good-natured shrug. One couldn't take offense when something was true. Polishing off a buttery lemon tart, she said, "If they had these in Tartarus, I'd jump right in. You really ought to try one."

"Mama and I are off to Madame Rousseau's for a fitting afterward, so I shan't risk it," said Primrose, Marianne's eighteen-year-old daughter. "With the descending waistlines this Season, gowns aren't nearly as forgiving, and no amount of tight lacing will erase a plate of cakes."

Rosie, as the girl was affectionately known, had inherited not only her mother's fair beauty but also the other's wit and self-confidence. Since Marianne's marriage to Ambrose a decade earlier, the Kents had considered Rosie one of their own. She'd formed a particular connection with Polly, who was the same age. The two girls presently shared a chaise, their arms linked and pale muslin skirts overlapping like petals of a single flower.

"You always look beautiful, Rosie," Polly said with quiet sincerity.

Rosie's jade-colored eyes danced. "You're a dear for saying that, but I'd rather not be squeezed like a sausage into a corset if I can help it."

"I'll have a cake." The pink ruffles on Gabriella Billings' bodice fluttered as she shrugged. "Since I'm a sausage anyway, I have nothing to lose."

"That's not true, Gabby. You're lovely," Emma protested.

"I have freckles and hair the color of carrots..."

Violet was distracted by the arrival of Tabitha, Em's grey striped cat. Ever since an unfortunate slingshot incident, Vi had been trying to get back into the feline's good graces. She held out a bit of cake as a peace offering; Tabby turned her nose up at it and curled up next to Em.

"... what harm is a piece of cake going to do?" Gabby finished.

Hearing the word "cake," Vi obligingly passed the silver tray of confections to her friend.

"Violet." Emma gave her a chiding glance.

"What?"

"Cake isn't the point."

To Vi, cake was always the point. With the tray held out, she said, puzzled, "It isn't?"

"Gabby is concerned about her looks," Em said pointedly.

"Oh." Vi looked at Gabby. With her ginger curls and bright blue eyes, the other girl looked like a friendly wood sprite. She was one of the few truly nice girls Vi had met in London, and that gave her indisputable appeal in Vi's book. "Why? You're pretty."

"You're ever so kind." Gabby's smile was tremulous. Using the silver tongs, she selected a slice of black currant cake (an excellent choice—Vi could vouch from experience). "I'm sorry to carry on like this. I think my nerves are frazzled because I'll be hosting my first house party in just a week." She ate a forkful of cake, mumbling, "I hope I do it correctly."

"Generosity and kindness are the marks of any successful hostess. And you, my dear Gabby," Marianne said, "have both in spades. You have nothing to worry about."

"I wish that were true. Father has spared no expense for the fete. He purchased a whole new wardrobe for me and jewels to match."

"I read about your jewels in the papers; the auction at Rundell's was quite a to-do, wasn't it? Were those *divine* pearls part of the collection?" Rosie said brightly.

Touching the lustrous strand around her neck, Gabby gave a glum nod. "You should see the sapphire necklace. It was owned by a *comtesse* of something or another, and I feel like an utter imposter wearing it. But the jewels are the least of it. Father's had an amphitheatre built to showcase the entertainment. He's hired The Great Nicoletti to perform magic tricks, and there's a troupe coming from Astley's—"

"Astley's?" Violet's mind had drifted off during the jewelry discussion, but now she bolted upright. "As in *the* Astley's Amphitheatre?"

"The one and only. Madame Monique and others will be performing."

"*Gadzooks*," Violet breathed.

Excitement blazed through her. She adored Astley's—and Monique Le Magnifique, the famed French acrobat, was her ultimate idol. "That's smashing news! I cannot wait to meet Madame Monique. Do you think she'll share the secrets behind how to stand on a moving horse or how to balance on a tightrope—"

"Have a seat, dear," Marianne said mildly, "and let Gabby finish."

Violet hadn't realized that she'd risen. She sat again, her heart thumping. *Meeting Madame Monique in the flesh. Absolutely brilliant!* Through the years, she'd practiced countless moves inspired by the acrobat; she wondered if the diva would mind giving her some tips.

"... Father wants me to be a success ever so much, but the fact is I'm just a wallflower," Gabby was saying. "What if nobody deigns to come to my party?"

Understanding suddenly perforated Violet's delight. Gabby's father was a banker whose fortune came from clients who were, well, a bit unsavory. In fact, while the Kents adored Gabby, they were not fans of Mr. Billings, whom they'd first met during the course of a murder investigation. With his wealth, Billings could purchase his daughter's entrée into the upper echelons, but acceptance was another matter altogether.

The banker's background and lack of blue blood made him and his daughter parvenus in the eyes of the *ton*, who treated them with barely disguised scorn. In fact, some cruel wit had saddled Gabby with the title of "Paper Princess" due to her papa's trade in banknotes. Like Violet, Gabby knew what it was like to be an outsider.

Vi summoned a teasing grin for her friend. "What are *we*—chestnuts? We Kents will be there in full regalia to support you. Even Thea and Tremont will be coming, although they'll arrive a bit late."

Thea, the second eldest Kent sister, had recently married the Marquess of Tremont. Given the adventures that had brought the pair together, they'd opted to spend their honeymoon rusticating at Tremont's country seat.

"We wouldn't miss your fete for the world," Rosie chimed in. "We *adore* parties."

"Society is agog to see what has been done to Traverstoke since the Earl of Woldier sold it to your father," Marianne said. "I predict you'll be bursting at the seams with houseguests, albeit curious ones."

"I don't care if they're curious—only that they *come*. I'm so grateful to all of you. I'm terribly afraid of disappointing Father: he wants so badly for me to make a splash."

"Be careful what you wish for." Eyes sparkling with mischief, Rosie said, "Or haven't you heard about the most recent *splash* in Society?"

Violet's stomach plummeted. *Crumbs. Not this again.*

"You mean Viscount Carlisle?" Gabby said, an odd note in her voice.

Rosie's golden ringlets bobbed as she nodded, giggling.

"It's not funny. It isn't Christian to laugh at another's misfortune," Vi blurted.

All eyes turned to her.

Em blinked. "Well, I suppose that's true. But usually you're the first one to laugh at the ridiculous, Violet."

"Carlisle's not ridiculous. He just slipped and fell..." Violet's face heated; she bit the inside of her cheek to stop herself from revealing more.

"I didn't say *he* was ridiculous, just the fact that a grown man managed to tumble into a fountain." Emma's head tipped to the side, her clear brown gaze narrowing. "You weren't somehow... *involved* in the incident, were you? At the time, we were looking all over for you, and you were nowhere to be found."

Vi didn't like the keen look in her sister's eyes. Before becoming a duchess, Em had aspired to join Kent and Associates, Ambrose's private enquiry firm. In fact, it was during the course of Em's first investigation that she had captured Strathaven's eye and his heart. Even now, with her husband's permission—and, on occasion, without his knowledge—she participated in the odd case.

Vi tried not to squirm. "Like I said before, I witnessed some of it, but I didn't linger." *I hightailed it out of there as fast as I could.* "I just don't think it's fair to laugh at the man."

Marianne's lips thinned with distaste. "I wouldn't think you'd defend Carlisle, of all people. After the abominable rumors he started—why, Ambrose had half a mind to call him out."

"So did Strathaven," Em said, "but doing so would have damaged Vi's reputation further. It was best to ignore the whole thing and let it blow over. Which it has, thank heavens. Otherwise His Grace would have had Carlisle's head on a spike—and I would have encouraged it."

"You always were a bloodthirsty thing, pet," a deep masculine voice said.

Strathaven entered the room. He was tall, dark, and wickedly handsome, his debonair image somewhat marred by the dark-haired baby girl in the crook of his arm. With a chubby fist wrapped around one end of His Grace's cravat, little Olivia tugged with stubborn insistence, cheerfully drooling all the while.

"Speaking of bloodthirsty, Livy is murdering your cravat." Emma held out her arms. "You'd best give the little imp to me."

As Strathaven handed over the babe, his knuckles brushed with casual intimacy against his wife's cheek. "I thought she might be lonely so I got her from the nursery."

"Lonely? With the army of nursemaids you hired to look after her?" Emma slanted a mischievous look at her husband and said in conspiratorial tones to their daughter, "Who was the lonely one, poppet—you or Papa?"

Livy flashed a toothless grin. An instant later, she grabbed at Emma's bodice.

"Ma ma ma," she said.

"By God, she's *talking*." Strathaven looked thunderstruck—as if his offspring had just recited a sonnet.

"She's hungry," Emma said ruefully. "I had better get Her Highness fed."

"On that note, Rosie and I must be off as well, or we'll be late for our fitting." Marianne rose, her daughter following suit. "We look forward to your party, Gabby."

The Strathavens and Kents departed, leaving Violet with Polly and Gabby.

"I wish someone would look at me the way His Grace looks at your sister," Gabby said wistfully into the quiet room.

"He loves her very much," Polly agreed. "I always knew he did, even before..." She trailed off, biting her lip.

"Before what?" Gabby asked.

Seeing her sister's flustered expression, Vi knew that Polly didn't want to reveal her uncanny ability to read other people's emotions. Back in Chudleigh Crest, Polly's acuity had led others to consider her a bit "strange," something she feared more than anything.

"Seeing as we Kents always marry for love," Vi said hastily, "it wasn't hard to guess that Emma and Strathaven would wind up a love match."

Polly sent her a grateful look.

"A love match. I see." Gabby sighed.

An odd pang struck Vi. She'd spoken the truth: Kents did marry for love, and, consequently, she'd been surrounded by passionate couples all her life. Yet why hadn't *she* encountered love's magic? She'd spent a good deal of time in the company of boys, but she'd never felt that mysterious—and supposedly irresistible—pull of attraction.

Quite frankly, she'd never understood what all the fuss was about.

Out of nowhere, Carlisle intruded upon her mind's eye. His stern, rugged features... his large and unyielding physique. Sensation washed over her: the rush of being contained by his rigid strength, his manly scent filling her nose, his breath coasting warmly over her ear...

Gadzooks, what's the matter with you? Why are you thinking such things? Bewildered, she realized that her pulse was racing—as if she'd run a race or climbed a tree.

"I have some bad news to share," Gabby announced. "About Carlisle."

Vi twitched. "Um, pardon?"

"He'll be at my party."

Butter and jam, Carlisle and I are going to be trapped together in the same house... for an entire week? Horror flooded Vi.

"What is more, Father says that I must be extra nice to him. Nice—after what he said about you, Violet! And I've heard that Carlisle is a large, stodgy, and intimidating man." Gabby shuddered. "Not the sort that I'd want to be nice to *at all*."

Vi cleared her throat. "Maybe you can avoid him?" *Like I'll be doing.*

"Father will be watching like a hawk. No, I need a better plan—reinforcements." Gabby brightened. "You'll help me, won't you?"

"Of course," Polly said at once. "What do you want us to do?"

"If you see me with him, you must come rescue me," Gabby pleaded. "Promise me you will? Pinkie swear on it?"

"What are friends for?" Polly hooked her little finger with Gabby's.

"Violet?" Gabby's eyes beseeched her.

Parsnips. This'll be interesting.

She muttered, "All right," and sealed the vow.

4

Passing the magnificent black iron gates that marked the sprawling lands of Traverstoke, Richard was not in the best of moods. To him, the prospect of being confined in a house for a sennight with several dozen party guests was only slightly preferable to being drawn and quartered. His chest burned as he thought of the ridicule he'd faced in the two weeks since his run-in with Violet Kent.

If anyone dares to bring the subject up...

His gloved hands fisted at his sides. He told himself that the latest gossip—Lady Esterby running off with her groom—had surpassed that concerning his stupid dip in the fountain. He was old news, and anyone who disagreed would answer directly to him.

The carriage jostled its way down a majestic oak-lined drive toward the main house, glimpses of fields and woods appearing between the ancient trunks. Richard made himself focus on the business at hand. He was here to settle Wickham's future—and perhaps his own. He would approach the party as he would any unpleasant obligation.

The manor came into view, and its grandeur lifted Richard from his brooding. By Jove, Traverstoke was a jewel of a country house. Built of golden Cotswold stone, it struck a kingly profile against the dull February sky. As the carriage rounded the circular drive, which had a grand fountain featuring Triton and a pair of sea nymphs at its center, Richard took in the imposing Palladian entrance of the main building.

Six carved columns held up a pediment worthy of a Roman temple. The large central edifice was flanked by two narrower buildings. The wings extended back farther than the main house, creating, Richard guessed, what must be an ample courtyard. He glimpsed a small wooden dome at the end of one of the wings— the highly touted amphitheatre, no doubt.

Richard shook his head, baffled. He couldn't imagine being that plump in the pockets. The things he'd do with such funds... the list of improvements that his estate required was a mile long.

His carriage stopped behind a line of other conveyances. He saw the host and his daughter greeting new arrivals at the foot of the grand staircase leading into the house. The latter, Richard saw with a sigh, was short and plump, dressed in a gown that reminded him of an overly decorated cake. Her bonnet was even fussier with floral protrusions that could take a man's eye out.

Then Richard saw something else that wiped all thoughts of his hostess from his mind. He yanked open the door and jumped to the ground. Gravel crunched beneath his boots as he stalked toward the fountain where Wickham stood—*flirting* with bloody Violet Kent.

They made quite the stunning couple, he noted grimly. Young, modern, and charismatic, they were sharing some private joke that made onlookers want to be in on it, to be part of the charming warmth they shared. They turned at his approach, and their laughter faded. Instantly, he felt like an outsider, old and taciturn compared to the dazzling duo.

Miss Kent was dressed in a travelling ensemble the color of her given name. Her carriage dress had those billowing sleeves which looked absurd on most ladies, but she managed to carry them off, Richard noted reluctantly, because she was above average height for a female. The frock also had a saucy buckled belt that drew the eye to her slender waist. From there, the flare of the skirts obscured her slim hips, the bottom he knew to be pert and firm by the way it had wriggled against his—

Devil and damn, man. Concentrate.

He gave a cutting bow. "I didn't expect to see you here, Miss Kent."

"My lord." Beneath the brim of her canary silk bonnet, her tawny eyes were wary. They darted to the right, where—of course —the bleeding fountain stood.

Heat lashed his cheekbones.

"Carlisle." Wickham made an elegant leg. "I was wondering when you would arrive."

"Wondering or worried?" Richard said caustically.

"Now why would I be worried?"

Because you're destroying your future, and you know I won't let you do it. I won't let you get ensnared by the likes of Violet Kent.

Richard scanned the crowd. He jerked his chin subtly toward the thin and colorless miss standing by a richly outfitted barouche. "Have you paid your respects to Miss Turbett yet?"

Thunderclouds descended upon Wickham's brow. His chin rose to a mutinous angle.

It was Miss Kent who spoke. "By Golly, do you always issue orders upon first arrival?" she said smartly. "Can't you at least wait until the bags are unloaded?"

Fury, already smoldering, ignited in Richard. He faced her, her boldness making his blood burn. "I'll thank you not to interfere with business that does not concern you, Miss Kent."

"That's ironic, isn't it? Seeing as how you were just telling Wick how to run his life."

His jaw clenched. "He's my brother. He'll be guided by me."

"Like a dashed horse? Wick is his own man. You ought to let him do as he pleases."

"And you ought to stop trifling with him." The words were filtered through his teeth, if not his brain. Through the haze of anger, he registered that Wick had slipped away. Bloody coward. Well, he would deal with his brother later—after he dealt with this recalcitrant little flirt.

"For crumpet's sake, I'm not trifling with him. He is my *friend*," she insisted.

"Your *petit ami* perhaps," he said scornfully.

Her cheeks flushed. "Not all of us have that... that lovey-dovey nonsense on our brains, you know. I don't even understand what that fuss is all about!"

That startled him momentarily. A coquette like her didn't understand that... *fuss*? Surely, she was being coy—playing one of her little games.

In tones that brooked no refusal, he said, "I want your word that you'll stay away from Wick."

"You'll get no such promise from me."

Enmity crackled between them. His blood pounded, the pressure in his veins rising.

"This is no lark, by Jove. Wickham's life is at stake," he growled. "You're no good for him."

"I'm *no good*?" Her eyes blazed.

God, he hated how women always twisted his words. "That is not what I said—"

"Well, you're nothing if not consistent when it comes to judging my character," she snapped. "To think I was going to *apologize* for our prior encounter."

"I don't expect an apology from you," he said flatly.

Females, as far as he knew, didn't admit a wrong. They were more apt to feign innocence over their wrongdoing (as the erstwhile object of his affections, Miss Lucinda Belton, had done), burst into tears (Lady Audrey's wont), or pretend it never happened (his mama's preferred strategy).

"I'm not going to apologize *now*. Now all I want to do is push you into a fountain again," Miss Kent said, her hands balled into little fists.

"You didn't push me. I slipped," he bit out.

"Care to give it another go and see what happens?"

Raw and powerful emotion tested his restraint, yanked at his self-control the way an unbroken stallion might at the reins. Staring into her flashing eyes, he knew an unholy urge. A crazed desire to grab her, hold her, *make* her surrender to him. He leaned in—

"There you are, Violet."

The crisp female tones jolted him back to reality. Chest burning, he forced himself to step back at the approach of the Duchess of Strathaven. A petite and buxom brunette, Her Grace had clear brown eyes which were probably quite fine when they weren't narrowed suspiciously upon one's face. She arrived at her sister's side, her tall, black-haired husband a step behind.

Gathering himself, Richard bowed. "Your Graces."

"Carlisle." Strathaven's acknowledgement was cool.

Despite the fact that both he and Strathaven were Scotsmen, and their estates were located in neighboring counties, their acquaintance was passing at best. They had little in common, and, frankly, Richard didn't approve of the other's lifestyle. For years, the wealthy duke had filled Society's scandal pages with his affairs, each more licentious than the next. It was widely said that Strathaven's second marriage had transformed him from rake to devoted husband; judging from the duke's protective stance behind the duchess, Richard judged that this was likely true.

It still didn't make him like or trust the man.

"Come along, Violet," Her Grace said briskly. "You're wanted elsewhere."

The duchess took her sister by the arm. Miss Kent aimed one glowering look back at him before allowing herself to be led away.

Strathaven lingered. His celadon gaze was icy. "Watch your step around my family, Carlisle."

The warning got Richard's back up. "Is that a threat?"

"I don't make threats. Only promises." Strathaven turned smoothly to follow the ladies, his voice trailing behind him. "I'll be watching."

Richard remained where he stood, hands clenching and unclenching at his sides.

It took some finesse, but Violet managed to deflect Emma's questions about Carlisle. The last thing she wanted was to cause her sister worry, not only for her sister's sake but for her own. If Em found out that Vi had pushed the viscount into a fountain, she wouldn't leave Vi alone for a single minute during the house party. Vi's freedom would be utterly curtailed.

Worse yet, there'd be more sermons. Exasperated glances exchanged amongst her siblings that said plainer than words, *There goes the idiot sister again, making a mull of things...*

Vi would rather eat rotten cheese than witness those looks.

I'll just have to handle Carlisle on my own, she decided.

She couldn't believe that he thought she was *trifling* with Wick. That he'd tried to warn her away from his brother—because, according to him, she was "no good." Her heart thudding furiously, she told herself she didn't give a whit about the cad's opinion of her.

About what Viscount *Killjoy* thought.

Was it childish to call him names? Perhaps. Did it make her feel better? *Absolutely.*

As she went along with an animated Gabby, who was giving

her and Polly a tour of the house, she amused herself by thinking of other choice sobriquets for Carlisle. *Lord High and Mighty, Lord High Horse, Pompous Prig...*

They entered the main atrium, and awe interrupted her musings, dissipating any remaining ire. Eyes wide, she gazed upward at the fluted marble columns that rose two stories high to support a frescoed ceiling. Checkered marble gleamed dully underfoot.

"Thunder and turf, Gabby," she said, her words echoing in the vast space, "I can't believe you're the mistress of this place. It's grander than a palace."

"I'm not the Paper Princess for naught," Gabby said with a rueful grin.

As much as Vi disliked the unkind moniker, she admired her friend's pluck for taking ownership of it, for turning meanness into humor. She slid one arm through Gabby's, another through Polly's, and said, "Well, don't just stand there. Give us a tour, Your Highness!"

Her grin turning into a true smile, Gabby obliged.

From the atrium, their hostess took them through a set of public rooms. The main salon was an elegant chamber with yellow silk-covered walls, rosewood furnishings, and three multi-tiered chandeliers. In the dining room, five tables had been impressively laid out to accommodate the many guests. The cameo blue music room boasted a gleaming pianoforte that Vi knew her sister Thea, the family musician, would adore.

The girls arrived at the library, a long, cavernous room which occupied the back of the building. Unlike the spaces they'd seen thus far, this one was more old-fashioned, with dark paneled walls and a massive, ancient-looking stone hearth carved with flora and fauna. A labyrinth of bookshelves took up half the room.

Gabby led the way to the mullioned windows, which gave an expansive view of the courtyard. The garden was beautifully designed with statues, manicured hedges, and graveled walking paths.

"The west wing houses the family quarters and guest chambers." Gabby gestured to the building on the left side. "Over to the right is the east wing, which has a few galleries as well as all the servants' rooms."

"Is that the amphitheatre?" Violet asked excitedly, pointing to the small domed structure just beyond the west wing.

"Yes. Its construction just wrapped up and has put all the renovations behind schedule," Gabby confided. "The architects couldn't get to this room and Papa's study around the corner."

"Oh, but the library is lovely just as it is." Polly's aquamarine eyes were dreamy as her fingers brushed one of the green velvet drapes. "One can practically feel the history that's taken place here."

"As a matter of fact, Traverstoke has a *very* interesting history. For instance, a Catholic family once owned the estate and built a secret worship room in the house."

Secret room? Brilliant! "Can we see it?" Vi said eagerly.

"It's just a plain old gallery now. But back then the owners had the chamber's dome concealed under a fake roof, and there's still a Priest Hole in there."

"What's a Priest Hole?" Vi wanted to know.

"A place where the Catholic priest would hide if the soldiers came knocking. In fact, there might be other hidden passageways in the house, although we've only found the Priest Hole—"

Loud voices sounded in the corridor, followed by a loud crash.

"Oh dear," Gabby said in flustered tones. "I'd better go check on that. I'll be right back."

When their friend hurried off, Violet said to Polly, "We must see this Priest Hole first thing!"

"Shouldn't we settle into our bedchambers first?"

"What's so interesting about a bedchamber? You've seen one

bedchamber, you've seen them all. We're talking about a *secret hiding place* here."

"Well... all right. If you put it that way. Um, may I ask you something, Violet?"

"Hmm?" Vi said absently. She was craning her neck, trying to get a better view of the amphitheatre. Had Madame Monique arrived yet? she wondered.

"What's going on between you and Lord Carlisle?"

Vi started, her gaze colliding with Polly's. The latter's eyes were wide, glimmering with a disconcerting mix of curiosity and knowledge. The last thing Vi wanted was for her sister to intuit the state of affairs between her and the viscount.

"Nothing's going on," she said uneasily. "Why do you ask?"

"I saw the two of you outside. You looked like you were arguing."

"Carlisle and I, um, had a small misunderstanding."

"Over what?"

Think, Violet. "He... he doesn't like the fact that Wick and I are friends."

Which was true. As a rule, Vi didn't like to lie... mostly because she wasn't any good at it. She would forget the fib she told, get caught in the details, and wind up giving herself away.

Polly's light brown curls tipped to one side. "Why doesn't Carlisle approve of your friendship with his brother?"

"Because he's Viscount Killjoy, that's why. A stuffed shirt."

"But you don't really know him, do you?" Polly said dubiously.

"I know what he said about *me*." Crossing her arms, Vi said with a surge of defiance, "What is more, Wick told me that Carlisle lost the family fortune and is forcing Wick to marry an heiress in order to bail the estate out of trouble."

"How *dreadful*."

Vi's nod was emphatic. "Carlisle despises me because he thinks my friendship with Wick will jeopardize his plans. Because I won't stand there and let him bully Wick around."

Polly's brows knitted. "I don't think the viscount despises you."

"He hates me as much as I hate... hold on. What makes you think he doesn't despise me?" Vi's pulse skittered. "Did you, um, sense something?"

Polly plucked at a pleat in her skirts. "He seemed angry and frustrated to me, but hate wasn't part of the mix." She slid Vi a glance from beneath her lashes. "For him or for you."

Vi ignored the flutter in her belly. "That's odd. Because I'm quite certain I *do* hate him."

"You know better than I, of course," her sister mumbled.

"Well, I'm not going to let him ruin my friendship with Wick. Or this party."

No one—*especially* not a stick-in-the-mud like Carlisle—was going to control her. To tell her what and what not to do. To make her feel badly about herself.

Gabby returned, her expression harried. "I'm so sorry, but there's a brouhaha I must attend to. One of the maids will have to take you to your chambers."

"Not to worry." Vi hitched a thumb toward the hallway. "What's going on out there?"

Lowering her voice, Gabby said, "One of the guests, Mrs. Sumner, discovered that another guest, Lady Ainsworthy, has a better view from her chamber. Mrs. Sumner is insistent that she have a room equal to the latter's." Gabby bit her lip. "It's not easy sorting out who should go where as we've a very mixed guest list. And don't get me started on the seating charts for supper: the rules of precedence are impossible to figure out."

"Why don't you ask Marianne for help? She's first-rate at that sort of thing," Vi said.

"A splendid suggestion. I'll ask her. See you both later?" Gabby rushed off again.

"Poor thing. Hosting a party seems like an awful lot of work—

imagine trying to please so many people." Polly shivered. "I'd never be able to do it."

"You could if you wanted to. But speaking of parties, let's not waste a second more." Vi grabbed her sister's hand and tugged her toward the door.

"Wh-where are we going?" Polly stammered.

Vi grinned back at her. "To have *fun*, of course!"

5

"This is an interesting party, isn't it?" Marcus, the Marquess of Blackwood, commented.

"That's one way to describe it," Richard said.

Standing with his friend by the marble mantelpiece, Richard watched the guests drift into the salon after an elaborate twelve course supper. They milled awkwardly within the room's silk-covered walls, a motley bunch and reflection of Billings' position as a man with a foothold in two worlds. The noblemen present represented the social stratosphere to which he aspired. The other guests—powerful and shady characters—were those who'd boosted Billings to his present position as the premier banker to London's Underworld.

Billings' reputation for flexible morality coupled with utmost discretion had earned him a dedicated clientele amongst the underbelly of society. Tonight, owners of prosperous gaming hells, gin factories, and other questionable businesses strutted like peacocks amongst the old establishment, most of whom hadn't a feather to fly with.

Blackwood was an exception, being both titled and wealthy. A former military man, he'd inherited a marquessdom and ran his estates with a capable hand. He was one of Richard's closest friends, the two of them sharing an avid interest in sporting and outdoor activities. As neither man cared for stifling social events, Richard guessed the other was here to please Lady Black-wood, who happened to be friends with the hostess and the Kents.

The thought of Violet Kent made Richard's temperature rise several degrees. At supper, the damned chit had been seated at a table several feet away from him, her companions including Wick and his cronies. At the host's table, Richard had endured a double displeasure. He'd had to watch Miss Kent flirt and laugh with the rakehells—all of whom appeared to be captivated by her—*and* he'd been subjected to Miss Billings' company.

To his consternation, his hostess was the epitome of all he found annoying in the opposite sex. Her inane chatter had bombarded his head like heavy artillery. If he'd had to hear one more word about the latest fashions, he'd have shot his own brains out. She'd also had the irritating female habit of pushing food around her plate, wasting what looked like an excellent repast. Not that he would know if the food was good or not: whenever he'd been about to eat, she'd ask him a silly question that obliged him to put down his fork and summon up an equally silly reply. He thought longingly of the turtle soup and beef cutlets that had come and gone untasted.

Moreover, he'd never been able to read females, and Miss Billings' demurely averted gaze had confounded his attempts to gauge her reactions. Not that she'd expressed any true opinions; she simply agreed with everything he said. If he'd claimed the sky was falling, he was certain she'd have dived for cover.

One supper was enough to cure him of any notions of marriage. Miss Billings might make some man an admirable wife but not him, by Jove. He'd find another way to fund the estate.

"I confess I'm surprised to see you here." Blackwood's voice joggled him out of his brooding. His friend was looking at him with perceptive blue-grey eyes. "As I recall, house parties aren't your entertainment of choice."

"You recall correctly," Richard muttered. "It couldn't be helped. I'm here to keep an eye on Wickham."

"Ah." Blackwood quirked a brow. "Still hoping he'll land an heiress?"

"Hoping won't save him, only planning will. I'm going to make it happen."

"And your brother agrees with your plan?"

"My brother will do as I tell him."

"A strategy that has yielded sterling results in the past." Blackwood's mouth took on a wry curve. "Remember the time you forbade young Wickham from entering that wager at White's?"

"He damned near broke his neck racing in the rain. And he *still* lost five hundred pounds." Which, of course, Richard had had to pay. "Foolish pup."

"Foolishness is repeating a failing strategy and expecting success."

Richard shot the other an annoyed glance. "Are you calling *me* a fool?"

"I'm merely suggesting that you consider the reality," Blackwood said, not without empathy. "You cannot protect your brother forever. Eventually, he'll have to answer for his mistakes."

"The price is too high," Richard said tightly. "He owes a cutthroat."

"Then he'll have to decide to save himself. I saw it time and again with the soldiers under my command. You can only bring a horse to water..."

Blackwood trailed off. Richard followed the direction of the other's gaze, his muscles tautening when he spotted the group entering the salon. Guests parted to make way for the Strathavens, who made a regal pair. They were followed by a couple Richard did not know. A lanky, dark-haired gentleman with silver at his temples and an earnest air accompanied a stunning blonde who seemed his natural opposite. She radiated worldly confidence in a daring gown of silver-shot silk.

Then Violet Kent made her entrance, and for Richard the rest of the room faded. Heat gathered beneath his collar as he took in the way her dress, the color of ripe peaches, clung to her nubile form. Her curves were alluring in their subtlety, enticing him to imagine what lay beneath the scooped bodice, the full sweep of her skirts. She radiated feminine vitality, her tawny eyes glowing as she laughed at something the two girls with her were saying.

"Ah. There's my wife now." Blackwood waved, and Lady Blackwood, who'd come in behind Miss Kent, headed over.

To Richard's dismay, she brought the Kents with her.

"There you are, darling." Lady Pandora Blackwood, a raven-haired beauty, arrived at her husband's side in a swish of wine-colored satin. "I'd wondered where you'd gone."

Not long ago, the Blackwoods had had a falling out, and Richard had witnessed first-hand the depth of his friend's angry despair. Now the breach seemed to be entirely healed, the pair more like lovebirds than ever. As Blackwood murmured something in his lady's ear, causing her cheeks to turn the same color as her frock, Richard wondered, not for the first time, why love came naturally for some yet remained an utter mystery to him.

"Lord Carlisle," Lady Blackwood said, "do you know everyone?"

Meeting the stares of the group, most of them decidedly hostile, Richard felt his muscles bunch. Before he could respond, however, the lanky gentleman stepped forward.

"I don't believe we've been introduced. I'm Ambrose Kent." The man's amber eyes assessed him. "This is my wife, Mrs. Kent."

Of course. Kent was the eldest brother and patriarch of the family. A professional man, he owned a successful private enquiry firm and had the reputation for being fair-minded and just. Per Richard's recollection, Mrs. Kent had been a wealthy and rather notorious widow prior to her second marriage.

Richard bowed. "Good evening, sir. Madam."

"How do you do, my lord." Mrs. Kent's emerald gaze was cool. "May I present my daughter Primrose and sister-in-law Polly? Come make your curtsies, girls."

The two obeyed. The blonde, a vivacious replica of her mama, said prettily, "How are you enjoying the party, my lord?"

"Very well, thank you—" He stiffened when he heard a snort. His eyes cut to the source. "I beg your pardon. Did you say something, Miss Kent?"

"No, my lord." Her whiskey eyes widened—the worst attempt at innocence he'd ever seen. "'Twas merely a sneeze."

"I hope you are not catching a cold."

"Oh no, I'm quite robust. I must have a sensitivity to something in the room," she said airily.

His jaw clenched.

"There you are, Carlisle." Wick sauntered up, followed by his band of merry ne'er-do-wells. With an ease that Richard could only envy, he introduced himself and his friends to the group.

Richard had made it his business to know his brother's associates and thus recognized Lord John Parnell and Mr. Tom Goggston. Both were second sons, neck-or-nothings who treated drinking, whoring, and gaming as competitive sports.

"Splendid party, eh?" Wick said.

"Quite." Miss Primrose dimpled. "Except there hasn't been any dancing."

"Rosie," Mrs. Kent said quietly.

"But it's true, Mama," her daughter said with a pout. "What's a party without at *least* a quadrille or two?"

"I love a good dance myself, and I'll wager you dance like an angel, Miss Kent." Stout and full in the breadbasket, Goggston said eagerly, "If your card ain't full, I'd—"

"There'll be no dancing this eve," Ambrose Kent said. "It's getting late, girls. Time to go upstairs."

"But *Papa*. It's not even midnight." His daughter's bottom lip quivered, her green eyes shimmering. "That's not fair."

"Upstairs," Kent repeated firmly.

He and his wife herded the girls toward the door. Miss Polly looked as if she was trying to console Miss Primrose, but the latter flounced away. Richard predicted trouble ahead for Kent.

Goggston turned to Violet. "You'll be a sport and dance with me, won't you?"

"Why, I'd love to be second choice. Thanks for asking." She rolled her eyes.

Wick chuckled. "She's got you there, Goggs."

"Yes, Goggs, leave the flirtation to Wickham. He's the Casanova of our group," Parnell said in drawling tones. The younger son of an earl, he had fair coloring, a narrow, aristocratic face, and an endless supply of ennui. It was reputed that there wasn't anything he wouldn't try once. "You'd best stick to what you do best: collecting jug-bitten tavern wenches at the end of the night."

Goggs flushed to the roots of his thinning brown hair.

"Besides, dancing is deuced dull," Parnell went on. "This curst affair needs more than a few country sets to liven it up."

"Agreed," Wick said instantly. "A game, perhaps?"

"Precisely." Parnell's expression turned thoughtful.

At that moment, Miss Billings approached the group in a flurry of ribbons. She avoided Richard's gaze. Egad, the feeling was mutual.

Addressing the others, she blurted, "I am in *desperate* need of your help."

"With what?" Miss Kent said.

"The guests aren't mingling. It's gone awfully quiet in here. The performers don't arrive until tomorrow, so I'll have to think of something to keep the party lively in the interim. Father says perhaps setting up card tables—"

"Cards are fine for the older set, Miss Billings, but I have a better suggestion for the younger guests," Parnell said with studied insouciance.

Looking hopeful, Miss Billings said, "You do, my lord?"

"A parlor game. Hide-and-Go-Seek is all the rage in the upper echelons, especially amongst the unattached guests."

"What a brilliant idea," Miss Billings exclaimed. "Do you think everyone will play?"

"We'll round 'em up for you. Just give us the word," Goggs said helpfully.

Richard stood at the periphery with the Blackwoods, watching as Wick and his posse worked their charm, enticing all the single ladies and gentlemen into joining the game. Within minutes, a dozen or so players stood in a circle as Parnell dictated the rules. Miss Billings would be the seeker; everyone else had to go hide somewhere on the ground floor, and the last one to be found would be the winner. The guests milled excitedly, Violet Kent amongst them, her eyes vivid against her flushed cheeks. Looking far less enthused, Miss Turbett joined the group as well.

Wick came over and clapped Richard on the shoulder. "Ready, old fellow?"

Richard stared at his younger sibling. "I'm not playing."

"Course you are. All unattached guests—that's the rule."

"That's absurd."

Although Wick's expression remained pleasant, his tone hardened. "No more absurd than your plans for me. What happened to *we're in this together?*"

Hell and damnation. Richard searched for an excuse. "I'm too old for games."

"You're hardly ancient, Carlisle." Mischief danced in Lady Blackwood's violet eyes. "Why, Lord Wormleigh is playing, and he's got a couple of decades on you."

Richard glanced at Wormleigh. The aging Lothario looked well into his cups and was winking broadly at all the single ladies.

"Don't interfere, Penny," Blackwood muttered to his wife.

Miss Kent ambled up. "Ready to play, Wick?"

"I'm not playing unless my brother does so as well," Wick said stubbornly.

Miss Kent's fine brows lifted. "Won't you deign to join us, my lord?"

"No, thank you," Richard bit out.

"I understand," she said sweetly. "Losing is more difficult for some people than others."

By Jove, why did the chit provoke him beyond bearing? In his entire life, no one had questioned his sportsmanship before. He might not be charming or popular, but he *always* conducted himself honorably in the realm of competition.

"I wouldn't know. I play to win," he growled.

"Excellent." Wick grinned. "In that case, may the game go to the best man—or lady."

6

Violet raced merrily toward her destination. She'd wound her way through several rooms, deliberately taking detours to throw others off her scent. She knew exactly where to hide and didn't want anyone else hedging in on her territory. She *loved* games; Carlisle wasn't the only one who played to win. With glee, she imagined Lord High and Mighty's face when she was declared the winner.

She passed through the library, hurrying past the carved stone hearth and the seats clustered around it. At the sound of female giggles and male murmurs emerging from the maze of bookshelves, her eyebrows rose. Clearly, the room was already occupied.

Not that she cared. Bookshelves were such an *obvious* place to hide.

Leaving the room, she made her way stealthily toward the floor of galleries in the east wing. She heard occasional voices, but they grew dimmer as she located the small, chapel-like room that she'd explored with Polly earlier that day. Shaped like a cross, the room's mint green walls were hung with gilt-framed paintings, and the ceiling was covered in a field of plasterwork flowers. She and

Polly had scrutinized those exquisite white blooms and, in awe, concluded that each of them was unique, slightly different from the rest.

Vi had also discovered something else.

With unerring steps, she went to the head of the room, where five steps led up to a platform; here, one could look out a picturesque window framed by billowing silk curtains. She ran her fingers under the ledge of the third step, nimbly searching out the hidden mechanism. She pressed and heard the familiar click. Grinning, she watched the steps move as one, swinging open like a door to reveal the gloomy depths of the Priest Hole. She crouched, readying to jump inside—and squealed when a large, masculine hand reached out of the darkness.

She gawked at the stern face staring out at her.

"Thunderbolts." She planted her hands on her hips. "What are *you* doing here?"

"Hiding," Richard said curtly. "That is the purpose of the game, is it not?"

When Miss Kent continued to stare down at him as if he'd grown three heads, he sighed and heaved himself out of the Priest Hole. Even though she was on the taller side for a female, he still towered over her by half a foot. He preferred this position to looking up at her from the hole. As far as he was concerned, he'd take every advantage he could get when dealing with the brazen minx.

"How did you know about my hiding place?" she demanded.

"Pardon. I didn't realize this niche belonged to you," he said sardonically.

Pink bloomed in her cheeks. "I meant how did you know about the Priest Hole?"

"Billings gave me a tour. He mentioned that this gallery used to be a Catholic chapel. I put two and two together."

Miss Kent's brows drew together. "You figured out where the Priest Hole was *by yourself?*"

Richard resented the incredulity in her tone. As if she didn't expect him to be able to put his own boots on, let alone figure out a simple secret mechanism. "Why is this a surprise, Miss Kent, when I assume you did the same?"

"Well, I'm a hoyden, aren't I?" Her smart words made heat crawl up his jaw. "Let's face it, we adventurous and modern females are known to show a bit of ingenuity. But a gentleman such as you,"—she shrugged—"well, you're..."

He waited, arms crossed over his chest.

"... conventional. A traditionalist." Her eyes taunted him. "I wouldn't expect *you* to be capable of locating a clandestine place."

In other words, she thought him a dullard. An unexciting—and stupid—stuffed shirt. That she held that opinion of him should come as no surprise. He'd never been the kind of man that women swooned over: a brooding, enigmatic Lord Byron... or a charming Wickham.

When Miss Belton had turned down his suit, his mama's words of consolation had been the following: *You can't blame her, Richard. Next time, try being less dependable and direct. Such earnestness grows tedious, you know.*

"Just because I don't go looking for trouble doesn't mean I can't find a bloody Priest Hole," he said shortly. "Like I said, I play to win."

"But I was going to hide here," Miss Kent protested.

"As they say, finders keepers, losers..." He imitated her shrug.

"I am *not* a loser—" Her head swung toward the door.

Footsteps and voices approached.

"*Crumpets,*" she breathed.

They stared at one another. Then, without another word, they both turned to the hole, Miss Kent jumping in first, Richard following and pulling the steps closed behind them.

Footsteps entered the gallery... whispers of other guests looking for a place to hide. Violet waited in the darkness, her heart thumping in her ears. And not just because she didn't want to be discovered.

The Priest Hole had clearly been designed for one person. For a withered cleric, there would be just enough room to stand or sit with his legs outstretched. But now there were two bodies in the tight space—and one of them was deuced *big*.

She and Carlisle stood facing one another; she was squished between his hard frame and the wall. Heat radiated from his body: it was like being trapped against a steel furnace. In the dimness, she could make out the harsh outline of his features, and his clean male musk pervaded her nostrils, affecting her... strangely. Warmth bloomed beneath her skin, the air in her lungs growing heavy and humid.

"Stop wriggling about." His quiet words brushed hotly against her ear.

Perspiration trickled beneath her bodice. She felt tingly... squirmy.

"For God's sake, stop moving." His voice sounded oddly husky. "Do you want us to be found?"

"I'm not... comfortable," she whispered back. "What in blazes do you have in your pocket? It's hard and poking into me."

He tensed, his caged potency jolting through her at the same time that recognition struck her.

Oh. Gadzooks. It's... that.

'Twas as if someone had attached an electrifying machine to the hole and was cranking with all their might. Charged awareness crackled over her senses, muting the footsteps and whispering voices just beyond. Everything faded but him. His scent. His heat and closeness. All the hairs lifted on her skin, butterflies swarming in her belly.

Don't do it. Don't look at him...

Anticipation brimmed over. Unable to stop herself, she tipped her head back.

His eyes gleamed in the dimness.

In the next instant, his mouth was on hers.

His kiss—her first—was a shock and a revelation at once. In the steamy darkness, his hard, firm lips ignited a dormant need. Hunger for something she'd never known came roaring to life inside her, and the feeling was astonishing. His taste poured through her, as dark and sweetly addicting as a cup of chocolate, and it made her *ravenous*. 'Twas as if she were starving and someone suddenly plunked her in front of a buffet.

Instinct took over, all thoughts abandoning her save one. *More.*

A desperate moan escaped her. He swallowed the sound, tilting her head back, and then the kiss caught fire. Senses aflame, she felt the hot, invading thrust of his tongue, and she answered naturally with a parry of her own. His low growl shivered through her. Their tongues twined, the slippery slide releasing a molten rush between her thighs.

Before she could fathom her body's startling response, she was lifted against the wall. Pulse galloping, she felt his thigh boldly insinuating between her legs, lifting her toes off the ground. The heat of that thickly muscled ridge burned through the layers of her petticoats; when she squirmed against him, the friction made bliss ricochet against her insides. She didn't even realize she'd moaned again until a hand clamped over her mouth.

"Shh, lass." The raw hunger in his voice mesmerized her. "We must be quiet..."

The warm, wet tug on her earlobe caused her head to loll dazedly against the wall. Butter and jam, who knew that that organ could be so sensitive? Her fingers bit into the unyielding sinew of his shoulders as pleasure came to her like a cart of desserts, each offering more decadent than the one before.

He licked the shell of her ear, invading wetly, suckling the tender lobe until her toes curled inside her slippers. When his lips travelled lower, branding a trail down her neck, she wriggled in helpless delight. His big hands spanned over her ribs, just beneath her surging bosom. Her breasts strained inside her bodice, the tips taut and needy, and when his thumbs brushed against the undersides, she couldn't help nudging into his caress.

"You're so soft. Sweet," he muttered.

His finger trailed over the bare skin of her décolletage, leaving goose pimples in its wake. He traced the low neckline of her dress... then dipped beneath. The breath whooshed out of her lungs when he found the stiff peak of one breast, circling gently. Desire flooded her.

"Do you like that?" his voice growled in her ear.

"Oh, yes—" Her gasp was swallowed by his kiss.

Exhilarating pleasure swept through her. Spun her more powerfully than any dance. Darkness amplified the sensations, and she was whirling in them, lost, guided only by his scorching lips and masterful touch. She rocked wantonly against the granite ledge of his thigh... and felt an iron-hard bulge poking into her own leg. This time, a sense of discovery sizzled through her.

She'd been around farmyard animals most of her life. Carlisle was... potent. Like a stallion she'd once seen brought to stud.

His shocking arousal made her feel both dizzy and powerful. Her spine bowed as he gently tweaked the tip of her breast, his tongue tracing a scorching line on the swells just above. Her breath jammed, her fingers spearing the rough silk of his hair as need soared to a feverish pitch—

"Hullo? Anyone in here?"

The voice—Gabby's?—cut through Vi's haze. She froze; Carlisle did the same. Footsteps padded closer. She didn't dare breathe, every muscle quivering with the fear of discovery...

"Got you!" Gabby announced cheerfully.

Taut as a bowstring, Vi fully expected the steps to swing open, to be exposed—dear God, *with Carlisle*. Instead, she heard the sound of whipping fabric, followed by male groans and shuffling on the platform overhead.

"I told you the curtains were a curst silly place to hide, Goggs."

Through her panic, Vi recognized the disgusted voice as Parnell's.

"You didn't have a better plan," Goggs said plaintively.

"You both did ever so well." Gabby's tone was consoling. "In fact, you're amongst the last to be found. There are only three more—oh my goodness, did Lord Wormleigh just run past in the hallway?"

"We'll help you hunt old Wormleigh down," Goggs offered.

A stampede of footsteps... and then the room went quiet.

The door to the Priest Hole swung open, the light momentarily blinding. When her pupils adjusted to the brightness, she saw that Carlisle had hoisted himself out. He was looking down at her, and the severe set of his features obliterated the remnants of her passion-daze.

Emotion roiled in his scorched-earth eyes... anger? Regret?

Shame and confusion crashed over her. *Why did I... with Carlisle of all people? God, what have I done? What must he think of me?*

She didn't even *like* him. Yet his dark hair and cravat lay crumpled by her hand, and her nerve endings still sparked with lustful sensations. Her cheeks flamed.

Laughter rang in the distance. Carlisle's muscular frame went rigid.

"We can't be found together. You stay," he commanded. "I'll go."

She could only nod. Moments later, the hole sealed shut once again, leaving her alone in darkness. Alone and shivering with discovery... because she now finally understood what all the fuss was about.

7

The following afternoon, Richard entered the amphitheatre. The magnificence of the domed interior momentarily lifted him from his dark musings. A forty-foot ring stood in the middle and, behind it, a raised stage backed by red curtains. The strains of an orchestra emerged through the closed drapery and added to the crackling anticipation. Guests were already filling the velvet-cushioned benches, eager to see the newly arrived performers from Astley's.

Standing near the back wall, Richard scanned the crowd—and spotted Violet Kent near the front of the theatre. As usual, she was surrounded by male admirers. Scowling, he noted how delectable she looked: she wore a pink frock topped with a cherry-colored pelerine that matched the shade of her lips. Thinking of how sweet her mouth had tasted brought a throbbing heat to his loins.

Rationally, he knew that she was a mistake. A part of him had always known that she posed a particular danger to a man of his temperament. The curse of his ancestors flowed in his blood: like the Carlisles before him, he bore that fatal attraction to his opposite. He was naturally drawn to beautiful flirts, found that combination of feminine exuberance and delicacy fascinating. Such women roused his basest instincts, an elemental need to protect and claim. Unfortunately, his past had demonstrated repeatedly that that way lay disaster.

His jaw clenched. Courting Violet Kent would undoubtedly lead to catastrophic results. Hell, he didn't even know the specifics of her dowry, whether it would support the needs of his estate. Yet for the first time in a long time, his personal desires overrode all other considerations.

Things had gone too far last night. He was furious at himself for taking advantage of an innocent. For losing control and violating his own code of ethics. Nonetheless, he was a gentleman, and his honor dictated that he now do the right thing. That he make amends for the liberties he'd taken—albeit with Miss Kent's cooperation.

Her very *generous* cooperation. The memory of it flashed like a fever.

Returning to his chamber last night, he'd finally succumbed to the raging lust that she'd ignited in him from the start. Lying in the dark, he'd given his fantasy free rein. He'd envisioned Violet spread on the bed, his head between her thighs. He'd eaten her pussy until she'd cried out, her surrender honey-sweet on his tongue. Then he'd flipped her onto all fours, hoisting up her slim hips and plunging home. Her tight, wet pussy had milked his cock like a *fist*, wringing his seed from him, making him come harder than he ever had before...

In all his years, he'd never experienced anything like her feminine passion. So vibrant and uninhibited—yet innocent too. In the Priest Hole, her inexperience had been evident and, he admitted to himself, powerfully arousing. At the same time, he wanted to shake some sense into her. Didn't she know the danger she'd courted, hiding with a man in the dark? Didn't she realize how vulnerable she was?

She's not yours to protect, his voice of reason warned. *Recall your past mistakes.*

His jaw tautened as he watched Violet laugh at some quip of Parnell's. Her laughter lit her whiskey eyes, her entire face aglow. For an instant, he found himself wondering what it would be like to be on the receiving end of such radiant warmth.

Seeing her with the fashionable buck made Richard feel old and taciturn. The ten-year age difference between Violet and him might have been a hundred. Even as a younger man, however, he'd never been the dashing type, the kind of suitor a lady might wax poetic about. He didn't like to mull over past failures, yet now his mistakes itched like old scars.

His judgement when it came to the fair sex had been proven unreliable. He couldn't read females, couldn't decipher what they were truly thinking or feeling. Both Lucinda Belton and Audrey Keane had seemed to welcome his addresses, greeting him with winsome smiles, their dispositions lively and sweet. Yet in the end, his offers had come to naught. He could have understood their rejections... had they not been steeped in duplicity as well.

He refused to make those same errors in judgement—hence his level-headed approach toward finding a wife. His title for her money: wasn't that the strategy? When had the plan altered to include seducing a hoyden in a Priest Hole?

Damn Violet Kent for muddying the waters.

"Have you recovered, brother?"

Wick's voice returned Richard to the present. His brother approached, every inch the dapper country gentleman in a checked brown jacket and matching silk cravat.

"Recovered from what?" Richard said.

"Your loss at Hide and Seek, of course." His sibling bestowed a beatific smile upon him. "Don't take it too hard, old boy. When it comes to games, our dear Vi is a ripping competitor."

"Don't refer to her in that manner."

Wick's brows shot up. "Beg pardon?"

"You ought to show more respect to Miss Kent. She is a young lady, not one of your wild scapegraces," Richard said curtly.

"*Miss Kent* is my chum, so I'll call her what I please."

"Since when can a woman and a gentleman be chums?" Richard scoffed.

He didn't believe for an instant that his brother's motives were pure. How could they be when a female as tempting as Miss Kent was involved? This meant that he had yet another problem to contend with. Not only had he kissed the troublesome baggage, he might also be treading on his brother's territory.

The notion made his molars grind together. He told himself this was only because Wick's future was at stake; his sibling needed to court Miss Turbett, not dally with Violet Kent.

"You really do have antiquated notions, you know," Wick said.

Miss Kent would have agreed. A traditionalist, she'd scornfully called him.

Then she shouldn't have let me kiss her, he thought savagely.

In a tight voice, he said, "Do you have any intentions toward her?"

"Toward who... *Violet*? Of course not. She's like a sister to me."

His brother's incredulity sounded sincere and told him what he needed to know. *One barrier out of the way.* Then he watched as more gentlemen joined Miss Kent's group, and his relief vanished. *Only a dozen bloody more to go.*

Wick's hazel eyes narrowed. "Why are you so interested in her anyway?"

He told himself it was a matter of honor. Of doing what was right.

"What's going on? Surely you can't mean..." Wick gawked at him. "Violet... and *you?*"

His brother's tone implied that the likelihood of such a pairing was akin to pigs taking flight.

"Why would that be so surprising?" Richard said brusquely.

"Because Violet's my friend—and, trust me, you're not the

sort of man she'd want to wed. She doesn't even *like* you." Wick dragged a hand through his hair, furthering its fashionable disarray. "And I know for a fact that she enjoys her freedom and has no interest in marriage."

The words planted like a dagger in Richard's chest, piercing the hope that had been insidiously burgeoning there. He knew his brother was right: his rational mind had been saying those exact things all along. Lust had blinded him, given him foolish notions. One illicit embrace didn't mean that Miss Kent would want to marry him.

Hell, just because she'd *seemed* innocent didn't mean that she was; had he forgotten Miss Lucinda's beguiling façade, Lady Audrey's calculating ways?

It was telling that, at present, Miss Kent took no notice of him, was too busy bantering with all her other gentlemen to even spare him a glance. Well, his sense of honor might demand that he offer for her, but he wouldn't play the dupe again. He'd go into the business with realistic expectations and keep his proposal cursory. Most importantly, he'd leave with his pride intact.

Just another duty to perform. The thought struck a stark note.

Music swelled, signaling that the show was about to begin.

Wick studied him. "I'm sitting with her and the fellows. Care to join?"

He glanced over to see that Miss Kent was now surrounded by her family. Another public scene was the last thing he needed. He'd find an opportunity to talk to her in private later on; God knew that interview was going to be brief.

"I'll find my own seat. Enjoy the show," he said flatly.

It required all of Violet's willpower not to look at Carlisle. She was acutely aware of him standing at the back of the theatre. His mere presence quickened her pulse, flooding her with remembered sensations, the most extraordinary she'd ever known. The raw silk texture of his hair between her fingers, the flexing of his virile body against hers, the devouring fire of his kiss...

"Is everything all right, Violet?"

Her gaze swung to Emma, sitting on her right. "Yes. Perfectly. Er, why do you ask?"

"Because your cheeks are flushed. And you're all out of breath," her overly observant sister said. "I think I know why."

Vi swallowed. "You... you do?"

"It doesn't take an investigator to figure out the cause of your excitement." A grin tucked into Em's cheeks. "You'll soon be seeing your idol, after all."

Her idol... *Oh, right.*

"Yes. Madame Monique. Can't wait," she mumbled.

"It won't be long, dear." Smiling, Emma turned to catch something that Polly was saying.

Unable to help herself, Vi cast a discreet glance in Carlisle's direction. He was now seated in the back row of the theatre; with his brawny form, he stuck out like a stallion in a pen of geldings. Just as she was about to look away, his gaze collided with hers.

Her stomach plummeted. His eyes were shuttered, his features set in foreboding lines. There was no trace of the passionate lover who'd awakened all her dormant needs. Who had, in one fell swoop, made her understand what desire was.

She turned away, mortification pulsing through her.

Don't be a ninny. Don't let him see how he affects you.

Why, oh why, had she acted so wantonly? He'd called her a flirt, said she wasn't good enough—and in the Priest Hole she'd gone and proved the dratted man right. Yet, to be fair, she wasn't *entirely* to blame, was she? After all, he was Viscount Killjoy, a stuffed shirt: he had no business kissing her like that! Why, he'd issued a sneak attack, she thought with growing indignation. Lured her into complacency with his starchy exterior, only to ambush her with his sensual and irresistible lovemaking...

Wait a minute. Carlisle—sensual? Irresistible? Did the kiss rot your brain?

She couldn't deny that during the encounter he'd absorbed her senses completely. In fact, the effect of his kiss had been like that of playing a sport: her mind had been focused, centered on naught but him and the moment. She'd felt utterly alive in her own skin...

Her mind roiled with confusion. *Why* had he kissed her when he didn't even like her? And why did she have to discover what passion was in the arms of a man who despised her? Another thought seized her. By Golly, did that make her a *trollop*?

"Ready for the show to begin?"

Her attention jerked to Wick, who'd taken the seat she'd saved for him. She mustered up a smile. "I can't wait to see Madame Monique. She's tip-top."

"Indeed." Something flitted through his gaze, something she couldn't read. "By the by, I was chatting with my brother just now."

Wings of panic beat in her chest. Carlisle hadn't told Wick about the Priest Hole, had he?

"Anything, um, interesting come up?" she croaked.

"Not really. It's always the same old tune with him. Miss Turbett this, Miss Turbett that."

"Oh." She told herself she was relieved.

"He did, however, call into question my friendship with you."

Outrage surged. "He did *what*?"

Wick's expression was solemn. "It seems he cannot fathom how a girl like you could be friends with me."

A girl like you. The words branded on Vi's brain, releasing sizzling reminders of the other things Carlisle had said about her. *You're no good... You can't spell propriety let alone put it into practice...*

A terrible suspicion arose. Had Carlisle kissed her *to make a point*? To prove that she was naught but an improper hoyden— and not good enough to be friends with his brother? Anger and humiliation quivered through her.

"I told him to mind his own business, of course," Wick said.

At least she had Wick's loyalty. She managed a smile. "Thank you."

"What are friends for?" he said with a wink.

As the music soared to new heights, the crowd tittering with excitement, she shoved her tumultuous emotions into a box and slapped on the lid. What did she care what Lord High And Mighty thought of her? So what if he judged her and found her lacking? It wouldn't be the first time someone did so and likely not the last.

Pull yourself up by your slipper laces. She squared her shoulders. If Carlisle dared to approach her again, she would tell him in no uncertain terms what she thought of him and his blasted tactics. She might even plant him a facer for good measure.

"Ladies and gentlemen," a voice announced from behind the curtain. "May I present... Mr. Cedric Burns and Miss Josephine Ashe!"

Determined to put Carlisle out of her mind, Vi sat forward in her seat. The red curtains parted, revealing a flaxen-haired duo juggling brightly colored balls back and forth. Handsome and wiry, Cedric Burns' smile was a flash of white in his tanned face. Flames of red and orange sequins glittered on his black waistcoat. His partner, the petite Miss Ashe, wore a matching vest over a tailored blouse and black skirts. The two circled each other on the stage, balls arcing between them.

From off stage, an assistant began tossing more balls at Burns, and without missing a beat, he incorporated them into the colorful flow until Vi counted a dozen balls being kept afloat between the jugglers. Excitement buoyed her spirits, and when the set ended, she applauded enthusiastically with the rest of the audience.

The pair took their bows. Turning to his partner, Burns said in a loud stage whisper, "What shall we do next, my dear?"

"I don't know." Ashe tapped a finger against her pointed chin, her light eyes inviting the audience to join in the repartee. "Does anyone have a suggestion?"

"Play with fire!" Parnell's voice came from behind Violet.

"Fire, fire," the crowd began to chant.

"Heavens, this is a raucous bunch, isn't it?" Emma muttered.

Violet didn't respond; she was too busy stomping her feet with everyone else. The next minute, an assistant appeared on stage, with a flaming taper in one hand and a bucket of unlit torches in the other. He lit them one by one, tossing them alternately to Burns and Ashe, the audience cheering as the performers each maintained fiery, ever growing circles in the air. Then, with skill so seamless it appeared to be magic, the pair began exchanging the flaming torches, their independent circles melding into one blazing loop.

When the act was over, Vi hooted and clapped wildly.

Burns bowed and made a flourish with his arm. "My partner, Miss Josephine Ashe!"

Ashe came forward, about to curtsy—when a white Arabian seemed to come out of nowhere, soaring into the ring in front of the stage, obscuring the jugglers. Vi gasped along with the rest of the crowd at the fantastical sight: the snow-white horse flew around the circle, a raven-haired lady standing on its back.

Madame Monique!

Clad in a white dancer's costume with a fitted bodice and short draped skirt, the acrobat embodied elegance. She lifted a leg, bending the pink-stockinged limb behind her with graceful ease as the horse galloped on. The audience went wild, leaping to their feet, Vi along with them. Breathlessly, she watched her idol perform one trick after another in the saddle. Madame Monique twirled on her toes, rode backward, even did a flip in the air. During the finale, Violet's hands clutched in front of her as Monique and her mount sailed through a fiery ring.

Deafening cheers erupted.

"She's incredible, isn't she?" Vi shouted happily to Wick.

"Indeed." There was an odd note in his voice, his gaze fixed on the regally bowing acrobat.

After the final round of applause, the curtain closed, and guests departed en masse for afternoon refreshments back at the house. Standing behind Wick, who was waiting politely for the aisle to clear, Vi couldn't resist looking for Carlisle; he was nowhere to be seen.

Good riddance, she told herself. *Now stop acting like a feather wit.*

Aloud, she said, "Madame Monique was smashing, wasn't she?"

Wick turned. "She certainly knows how to give a good performance."

"I do hope we'll get an opportunity to meet her. I have so many questions I want to ask. Perhaps Gabby could arrange it..." Vi trailed off, staring at her friend. "Wick? Are you all right?"

The color had suddenly drained from his face. His pupils were dilated, his breaths rapid and shallow. He was looking past her to the entrance of the amphitheatre...

Craning her neck, Vi glimpsed a black-haired gentleman standing there. Of medium height and elegantly trim, he exuded an aura of cold ruthlessness that she could sense even from a distance. The pair of hulking brutes flanking his sides added to his menacing presence.

"Who is that?" she whispered.

Wick raked his hair with a visibly shaking hand. "Who do you mean?"

"That man over there with the guards. The one who's staring at you?"

"I haven't the faintest," he said unconvincingly. "Look, I just remembered that I, er, promised to meet up with someone. See you later?"

"Wick, what is going—"

Before she could finish, he pushed his way into the aisle, eliciting disgruntled exclamations from other guests. He waded his way toward the rear of the theatre—in the opposite direc-

tion from the ominous stranger—and exited through a back
door.

Stupefied, Vi turned to her sister. "Em, do you know that man
by the entryway?"

Her sister followed her gaze. "I don't recognize him. But
judging from his charming entourage, I'd guess he's one of
Billings' infamous associates. Why do you ask?"

"Wick seemed taken aback when he saw the man looking at
him," Vi said.

Em's sable brows lifted. "Wouldn't you feel the same way?"

Both of them glanced at the stranger. Vi's nape prickled. The
cutthroat was looking at the door through which Wick had
exited, his gaze as hard and unblinking as a snake's.

8

"How absolutely *sporting* of you to arrange this, Gabby," Vi said.

It was an hour before supper, and she and Polly were following their hostess down the hallway toward Madame Monique's suite, where they would have a private audience with the diva. The skirts of the girls' evening gowns swished over the thick carpeting.

Gabby chuckled. "You're welcome. This meeting will be brief, but you'll have more time to converse at supper. I've put you and your family at my table with Madame Monique."

"Smashing," Vi breathed.

"There's only one hitch to my seating plans." Gabby huffed out a breath. "Father insisted that I place Viscount Carlisle next to me."

At the mention of Carlisle, Violet experienced—on top of everything—a swift tug of guilt. She'd engaged in an illicit (albeit entirely unplanned) embrace with Gabby's potential suitor. It went against her code of honor, her very nature, to betray a friend. True, the other girl hadn't seemed at all interested in Carlisle... but what if her feelings had changed?

As Violet searched for some casual way to bring up the topic, Polly said, "How are things going with Carlisle?"

"*Terribly*. I dread each and every encounter," Gabby said with feeling. "He never smiles, we have naught in common, and I've had better luck carrying on a conversation with a house plant. The truth is he makes me horribly nervous. And you know what I do when I'm nervous: I chatter. And chatter. Over supper last night, I carried on a conversation with myself for two whole hours."

"I'm sure it wasn't as bad as all that," Polly said soothingly.

Vi wasn't so sure. Because Gabby *could* out chatter a magpie. It was part of her charm.

"Trust me, it was." Gabby came to an abrupt halt, her blue eyes beseeching. "If you see me talking too much tonight, give me a kick under the table, will you?"

"I can't kick you," Polly protested.

"I'll do it." Vi figured she owed Gabby the favor. Clearing her throat, she said, "Are you *certain* you're not interested in him, Gabby?"

"Yes. Absolutely. Not only does he lack conversational skills, he's so..."—Gabby shuddered—"*large*."

Vi flashed back to the feel of Carlisle's hard, aroused body pinning her to the wall. Heat fluttered at her core, the tips of her breasts tingling. She couldn't deny that she found his brawny physique powerfully stimulating. His thick, muscular thigh had felt so good wedged between her legs, and the way he'd touched her, his big hands roaming with such exquisite care...

No, get your mind out of the gutter! Remember he used you—merely to prove a point.

She swallowed. "You have a problem with his, er, size?"

Gabby's red curls bobbed emphatically as she led them around a corner. "I prefer a gentleman who is less overwhelming in every respect. More refined, if you know what I mean. Not short, but a nice manageable height that doesn't give one a crick in the neck when one is speaking to him." Her eyes grew dreamy. "Someone who likes to spend hours having cozy chats in front of the fire, who likes to shop, who likes cats more than dogs—"

"Why does he have to prefer cats over dogs?" Vi wanted to know.

"Because *I* do. And my ideal husband and I would agree in all things."

Polly looked doubtful. "I'm not sure marriage works that way."

Vi had to agree with her sister. The couples in their family tended to be as passionate in their conflicts as they were in their love for one another.

"That's how *my* marriage would work," Gabby said fiercely, "if I were given a chance to decide my own fate."

"Won't your father allow you to choose your husband?" Vi asked.

"He'll consider my wishes, but he has his own ideas as well."

"Surely you would be the best judge of the husband you'd want," Vi said reasonably. "You're the one who has to live with the fellow after all—"

A loud shatter startled her, drowning her out. She heard raised female voices coming from behind the closed door up ahead. For once, she wished she'd paid more attention during her lessons with Monsieur Le Roche. The argument was happening in rapid-fire French, and she couldn't comprehend a thing.

"What's going on?" she said.

Polly shook her head. "They're talking too fast for me to—"

The door flung open, and Josephine Ashe stormed out. She was still dressed in the clothes from her performance, angry color blotching her cheeks. She stopped short at the sight of them.

"Miss Ashe." Brow furrowed, Gabby said, "Is something amiss?"

"It's nothing—nothing at all." Miss Ashe dropped a hasty curtsy. Ran a hand through her cropped blond locks. "I was just on my way."

"Oh. Well, of course. Don't let us detain you—"

Before Gabby finished speaking, the juggler was already halfway down the hall.

"Crumpets." Vi stared after Miss Ashe. "What was *that* about?"

"As the English like to say, it was much ado about nothing."

Vi spun in the direction of the sultry, accented voice. Posed in the doorway, Madame Monique was draped in a flowing robe of pink chiffon, her dark coronet studded with pearl-tipped pins. "My visitors have arrived, I see." She waved an imperious hand. "Come."

Polly slid Vi an uncertain glance.

Vi wasn't going to let some squabble get in the way of meeting her idol. Tugging Polly along, she led the way toward the acrobat's suite. "Thank you for the invitation, Madame."

"I must be off. See you all at supper?" Gabby said.

The diva inclined her head. "And if you could be so kind as to have a new looking glass delivered, Mademoiselle Billings? The current one has suffered a mishap."

As Violet followed Madame Monique into the suite, she thought *mishap* might be a euphemism. The looking glass above the vanity had been smashed to smithereens. The remnants of a broken vase mingled with shards of glass upon the vanity and surrounding carpet. A maid with a severe grey bun and weathered countenance was on her knees, cleaning up the mess.

"*Laisse*, Jeanne," Madame Monique chided. "I'll send for someone to take care of it."

"It is no trouble, Madame—"

"Have a care with your hands, yes? They are far too valuable to risk doing such work." The acrobat's tone was gentle yet firm.

Jeanne rose stiffly. "As you wish, Madame. I shall prepare your toilette." For an instant, she studied Vi and Polly with rheumy, shrewd eyes before shuffling off.

Vi and Polly followed Madame Monique into the adjoining

sitting room, which boasted a view of the gardens on the west side of the house. Dusk saturated the sky with red, purple, and orange. The lights of the stables winked in the distance.

As soon as they were all seated, Vi blurted, "I've been following your performances since I was a girl, Madame Monique. It is the utmost honor to meet you."

"How kind, Miss Kent." The Frenchwoman reposed as sinuously as a cat, curling her feet beneath her on the damask chaise. "Let us be friends. To you, I am Monique."

Madame Monique wants to be friends... with me?

"Then I'm Violet, and this is Polly," Vi said in a giddy rush.

Polly shyly wriggled her fingers in greeting.

Leaning forward, Vi said, "Your feats, Monique—they are incomparable! I have so many questions I want to ask you. How do you keep your balance standing on one leg on a moving horse? I've practiced and practiced and whilst I can stand, the instant I try to lift the other leg—"

"Pardon." Monique's brows arched. "Am I to understand that *you* were attempting acrobatics?"

"Yes—though not in London, of course," Vi said hastily. "Back in Chudleigh Crest, the village where I grew up, there was an open field behind our cottage. I'd just put on my trousers and—"

"Your *trousers?*"

"Well, not mine, really. I filched them from my brother Harry. The point is," Vi said, "I practiced and practiced but could never sustain a one-legged pose for more than a second."

The Frenchwoman stared at her. "You *are* an unusual miss, are you not? Quite the *ingénue*. I see now why you are so popular with the gentlemen."

Something about the other's scrutiny made Vi uncomfortable. "But I'm not—popular, that is."

"There's no need to play the coquette with me, *chérie*. I saw you at the performance this afternoon. Surrounded by a herd of young bucks," Monique said in light tones, "and sitting next to a handsome young Adonis."

"You mean Wick? He's a chum," Vi said quickly, "as are the others."

After a pause, the acrobat gave a laugh as floaty as her leaps. "How delightfully modern you are. A woman after my own heart."

The awkward feeling ebbed from Vi, pleasure thrumming in its place. The heroine of her childhood had complimented her on being modern and thought they were similar? *Outstanding.*

"Now you were asking about balance," Monique said.

"Yes?" Vi was poised at the edge of her seat.

"The secret, my dear, is to trust one's natural instincts. Those who fear to let go end up falling. To succeed, do not fight the moment, but rather,"—the diva flicked her fingers—"reap its glorious uncertainty."

Vi tried to make sense of the advice. "You mean I shouldn't be afraid of falling?"

"Fear leads to failure. To conquer fear, one must lean into it, laugh in its face. One must be bold, remorseless, willing to take any risk when it comes to art and life. *Alors*, you wish to know the secret to success?"

Vi nodded fervently.

"Don't be fooled by love. Trust no one but yourself, and let nothing stand in your way." A feverish glow lit Monique's eyes. Although she was looking at Violet, her gaze seemed focused on something only she could see. "Be *La Belle Dame sans Merci.*"

A shiver coursed down Vi's spine. As much as she admired Monique, the other's philosophy seemed a bit... ruthless. Then again, she told herself, if one's job was to jump through a ring of fire day in and day out, such an unflinching attitude was probably necessary.

"Do you have, um, any specific pointers?" she asked. "When it comes to technique, I mean?"

Monique's attention snapped back to her. "Lean into gravity's pull rather than away from it. Use your arms for balance." The Frenchwoman's tone was crisp. "And train your horse so that you ride as one, each compensating for the other. I practice riding blindfolded."

"Blindfolded? Now why didn't I think of that?" Thoroughly impressed, Vi said, "I shall try that at the first opportunity—"

Jeanne's voice came from the doorway, a diffident murmur of French.

"I am being summoned." Monique rose in a graceful swirl of pink chiffon. "Please excuse me."

Vi hopped up, as did Polly.

"Thank you for your time," Vi said gratefully, "and for your excellent advice."

"*Tout le plaisir était pour moi.*" Monique's lips curled up at the corners. "I look forward to furthering our acquaintance over supper, *ma chère*. A performer must know her audience, after all."

9

The pungent odor tickled Richard's nose, and, before he could stop it, he sneezed.

For the third bloody time.

"Bless you. Er, again." Seated to his left at the head of the table, Miss Billings paused in her monologue about bonnets long enough to remark, "I hope you haven't contracted an ailment, my lord?"

"I'm fine." *Or I would be—if someone wasn't wearing that blasted perfume.* He didn't know where the noxious scent was coming from, but every now and again, it wafted over to him, irritating his nostrils. "Thank you for your concern," he said curtly.

His hostess launched into chatter again. About gloves this time. Egad.

Suppressing a sigh, he listened with half an ear. He'd been on edge all evening, and one reason for his disquiet was sitting directly across the table. Miss Kent was acting as if he didn't exist. When he'd tried to approach her in the drawing room before supper, she'd been as slippery as a lamprey, wriggling her way through the guests, eluding him at every turn. At present, she was polishing off her fish course with gusto, and he'd have found her hearty appetite endearing if she wasn't simultaneously presenting him with a cold shoulder.

That said shoulder was left bare did not improve his mood. The neckline of her daffodil satin frock invited far too much attention, and he had to quell the urge to rip off his jacket and throw it over her. His grip tightened on his knife as Goggston, sitting to her left, snuck yet another look at the exposed swells of her bosom. Richard wanted to strangle the prat... even if he couldn't precisely blame him.

Because it was taking all of Richard's willpower not to join in the ogling like some randy schoolboy. His only excuse was that he knew first-hand how soft and firm those breasts were, how perfectly they'd fit in his palms. His skin slickened beneath his cravat; he tried not to think about how her nipples had budded so sweetly at his touch, not to wonder at their color, if they were the same berry pink as her lips...

Her eyes suddenly met his. The impact of that tawny gaze was like a blow to the gut during a practice round at Gentleman Jackson's. Her throat rippled, and she quickly looked away.

He became aware of the hot, thick throbbing in his groin, and he wanted to groan in frustration. God's wounds, what was the matter with him? Why did one look from the little baggage affect him this way? He didn't have time for this nonsense; he had more pressing concerns.

He looked around the dining hall, its dark paneled walls hung with portraits of the aristocracy. Billings had undoubtedly purchased some impoverished peer's ancestors to decorate his house, and now they looked down their noble noses at the motley guests supping at banquet tables set with gleaming silverware and hothouse arrangements. A quick survey revealed that Wickham still hadn't shown. Richard had no idea where his sibling was—but he had a good idea why the other had absented himself.

Richard looked to the foot of his table. Billings occupied the end seat, the Duchess of Strathaven to his right. But it was the man across from her, dark-haired and ruthlessly elegant, who held Richard's attention.

What is that bastard doing here?

Turning to Miss Billings, he said, "Are you acquainted with the man talking to your father?"

"Mr. Garrity, you mean?" she replied without missing a beat. "Actually, I only met him today. He wasn't precisely invited, you see, but he is one of Father's business associates, and Father says we must do everything to make his visit a pleasant one."

"What does Mr. Garrity do, precisely?" This came from Miss Kent, whose brow was furrowed.

"He supplies funds to those in need," Miss Billings said guilelessly. "Father says he's an important man."

Billings wasn't wrong. Garrity was one of the most powerful cutthroats in London. He'd built a thriving empire from moneylending at an outrageous margin. Any sod stupid enough to take a loan from Garrity was putting his neck on a bloody chopping block.

God's blood, why were you so stupid, Wick?

A footman placed the next dish in front of him, and Richard sliced his *roulade de boeuf* with a savage stroke, guts of asparagus and leek spilling out against the Sèvres china. He told himself Wick still had three months to pay off the debt. As dangerous as Garrity was, the moneylender was known to be a man of his word. He wouldn't come after Wick... yet.

"Has anyone seen Mr. Murray?" Miss Kent ventured.

The worry in her voice made Richard wonder if she knew about Wick's connection to Garrity. He shook his head, answered gruffly, "Not since this afternoon."

"Maybe the old boy's taking a nap and slept through supper." Goggs slurped at his wine.

"When have you known our Wick to nap?" The scoffing reply came from Parnell, sitting two chairs down from Richard. They were separated by Mrs. Sumner, an auburn-haired, voluptuous widow whose crimson dress left little to the imagination.

"Once he and I wagered on who could stay up the longest," Parnell continued, his pale features smirking, "and Wick managed to go three days and nights without sleep."

As if Wick wasn't addled enough, he had a friend who encouraged sleep deprivation. Just bloody perfect.

"A fellow with staying power, eh? Mr. Murray sounds like someone I'd like to get to know better." Mrs. Sumner's blackened lashes lowered in a roguish wink.

Why was his brother such a damned magnet for trouble? Gritting his teeth, Richard prepared to reply, but Miss Kent beat him to it.

"Mr. Murray is very busy these days," she said primly. "He has to think of his future."

Mrs. Sumner's plucked brows shot up. "You speak for him, Miss Kent?"

"As a friend, I do."

Her steady reply ignited a sudden, unpalatable sensation in Richard. It took him a moment to recognize the feeling as... jealousy. Of his own brother? The possibility flummoxed him. All his life, he'd looked after Wick—would give the other the shirt off his own back if necessary. Yet Miss Kent's loyalty and concern made his chest constrict with a contemptible emotion.

Longing. For something that would never be his.

Blocking out the unacceptable thoughts, he turned to Mrs. Sumner. "As Mr. Murray's brother, I can assure you that his plate is presently full. He has no time for diversions."

"Pity." The widow's gaze roved over him. Then she leaned forward, giving him an unobstructed view of her twin assets. "Tell me, my lord," she cooed, "does stamina run in the family?"

His neck heated. How the hell was he supposed to respond to that? This was one of the many reasons he loathed flirtation. He'd never had a talent for navigating the labyrinth of hidden meanings and innuendo. He preferred honesty and straight dealing. When Lucinda Belton had laughingly declared, "I've never met a man as direct as you, Carlisle—why, you're as blunt as a mallet," she hadn't been wrong.

As he struggled to come up with an acceptable reply, Miss Kent spoke up.

"It seems you've fallen into your dish, Mrs. Sumner," she said with studied candor.

He saw that the widow's bodice was indeed soaking up the sauce from her plate. Straightening, Mrs. Sumner reached for her napkin and rubbed at the greasy spot on her bosom—slowly, her fingertip tracing a suggestive circle. She winked at him.

By Jove. Appalled, he looked away.

The widow said casually, "How kind of you to notice, Miss Kent."

"Rather difficult not to," Miss Kent said.

Her disgruntled tone lifted Richard's spirits.

Abruptly, she turned her attention to the acrobat seated on the other side of Goggston. "Monique, I'd love to hear more about the secrets behind your performances. And yours as well, Mr. Burns," she added.

Next to Parnell, Cedric Burns flashed white teeth that sparkled against his tanned complexion. "I haven't any secrets, m'dear. What you see on the stage is purely the result of practice and skill."

Monique reached for her goblet of wine, smirking. Richard thought that her beauty was like beveled glass: it had a hard, polished edge. Unlike Miss Kent, whose fresh prettiness owed nothing to artifice, the acrobat honed her charms with rouge and paint.

"Pure fustian, Monsieur Burns. The Great Nicoletti claims the same thing," she said, "yet he cuts his assistant in half with a saw and then puts her back together again. Tell me, what sort of *prac-*

tice makes such a feat possible?" Her smile was derisive. "Every great performer has secrets."

"If you don't care to share the tricks of your trade, Burns, just say so," Parnell drawled.

"Hard work is the trick," Burns protested. "My partner and I practice for hours each day."

"Where is the lovely Miss Ashe, wot?" Wormleigh said from halfway down the table. As usual, the aging dandy appeared foxed, his jowls ruddy above the elaborate folds of his cravat.

"She developed a megrim. Sends her regrets," Burns said.

"Too bad. Never met a gel who could handle fire." Wormleigh leered. "Would like to know her secrets, wot."

"A woman must guard her secrets as closely as her jewels." Monique raised her glass to her rouged lips. "They are her most valuable commodity."

"What if she doesn't have any secrets?" Miss Billings piped up.

"Then she has no choice but to rely on her jewels." Smirking, Parnell said, "Stunning necklace, by the by."

Miss Billings beamed. "You're ever so kind, my lord. It's a French heirloom."

By Richard's reckoning, Parnell hadn't given her a compliment but an underhanded barb. And while Richard, himself, found some of Miss Billings' habits annoying, she was, in general, an artless, well-meaning sort of female. She did not deserve to be publicly insulted—and in front of guests who were, at that very moment, dining on her generosity.

"You look lovely, Miss Billings," Richard said brusquely. "With or without the jewels."

His hostess blinked, her jaw slackening.

"I agree, Gabby," Miss Kent declared. "You look marvelous."

She glanced at him—her tawny eyes surprised and... approving? Warmth spread through his chest like sunshine.

The others launched into superlatives about Miss Billings' jewelry. Richard was no connoisseur of gewgaws, but even he could guess that her necklace must have cost a king's ransom. Deeply hued sapphires, each the size of a thumbnail, were set in a web of icy, glittering diamonds.

"Now Miss Billings," Monique cut in silkily, "with your earlier statement I must disagree. Everyone has secrets."

The hum of conversation faltered; guests shifted in their seats. Richard guessed that the Frenchwoman's pronouncement had made each and every one acutely aware of whatever knowledge he or she didn't wish others to know. Memories of his rendezvous with Miss Kent smashed through his mental barriers. How indescribably good she had tasted, how soft and perfect she'd felt in his arms...

Beneath the table, he hardened with shocking swiftness.

"Well, I don't have any. Truly," Miss Billings chirped. "I'm ever so boring, nothing mysterious about me at all. Father says I'm like an open ledger..."

For once, Richard was grateful for the girl's droning soliloquy. As she went on and on, it gave him a chance to recover from his disreputable state. He'd gotten to about half-mast when the soft underside of a slipper slid up his calf. All the muscles in his body went rigid; he shot a disbelieving gaze across the table. From the way Miss Kent was angled subtly forward in her chair, there was no doubt it was she who was caressing him under the table.

Good Lord, was she *playing footsy* with him?

Lust clawed at him. In an instant, he was rock-hard again.

She froze, her gaze lifting slowly to his. He didn't have time to mask his reaction, the hunger raging through him. Her eyes widened... she looked *startled*? What the hell did she expect when making such a bold advance?

She sprang from her seat. Which obliged the gentlemen around her, himself included, to rise as well. He cast a quick glance downward; thank God his jacket hid his rampant cockstand.

"Pardon me," she blurted.

Cheeks pink, she took off like a doe.

It took every ounce of his willpower not to follow her immediately. To track her down and finish what she'd started. But to do so would elicit talk... so he forced himself to bide his time. The ten minutes he waited felt like ten years. Finally, he excused himself. With anticipation roiling in his veins, he went in search of the naughty minx so that he could settle the score between them once and for all.

Violet walked through the halls of the mansion in an agitated state, barely noticing where she was going. She couldn't believe what she'd done... *again.* Carlisle was like a bad luck penny. His mere presence brought out her worst behavior. First the fountain, then the Priest Hole, now *this.*

Her heart thumped with mortification. She'd only meant to give Gabby a nudge beneath the table—to keep her promise to stop the other from chattering on. But her foot had missed its mark. Drat Carlisle and his overly long and muscular legs!

Now he had further proof to use against her: more evidence that she was an improper hoyden—the awful flirt he'd accused her of being. Despair welled beneath anger; for once, she couldn't keep it at bay.

Why, oh why, can't I get anything right?

Her heart squeezed as she recalled how Carlisle had looked at her, his eyes forge-dark and smoldering, his nostrils flaring, that muscle ticking in his jaw... for one panicked moment, she'd feared that he might do something crazed. What, exactly, she didn't know and didn't want to find out. He'd looked like a man pushed to the very limits of his self-control.

Calm yourself. Pull yourself up by your slipper laces...

She tried telling herself that Carlisle was nothing but a judgmental ass. Yet over supper he'd shown surprising sensitivity and kindness toward Gabby. He'd stepped in, turning Parnell's mean-spirited remark into a compliment.

So maybe he's not always a judgmental ass, her inner voice amended. *Only to you.*

The notion offered no comfort. Dash it, why did Carlisle confuse and vex her so? Why did his opinion of her matter so much?

"For crumpet's sake, stop obsessing over it," she muttered to herself as she paced down the corridor. "Think of something else."

Her thoughts veered to Wick, and worry for her friend distracted her from her own frazzled state. Thunder and turf, Wick had looked *terrified* when he'd seen Garrity at the performance, as if his worst nightmare had come to life—and now she'd come to discover that Garrity was a moneylender?

This could be no coincidence and didn't bode well. The fact that Wick hadn't shown for supper increased her concern. She decided to go look for him, make sure he was all right.

She headed up the grand stairwell toward the guest wing where Wick's room was located just around the corner from Monique's. She arrived and knocked on his door. No answer.

"Wick, it's me, Violet," she said softly. "Are you there?"

Still no reply.

Reaching into her reticule, she pulled out a scrap of parchment and a pencil stub and scribbled a hasty note against the wall. As she was about to slip the message under Wick's door, her nape tingled. Her head whipped up, her gaze sweeping the empty hallway. There was no movement in the corridor save the flickering of the wall sconces.

She exhaled. Her overactive mind was playing tricks on her. Bending, she slid the paper beneath the door and hurried back to supper.

10

With simmering anger, Richard watched the door of the library open at three in the morning. She'd arrived exactly as her note had promised, the glow of her taper licking the paneled walls. She was wearing a frilly wrapper over her night-clothes, her hair a gleaming, luxuriant cascade down to her waist: perfect for the assignation she'd planned, he thought grimly.

He rose from a chair in the shadows. "Good evening, Miss Kent."

She gasped, her candle wobbling precariously in its holder. "*Carlisle.* Gadzooks, you startled me. Wh-what are you doing here?"

"I could ask you the same thing. But I don't have to, do I?"

He held up the piece of paper between finger and thumb. The incriminating note he'd watched her slip under his brother's door. He knew the brief message by heart, having read it over several times in furious disbelief.

W.,
Urgent that we meet. Library—three o'clock, whilst everyone's abed.

V.

By God, over supper she'd been trifling with him, Richard—even *he* couldn't mistake a foot running up his leg as flirtation—and the next minute she'd gone running after his brother! Rage seared his chest. The little *trollop*. She was no different from the others. Well, if the shallow flirt thought she could play him like a puppet, she was in for a rude awakening.

Her eyes widened. "Why do you have the note I left for Wick?"

The coquette didn't even bother to deny that she'd set up a lover's tryst!

"Because I saw you put it there and retrieved it. Because I'm saving my brother from a world of trouble where you're concerned," he bit out.

"Hold it right there." She slapped her candle down on a table and approached him. "You *stole* the note I left for Wick?"

God, why did she yank on his tether like no one else?

"I didn't steal it, you brazen minx," he said through gritted teeth. "I took what should never have been put there in the first place."

"First of all, you have *no right* to take what is not yours. Second,"—her arms folded over the ruffled front of her wrapper, her eyes bright with anger—"why do you insist in interfering in my friendship with Wick?"

"Friendship? So that is what you *modern* sorts call it?" he said scathingly.

"It's what anyone who has more than a speck of pea gravel for a brain calls it. Gadzooks," she burst out, "why must you plague me so? What have I ever done to you?"

"Other than pushing me into a fountain? Or running your foot up my leg during supper?"

That shut her up. For nearly an entire minute.

Huffing out a breath, she said, "Fine. I apologize. Both were accidents." As if that half-arsed attempt at remorse wasn't bad enough, she followed it up with a glower. "Now why did you follow me to Wick's room?"

It was on his tongue to deny that he had. His pride made him balk at admitting that he'd gone after her for any reason. At the same time, he refused to stoop to her level—to play games.

Satisfy your honor, and be done with this madcap business.

"I wished to speak to you," he said shortly.

"To me? Really?" If sarcasm could drip from words, she'd have flooded the library. "I'd never have guessed given the way you were scowling at me through supper."

"Me, scowling at *you*? How would you even notice when you scarcely looked my way?"

"Why would I look at someone who blatantly disapproves of me?" She stepped right up to him, toe to toe, her stance fearless. "Who thinks I'm a no-good hoyden?"

He fought to hold onto his temper. "I never said you were no good. I said you were no good *for Wick*. He needs a wife who can manage him."

"For the last dashed time, Wick is my *friend*. Get it through your thick skull: I have no designs on your brother whatsoever. In fact, I don't want to get married *at all*."

"That's inconvenient, isn't it," he said acidly, "since I'm offering for you."

A heartbeat passed.

She glared at him. "That is not amusing, Carlisle."

"I don't think so either. Unfortunately, it must be done, given what happened between us in the Priest Hole." He managed to adopt a pragmatic tone, despite the fact that his heart was beating like a fist against his ribs. "I am not in the habit of seducing innocents, Miss Kent, and my honor demands that I answer for my mistake."

"Your... *mistake?*"

Her incredulity made his neck heat, yet he blundered on. "Obviously, I wasn't in my right mind. If I had been, I wouldn't have gone near you. You're obviously not the type of female who would suit a man of my temperament."

"*I* don't suit *you?*"

"Well, yes," he said impatiently. "It's obvious that we are opposites in nature. As you yourself have said, I respect tradition. I envision a calm, orderly sort of life, one centered on my duty to my title and estate. Ideally, my wife would share my goals and views on marriage." Finally, he was on stable ground; he could talk for days about duty. "She would understand the importance of abiding by rules of convention and propriety. She would not be prone to flights of fancy or the silliness which plagues most of your sex. Rather, she would strive to live up to the honor which I would bestow upon her."

"What lottery did she enter to be so lucky?"

Ignoring the interjection, he said, "You, on the other hand, are a modern female, which means... well, I don't know what it means exactly, other than you're prone to scrapes, flirtations, and generally wreaking havoc wherever you go. In sum, you are nothing like the sort of wife I had imagined for myself. Nevertheless," he said, holding up a hand when she made to speak, "I am willing to overlook those differences between us because of the weakness of a moment. It happened, there's no going back, and thus, I must do the honorable thing. So will you?"

She was staring at him. "Will I... what?"

"Marry me," he said.

Violet was not a girl prone to romantic delusions. Growing up, she hadn't been one to dream of a knight in shining armor sweeping her off her feet because she'd wanted to be the one *riding* the steed—and not side saddle either. Knights, to her mind, received the better end of the bargain: they got to ride off on exciting quests while their poor wives were left to slave away in some drafty old castle.

So, no, she wasn't a particularly sentimental girl. But that didn't mean she expected her first and only marriage proposal to be slung at her like mud. Anger blasted through her.

"I'd sooner... eat a horse than marry you!" Her voice shook. "And I *adore* horses."

She had the satisfaction of seeing Carlisle's expression harden. "So your answer is no."

"You have a screw loose if you think I'd say yes to such a proposal!"

Emotion smoldered in his eyes; it was quickly banked. "Then my duty is done."

"I wouldn't marry you if you were the *last man on earth*."

"Spare me the clichés," he clipped out. "Your answer has been duly noted, and, I might add, with no little relief."

Relief? Her fury found fresh legs. "Your relief could not be possibly greater than mine. As wrong as I may be for you, you are *infinitely* more wrong for me. You're nothing like the sort of man *I* would wish to marry."

A muscle ticked in his jaw. "Your behavior in the Priest Hole would suggest otherwise."

Heat scalded her cheeks. "It was dark. A moment of weakness."

"Admit it, you little baggage. You wanted me," he gritted out.

She refused to give him the satisfaction. "You could have been *any* man."

A dark flame leapt in his eyes as he leaned over her. "So you would have allowed any man's tongue between your lips? Any man's hand down your bodice? You'd ride any man's thigh and pant in his ear?"

"You... you're no gentleman." Not the strongest riposte, but it

was difficult to think when she could scarcely breathe. His nearness made her feel lightheaded. More than a little crazed.
Clinging to her last vestiges of rationality, she shot back, "Only a
troglodyte would say such things."

"Troglodyte? Impressive word." His eyes glinted like raw ore.
"But can you spell it?"

That does it.

Black lines exploded across her vision. Her hand raised to
slap him.

He caught her wrist. Her other hand automatically came up,
but he caught that one too. Before she knew what was happening,
he'd driven her backward, her spine pressing up against the end of
a bookshelf. He caged her, pinning her hands above her head with
one big hand. Bosom heaving, staring into his dark impassioned
eyes, she felt... *anticipation*.

"By Jove, you drive me mad, woman," he growled.

Her heart hammered in her ears. "Not as mad as you
drive me."

Pure masculine triumph flashed in his eyes.

"Then let's go to Bedlam together," he rasped.

His mouth slammed onto hers.

All thoughts of honor and duty were washed away by a flood of red—
anger and desire so intertwined that there was no hope of separating
them. Together, they lashed at him, whipping him into an animal
frenzy. Control slipped from his grip, replaced by the burning,
driving need to tame and claim the recalcitrant goddess in his arms.

He ravaged her soft lips, shuddering when they parted on a
breathy moan. When she licked his invading tongue, he felt that
lush swipe all the way down in his groin. His balls swelled, his
engorged cockhead butting against his trousers.

Her sweet, hot flavor wiped reason from his brain. He was driven by one imperative.

Make her mine.

He released her wrists, growling with satisfaction when her fingers speared his hair, pulled him closer. He loosened the tie of her wrapper, his palms roaming over her night rail. Cupping one sweetly rounded breast, he found the stiff peak, working it between finger and thumb, swallowing her sensual little gasp. He dragged up the voluminous fabric of her shift, bunching it between them.

His hand closed around one sleek, soft thigh and moved upward. *Goddamn—yes.* She was drenched for him, her plump petals soaked with dew.

"Wh-what are you doing?" She looked dazed. "You can't, shouldn't...*ohh, by Golly...*"

He stroked her leisurely. "Shouldn't what? Touch your pearl? Tickle it like this—or like this?"

She whimpered; her thighs clamped with erotic insistence around his hand.

"Work yourself against me," he said thickly. "There you go, lass. Exactly so."

Eyes glazed, she wriggled against his hand, her bottom lip caught beneath her teeth. Her wanton innocence undid him: no woman had ever responded to him with such unschooled passion, such pure feminine desire.

His cock had risen fully, the blunt dome nudging past his waistband. He spurted a little as he petted her, diddling her pearl, coating it with her own cream. Maddened by her moans, he went lower, delving deep into her slick folds. As his thumb rocked over her nubbin of pleasure, his middle finger circled her quivering hole.

"Do you feel empty here?" he rasped. "Does this little mouth wish to be fed?"

Her hips lifted, her eyes passionate and needy. "Carlisle, *please*..."

His name on her lips and her breathless plea—a siren's song.

Triumph blasting through him, he nudged his finger deeper, groaning at the exquisite restriction. Her shiver coursed through him, his cock straining desperately toward the virginal paradise flowering around his digit. Mindful of the snug fit, he touched her carefully, raging lust tempered by tenderness he'd never felt with any woman before. He plunged and withdrew in measured increments, shuddering when she finally took him to the knuckle.

When she chanted his name, he claimed her mouth once more, screwing his finger in deeply, his thumb working her pearl. She stiffened in surprise when her climax broke, her sweet cries of release vibrating down his throat. As her cunny massaged his finger with mind-obliterating spasms, sweat misted his brow. His erection pulsed, more pre-spend leaking. By God, to feel that tight little sheath stretched around his shaft. One flick and he could release the fall of his trousers, could bury himself to the balls—

Faint voices jerked him from feverish temptation. He tensed, ears straining. A man and a woman... out in the hallway?

The peril of the situation struck him like an icy wave. Violet's reputation would be ruined if they were caught like this. With fathomless regret, he pulled away. He yanked her nightclothes down, grabbed her hand.

"We have to go," he said.

"Hmm?"

Despite the looming disaster, his lips twitched at her dreamy response. Well... damn. If he'd known he could get her acquiescence this way, he'd have seduced her weeks ago.

In low tones, he said, "People are out in the corridor."

He saw reality return, her eyes widening. "Crumpets, what are we going to do?"

"We'll wait in here until they pass." He tugged her into the dark labyrinth of bookshelves. Positioning her behind him, he stood on guard at the mouth of the aisle, peering around the shelf to monitor the entrance to the library. His senses strained to catch what was going on outside.

"*Carlisle.*" Her urgent whisper came from behind him.

"It'll be all right." His eyes were trained on the door. "They've passed us by—"

"Never mind them. There's someone else in here. *With us.*"

He swung around, saw her pointing shakily toward the far end of the aisle. Squinting, he made out a form in the gloom... someone sitting on the floor against the shelves? The back of his neck prickled.

"Stay here," he said tersely.

He went to grab the taper she'd set on the table earlier and headed back down the aisle. She ignored his instruction—of course—and followed right on his heels.

The flame cast an eerie mix of light and shadows over the aged spines, and as he neared his destination, the form on the ground took the shape of a woman. Crouching, he held out the candle: Madame Monique. His gut iced over. She was slumped like a ragdoll against the shelf, eyes staring out of her bloodless face, hands balled at her sides.

He heard Violet's sharp intake of breath. "Dear Lord, is sh-she...?"

He placed his fingers on the acrobat's throat. Cool skin, the flatness of nothing.

"She's dead," he said grimly.

"H-how did this happen?"

He raised the flame higher, saw blood streaking from a wound on her right temple. He ran the light over the rest of her; something glinted within her furled fingers.

"Hold this." He handed the taper to Violet. "I see something..."

Reaching down, he gingerly removed the object from the dead

woman's grasp. His breath rammed into his throat as he lifted the distinctive signet ring, the ornate initials gleaming.

No, it can't be...

"*Gadzooks.*" Violet sounded as shocked as he felt. "That ring... it belongs to Wick."

Ambrose Kent didn't take vacations often, and now he wondered why. The verdant meadow was paradise. He was having a picnic with his wife, the scent of honey wafting on the summer breeze, birdsong echoing in the blue skies. And that wasn't even the best part of it.

With his back against the sun-warmed blanket, he stared up into his spouse's gorgeous face. The two of them were as naked as Adam and Eve. Marianne's pale blond tresses streamed over her shoulders, one end curling around a lovely coral nipple.

His hands tightened on her soft hips.

"Ride me, my selkie," he urged.

Emerald eyes heavy-lidded, she obeyed, rolling her hips, teasing him by rising until her pussy clamped just the tip of his cock... and then sinking down slowly. She took his turgid shaft all the way, her swollen lips smacking wetly against his bollocks.

God, yes.

"Faster, you little tease," he growled.

With a sensual smile, she obeyed. Her rhythm was exquisite, mind-blowing, nearly drawing his fire. But he wouldn't come—not until she did. Gripping her hips, he slammed upward as she came down, the intensity of the penetration wringing moans from them both. Seed swelled in his balls, his climax building. The breeze grew stronger, and the birds began to squawk, some damned woodpecker knocking with distracting insistence...

He blinked, chest heaving, disoriented by the dimness. He was lying on his side, his wife's plush backside tucked up against him. Groggily, he took in the strange bedchamber... then it returned to him. The damned house party.

Being a man of simple tastes, he preferred hearth and home. Marianne enjoyed doing the social rounds, however, and for her sake, he would make any sacrifice. Lifting the blanket, he peered down and saw his fiercely erect cock wedged against her bare buttocks.

Maybe this won't be a wash after all.

Of late, they'd dealt with constant interruptions at home. Between the antics of their nine-year-old son Edward, the theatrics of their eighteen-year-old daughter Rosie, and the adventures of the rest of the family, he and Marianne had hardly had a moment alone. Now that they did have some blessed privacy, he wasn't going to waste it.

He nuzzled his wife's neck, his palm sliding forward to cup her full breast. She made a sleepy, sensual sound, all the encouragement he needed—

Knock, knock, knock.

"Darling?" his wife said drowsily. "Is someone at the door?"

"Ignore them." He nipped at her earlobe, tweaking her nipple lightly. "They'll go away."

KNOCK. KNOCK.

"Ambrose? Marianne?" It was Violet's voice. "Are you awake?"

"Bloody hell." He inhaled for patience.

"You should get that," Marianne said.

With a grumbled oath, he released his plump bounty.

"I'm coming," he said through clenched teeth. *And not the way I wanted to.*

He shoved on his dressing gown and cast a longing look at the bed, where his better half was now sitting up. Her breasts were on spectacular display as she stretched her arms, yawning.

Soon, he promised himself.

He stomped to the door and yanked it open. "Violet, this had better be an emergency..."

He trailed off—because his sister wasn't alone. *Viscount Carlisle* was with her.

Pulling his sister protectively to his side, Ambrose said tersely, "What's going on? Why are the two of you together? And at this hour?"

"We happened upon each other in the library. It was, um, a coincidence," she said.

His middle sister had never been an accomplished liar; he didn't believe her overly innocent expression for an instant. More damning yet was how disheveled she looked: her frock was rumpled, her hair bound in an untidy braid.

His gaze swung accusingly to the Scot. Carlisle's face was set in grim lines, his posture tense. Before he could interrogate the bounder, Vi blurted, "But that's beside the point. Ambrose, we discovered something terrible in the library. Madame Monique—she's *dead*."

"Dead?" he said, astonished.

Violet nodded, her eyes wide.

Ambrose's surprise didn't last for long. For a man in his profession, it rarely did.

"Tell me everything," he said briskly.

12

V iolet paced the length of Billings' study. Located next to the library, where her brother was presently examining the scene of death, the room had the same old-fashioned ambience with dark paneled walls, mullioned windows, and an ancient hearth crawling with stone roses and vines. A burgundy Aubusson added a splatter of color...

Monique's face, streaked with blood, flashed in Vi's mind. Horror penetrated her veil of numbness. Her throat thickened.

What happened to you, Monique? How can you be so full of life one moment... and gone the next?

"Are you all right, my dear?" Marianne was standing by the window. Dawn's watery light highlighted the fine lines of worry around her eyes. "Perhaps you'd prefer to go upstairs—"

"I'm fine," Vi said at once. "I want to be here."

Determination anchored her. There was no way she was going to miss the upcoming meeting. It was bad enough that Ambrose had barred her from revisiting the library. Her big brother had put his foot down, saying that she'd seen too much as it was; he'd taken Carlisle, Emma, and Strathaven into the library with him, and Billings had joined them. Violet had been made to wait in the study like a child under Marianne's watchful eye.

Annoyance warred with guilty unease. *What's taking them so long in the library? How is Carlisle handling the situation? Is he following through with our plan?*

After stumbling upon Monique, she and Carlisle had faced a difficult dilemma. If they revealed that they'd found Wick's ring in the dead woman's hand, they'd be incriminating Wick—something neither of them wanted to do. She and Carlisle had gone directly to find Wick and clear up the matter... but his room had been empty, the bed still made.

Where on earth had Wick gone?

Since they could tarry no longer, Vi had made the only proposal she could think of to protect her friend: she and Carlisle had to keep Wick's ring a secret for the time being.

Carlisle's features had been even starker than usual. He'd looked as if he were grappling with an army of inner demons. "I cannot in good conscience embroil you in my brother's affairs. To ask you to lie for him," he'd said flatly.

"We don't have a choice," she'd replied. "We can't risk endangering Wick."

As much as she hated keeping anything from Ambrose, she hated the idea of Wick being accused of murder even more. Her chum might be a reckless rake, but he was no killer.

Carlisle's ravaged expression had spoken volumes about his moral conflict. Protect his brother by lying... or tell the truth and condemn his sibling? At times, being Lord High Horse couldn't be easy.

Taking pity on him, she'd said, "Why don't we do this? Let's at least wait until we have the chance to talk to Wick. Once we ascertain his innocence, *then* we'll tell Ambrose everything."

Sin first, beg forgiveness later—not exactly a new strategy for her. Although Carlisle hadn't been entirely convinced, he'd relented. She'd changed quickly into more proper attire, and then together they'd gone to Ambrose.

Which brought her to now. What was taking them so long in the library?

"Pacing a trench into the Aubusson won't get them in here any faster," Marianne said mildly. "Do you want to talk about what's troubling you?"

Vi went through a mental checklist of her problems. Concealing evidence in an investigation... no, she couldn't talk about that. Engaging in repeated intimate acts with Carlisle... mum's the word on that as well. Discovering desire for the first time and with a man who utterly confounded her... right.

"There's nothing I want to talk about," she said truthfully.

Just then, the door opened—*at last*—and Billings marched in first. He was a small, wiry man with thinning grey hair and papery-looking skin. The others filed in behind him, their expressions somber. Carlisle brought up the rear and closed the door.

Despite the situation, Vi's pulse skipped faster at the sight of him. His smoky gaze met hers, and awareness thrummed between them. After the steamy interlude in the library, there was no point in denying their animal attraction. With a flash of insight, she realized that the perilous secret they now shared bound them together as well. They were... co-conspirators.

"Did you find anything?" she blurted to the group.

Ambrose nodded gravely. "Why don't we sit first?"

Billings took his position at the large mahogany desk which dominated one end of the room. On the wall behind him hung a rather grisly painting of dead, glassy-eyed pheasants lying in a heap, waiting to be plucked. Everyone else gathered around the desk. Violet was glad when Richard chose the chair next to hers.

Ambrose remained standing, taking the place next to their host.

"I'll begin with a summary of what we know thus far." His tone was brisk and professional. "Madame Monique was discovered in the library at approximately three this morning by Violet and Carlisle. By the state of the corpse, I would judge that the victim had been dead no more than an hour or two before she was found. She suffered a blow to the right temple."

"Dear heavens," Marianne murmured.

"I can't confirm that the blow killed her," Ambrose went on. "We'll need a medical man for that. But the shape of the wound suggests that it was caused by a long, thin object. When I searched the library, I found traces of blood on the ledge of the stone mantelpiece. It's likely that Monique hit her head there."

"An accident... or do you think she was pushed?" Marianne said, her brows knitting.

"There's no way of knowing for certain at this point," Ambrose replied.

"But the fact that she ended up in the bookshelves is highly suspicious, don't you think?" Em's brown eyes were pensive. "If she hit her head on the mantel, how did she wind up halfway across the room? And don't forget the dust on her gown. It looked as if she'd swept the floor with her skirts. She was clearly dragged into the shelves."

Gadzooks. The image of Monique's limp body being hauled through the library released an icy trickle down Vi's spine. Her hands grew clammy in her lap, her lips trembling.

She felt a brief touch on her shoulder. Carlisle—somehow he'd sensed her disquiet. The warmth of his hand lingered, and his gaze was steady, reassuring.

"The windows to the library were locked," Strathaven was saying, "and there were no signs of forced entry. If the victim was attacked, whoever did it was already inside."

Ambrose gave a decisive nod. "We'll convey all this information to the magistrate who takes on the case."

"No." Billings spoke up for the first time. "I don't want the magistrate involved."

Ambrose frowned. "We're likely talking about a murder, sir. You don't have a choice."

"Like hell I don't," Billings said. "I know Jones, the local magistrate, and he's a damned zealot. If I give him free rein, he'll run roughshod over the place and inconvenience my guests."

"Tiresome business, murder," Strathaven said with irony.

Emma's forehead furrowed. "I'm sure your guests will understand, Mr. Billings."

"Not my business associates. They are *important* people, do you understand? They're used to making their own rules, and they have no liking for authorities. If the magistrate comes in with guns blazing, I'll have a revolt on my hands—and my reputation will be *ruined.*" Sweat beaded on the banker's upper lip. "Under no circumstances will I allow that to happen. My guests were promised a party, and they must not be disappointed. So name your fee, Kent."

"My fee... for what?"

"Your services," the banker said impatiently. "You're an investigator, aren't you? The best in London and I know that firsthand. Thus, I am retaining you to clear this matter up as quickly and discreetly as possible before Magistrate Jones takes over."

Ambrose's brows slammed together. "I have no authority over the magistrate—"

"No, but your excellent reputation has sway, and it goes all the way back to when you were with the Thames River Police." Billings' eyes glittered with determination. "You leave Jones to me. I'll tell him I have a man on the case, one of the best, and you'll keep him apprised of everything. Of course, you and I will know the truth: that you're working for me to resolve this business with all due haste."

"A woman has died, sir, and she deserves justice." Ambrose's tone had a steely edge. "Her death is not a fact that can be swept under the carpet nor should it be."

That's my brother, Violet thought with pride.

"That's not what I'm suggesting. Do what you must,"— Billings waved impatiently—"but do it with discretion. That's all I ask. Can you do that?"

"Until I pursue the matter further, I don't know yet if the victim's death was the result of an accident or foul play. Given the circumstances, I suspect the latter. Which means I'll have to interview potential suspects—including your guests."

Billings gave a terse nod. "Conduct your interviews with tact, and keep me informed. The investigation mustn't interfere with the party or diminish its pleasure in any way."

Vi couldn't refrain from speaking up. "Don't you think the fact that a woman was found dead in the library will dampen the party spirit?"

"Leave it to me. Handled properly, the guests will have nothing to concern themselves over." The banker smiled humorlessly. "To be frank, half of the guests see death every day and will think nothing of it. The other half see Madame Monique as naught more than a glorified servant—and thus will think nothing of it."

Disbelief and indignation made Vi speechless.

"So we have a deal, Kent?" Billings said. "I'll double your usual fee."

Ambrose growled, "You can take your money and—"

"If you won't do it for the money, do it for Gabriella. My daughter claims you are her staunchest allies, her... friends." The banker spoke the last word as if it were in a language foreign to him. "We all know that she is a wallflower, and her reputation is riding on the party's success. It's her last chance to gain a foothold in Society. So will you help her—or let her fall?"

Although Billings' assessment was uttered without emotion, to Violet it had the ring of truth. Gabby did need the Kents' support. But even more important was gaining justice for Monique. If anyone could discover what had happened to the acrobat, it would be Ambrose. And by finding the true killer, he'd ultimately be clearing Wick of any wrongdoing as well.

"Please take the case, Ambrose," Vi blurted. "For Monique and Gabby." *And for Wick.*

"I'll help," Emma said immediately.

Beside her, Strathaven let out a sigh.

Marianne placed a hand on Ambrose's arm. "I think your assistance is needed, darling."

A silent exchange passed between the two; Ambrose gave a reluctant nod.

"All right." Turning to Billings, he said evenly, "I will conduct this investigation, but I will do so on my own terms. Know this, sir: I will pursue the matter to its end—even if the result is not to your liking."

"Just keep me apprised and act with discretion." Billings stood. "Now I must make arrangements to have the body removed."

"It would be best to move the victim to a cool place, to preserve the body as much as possible," Ambrose said quietly. "I want a colleague of mine to examine her."

"As you wish." Billings was already heading toward the door, his stride brisk. "Carry on."

The door closed behind him.

"Bloody hell." Ambrose dragged a hand through his unruly hair. "What did I just sign on for?"

"You did the right thing, my love," Marianne murmured.

Ambrose's golden gaze grew focused. "There's much to do," he said. "I have to send for Dr. Abernathy; hopefully he can arrive from London by tomorrow or the day after and give us a more definitive opinion on the cause of death. I'll need to contact Lugo and McLeod as well. My partners can search Monique's residence in London; perhaps there'll be clues there as to why someone might want her dead. In the meantime, I want to interview those closest to her: her maid and colleagues, to begin with. We'll start compiling a list of suspects."

Suspects... people who might want Monique dead...

The memory struck Vi with the force of lightning. She jumped to her feet. "I want to help too! In fact, I know who—"

"No."

"Out of the question."

Ambrose and Carlisle frowned at each other; they'd spoken simultaneously.

"But I can help," Vi protested.

Carlisle shook his head. "You've seen enough for the night, Miss Kent. I am sure your delicate constitution would not benefit from further exposure to this macabre business."

And there goes our armistice. It was nice while it lasted.

"I've got the constitution of an ox," she said with a snort, "and everyone here knows it."

"Now, Violet—" her brother began.

"This is important," she insisted. "I know someone who had an argument with Monique *just last night*."

Finally, she had everyone's full attention. They were all staring at her.

"Who?" Emma said.

And the idiot sister shows her ace...

"Josephine Ashe," Vi said triumphantly.

13

An hour later, Richard found himself in a private sitting room that their host had arranged for their use during the investigation. He shared a settee with Violet; the Duchess of Strathaven occupied an adjacent chair, her husband standing behind her. They were all awaiting the return of Kent, who'd gone to perform a search of Monique's room and speak to her maid. The investigator had wanted to know as much as possible about the victim before interrogating Josephine Ashe.

As the other three talked in low murmurs, Richard couldn't bring himself to join in. Inner turmoil consumed him. His profound worry for Wick. His unsuitable and undeniable attraction to Violet. The right thing to do on both counts.

As the shock of Monique's death had worn off, an awful suspicion had arisen in Richard: was his brother somehow mixed up in the business? He didn't believe for a second that Wick would harm anyone... but what if his brother had had a connection with Monique? An amorous one?

He recalled the noxious scent that had clung to Wick when he'd shown up at Richard's townhouse several weeks ago... what had Wick said about it?

It's French and expensive.

Richard had asked if Wick was referring to the perfume or the tart who'd worn it.

And Wick had said, *Both*.

That same vile smell had irritated Richard last night at supper. Could Monique have been the one wearing it? Had she and Wick been carrying on some sort of affair?

A vein throbbed near Richard's temple. He prayed that his suspicions were unfounded because a connection between Wick and the Frenchwoman might make Wick a suspect. And there was still the matter of the ring: how had the deuced thing ended up in Monique's hand?

Which brought Richard to the second source of his disquiet. Somehow, he'd allowed Violet to get entangled in this mess. He hated the fact that she was concealing evidence for his brother's sake, but at the moment he didn't know a better option.

He glanced at her. As she discussed the case with her sister, her features were animated—no doubt because she'd wrangled her way into the interview with Ashe. Watching her, he felt a stirring of a deep hunger, yearning beyond anything he'd experienced before. He knew his desire for her wasn't wise, but that no longer seemed to matter.

It just *was*—and he was tired of fighting it.

Moreover, as far as he was concerned, they *had* to get married now. He'd taken advantage of her innocence not once but twice, and he needed to do right by her. His honor depended upon it. But how would he convince a free-spirited miss like Violet to marry a man she thought was a bloody stuffed shirt?

The door opened, and Kent walked in.

Richard put a lid on his rumination. *You'll talk to Violet soon. For now, focus—for Wick's sake.*

"How did it go?" Her Grace said. "Did you find any clues in Monique's bedchamber?"

Kent cleared his throat. "No. Nothing in particular." For some reason, his jaw reddened. "At least, nothing that would suggest a reason for her death."

"Perhaps I ought to have a go at her bedchamber—" Her Grace began.

"That's not necessary, Emma," the investigator said firmly. "Heed me on this."

"Did you learn anything from Monique's maid?" Violet said.

Kent sighed. "When I informed her of the news, she became hysterical. 'Twas impossible to interview her in such a state. The housekeeper gave her a sleeping draught; I'll talk to her again after she wakes." He sat, stretching his long legs in front of him. "In the interim, I've summoned Miss Ashe. She's on her way."

"I can't wait to hear what she has to say," the duchess declared.

"Billings has yet to make an announcement concerning Monique's death, so Miss Ashe should be in the dark about the business—unless, of course, she was involved. Your job is to observe her reaction, Em." Kent aimed a stern look at his sister. "Let me take the lead."

"Whatever you say," Her Grace said brightly. "When do I ever interfere?"

Behind her, Strathaven looked... amused.

As Kent and the duchess discussed their strategy for the interview, Violet said under her breath, "Emma can be a bit managing, you see."

Being neither deaf nor blind, Richard had surmised as much. Yet he heard the affection in Violet's tone, a matter-of-fact acceptance of her sibling's foibles. From what he'd observed thus far, the Kents seemed to share a rare respect for one another. Or perhaps they were too unconventional to notice each other's eccentricities.

"Is this a problem for you?" he ventured.

"It's part of Em's charm." Violet's lips tipped up. "Just as dodging her is part of mine."

The playful and unconditional warmth she had for her family

was foreign to his own experience. In the Murray household, affection had been measured and expectations strict; any deviation from one's role had led to repercussions. He'd always been the responsible son. Ever since he could remember, his father had pressed upon him the importance of duty, of taking care of the family. After Papa's death, when Richard hadn't been able to keep Mama in the style she'd been accustomed to, she'd made her displeasure clear.

Whereas Wick... Wick had always been the prodigal son for whom no repenting was necessary. He'd been cosseted by the entire family, Richard included.

And look at where that has gotten him, Richard thought heavily.

"You're worried about Wick, aren't you?" Violet said in an undertone.

Her insight surprised him. He wasn't used to someone reading his thoughts—to having anyone care to do so. He cast a quick look at her siblings still engrossed in their conversation.

Quietly, he admitted, "Aye. I am."

She nibbled on her lip. "Perhaps he and the others went on a jaunt to the village last night? It'd be just like them. Maybe they got three sheets to the wind and are just now waking up in some tavern."

It was a heartening possibility. Much more so than the others rattling in Richard's head.

"You ease my mind, lass," he said.

A bemused look came over her. "I don't think anyone has *ever* said that to me before."

Before he could reply, a knock sounded on the door.

"Come in," Kent said, and Richard rose with the other men.

Josephine Ashe entered the room. She was dressed in a plain bombazine gown, her manner as watchful as that of a governess. With the exception of her daringly short coiffure, she appeared quite ordinary. Nothing suggested that she juggled fire for a living.

"Good morning," the duchess said. "Thank you for coming."

"Of course, Your Grace." Miss Ashe's curtsy was diffident, her wary gaze circling the room's occupants and lingering for an instant on Violet. "You, er, wished to see me?"

"Please have a seat." Kent gestured to a chair. "We'd like to ask you some questions."

Perching on the very edge of the chair, Ashe said, "About what, exactly?"

"Your relationship with Madame Monique."

At Kent's direct reply, Ashe's eyes narrowed. "Why would you wish to know about that?"

"Because Monique is dead," Kent said.

Richard wasn't the best judge of women, but even he saw the surprise flash through Ashe's eyes. "Dead... *Monique*? But how?"

"That is what we are trying to determine," Kent said briskly. "To do so, we are interviewing those with connections to her."

"You don't think *I* had something to do with it?" Ashe sounded aghast.

Violet spoke up. "I saw you and Madame Monique having an argument yesterday."

Ashe ran a hand through her cropped blond locks. "That was nothing. Monique and I, we have never rubbed along—but that doesn't mean that I would harm her."

"What was the source of friction between the two of you?" Her Grace asked.

Color seeped into the juggler's pale cheeks. "Monique wasn't an easy person to get along with. She thought only of herself, never spared a thought for others. Sharing a stage with her was akin to sharing a bed with someone who hoards all the blankets." An angry tremor entered her voice. "I was constantly left in the cold."

Richard recalled yesterday's performance. Monique's dramatic entrance had cut short Ashe's applause. Could professional jealousy be a motive for murder?

"I wasn't the only one who felt that way," Ashe added quickly.

"Ask my colleague, Mr. Burns—or any of the other performers at Astley's. Monique de Brouet was a selfish, unpleasant woman."

"De Brouet is her true name?" Kent had removed a small notebook and was jotting into it.

"So she claimed." Ashe's eyes glittered with a hostility that she couldn't hide. "Monique boasted that she came from *la noblesse*, you see. Liked to lord her origins over me just because my father was a fisherman from Marseilles. As if any of that mattered." Her arms folded over her thin chest. "Even if her family was aristocratic, they lost everything in The Terror before she was born. Monique might like to act all hoity-toity, but the fact was she was a performer at Astley's just like me. No better, no worse."

"What were you arguing about yesterday?" Violet said.

"I did not appreciate the way her entrée cut short my ovation. It was not the way we had practiced; she was always up to such tricks."

"I'd be annoyed, too, if someone altered a routine I'd practiced." Violet's matter-of-fact empathy seemed to calm the other. "Was that why you broke her looking glass?"

"For months, I'd been frustrated by her selfishness—and yesterday I gave in to my feelings. But it was a fit of pique, nothing more. On this, I swear."

"Where were you last evening, Miss Ashe?" Kent said.

"I was indisposed." Above the dark collar of her dress, Ashe's throat rippled. "It had been a long day, with travel and the performance. I had dinner on a tray in my room."

"Can anyone vouch for that fact?"

"I am an *artist*, sir. Not a harlot like Monique de Brouet." Her voice quivered with outrage. "Unlike her, I do not entertain guests in my room."

"I was referring to a maid or any other servant who might have seen you," Kent said patiently.

"Oh." Some of the wind left her sails. "Miss Billings did

provide me with a maid... Mary, I think her name was. She helped me get ready for bed."

As Kent scribbled in his notebook, Her Grace cut in. "Why do you call Monique a harlot?"

"Because she is... or was, rather." Ashe cleared her throat. "Everyone knew she had lovers."

"Do you know the identities of these lovers?" Kent said.

An invisible vise gripped Richard's insides. *By Jove, don't let her say Wick...*

"Monique was discreet," Ashe said grudgingly. "Although she didn't name names, she was constantly showing off this gewgaw or that, bragging that it came from some wealthy admirer. Her dressing room was bursting at the seams with gentlemen."

Pencil poised, Kent said, "Do you recognize any of them here at the party?"

"I had better things to do than pay attention to Monique's adoring hordes," Ashe said with a sniff. "All I know is that she played fast and loose with her virtue."

"What about enemies?" Richard spoke up. "Did Madame de Brouet have any?"

"With the way she conducted her life, I would be surprised if she didn't," the juggler said righteously. "If you wish to know particulars, ask that maid of hers, Jeanne. That one was the gargoyle at the gates, guarding all her mistress' dirty secrets."

"We'll speak to her," Kent said. "Thank you for your time, Miss Ashe."

After the performer's departure, he turned to the group. "What do you think?"

"She sounded like she was telling the truth," Violet said.

"I can speak to the maid, Mary, to verify Miss Ashe's alibi," the duchess offered.

Kent nodded. "Good idea, Emma. You have a way with interviewing staff."

Her Grace beamed, and Strathaven murmured, "I'll go with you, pet."

"I want to help too," Violet said.

"You've done enough, Vi," Kent said firmly. "Thank you for the help with Miss Ashe. We can handle the rest."

"But *Ambrose*—"

"I'll escort Miss Kent back to her room, if I may," Richard intervened.

Kent's gaze thinned. Although Richard lacked the ability to read women, he had no problems understanding masculine communication. A silent exchange passed between him and Kent.

The twitching muscle in Kent's jaw warned, *Harm my sister, and I'll string you up.*

My intentions are honorable, Richard's jerk of the chin affirmed. *You have my word.*

After a minute, the investigator said aloud, "*Directly* to her room, my lord."

"Thank you, sir." Richard offered his arm to Violet. "Shall we, Miss Kent?"

14

Violet had never been a shrinking testament to her namesake, yet she was unaccountably tongue-tied as Carlisle escorted her back to her room. There was much to discuss concerning Wick, yet her brain refused to cooperate. Perhaps the lack of sleep combined with the excitement of the last several hours was finally taking its toll. She felt giddy, her pulse skipping erratically; she couldn't control the wave of aware-ness flooding her senses.

Despite his brawny build, Carlisle moved with undeniable grace, his stride athletic and assured as they climbed the steps up to the floor of her room. Glancing beneath her lashes at his unsmiling mouth, she recalled the sensual firmness of those lips—and had to wet her own. Her gaze dipped lower, to the long-fingered hands at his sides, and molten heat welled inside her.

In the library, he'd awakened her to pleasure that she hadn't known existed. His kisses had been so hot, his words even hotter. Then there was the way he'd touched her: *inside* and out until bliss had exploded, catapulting her over that dazzling, ecstatic edge... It had been, without question, the most exhilarating experience of her life. Better than any sport. Better than riding, climbing, and dancing *combined*.

"We should talk."

Carlisle's pronouncement pulled her from her reverie. His brusque tone and the intent look in his eyes instantly filled her with wariness. Although she couldn't deny her physical attraction to him, their differences were far from settled. The memory of his shoddy marriage proposal surfaced, along with all his past comments about her character.

And he'd sided with Ambrose in trying to shut her out of the case.

Nothing has changed, her inner voice said. *Just because he dallied with you doesn't mean he likes you.*

Something inside her deflated like a soufflé. As much as she'd told herself that his opinion didn't matter, for some infernal reason, it did. The fact made her feel exposed, vulnerable in a way she didn't like.

As they passed the landing, which featured a Grecian urn gleaming in its recessed niche, she tried to bluff her way through. "Yes, we need to figure out how to help Wick—"

"There's no *we* in that endeavor, Miss Kent. Wickham is my brother and my responsibility. I don't want you involved."

His rejection worse than stung—it *hurt*. A fragile connection had sprouted between them since finding Monique's body. For a short time, they'd actually been working together, and it had felt surprisingly... right.

Swallowing, she said, "I'm already involved. Wick's my friend. Don't forget I'm protecting his secret, too."

"I'm in no danger of forgetting. I've never regretted anything more in my life." While she struggled to absorb that blow, Carlisle went on impatiently, "My brother aside, you and I have a matter to settle between us. A matter of honor."

At the word "honor," she stopped short in the deserted hall-way, just a few doors down from her chamber. Anger shot up like a geyser. She welcomed the sudden surge of energy because it felt better than humiliation.

"You're not going to propose again, are you?" she said acidly.

His eyes flickered. Did he flinch?

When he spoke, his words were harder than iron. "Is it the notion of marriage that you find offensive or the notion of marriage to me?"

"I don't find the notion of marriage offensive."

"It's me, then." His expression was darker than a forge. "At least you're honest. So none of that meant anything to you, is that it?"

"None of what?" she shot back.

"Kissing, making love." Iridescent ore glittered in his eyes. "You're like the rest of your sex. Flirtation is a game to you. You string men along for fun and then toss them aside when you grow bored."

The unfairness of the accusation rendered her speechless for a moment.

She planted her hands on her hips. "I'm not playing any games!"

"In case you've forgotten," he said in scathing tones, "you and I have played twice now in the dark. Yet you won't even listen to my proposal."

Then and there, her temper snapped.

"Because I don't want to be insulted, you lummox!" she yelled.

"Insulted?" he said coldly. "Why would *you* be insulted?"

Could the man honestly be that obtuse?

"Because your last *proposal* was a lecture on duty and responsibility. Despite the fact that I am not the paragon you want for a wife—that I am a *mistake,* as you so charmingly put it—you charitably offered to take me on anyway, in spite of your good judgement."

Heartbeats pounded by as he stared at her, looking...

surprised? Ruddy color tinged his broad cheekbones. Lifting a hand, he rubbed the back of his neck.

"I didn't mean it that way," he muttered.

"Well, that's the way it came out. And I have no desire for a repeat performance. Trust me, I'm fully aware of my flaws and don't need to have them pointed out to me." Her breath grew choppy; she had the sudden panic that she might burst into tears. "If you'll excuse me," she said, her vision blurring ominously, "I'll see myself to my room."

"Wait." He caught her by the arm.

"Just let me *go*." Determined not to let him see her cry, she struggled against his hold.

"Violet, please. I... I'm sorry."

At his hoarse words, she stilled. He was... apologizing? To her?

"I didn't mean to insult you. I'm not skilled when it comes to dealing with... affairs of a personal nature." The gruffness of his admission made her throat swell. "I haven't my brother's charm or ease with your sex. Sometimes I say things, and they don't come out as I intended. That is my failing entirely—and not a reflection of my regard for you."

Violet stared at his sincere, rough-hewn features, unable to form words.

He released her arm. His gaze fixed on the carpet as if the pattern explained the mysteries of the universe. "I don't expect your forgiveness. I've not acted like a gentleman where you are concerned. But even so,"—his voice was gravelly—"I cannot regret what has passed between us."

The thumping of her heart grew loud in her ears. All at once, emotion surged. She didn't have the wherewithal to push it back.

"You're crying? *God,* I'm such a bastard." Looking stricken, Carlisle cupped her jaw with both hands, his thumbs wiping clumsily at her tears. "Damnit, I'm so sorry..."

His tenderness was unexpected and... *awkward.* Endearingly so. It unleashed a tempest within her, and she began to weep.

With a groan, Carlisle gave up trying to dash away her tears and pulled her into his arms instead. His embrace was too tight, the buttons of his waistcoat jamming into her cheek, but he stroked her back, murmuring bits of nonsense against her hair.

Vi didn't cry often, but when she did it was oft like this: as intense and brief as a summer storm. When the tears subsided, awareness returned to her... along with a feeling of supreme foolishness. Embarrassed, she pushed at his chest. He let her go and silently handed her a handkerchief.

Fighting a sniffle, she wiped her cheeks. "Just so you know, I'm no watering pot. I don't know where that came from."

"'Tis the stress, I expect. You've been through a lot. First there's the assignation in the library, then finding a dead body. And I had to go top it off with the worst proposal in living memory."

His dry humor startled a hiccupping laugh from her. His expression remained stoic, but the line of his lips bent a little. A rueful curve.

"When did you become so understanding, Lord Carlisle?" she said.

"Just now, when a young miss put me in my place and deservedly so."

In his iron-dark gaze, she thought she glimpsed a smile. Her heart fluttered.

"Feeling better now?" he asked.

"Yes," she said shyly. "Thank you."

He reached out, brushing his knuckles against her cheek, his touch mesmerizingly sweet.

The sound of footsteps dispelled the magic of the moment. They sprang apart just as Miss Turbett appeared at the end of the hall. She was walking with her head down, apparently lost in her thoughts. When she was in danger of plowing right through them, Vi spoke up.

"Um, hello, Miss Turbett."

The other miss started, her grey gaze flying up. "Oh! My, you gave me a fright. I'm afraid I didn't..." She bit her lip, bobbed a curtsy. "Good afternoon."

Violet and Richard both returned the courtesy. Vi noticed that the other girl looked paler than usual—which was saying something. Beneath Miss Turbett's fine, translucent skin, tracings of blue veins could be seen, and purple smudged below her eyes.

"Are you all right?" Vi said with concern.

The other's light brown lashes swept rapidly. "Oh, yes. I'm perfectly fine—"

"Amelia! There you are." Mr. Turbett came marching up. He was a tall, sparse man; during the party, Vi had observed that the merchant had a brusque and domineering manner, especially when it came to his daughter.

"What have I told you about wandering off without me?" he demanded.

Cowering, Miss Turbett whispered, "I'm sorry, Father. I... I was just..."

"She was just chatting with us," Violet said brightly. "Good day, sir."

"Turbett." Carlisle inclined his head.

The merchant grudgingly bent at the waist. "My lord. Have you seen Mr. Murray?"

Carlisle's jaw tautened. "My brother is around, I'm sure."

Neatly done, Violet thought.

"But not where he's supposed to be." Turbett's gaze narrowed. "I've seen neither hide nor hair of him since yesterday afternoon."

"Father, please—"

"Be quiet, Amelia." Her father held up a hand to silence her. "Now, Carlisle, you and I had an understanding. I didn't come all the way to this bloody house party to twiddle my thumbs. And now there's the inconvenience of that woman's accident. God knows how an acrobat managed to meet her maker tripping over something in the library."

Violet exchanged a quick look with Carlisle. Apparently, Billings had made the announcement about Monique's death, and he'd skimmed over the facts.

"Now we're all stuck here until the matter is wrapped up, and I refuse to have that time be wasted. Mr. Murray had better pay his respects to my daughter soon, or our deal is off." Turbett crossed his arms over his puny chest. "He's not the only fish in the sea."

A muffled sound of embarrassment escaped Miss Turbett. Violet's heart went out to the other. Simultaneously, she noted the ominous ticking of the muscle in Carlisle's jaw.

With an obvious force of will, he maintained his temper. "Wickham knows his duty. You may expect to see him soon."

"I had better." His message delivered, Turbett grabbed his daughter's arm. "Come, Amelia. 'Tis time for our afternoon constitutional."

The girl looked so miserable that Violet said impulsively, "I was wondering, Miss Turbett, if you'd care to join my sisters and me for, um, a game of cards some time?"

Miss Turbett blinked. "Oh. That's nice of you—"

"My daughter doesn't play games. She hasn't time for frivolity. Good day." Without another word, Turbett dragged his offspring away.

"He's not a friendly chap, is he?" Violet muttered under her breath.

"To Turbett, friendliness is a waste of time." Distaste was evident in Carlisle's austere countenance.

Then why are you bullying Wick into marrying his daughter? Why are you using him to clean up the mess you made?

Confusing questions tangled in Vi's brain. At the same time, weariness rolled over her like a fog. She wavered on her feet; Carlisle caught her.

"You haven't slept all night. You must be exhausted." He steered her the remaining distance to her room. "Time for a nap."

She opened her mouth to argue that she wasn't a child—and a yawn emerged instead. Crumpets, she *was* drowsy. "We have to talk. 'Bout Wick," she mumbled.

"We will. After you've rested."

"Promise?"

He nodded. "Now get inside, lass."

She let him open the door for her, was halfway in when she turned around. "Carlisle?"

"Yes?"

"Thank you... for being nice."

His lips tipped up slightly at the corners. "You're welcome."

Smiling to herself, she closed the door. Without bothering to take off her clothes, she stumbled to the bed and flopped onto the mattress. She gazed up at the canopy, her eyelids already heavy, and within minutes, she fell asleep... thinking of him.

15

"Violet, dear, it's time to get dressed for supper."

Vi ignored the soft, familiar voice and snuggled deeper into her dream. Cuddled against a hard chest and held by strong arms, she was riding into a glorious sunset with her prince. They were astride a majestic white horse, and she sat in front of him, relaxed and comfortable in her... trousers?

"Poor thing's all done in."

She disregarded the second voice, too, because she'd turned her head to look into her prince's eyes: they were as dark and smoky as a smithy. He bent his head, his mouth slanting deliciously over hers...

"Violet never naps. I hope she's all right..."

As the voices murmured on, the vestiges of the dream slipped away. Violet blinked groggily at the pink canopy; never a sound sleeper, she wasn't used to the disorienting lethargy of waking from a deep slumber. Then it all came back to her.

Monique... Wick... *Carlisle.*

The stress of events and that crying jag must have worn her out. How long had she been asleep? Leaning up on her elbows, she saw two figures standing by the wardrobe. Emma... and Thea!

She threw back the covers. "Thea, when did you arrive?"

The second eldest Kent sister, now the Marchioness of Tremont, turned, her pretty, gentle face wreathed in smiles. She opened her arms, and Violet bounded into them.

"Just an hour ago." Thea gave her a hug and stepped back, studying her with warm hazel eyes. "It's only been a few weeks since we were last together, but I vow there's something different about you."

Vi squirmed. "I'm, um, just the same as I ever was. Same old Violet, that's me."

"Now that you mention it, Thea, I see it too." *Parsnips*—now Em was scrutinizing her too. "There *is* something different about you, Violet. A certain glow."

Do not blush. Do not blush.

"I had a good nap, that's all." Running her fingers through her tangled tresses, she said, "How was your journey, Thea?"

"Not as eventful as what's been going on here." Thea shook her head, her gilded oak curls gleaming. "Emma told me everything. I can't believe it. How dreadful for Madame Monique. And for you and Lord Carlisle to discover her."

"It was a shocker," Vi admitted.

"We'll have to do our catching up whilst we get Violet dressed," Emma interjected. "There's only an hour before supper."

Vi noticed then that her two sisters were already dressed for the evening. Emma's cerise taffeta complemented her rich brunette coloring, a pink sapphire and diamond choker circling her neck. Thea's celestial blue *crepe de chine* was trimmed with seed pearls and suited her ethereal beauty perfectly.

Violet scratched her ear. "I suppose I'd better get cleaned up, hadn't I? Next to both of you, I look like something the cat dragged in."

"Silly girl," Thea said, smiling. "We'll get you shipshape in no time."

Back in Chudleigh Crest, the Kents had no servants. They'd

done their own chores and helped each other dress. As her sisters fussed over her, Vi was reminded of those times, so simple and good. Now that Em and Thea had married, things had changed; these moments together were becoming more rare and precious. She could feel her own girlhood slipping away—torn away, in truth, by new experiences.

Mere days ago, all she'd desired was freedom. To carry on as she wanted, with no one to judge her or tell her what to do. Now she was tantalized by a different possibility, and she couldn't deny that Carlisle had been the one to plant the seed. To awaken a dormant longing inside her.

Kents had a tradition of falling passionately in love. Although she couldn't label her feelings toward Carlisle as love, precisely, she couldn't deny that they were passionate. All her life, she'd adored physical activity for the way it made her feel: fully present in her own skin. Carlisle had the same effect on her... only *more* so.

Being with him was more exhilarating than any sport. And it wasn't just the lovemaking. Thinking about the unexpected gentleness beneath his gruff exterior made her pulse speed up.

Could she have misjudged his character all along? But there was what Wick had said about him. What sort of man would force his brother into an unhappy marriage to correct his own mistakes? Yet Carlisle was clearly concerned for his brother's welfare. Thunder and turf, he was *concealing evidence* to protect Wick.

She couldn't reconcile these facts. Clearly, she didn't have all the pieces of the puzzle. She resolved to ferret out the truth at the first opportunity.

"Breathe out," Thea said.

Air whooshed from Vi's lungs as her sister knotted the corset strings.

"So tell me more about Lord Carlisle," Thea said. "It sounds as if things have changed between the two of you."

Crumbs. Her emotions already felt raw and exposed; she didn't know if she wanted to share them. "Um, changed?"

Emma jumped in. "Before the party, you couldn't stand him— and understandably, given the gossip he'd started. But now the two of you seem as thick as thieves. In the study this morning, Carlisle appeared inordinately protective of you and concerned for your well-being."

Em's observation gave Vi a little thrill. She was beginning to see that perhaps her judgement hadn't always been sound when it came to Carlisle. It was comforting to have her sister's opinion. Hmm, maybe she ought to try confiding a little more.

Testing the waters, she ventured, "What if I said Carlisle's not as bad as I once believed?"

"What changed your mind?" Em said.

His kisses... how kind he can be... the fact that we're presently concealing evidence together?

"I think he and I got off on the wrong foot," she said.

Em's brows lifted. "That's it? A simple case of misunderstanding?"

If she wanted her sisters' advice on relationship matters, she couldn't furnish them with half-truths. They needed to know how she and Carlisle had started off.

She sighed inwardly. *Time to face the firing squad.*

"Do you remember the Yuletide ball where Carlisle fell into the fountain? He, um, sort of... had some help. From me." Her breath held as she awaited their response.

Thea paused in the adjusting of petticoats to look at Emma. "You were right after all."

Instead of looking surprised, Em looked pleased with herself. "It wasn't difficult to deduce."

Vi stared at her siblings. "You mean you *knew* the entire time that I was responsible for Carlisle's fall?"

"Well, not for certain," Em said. "But I guessed."

"How?"

"Let's face it, dear, you were never good at prevaricating. Your accounting of your time at the Yuletide ball was always a bit suspect, and there were those champagne stains on your gown." Her sister's tone was dry. "Then there was the way you leapt to Carlisle's defense when we were making light of the accident. It smacked of guilt."

"I was that obvious?" Vi muttered.

"Only to someone who knows you." Em canted her head. "Why didn't you just tell us what happened, dear?"

Vi studied her toes. "I was embarrassed. And I didn't want you to be cross at me, Em."

"Why would I be cross?" Her sister sounded puzzled.

"Because you're always reminding me to act less like a hoyden. To curb my behavior." Vi hitched her shoulders in a self-deprecating shrug. "You know, to be less, well, *me*."

"But that's not true. I want you to be you. I'm just worried that—"

"I know you have my best interests at heart," Vi said quickly. "It's just that sometimes I can't help being who I am."

"Who else would you be?" A notch formed between Emma's brows. "The *ton*—it's not a forgiving place, and I don't want you to get hurt. But neither do I want you to change the essence of who you are."

A tremulous warmth crept through Violet's chest. "You mean that, truly?"

"I do. Darling girl,"—Em reached out, tucked a stray curl behind Vi's ear—"you're special and wonderful. Can't you be that... *and* a little more careful?"

Vi loved her sisters. She truly did.

"You're right. I really ought to think before I act." Expelling a breath, she confessed, "I didn't *intend* to push Carlisle into the fountain. But I lost my temper, and the next moment he was bathing in champagne. I felt horrible about it for days."

Her sisters looked at one another—and erupted into gales of laughter.

"It's not amusing," Vi protested.

"I know, dear," Thea said between gasps, "but I can't help it. If you felt horrible, imagine... imagine how poor Carlisle felt!"

"Felled by a female. I'm sure that was a blow to his pride," Emma said with a chuckle.

Feeling lighthearted now that a burden had been lifted from her chest, Vi gave a snort. "He'll recover. After all, he has plenty of pride to spare."

"He is a bit of a stuffed shirt, isn't he?" Em said.

"He has good qualities, too," she protested.

"What are they?" Thea said slyly.

"Although he can be a bit old-fashioned... he's an honorable man."

As she said the words, she realized the truth of them. Carlisle had protected her reputation after she'd made him a laughing-stock. After they'd kissed, he'd made her an offer—true, it was the worst marriage proposal in the history of Christendom, but it was the intention that counted, wasn't it? He'd even owned up to his mistakes, apologizing when he realized that he'd hurt her.

"And despite his bluster, he's kinder than he lets on," she mused.

Thea returned from the wardrobe with Vi's evening gown. "According to Lady Blackwood, her husband has the highest opinion of Carlisle. Says he's a gentleman's gentleman, the kind of man you'd want at your back in a battle."

She thought of the Priest Hole, how he'd found it before she had. He was competitive, a man of action, and she admired that. And as annoying as his stubbornness could be, there was no denying his strength of will and commitment.

"There *is* something reliable about him. And he's a solid, quick-witted chap." Why hadn't she recognized his good qualities earlier?

"Some gentlemen improve upon acquaintance," Thea said as if reading her mind. "What we think of as pride might in actuality be a reserved nature. A sort of discomfort around others. I should know: when I first met Tremont, he seemed standoffish as well."

"His reserve didn't last long around you, Thea," Em said with a wink.

Thea blushed.

Emma adjusted a floaty sleeve. "Now, Vi, are you forming an attachment to Carlisle?"

Leave it to her sister to hit the nail on the head. In the past, Violet might have tried to evade the question out of embarrassment. She was still far from comfortable sharing her feelings, but she was learning the benefit of being more open.

"How would I know?" she asked. "How did the both of *you* know?"

"I was attracted to Tremont from the moment we met. He was so handsome, and I felt tingles whenever he was nearby," Thea said dreamily.

Vi started a mental list.

Tingles. Check.

"Did you feel tingles too, Emma?" she asked.

"Yes, but they were overshadowed by a strong desire to throttle Strathaven. His Grace was, without a doubt, the most frustrating man I'd ever met." A grin tucked into Em's cheeks as she worked on the buttons on the back of Vi's dress. "He still is, bless him."

Frustration. Double check.

"I know what you mean," Violet said with feeling. "At times, Carlisle and I seem to bring out the worst in each other."

"In what way?" Em said.

"Well, he has a tendency to be domineering and conservative. Whereas I'm, you know... *me*. I'm not exactly a run-of-the-mill miss."

"A hereditary condition, I'm afraid. Luckily, normality is an overrated quality." Em shook Vi's skirts into place. "Just ask our husbands who couldn't give a whit about it."

"Tremont thinks I'm normal," Thea said.

Emma's brows lifted. "You... who foiled the plot of a nefarious spy?"

"Well, I can *pass* for normal." Thea's smile was demure. "Under exigent circumstances."

"The point *being*, the most important thing one can be in a relationship is oneself. Who else can one be after all?" Stepping back, Em inspected Vi. "I think you're ready, dear. Go have a look in the looking glass."

Vi trotted over to the long oval mirror—and her lips tipped up in her reflection. She loved the rich hue accomplished by layering pale golden gauze over saffron satin. When she moved, the golden threads caught the light, glimmering. As the *coup de grace*, tiny golden blossoms had been embroidered onto the gauze, drifting playfully over the full skirts and piling up richly at the hem.

Twisting this way and that, she breathed, "This gown is the *utmost*."

Her sisters' smiling faces appeared behind her.

"How lovely you are. The gown suits you perfectly," Thea said.

"And, in the end, finding the right husband is no different from finding the right dress. One must consider the fit," Em said prosaically, "and whether or not he accentuates one's best qualities. In his presence, one ought to feel confident and at one's best."

Memories of Carlisle's kisses and his warmly possessive touch caused a melting sensation in Violet's midsection. Those times with Carlisle had been sublime. Despite the sisterly confidences shared this eve, however, she wasn't quite up to revealing *that* tidbit.

Passion aside, she wasn't sure of the fit between her and Carlisle. Their connection felt both vibrant and fragile, like a breathtaking gown that could snag at any moment. She was beginning to recognize his good qualities... but was he seeing hers? When it came down to it, she wasn't even sure he *liked* her.

Swallowing, she said, "Given how we started, do you think it's possible that Carlisle and I could learn to bring out the best in one another?"

"Conflict is oft the prelude to romance," Thea said in philosophical tones. "Remember how Emma and His Grace were when they first met?"

"We're still that way," Em put in cheerfully, "but we have learned to compromise and that makes all the difference."

Compromise. Well, she would try. And that reminded her of something else.

"Em, may I ask you a favor?"

"Yes, dear?"

"Would you speak to Ambrose about letting me join the investigation? I promise I'll be guided by you, will act under your supervision. Please, Em," she pleaded, "I *know* I can help, and I want to be a part of this."

Her sister studied her. "It's that important to you, Violet?"

"Remember how *you* felt when you were barred from helping Strathaven?"

During the murder investigation that had brought Emma and His Grace together, the former had had to fight to be included in the proceedings. To be taken seriously... as Violet wished to be.

"I remember. All too well." Em gave a brisk nod. "I'll talk to Ambrose, but I'm not guaranteeing anything will come of it."

"Thank you!" Vi threw her arms around her eldest sister. "You won't regret it."

Em returned the hug, sighing, "I hope you're right."

16

R ichard stood with Blackwood in the ballroom after supper.
The mirrored walls made the grand space appear even
larger, magnifying the effect of the pink marble floors and crystal
chandeliers. The night was surprisingly balmy, and the balcony
doors that lined one side of the dance floor were left open, navy
curtains stirring in the breeze.

Whatever one could say about Billings, the banker did indeed
know how to "handle" situations. As he'd predicted, the guests
seemed remarkably blasé about the fact that Madame Monique
had passed away the night before. The rough-and-tumble portion
of the crowd was enjoying the fine victuals as if nothing had
happened. The bluebloods, on the other hand, were speculating
with titillated abandon over the cause of the "accident." No one
appeared distressed by the fact that a woman had been found
dead in the library.

"No reason to let a little thing like death get in the way of a
good time." Blackwood's dry observation echoed Richard's own.
"Now if my sons were here, they'd be in tears. They adore Astley's
and Madame Monique in particular, God rest her. Speaking of

which, how are you holding up, old boy? It can't have been pleasant... finding her."

Although Kent's plan was to keep details from the general
public, the Blackwoods, being trusted friends, were an exception
to the rule.

"I'm fine." Richard straightened as he saw Violet enter the
room. By Jove, she was a vibrant bloom. The now familiar
yearning gripped him. They'd been seated apart at supper, and
he'd found himself missing her company. "It's Miss Kent I'm
worried about."

"Changed your opinion of her at last, have you?"

Richard's face flushed. Months ago, Blackwood had been on
the receiving end of Richard's tirade about Violet—those fateful,
damnable words that had been overheard and turned into ugly
gossip. Richard winced at the memory of his own stupidity,
wishing with every fiber of his being that he could take those
words back.

"I was wrong," he admitted. "In truth, my opinion has quite
reversed."

"Oh ho. Is that the way the wind blows?" Blackwood raised his
brows.

"If I can persuade the lady in question to accept my suit."

Deep down, Richard wasn't confident that he could. He'd
spent the afternoon looking for Wickham at the house and local
village, to no avail. When there was naught else he could do—
except go mad with frustration and worry—he'd gone for a ride to
clear his head.

As he and Aiolos had galloped through the estate's rolling
fields, he'd let himself mull over his interactions with Violet. He
was forced to conclude that he hadn't acquitted himself well.
Mostly he'd just harangued her and accused her of things. Self-
recrimination had filled him. The truth was she deserved far more
than the apology he'd given her.

Recalling her tears and insistence that she was no watering

pot, he felt a foreign and poignant ache in his chest. She was a spirited little thing and, he was beginning to understand, not one to wear her emotions on her sleeve. Beneath her carefree manner lay sensitivity and depth of feeling. She was nothing like the shallow flirt he'd first imagined her to be.

As he broodingly watched Parnell, Goggs, and other gentlemen swarm around Violet, he recognized just how wrong he'd been. She *wasn't* flirting with them. Now that he wasn't blinded by his prejudice, he saw none of the usual female affections. No eyelash batting, fan twirling, or coy laughter. Instead, Violet treated the rakehells the way she treated Wick... with warm and easy camaraderie. For God's sake, she'd just *punched* Goggs in the arm.

Those lads were her friends. Exactly as she'd claimed.

Even as the notion relieved him, possessiveness surged. Richard realized that he didn't want her consorting with other males, even if they were just her friends. He wanted her... for himself. To belong only to him. To achieve that, he would have to convince her to marry him. But he wasn't certain how to achieve his goal. His previous attempts at courtship had proved abysmal failures, and God knew his dealings with Violet had been less than stellar.

"Well you're not going to woo her from over here." Blackwood looked like he was fighting a smile—the bastard. "Go over and talk to her."

Richard was seized by uncharacteristic panic. "What should I, er, say?"

The only topics that came to mind were murder, mayhem, and his missing brother—not exactly things to engender tender feelings in a lady.

Grinning openly, Blackwood said, "Talk about the weather. The lovely music. How pretty her frock is."

"How pretty *whose* frock is?" Lady Blackwood asked, joining them.

Blackwood drew his marchioness close, kissing her temple. "Miss Kent's."

"Ah." Lady Blackwood's eyes sparkled at her husband. "So I was right?"

"As always, my love."

Richard muttered, "So talk about her gown—that's your advice?"

"Actually, knowing Violet, I daresay she'd prefer a dance to small talk." Lady Blackwood smiled. "And if you do converse, I'd recommend sporting topics over frippery."

"Sporting?" *That* sounded promising. Like something he could do with some level of competence. Yet he couldn't recall any lady in his past who'd shared his interest in the subject. Intrigued, he said, "What kind of sports does Miss Kent enjoy?"

"Come, Carlisle, it's not as if she's a stranger," the marchioness chided. "Just be yourself and go talk to her."

Clearly, she didn't know how disastrous being himself could be. But what other choice did he have? Very well, he would go over and do his best.

As he made his way through the throng, he told himself Lady Blackwood was right. Violet wasn't some stranger. He'd kissed her, known the inexpressible delight of bringing her to climax in his arms. But that was just it: in bedroom matters, he related to women just fine. It was in all other situations where they were enigmas to him. He didn't know what they wanted, what would please them.

Out of nowhere, an image sprang from a deeply buried place in his mind. His mama's bedchamber, viewed through his thirteen-year-old eyes. He was on a rare visit home from Eton, and walking through the estate, he'd stumbled upon a field of daffodils. Thinking they were as lovely as his mama, he'd picked a bunch, hoping that they might please her. As he clutched the droopy blooms in his dirt-stained hands, he felt nervous excitement.

Sitting at her vanity, his mama took his tribute gingerly, her face as cool and beautiful as the diamonds glittering at her ears and throat. *How... singular,* she'd said in her cultured tones. *Is that mud on your hands? You'd best go clean it off.* She'd turned back to the mirror.

Later that day, he saw the daffodils again. Ragged and wilted, they lay discarded on a tray that his mama's maid was removing from her room.

He shoved aside the memory. Why would he think of such stupid things now? Violet didn't have anything to do with his mother. Hell, she was unlike any other female he'd met.

Given how different she was, he thought with sudden insight, perhaps he should... set aside his preconceived notions? Lord knew his assumptions about women hadn't helped him thus far. Instead, he could try to discover what *Violet* wanted—and use that to win her over.

Strategy in place, he made his way to her side with a determined stride, swatting other would-be beaux out of his way like the annoying gnats they were. When he reached Violet and her sister, he bowed.

"Your Grace. Miss Kent," he said.

"Good evening, Lord Carlisle." The duchess' greeting was warmer than he expected. "Are you enjoying the ball?"

"Yes, thank you." Clearing his throat, he said to Violet, "That's a pretty frock."

Her chestnut curls, pinned in glossy bunches over her ears, tipped to one side. "You like it, my lord?"

"Indeed. It's very... yellow." God, he sounded like an idiot.

"I believe the proper term for it is saffron, my lord."

Her tawny eyes were sparkling, and he thought she might be teasing him.

"Are you perchance making fun of me, Miss Kent?" he said slowly.

"Perhaps a little?"

"Then in return I believe I shall claim a dance," he heard himself say. "With your permission, Your Grace?"

The duchess smiled. "Enjoy yourselves. I do believe the next one's going to be a waltz."

To his everlasting luck, it was.

He tucked Violet's hand into the crook of his arm. Her gloved fingers were slender, dainty, and fit perfectly there. He escorted her toward the dance floor, proud as if he'd accomplished a monumental feat. Maybe he was better at this courtship business than he gave himself credit for.

"Why are you smiling in that odd manner?" Violet eyed him speculatively.

"No reason. I'm just, er, honored that you agreed to this dance."

"Oh." Her lush sable lashes veiled her gaze. "It was, um, nice of you to ask."

Was she blushing? It gave him the courage to admit, "I've always wanted to."

She wrinkled her nose. "What a bouncer. A few days ago, you couldn't stand the sight of me."

"That's not true." He led her onto the crowded dance floor. Carving out a space just for the two of them, he said, "Even when you infuriated me, I still liked looking at you, lass."

Her cheeks turned pinker. By Jove, if she liked his straight talking, he might have a decent shot at this after all. His confidence grew.

"So, um, I still haven't seen Wick," she said. "Have you?"

Richard had spent the last eighteen hours worrying and searching frantically for his brother. Suddenly, he wanted a few minutes for himself. The respite of a single dance. Was that too much to ask?

He uttered words he'd never said before. "Wick can wait."

He positioned a hand above her waist, felt hers alight on his shoulder. Their free hands met and held in the air. Despite what they'd done in the dark, holding hands in the light filled him with sizzling awareness.

From the way she shivered, he knew she felt it too.

"Let's enjoy this, shall we?" he murmured.

The opening strains sounded. Gathering her close, he swung her into the waltz.

———

Dancing with Carlisle was nothing short of a revelation.

Before this, Wick had been Vi's favorite partner because of his daring, the sheer outrageousness of his spins. She'd liked his wild approach because you never knew if you were going to crash, and the danger made it fun.

Now she was discovering a far greater thrill.

Carlisle spun her again, the strength and assuredness of his movement rustling a breathless laugh from her throat. He possessed the grace of a true athlete, and he partnered her as if they'd done this hundreds of times before. They whirled in unison, their speed building with the music, her heart pounding even faster as she gazed into his ore-flecked eyes.

"Enjoying yourself, lass?" he said.

"You're a splendid dancer."

"That surprises you?"

"A bit? Not because I think you have two left feet," she hastened to say, "but I've never seen you dance before. I thought the activity might be too frivolous for you."

"Even we stuffed shirts like a good dance. And by now I should think you know that I enjoy physical activity of all kinds. When it involves you, that is."

His husky words turned her insides into sun-warmed honey, her nipples puckering beneath her bodice. Gadzooks, she'd found a gruff and scowling Carlisle attractive; now that he was flirting with her, he was *irresistible*.

The world faded away, and there was only Carlisle and her, the rightness of the moment. She'd never been more at home in her own skin than now, moving as one with him. Wrapped up in the lush music, the smoky intensity of his eyes, she had a sudden recognition.

The joy she was feeling came not from recklessness but... trust.

The wild dances with Wick couldn't hold a candle to the perfection of his brother's partnering. Carlisle was so steady and in command: he would never let her crash or fall. Knowing that his strength was a match for hers made it easy to let go. When she relaxed fully into the beauty of the moment, it was as if an invisible source of resistance dissolved. She was frictionless, flying across the floor with him in the most exhilarating dance of her life.

She never wanted it to end.

Alas, the music slowed, and Carlisle took her into one last, dizzyingly perfect spin. When her senses recovered, she saw that he'd led her out onto one of the balconies.

"How did we end up here?" she said breathlessly.

"I wanted a moment alone. If that is all right with you?"

She nodded because she, too, wanted whatever privacy they could find before her sister came looking. She rested her arms on the balustrade, and he followed suit. They stood side by side in companionable silence. Diamonds glittered in the black velvet sky, lamps flickering in the shadowy buildings that circled the courtyard below. The beauty of the moonlit scene struck her... along with a stab of poignancy.

Monique would never see such a view again.

He slanted her a glance. "Are you recovered?"

"Yes, I slept all afternoon." She cleared her throat. "What did you do?"

"I talked to Wick's cronies. Since none of them had seen him since the performance yesterday, I went to look for him in the village."

"Any luck?"

He shook his head, weary lines etched around his mouth. "I never thought he'd stay away this long. I don't know where he could have gone."

Worry trickled through her. Like Carlisle, she hadn't expected Wick would be gone for this long. She hesitated before voicing the possibility that had to be addressed.

"Do you think he might somehow be involved? In Monique's death?" she whispered.

Silence stretched between them, incongruously filled by the buoyant notes of the orchestra.

Carlisle's big hands gripped the stone railing. "Wick would never hurt someone... knowingly."

She swallowed because she'd been thinking the exact same thing. "But what if he and Monique were together and... an accident happened? And then he ran because he was afraid?"

Moonlight couldn't hide the pain that flashed in Carlisle's gaze.

"I'd trade my soul," he said in low, hoarse tones, "for that not to be true."

He looked so grim, so in need of comfort, that she reached out a hand to his lean cheek. The bristly beginnings of a night beard quivered beneath her palm.

"You're a good man, Carlisle," she said. "A good brother."

"I failed Wick. Father's parting words were to look after the estate and the family, and I've done a shoddy job of both."

So he *had* lost the family fortune... just as Wick had claimed. From the interaction with Turbett, she knew that he'd arranged for Wick to marry Miss Turbett, too. Wick had been telling the truth about Carlisle forcing him to wed.

Seeing the self-blame in Carlisle's eyes, however, she didn't have the heart to take him to task. Clearly, he regretted his behavior toward Wick. Moreover, she was beginning to see just how heavy his mantle of duty and responsibility was. He'd been left in charge of everything and everyone. Like a lonely giant, he shouldered the weight of his entire family.

"No one's perfect," she said softly.

"If anything happens to Wick, it will break our mama's heart. He's always been her favorite. By not protecting him, I've failed her too."

"That's a bit harsh," she protested. "Who made you king of everything?"

"Er... pardon?"

"King of everything," she repeated. "You know, someone who thinks he rules everything in his sphere. Who takes responsibility for everything... even when it's not his to take."

He blinked at her. At least she'd succeeded in halting his spiral of self-recrimination. Wanting to draw him out further, she said impulsively, "I used to have other names for you, too."

"Did you now?"

"Well, they were names I only called you in my head. And maybe once or twice aloud in front of my sister Polly," she amended. "When I was really angry."

"Now I'm not sure I want to know." He seemed fascinated. "But go ahead. Tell me."

"My favorite was 'Viscount Killjoy.' 'Lord High Horse' or its variation 'Lord High and Mighty' came a close second," she said candidly. "And, of course, there was the old standby."

His lips twitched. "And that was?"

"'Pompous prig'," she informed him.

He threw his head back and laughed.

The rich, rusty sound reached all the way to her toes, curling them.

Eyes gleaming, he inquired, "No 'Tyrannical Troglodyte'?"

"An excellent suggestion." She grinned. "I'll have to add it to the list."

"By Jove, you are an ease to me, Violet." There was a note of wonder in his voice.

It was the second time he'd said such a thing to her, and her heart burgeoned. She realized she'd never been that to anyone before, never felt... needed. Blood rushed beneath her skin, desire mingling with something deeper, headier.

They looked into each other's eyes. He bent his head slowly toward her. Before their lips could meet, something flashed over his right shoulder, distracting her. She blinked and instinctively shifted her head away to get a better look. A moving light in the courtyard below... a man with a lamp.

"Er, Violet?"

"Wick," she breathed.

"What did you call me?" Carlisle scowled.

"Not you. It's *actually* Wick. I think I see him in the courtyard!"

He spun around, and they both rushed to peer over the balcony. It *was* Wick, she saw with relief. His movements were furtive as he made his way down the walking path. A minute later, he turned into the amphitheatre.

"What's he doing?" she said.

Carlisle's eyes blazed with hellfire. "I don't know, but I'm bloody well going to find out."

17

Richard shoved open the door of the amphitheatre. He was alone; Violet had been waylaid by her chaperone, and for once he was glad for it. He was about to deal with his little brother, and he didn't want Violet around if things got messy—hell, he didn't want Violet involved in this business *at all*. But she'd been dragged into this mess by her loyalty to Wick.

Wick had *a lot* of explaining to do, and Richard meant to get answers, one way or another.

In spite of the dim lighting, he spotted his brother right away. Wick was sitting at the center of the stage, his back slumped against what appeared to be a massive oak wardrobe. His clothes looked bedraggled, as if he'd slept in them, and he'd lost his cravat, his collar hanging open. He seemed to be staring out at nothing as he lifted a silver flask to his lips.

"Where the bloody hell have you been?" Richard snapped.

Wick's head jerked up. His gaze—bleary and slightly unfocused—met Richard's. "Oh. It's you, Carlisle."

"Yes, it's me, and I've been looking all over for you." Richard took the steps up to the stage two at a time. Towering over his sibling, he repeated, "Where in blazes have you been?"

"Perdition, ol' boy. That's where."

Hearing the other's slurred tone, Richard reached out and grabbed the flask.

"Give that back," Wick protested. "It's mine."

"You've had plenty. We're going to talk right now, Wickham. Where were you last night?"

"What business is it of yours?" Wick retreated into belligerence. "I'm six-an'-twenty. Sick an' tired of being ordered 'bout like a witless child."

Then don't bloody act like one. Richard strove to hold onto his patience. "Listen, and listen carefully. Something bad happened last night. Do you know that?"

"Bad... yes. Very." Wick hiccupped. "I was verra, verra bad."

Sleet coated Richard's gut. "What do you mean?"

Wick crooked a finger at him.

His skin prickling, Richard crouched so that they were eye to eye.

"Broke in," Wick said in confiding tones.

"Where?" *Please God, don't let him say the library...*

"Woodcutter's cottage. Or maybe it was the gamekeeper's. I dunno,"—Wick shook his head sadly—"somewhere out in the woods."

"You were there all night?"

"Left before supper. Couldn't stand to be here." Before Richard could feel relieved, Wick added sullenly, "Didn't want to see *him*, did I?"

"You mean Garrity?"

"Who else? Bastard."

"Did he approach you?" Richard demanded.

"Didn't give 'im a chance. I ran off." Self-pity infused Wick's voice. "Like a damned mongrel with his tail between his legs."

"As long as Garrity knows you intend to make your payment on time, he has no reason to intimidate you. You have nothing to fear as long as you follow through on the plan to marry Turbett's daughter."

"Nothing to fear... and nothing to live for." Wick's voice hitched. "If I have to marry that cold fish—"

"It's either that or face Garrity. Your choice," Richard said bluntly. "Now focus because I have something very important to ask you..." He turned, hearing footsteps.

Violet was hurrying down the aisle toward the stage, her golden dress sparkling in the gloom.

Hell and damnation. "What the devil are you doing here?" he said.

"Hello to you, too," she said pertly. "I told Emma I had a megrim and needed to lie down." Clambering onto the stage, she passed him, kneeling on his brother's other side. "Where have you been, Wick? We've been so worried..." Her nose wrinkled. "Gadzooks, are you pickled?"

"He got soused and passed out at the gamekeeper's cottage," Richard cut in.

"Woodcutter's," Wick mumbled.

"Whatever. The point is," Richard addressed Violet, "he wasn't here."

She let out a sigh of relief. "So he's innocent."

"Wouldn't say I'm *innocent*, Vi"—Wick waggled his brows—"if you know what I mean."

Richard was tempted to punch his brother in the face. "Stop leering at her, you idiot—and her name is Miss Kent. You'll address her with respect."

Violet rose, facing him. "He can call me what he wants. He's my friend."

It irked him that she took his brother's side when *he* was the one defending her honor. "That's not an excuse for him to treat you shabbily."

"He's *not.*"

"I say he is. For God's sake, Violet," he bit out, "I'm looking out for your best interests."

"Trust me to be the judge of what that may be," she retorted.

"Did you just call her Violet?" Wick said.

He and Violet turned, saying simultaneously, "*Shut up*."

"Fine. But hand me my flask, will you?" Wick said sardonically. "If I must be submitted to this domestic drama, at least let me do it drunk."

Richard inhaled for patience. Collecting himself, he was about to address Monique's death, but Violet beat him to it.

"Wick, where's your ring?" she said.

Wick's cheekbones reddened. "Er, which one?" he said unconvincingly.

"The bloody signet with your initials," Richard said. "When was the last time you had it in your possession?"

"Why do you care about my damned ring?"

"Because it was found on a dead woman's body," Richard snapped. "Monique de Brouet had your ring clutched in her hand when Violet and I discovered her in the library this morning."

Wick stared at him. "Monique... she's dead?"

"Yes, and unless you can explain how she got your ring, you might find yourself the goddamned suspect in her murder," Richard gritted out.

"I would never hurt her." Wick sounded dazed. "Never. I... I cared for her."

Devil take it. Just as Richard had feared.

Violet said quietly, "You and Monique knew one another?"

"We met last year. For a time, we were... friendly. She's really dead?"

Richard heard the shock in his brother's tone. "Focus, Wick. Your ring. How would it have ended up in Monique's possession?"

"I gave it to her." Wick's words were hoarse, barely audible. "When I broke things off with her a fortnight ago. It was supposed to be a memento of our time together."

God. Wick had been involved with the dead woman just two

weeks ago.

"Why did you break things off?" Richard said.

"Because you said I had to marry Miss Turbett to pay off my debt to Garrity. You said that was the only way. And you were right."

"Hold up. *Your* debt? To Garrity?" Violet's eyes were wide with astonishment. "*That* is why you have to get married?"

Wick slid her a look that Richard couldn't quite interpret and nodded.

"Never mind your debt for now," Richard said impatiently. "How did the parting go with Monique?"

Wick raked his hands through his hair. "When I told Monique I was planning to be married, she flew into a rage. She was irrational, swearing revenge one minute and weeping the next. I had no idea that she'd even thought that we could have a future together beyond our..."—he glanced at Violet and mumbled—"... er, arrangement."

A divot formed between Violet's brows.

Richard thought that Wick's revelation about his peccadillo might have offended her sensibilities. Her next words proved him wrong.

"You and Monique didn't part on good terms? Oh Wick," she said, "don't you see how that might look now?"

An echo of Richard's own fears.

"But I—I would never hurt her," Wick stammered. "You must believe me!"

"Of course *we* do. But we're not the problem." Rising, Violet paced in front of him, her golden skirts swirling. "It's what everyone else will think."

"Bloody hell, are they looking for me?" Wick jolted upright. "Should I run, get away—"

"No one knows about your ring. Violet and I have taken care of it," Richard said curtly.

"What do you mean you've taken care of it?" Hope wobbled in

Wick's voice.

"We took it. We didn't tell anyone that we found it in Monique's hand." Violet bit her lip. "Not even my brother, who's heading the investigation."

Richard heard the tension in her voice. Hated that she'd been dragged into this fiasco.

"Investigation?" Wick blanched. He reached out, grabbing Violet's hand, making Richard's shoulders bunch. "Dear God, Vi, if our friendship means anything to you, you must *promise* me that you won't tell your brother about the ring."

"Bloody hell, Wickham, that's not fair," Richard bit out. "And for God's sake, unhand her."

Wick released her hand, but his expression remained beseeching. "Vi, come on, you know I didn't do it. *Promise me* you'll keep my secret. Or I—I'll have to run—"

"*No.* You mustn't run, Wick. If you do, you'll only bring suspicion upon yourself and look all the more guilty." Exhaling, she said, "I promise that I won't tell Ambrose about the ring... until we can prove that you're innocent. Then the ring won't matter, will it?"

"Thank you, Vi." Wick gave her a lopsided smile. "You're a true friend."

"Does anyone else know about you and Monique?" Richard asked.

Wick's brow wrinkled. "I don't think so. She insisted on discretion, so I never told anyone."

Reaching into the inner pocket of his jacket, Richard took out the signet ring and handed it over. "Then you must stay and act normally. Do not rouse suspicion."

"What if someone asks where I was?" Wick's hands trembled as he slid the ring into place.

"Did anyone see you last night? Anyone who can provide you with an alibi?" Violet asked.

Wick propped his elbows on his knees, his head dropping into his hands. "My sole companion was a bottle of whiskey I filched from the billiards room. I found the gamekeeper's cottage open and let myself in. I drank all night, passed out... didn't come to until dusk."

"That's *hours* unaccounted for," Violet said with clear dismay.

Richard came to a swift decision. "If anyone asks, Wick, say you were indisposed today. Don't elaborate on the details." The last thing he wanted was for his sibling to construct some elaborate Banbury Tale and get snared in the details. "For now, go directly to your room and get cleaned up. Then go to the ball and act as if nothing has happened. Do you understand?"

"I shall do my best." Wick got unsteadily to his feet. "But what about Garrity? What should I do if he approaches me?"

"You have three months left to pay off your debt," Richard said shortly. "Until then, he's not going to do anything to threaten his investment. But, if you're wise, you'll show your good faith by doing what you came here to do: secure Miss Turbett's hand."

"You're right, Richard." Wick hung his head. "You always were, and I'm sorry if I've been... difficult. You're a good brother to me, a better one than I deserve."

Richard's chest clenched. As a boy, Wick had worn that hangdog expression too many times to count, usually after he'd engaged in some mischief or another. Back then, Richard had always been able to help his little brother. Yet now Wick was a grown man, and it wasn't just some foolish prank he would have to answer for but *murder*...

He shoved aside his worry. Clapped a hand on his sibling's shoulder. "We'll see you out of this trouble, Wickham. I promise you that."

Wick gave a fretful nod. As he passed Violet, he paused and bent his head toward her ear. Her eyes widened at whatever he was saying to her. When he was done, he gave her arm a gentle squeeze and departed.

Richard waited until the door of the amphitheatre was closed.

"What did Wick say to you?"

"He apologized."

"For what?"

"For misleading me about you." Her lashes fanned rapidly. "And now I owe you an apology as well. It seems I've misjudged you for some time, Carlisle."

Richard frowned. "Misjudged? How so?"

"Wick told me that you were forcing him to woo Miss Turbett against his wishes."

"That's not untrue—"

"But Wick said it was to pay off debts that *you* had incurred. He told me that you'd made some bad investments that had paupered the estate. He claimed that you were coercing him into marrying for money in order to rectify the mistake that *you* had made."

Her words struck like arrows dipped in poison. A sharp, painful sensation spread through his chest.

"Wick... lied about me?" he said thickly.

She nodded. "And I believed him. Consequently, I think it's made me judge you harshly... *wrongly*. And for that I am truly sorry."

"It's not your fault. You couldn't have known." Disbelief seeped through him; he shook his head, trying to understand why his brother would betray him. "Why would Wick say such things...?"

"He said he was ashamed," she said quietly. "He's always measured himself against you, I think, and felt he came up short."

"Compared to *me*?" Richard was stupefied. "He's the one with all the good looks and charm."

Violet frowned. "That's not true."

"Of course it is. Wick's the golden boy of our family, every-one's favorite. He could have done anything, been anything had he put his mind to it." Richard rubbed the back of his neck, said gruffly, "In looks and manner, I can't hold a candle to him."

"That's *absurd*. You're very attractive," she said hotly.

His head snapped up. She didn't appear to be making fun of him. "You think so?"

She nodded vehemently. "How could you doubt it?"

Because you're the only female who's ever said it?

He coughed in his fist. "I wasn't certain you saw me that way."

"I don't go around kissing just any gentleman." Although she blushed to the roots of her hair, her gaze was steady and sincere.

"Just me, then." Hope bloomed in his chest. Curling a finger under her chin, he said, "Could it be that you've taken a liking to me, lass?"

Her tawny gaze turned troubled. "Maybe I have, Carlisle, but look at our history of misjudging one another. We're so different, you and I."

"Whatever our differences are, we'll overcome them. Learn to compromise," he said resolutely.

"Compromise," she murmured. "Just like Thea said."

"You spoke to your sister of me? Of us?"

"With the omission of certain details, yes." She nibbled on her lip—by Jove, he wanted a nip at that plump ledge, too. "Sisters talk, Carlisle. Don't take it to heart."

"Have you spoken of other men in this fashion?" Satisfaction rolled through him when she shook her head. "Then it *does* mean something." He took hold of her hands. "Violet, my sweet, give me a chance to court you. I know the timing isn't right, what with this mess involving Wick. But after I get this sorted, if you give me permission I'll—"

"The timing *is* right."

He frowned, not following.

"Don't you see, Carlisle? Fate has thrown us together time and again for a reason." Her beautiful eyes were beseeching. "We have to work *together* to find out what really happened to Monique and clear Wick's name. And, in doing so, we'll get to know one another better and see how we get on. If you want to court me, let me be a part of this."

Why did she have to want the one thing he couldn't agree to?

With simmering frustration, he said, "Don't you understand it isn't safe? You're more delicate than you realize, lass, and vulnerable too. I won't risk anything happening to you."

"For crumpet's sake, I'm not some shrinking flower—"

Approaching voices and footsteps cut her off.

Her eyes grew large as saucers. "We can't be seen alone in here. Emma will have my head!"

Richard scanned for possible hiding places. The voices were getting closer, no time to get off the stage. His gaze hit the wardrobe: big enough for two—barely. Grabbing her hand, he reached for the wardrobe door. He pushed her inside and followed, closing the door swiftly behind them.

In the darkness, he waited, Violet jammed up against him.

Laughter... people had entered the amphitheatre. Their voices were muffled by the heavy wood of the wardrobe, but he heard a woman and a man talking. He strained to hear their conversation, to gauge how long this might go on. At the same time, he was distracted by the exquisite torture that was Violet: her feminine scent, her lips within kissing distance, her sublimely perky bosoms pressing into his chest...

"There's something poking into me," she whispered.

Good God, not this again.

Before he could utter an apology, she wriggled against him, rendering the source of her discomfort—and his—harder than an anvil.

"It's against my back. I think I can reach it," she muttered. "I'll just push it aside..."

Before he could puzzle out what she was referring to, there was a soft click—and the ground dissolved beneath their feet. She gasped, and he threw his arms protectively around her as they plunged into darkness.

18

L ying in the musty gloom, Violet tried to catch her breath. When she did, she felt a sensation building up in her, rising from her belly, tickling her throat like champagne—

A hand clamped over her mouth just in time to muffle her giggle.

"Hush, you little minx." Carlisle's breath heated her ear. "They might hear us up above."

He was lying on his back, and she was sprawled atop him. They were in some sort of concealed compartment beneath the stage; above them, the trapdoor through which they'd fallen had closed again, a faint line of light seeping through.

Squinting in the dimness, she gauged that the low-ceilinged space was only a bit bigger than the Priest Hole. A short ladder rested on its side against one wall. Looking up, she guessed that she and Carlisle had fallen a good seven feet. She recalled him twisting mid-plunge to bear the brunt of the impact.

"Are you all right?" she whispered.

"I'm fine," came his reply. "There's a mattress beneath me."

"This must be The Great Nicoletti's *Wardrobe of Vanishing Wonders*. The wardrobe has a false floor—that's how he disappears. And, to reappear, he just climbs up the ladder." Tickled, Vi said, "I figured out his secret."

"Bravo," Carlisle said dryly.

Footsteps thudded overhead. Carlisle's arms closed around her, holding her still as hinges creaked. Vi's breath held; someone had opened the wardrobe up above.

"See? Nofin' inside," said a man's voice.

"But I could have sworn I heard something." Violet recognized the simpering female tones as Mrs. Sumner's. "You're certain there's no one in there, Tobias?"

Tobias Price, one of Billings' cutthroat clients, Vi recalled. A bearded, barrel-chested man.

"Look for yourself, dove: 'tis as bare as a babe's arse inside."

"You're right. It must be my nerves. They've suffered such a shock from Madame Monique's untimely demise."

"O' course they would, you bein' a true lady," Price rumbled. "But you've nothin' to fear when you're with me. Even the devil knows be'er than to cross Tobias Price."

"I do *adore* a strong gent. But it's not the devil I fear." A coy pause. "Can you keep a secret?"

"Did Mary 'ave tits?"

"Well, I heard from my maid who heard from one of Billings' servants that a footman came upon *Lord Wormleigh* and Madame Monique having words the night she died."

"That bloated old nob?" A snort. "'E's no killer."

"I read sensation novels. Killers are those one *least* suspects. Besides, my maid also said that Wormleigh was seen by the library later that night—and that, as you know," Mrs. Sumner said triumphantly, "was where Monique was found."

Another snort. "I'd put my blunt on one o' the filly's studs. She 'ad a stable o' gents, and talk 'as it that some are at the party. Any one of 'em could 'ave the done the deed."

"You weren't one of her studs, were you, Tobias?" Mrs. Sumner said archly.

A guffaw. "Not jealous, are you?"

"I don't like to bathe in dirty water," she said with a sniff.

"No need to be coy. I think you like to play dirty—that's why you approached me. Now come 'ere, dove, and let Tobias soil you some more..."

The door slammed on the wardrobe, muffling the laughter. The pair's footsteps moved over and off the stage. Their moans and grunts were distant, coming from the seating area.

"Did you hear that?" Violet said in an excited whisper. "About Wormleigh? And Monique's *other* lovers?"

"More leads to follow. In the interim, we'll have to, er, wait Price and Mrs. Sumner out."

At that moment, Violet became acutely aware of the fact that she was still lying atop of Carlisle, his arms wrapped around her. Beneath her cheek, his heart thumped in a potent, virile rhythm. Thrill, and a bit of mischief, wound through her. Despite his irritating tendency to be overprotective, here they were again, sharing another adventure together.

With her elbows on his chest, she propped her head in her hands and looked at him. The dim light limned his granite features, the sensual pools of his eyes. She recalled his gruff statement that he couldn't hold a candle to Wick—utter codswallop, as far as she was concerned—and the surprise he'd tried to conceal when she told him that she found him attractive.

In truth, he was the most compelling man she'd ever met. She admired him: his honor, strength, and loyalty. To think, all this time she'd believed he was bullying Wick when he'd been working tirelessly to help his brother! Remorse filled her; she wanted to make it up to him. She also wanted him to understand that she wasn't some fragile dandelion that would fly apart at a puff of air.

Why can't you accomplish both tasks at once?

The notion came out of nowhere, a spark that set her smoldering emotions aflame. She'd always been a girl of action: why not *show* him that she was no weak, missish female? That she could match him step for step, be a worthy partner... in every respect? Although her experience with lovemaking was limited, she could go by Carlisle's example: she'd do to him what he'd done to her. Everything else, she'd improvise.

Guided by impulse and desire she could no longer deny, she bent and touched her mouth to his. Tasting his surprise, she felt his animal shudder, and it thrilled her that she could arouse this primal response in so proper a lord. She ran her tongue along his bottom lip, and his breath gusted, his mouth opening for her.

With thrumming excitement, she dipped her tongue in and his surged to meet her lapping caress. The sensuous, moist tangling drew goose pimples on her skin, her nipples stiff and throbbing beneath her bodice. When his hands clamped on her waist, she batted them away.

"No. My turn," she whispered.

His brows rose... but his hands fell to his sides.

Tearing off her gloves, she cupped his jaw and slanted her mouth over his. The kiss caught fire, sucking the air from her lungs. Panting, she tugged off his cravat, tossing the starchy linen aside. Nuzzling his neck, she breathed in his arousing male musk. Then she licked her way down a strong, quivering tendon, drawing her tongue over the hard bump of his throat. A groan rumbled in his chest.

Dizzy with success and her own escalating need, she fumbled with the buttons of his waistcoat. In her eagerness, she tore off the last one, sent it skittering into the darkness. She tugged his shirt free of his waistband and slid her hands up under the linen.

"By... Golly." The words left her in a stunned whisper.

His eyes gleamed up at her. "Not what you expected?"

Having never touched a naked male chest before, she hadn't known *what* to expect. The combination of hair-dusted skin and flexing muscle filled her with wonder. Marveling, she ran her fingers up the lean ridges of his abdomen to the powerful slabs of his heaving chest.

She squirmed, arousal making her mind fuzzy. How badly she wanted him to touch her. But, no, she was in charge, trying to make a point... what was she supposed to do next? What would he do to her?

Remembering, she searched out his nipple with her fingertips. She circled the flat nub, caressing him as he'd caressed her. She'd loved it when he'd stroked her thus, but she could tell she wasn't getting the same reaction from him.

"Am I doing something wrong?" she whispered.

"I'm not complaining, lass, but it's not quite the same for me as it is for you." There was a catch of humor in his voice. "Now are you done playing your game?"

"I'm not playing—"

The air whooshed from her lungs as he rolled over in a swift motion, pinning her beneath him. Breathless, she stared up at his rugged features and smoldering eyes.

"You're done," he informed her huskily. "Now it's my turn."

Lust pounded in his veins as he took her mouth, swallowing her whimper of excitement. The little vixen had driven him nigh mad with her innocent explorations, her untutored caresses firing his blood more than the most experienced courtesan could have done. He didn't know what she was trying to prove, but he'd gone along until he judged she'd had enough and neither of them could take much more of her teasing.

Now his lips coursed over the exposed swells of her décolletage, his fingers hooking beneath the neckline to find her nipples. One of these days, he would have time to get all her clothes off, and he was going to spend *hours* paying tribute to her breasts. He was going to kiss and suckle her sweet tits to his heart's content. For now, he had to satisfy himself with fingering the stiff peaks, rubbing and pinching them lightly as she moaned.

She was so responsive. Made for him. Even the scent of her skin smelled right, ratcheted up his need to touch and taste her everywhere.

He grabbed a fistful of her skirts, dragging them upward. The dimness couldn't hide the fact that every inch he revealed of her was absolute perfection.

"Christ, you're bonny," he rasped.

He ran a hand reverently up one slender stockinged leg, from dainty ankle to shapely calf. His palm moved up to her bare thigh, so sleek and soft it put silk to shame. He made room for himself between her legs, and the view got even better.

"Carlisle..."

She squirmed bashfully, but he didn't let her close her legs.

"I'm right here, lass," he said thickly.

Aye, he was right where he wanted to be, looking his fill of the shyest, prettiest little pussy. He inhaled her earthy sweetness before running a finger through her silky thatch. His cock jerked against his smalls. Goddamn, she was wet. Her petals were dripping with nectar.

He *had* to have a taste.

"Carlisle, what are you... you can't..." Her fingers clenched his hair. "*Gadzooks...*"

He would have chuckled if his mouth hadn't been more pleasantly engaged. Humor and passion—he'd never known the two could go hand in hand. Yet they did with Violet. His amusement faded into the roar of lust: the taste of her was *indescribable*. Ambrosia. One taste and he knew he would never get enough.

Parting her with his thumbs, he took his time feasting on her plump and luscious slit. His tongue swiped upward, finding the little bud beneath the shy hood. When he suckled, her hips suddenly bucked, a dangerously loud squeal escaping her as she came.

Surging upward, he sealed his mouth over hers. He plunged two fingers inside her convulsing passage, rocking his thumb over her nubbin to prolong her climax. As her sheath continued to ripple around his fingers, his bollocks pulsed in tortured synchrony, his cock burgeoned past the point of pain.

"Carlisle," she whispered against his lips.

"Yes, love?"

"Do you want, um…"—he jolted, barely stifling his groan when her fingers fluttered over the throbbing ridge in his pants—"help with that?"

Be a gentleman. Don't make her do anything she might regret later.

Running his knuckles over her cheek, he tried to discern her expression in the dimness. How far ought he allow things to go? With the two misses he'd courted before, he'd never trespassed the boundary of chaste kisses. His other experiences were with paid and experienced bedpartners who had allowed him to go a great deal further. All the way, one might say.

But Violet… she was different from all the rest, a class of her own. Thus far, she'd defied all his attempts to categorize her based on his past experience. Perhaps what he ought to do… was trust her to tell him what she wanted?

"Do you want to, lass?" he said hoarsely.

At her game nod, his cock wept a tear of relief. Fumbling with the fasteners, he lowered the placket of his trousers, his rod springing eagerly free of its confines. She turned onto her side to face him, and he guided her hand. His member jumped at her touch.

"It's chomping at the bit, isn't it?" she said with a breathless laugh.

"You have no idea," he muttered. "Violet, are you certain…?"

She whispered, "Tell me what to do."

She was his every fantasy come alive.

He wrapped her slender fingers around his shaft, showing her the general motion. Violet, being Violet, caught on quickly. She tackled the task with a feminine energy that made his senses spin. Leaning back on his elbows, he gave himself up to the pleasure of her touch, of watching her work his turgid pole with her delicate hands.

"You're hard and soft at the same time," she marveled.

"Soft?" He didn't think so. At the moment, his truncheon was so big and thick that she was using two hands to pump him.

"Your skin is like velvet," she clarified. "Wrapped around a poker or something."

He choked back a laugh. "How, er, poetic of you."

"Books were never my forte." Her thumb rubbed against the slit in his cockhead, and his neck arched in bliss. "Why is it wet here?"

"Because you're touching me so well, lass."

"Oh... so this makes you feel good?"

Good wasn't the word for it. *Randier than a sailor*, maybe.

Like he was about to unload his cannon—definitely.

But all he could manage was, "Aye," because her thumb was drawing exquisite circles over his engorged dome, smearing his pre-spend, making him shudder with need.

"You're sensitive here," she murmured.

"'Tis like your pearl for you. In this, we're not so different."

To illustrate his point, he reached between her thighs. His cock seeped a little more when he found her pussy freshly dewy, her bud bold and slick. He diddled her, and she moaned, her grip tightening on him.

"That's it, lass. Do it harder, faster," he urged.

She instantly obeyed, and God, her *hands*—they were made to handle him, to bring him to the brink. He returned the favor, plowing his fingers into her cunny as she frigged his cock. Soon they were both panting, racing toward climax. His balls drew up, heat roiling at the base of his shaft. She came again, her pussy clenching his driving digits.

He bit down on his lip to prevent a shout, tasting blood as he erupted in her hands. He shot his seed again and again, drenching her palms, molten trails leaking through her fingers.

Flopping onto his back, he dragged her into his arms and tried to catch his breath. Dazedly, he thought to offer her a handkerchief, but that would presuppose that he could move. And he wasn't certain that he could. Ever again.

"Carlisle, that was,"—Violet's voice was breathy in his ear—"*tip-top*."

His lips curved up in the darkness. Because, Christ, she was right.

Making love with her *was* tip bloody top.

19

After lunch the next day, Violet was given permission to stroll around the courtyard with Carlisle. Others were also enjoying the graveled paths, which were bordered by hedges, scattered Greek and Roman statuary providing points of interest. Across the way, Vi saw Wick; thankfully, he looked back to his usual self. He was paying attendance to Miss Turbett, her father following at their heels. In front of them, Parnell and Goggs were escorting Primrose and Polly, the four laughing merrily.

Sitting on a bench at the center of the quadrangle, Emma kept an eye on everyone.

"Did your sister suspect that you left your chamber last night?" Carlisle asked as he and Vi walked along the path.

To an outside observer, Carlisle's expression would appear impassive. Beneath the brim of his hat, his rugged features were schooled, and he looked every inch the proper lord in his tobacco brown frock coat and biscuit trousers tucked into polished Hessians. But Violet recognized the intimate gleam in his eyes, and it made her insides as warm and gooey as a freshly baked treacle tart.

Trying not to blush, she said, "Not that I know of. To be on the safe side, I did arrange several pillows beneath the covers. So if she looked in, she would have seen a sleeping form."

"Enterprising." His lips twitched. "Done this often, have you?"

"You're the first gentleman I've snuck off to see," she said candidly.

"I meant pulling the wool over your sister's eyes." His gaze narrowed. "As to sneaking off to meet gentlemen, I'll be the first and the last. There's no going back, Violet. It's time we made things official between us."

Joy and trepidation warred within her, a confusing mix. On the one hand, there was their fierce and undeniable attraction—as evidenced by their most recent interlude beneath the wardrobe. Just thinking about those steamy moments quickened her pulse. Yet their desire and compatibility felt new; they'd been enemies longer than they'd been lovers.

A marriage could not succeed on physical attraction alone, she reasoned. There had to be friendship and respect for one another. She knew from experience that she couldn't change who she was; she couldn't bear it if they wed and he ended up... disappointed.

Running her gloved fingers along the top of a hedge, she strengthened her resolve. "I told you my terms last night, and they haven't changed. If you want to court me, you'll have to do it while we're working together to help Wick."

His forehead lined with frustration; she braced for his refusal.

"Why do you want to be involved in this dangerous business, lass? Why is working together so important to you?" He was looking at her intently, as if her answer truly mattered to him.

"Because I want you to like me," she blurted.

"I do like you."

"I'm not sure that's true," she said sadly.

He quirked an eyebrow. "If our time in the Priest Hole, the library, and, most recently, the wardrobe hasn't convinced you, I'd be happy to give it another go."

Heat rose in her cheeks. "Not *that* kind of liking. The other kind."

"What other kind?" He sounded genuinely confused.

"The kind where you admire my qualities and respect my views," she said in a rush. "Where we share common interests and, to put it plainly, we're *friends*."

"I don't want to be your friend," he countered. "I want to be your husband."

"The two are not mutually exclusive conditions. I don't want to be wed to someone I don't enjoy spending time with." *And I don't want you to regret marrying me.*

"Fine," he said quickly. "We'll be friends."

"Just *saying* it doesn't make it true."

"Tell me how to make it true, and I will."

His commanding tenacity made her heart stutter. Perhaps that was why she'd never known desire before him. She'd been around boys all her life, but Carlisle... he was all man.

"To see if we're a true match, we need to get to know one another, share confidences," she explained. "I want you to treat me as you would a friend—Lord Blackwood, for instance."

"That makes no sense. Of course I'm going to treat you differently from Blackwood," he said, his tone incredulous. "I want to share my bed with you, not pass the time playing billiards and talking about the hunt."

The mention of his bed made her knees wobble. "Why can't we do all those things?"

For an instant, he looked baffled. He recovered quickly. "If that's your wish, then we can."

"But physical attraction aside," she persisted, "do you trust me the way you trust Lord Blackwood? Value my opinion in the same way?"

"That's not a fair comparison. I've known Blackwood for years."

"Fair enough. Then we need more time to get to know one another," she conceded.

"How much time?"

"As long as it takes?"

"That's not an answer." Now he sounded annoyed.

"Are you certain you want to court me? We're so different."

"I'm certain," he said flatly. "You're the one who needs convincing."

"And I've told you how to accomplish that."

He came to a halt in front of a statue of Hercules, depicted performing one of his labors. Carlisle's expression was as fierce as the marble figure's. "All right."

"All right?"

"If it's your wish, we'll work together."

She felt like she'd imbibed champagne, bubbles of joy bursting inside her. "Thank you—"

"Don't thank me yet. There are rules."

She should have known.

He took her hand, tucking it into the crook of his arm and placing his hand over it for good measure. They continued walking. "If we do this, you'll be guided by me. You'll heed my advice and not act recklessly. Most importantly,"—he pinned her with a glance—"you're not to put yourself in danger, do you understand?"

"I understand," she said giddily.

"That's settled, then. When shall I speak to your brother?"

"Um... about what?"

"To make my suit known," he said with a hint of impatience.

Panic trickled through her. She'd thought they were talking about a private understanding, just between the two of them. She wasn't ready to expose their budding relationship to *public* scrutiny.

"It's too soon to speak to Ambrose. Everything has happened so quickly and—"

"There's no reason to drag your heels. Lord knows we're

already concealing too much from your family as it is. I must insist that I court you properly, out in the open."

She strove to come up with a compromise. One that wouldn't lock Carlisle into a decision he might later regret. "How about we decide at the end of the house party whether or not you ought to speak to my brother?"

"Why wait? The time for dithering is over."

"I'm not dithering," she protested. "This is an important decision, one that affects the rest of our lives. I just want both of us to be certain."

"I am certain," he said stubbornly.

"How can you be so sure?"

"Because I've been through this before."

"You *have*?" Surprise made her halt, but he kept going, dragging her along. "When? I mean, everyone says you're a confirmed bachelor. There's no talk of you being attached to any lady."

"The instances happened in my youth and were not widely known."

"Instances—as in *plural*? More than once?"

"That is the generally accepted meaning of plural." His tone tight, he said, "I won't go into details, but suffice it to say I believed I had the affections of the young ladies involved. With the first, I was her brother's friend. I helped squire her through her season and bailed her out of more than a few scrapes. She always expressed her gratitude and showed a certain preference for me—or so I thought. When I declared myself, she said she'd never thought of me in that manner."

"Oh... I'm sorry." Vi didn't know what else to say.

"I don't want your pity," he said with disgust. "I'm telling you this so you understand my perspective. The second instance started off similarly to the first. The young lady had given me every indication that she thought I was acceptable to her. When I asked for her hand, she agreed."

"What happened then?"

"She wanted our engagement to be kept secret for the time being. Said her sister was newly engaged and she didn't want to steal the other's thunder." His expression was stark. "After a month of skulking around, I told her that I wanted our courtship to be out in the open. It was then that she confessed she was in love with another man. She eloped with him a week later."

Butter and jam. He'd been strung along by ladies not once but *twice.* For a man as proud as Carlisle, that must have been difficult to bear. Vi recalled his earlier accusations about her being a flirt—and realized she now knew the origins of his prejudices.

Then another thought occurred to her: in these incidences, had his heart been broken? She found she didn't like that notion *at all.*

"Were you very... hurt?" she said cautiously.

"My pride was. I was angry as hell. After that, it was clear to me that I have no talent when it comes to reading females. I don't understand the hidden signals of your sex."

Her relief that his heart hadn't been involved faded at his disgruntled look.

Brows lifted, she said, "Why are you looking at me like that? I don't understand them either."

"Given my aversion to flirtation and such games," he went on grimly, "I avoided the Marriage Mart."

"What changed your mind with me?" She hoped that he'd say it was her character and charm.

"In the past year, marriage has become a necessity for me. From a financial standpoint."

Be still my beating heart.

"But I... I'm no heiress." It occurred to her that she knew very little about his monetary situation and the sort of dowry he might require in a bride. Anxiously, she said, "I'm quite certain Ambrose and my brothers-in-law will throw something in the pot, but—"

Carlisle let out a guffaw.

"What's so amusing?" she said.

"You talk as if you're a card game." He chucked her under the chin. "Throw something in the pot, indeed."

"But the stakes are high for you, are they not?"

His amusement faded. Soberly, he said, "Aye, lass. In the past year, I sold off my personal holdings to keep the estate afloat. I auctioned off my stables, the breeding program I'd been building."

She heard the thrum of longing in his voice. Although Richard didn't say it, he had sacrificed his own wants in the name of responsibility. The same way he'd gone beyond duty to rescue his younger brother.

He's a jolly fine chap. A truly decent man.

"I'm sorry you had to abandon your dreams," she said gently.

He looked briefly nonplussed. Then he shrugged. "I did what had to be done."

"Do you plan on rebuilding your stables one day?"

"Mayhap one day. There are more important considerations."

His reply was curt, but she saw the flicker in his eyes. His dream hadn't been completely snuffed out, no matter how he tried to discount it.

"What you want *is* important," she insisted.

He sighed. "It's not so easy, lass. There's the estate to think of and the lives of all who depend upon it for their survival."

"What is the situation of your estate now?"

"It's stabilized for the time being. I implemented fiscal measures that I'm told are Draconian. My mama has yet to forgive me for them," he said wryly.

"How could she blame you for doing what needed to be done?"

"She finds a way."

She didn't like his matter-of-fact acceptance of the blame. Richard's burdens were even heavier than she'd realized, and it seemed he got little thanks for all that he'd done. No wonder he had his curmudgeonly moments. Thinking of Wick's misleading lies about his older brother, she felt a stab of anger at her friend.

"You needn't worry that you'll be marrying a pauper." Apparently mistaking the cause of her silence, he said with determination, "I'll see to it that you have the necessary comforts."

"I'm not worried about money," she assured him. "My family had very little when I was growing up, and the truth is that I like a simple life."

He gave a gruff nod. "So are we settled or not?"

Romance really wasn't his forte. Luckily for him, she found his honesty irresistible—far more pleasing than flummery. The fact that he'd shared his past with her and was willing to work together to save Wick gave her hope.

Compromise—it made all the difference, Em had said. And compromise went both ways.

"All right." Vi prayed she was doing the right thing. "Speak to my brother, Carlisle."

He exhaled, and when she realized he'd actually been holding his breath, her heart hiccupped.

He brought her hand to his lips. "You won't regret this. Now I have one more favor to ask."

"Another one?" Oops. She didn't mean to sound ungracious.

"Yes," he said solemnly. "I want you to call me Richard."

"Oh... well, all right, um, Richard."

Given the physical intimacies they'd shared, it was ridiculous that saying his name could affect her so. Yet his heated gaze made her want to swoon like some silly debutante.

Reminding herself that their privacy would soon be over and there was still much to discuss, she took a breath. "Now about Wick. What are we going to do?"

The sensuality left Richard's eyes, replaced by sharp focus. "Do you know how the meeting between your brother and the magistrate went?"

It had been a busy morning. Not only had Dr. Abernathy

arrived to examine the body, but Billings had been unable to stave off a visit from the local official any longer. Magistrate Jones had descended upon the estate with constables in tow, and Vi had gotten a glimpse of him: his countenance would make the Grim Reaper's seem cheerful in comparison. Guests—especially those of the cutthroat variety—had scattered like marbles at his arrival.

A panicked Billings had begged Ambrose to meet with Jones in private.

"From what Emma told me, Jones barked a few questions but stood down due to Ambrose's sterling reputation," Vi said with pride. "Jones was willing to let Ambrose continue the investigation on the condition that he receive regular updates."

"That's good news, isn't it?"

She gnawed on her lip. "The thing of it is, we *can't* tell Ambrose about Wick's ring now. If we did, we'd be putting my brother in a terrible position. He'd either have to withhold evidence from the magistrate, which could land him in heaps of trouble... or he'd have to tell Jones and then Wick might be thrown in prison or worse."

From Carlisle's strained expression, she knew he saw her point.

"It isn't right that you have to lie to protect Wick," he said heavily. "But the evidence against him is so bloody damning. Not only was he intimately involved with Monique, but the affair ended recently and not on good terms. And he has no witness who can vouch for his whereabouts during the time of her death. Then there's the ring: how the hell did it end up in Monique's hand?"

Vi had been pondering that question, too. "Maybe she had it on her person? The ring is clearly a man's signet. The murderer would have known that planting it in Monique's hand would throw others off his or her scent."

"A logical deduction." Carlisle's approval warmed her. "And we have a fresh lead to follow. Mrs. Sumner mentioned that Worm-leigh was also Monique's lover."

"We could tell Ambrose we overheard some guest gossiping about it. He doesn't have to know the, um, specifics of how we obtained the information."

"If it can be avoided, I'd rather not meet him at dawn," Carlisle agreed.

Violet saw Strathaven enter the courtyard and go to Emma. From the way Em bounced up, Violet knew there was news. Sure enough, Em and His Grace headed her way.

"There goes our privacy," Carlisle sighed.

"I'm sure we can arrange some time alone in the not too distant future," she said.

His eyes lightened. "But your reputation—"

"*Now* you're worried about my reputation?"

"I'm always concerned on that front," he said, his manner lordly, "and take the necessary precautions. You'll note we've yet to be caught."

"That is because, Lord High and Mighty, *I* am a modern miss with more than a little ingenuity at her fingertips." To emphasize the point, she held up her hands, wiggling her fingers. "You'll recall that *I* was the one who found the hidden lever in the wardrobe."

"Yes, well, I'll grant you have a talent for manipulating hard objects." Although his mouth remained stern, crinkles fanned from his eyes, which were smiling wickedly at her.

She could actually feel the blush rising up her face. He laughed just as Emma and His Grace arrived. Both of them looked surprised, no doubt because seeing Carlisle with anything but a scowl was rare.

The men exchanged bows.

"Is there news?" Violet asked.

Emma nodded. "Dr. Abernathy is ready to share his results.

And I spoke to Ambrose: he's agreed to let you be a part of this—as long as you're careful and supervised by me."

Vi threw her arms around her big sister. "Thank you, Em!"

"No thanks needed, dear." Emma's glance slid to Carlisle. "I've been in your shoes, after all."

20

The meeting with Dr. Abernathy took place in Billings' study. Footmen were posted outside the door and ushered in Violet, Richard, Emma, and the duke, locking the door behind them. Clearly, Billings wanted no interruption and no gossip leaked out to the other guests.

Their host was at his usual position at the desk. Behind him, the painting of the dead game fowl formed a rather apropos back-drop, given the grisly topic of the meeting. Ambrose and Mari-anne were already present, and Dr. Abernathy, the beetle-browed Scottish physician, was talking with Thea and her husband, the Marquess of Tremont.

Violet brought Richard over to introduce him.

"It's a pleasure to meet you at last, my lord." Thea's hazel eyes twinkled. "My little sister has said so much about you."

"*Thea*," Vi said in mortification.

Richard's jaw turned ruddy. "Good things, I hope."

"Exceedingly good things," Thea said cheerfully.

Tremont, a handsome man with gilded hair and grave eyes, put his two cents in. "Anyone who can keep up with Violet is an intrepid fellow in my books."

More than once, her brothers-in-law had been placed on chaperone duty.

"Crumpets, I only lost you that once," Violet muttered. "Now I never hear the end of it."

"As everyone has arrived, we can begin." Ambrose, standing by the side of the desk, called the meeting to order. "Dr. Abernathy has graciously come from London to conduct an examination of the deceased, Monique de Brouet. If you would share your results, Doctor?"

Dr. Abernathy inclined his head. "Let me say at the outset that Mr. Kent charged me with discovering the cause of Madame de Brouet's death. Given that this is a science yet in its infancy," he said in his thick brogue, "I cannot guarantee the accuracy of my conclusions, only give you my best estimation of the truth."

"You're all we have,"—Billings gave a dismissive wave—"and that's better than nothing."

Bristling, the good doctor drew himself up. "What I have to share is based on careful observation and consideration of the facts. It is most assuredly better than nothing."

"Go on, Doctor." Ambrose shot a warning glance at their host.

"Verra well. I found a laceration on the victim's right temple, approximately an eighth of an inch deep, one inch wide and three inches long. Those dimensions match those of the mantelpiece ledge in the library. The blood on the mantelpiece corroborates its connection to the injury."

"We already know she hit her head," Billings said. "Was it an accident?"

"That I cannot conclude from the physical evidence."

"Then we're no better off than where we started," the banker said in disgust. "In that light, I don't want to drag this matter out any further. Kent, you will close the investigation and tell Magistrate Jones it was an accident—"

"On the contrary, Madame de Brouet's death was no accident," Dr. Abernathy said.

"You said so yourself: you don't know whether she fell or was pushed into the mantel," Billings retorted.

"That is true. But I do know what killed her. And it was no accident."

Vi worked it out first. "You mean... it wasn't the blow to the temple that killed her?"

"Precisely, Miss Kent." The physician gave her an approving nod.

"Then what caused her death?" Richard said.

"Asphyxiation." At the silence that greeted his pronouncement, the physician added, "I believe she was smothered."

Monique de Brouet was murdered... and Wick's ring was in her hand?

A deep chill pervaded Richard's gut.

Kent's brows drew together. "Will you elaborate upon how you arrived at that conclusion, Dr. Abernathy?"

"Of course." Dr. Abernathy's pedantic tones reminded Richard of his old professors at Eton and Oxford. "To begin, I do not believe that the wound at the temple was sufficient to cause a fatality. There would have been some bleeding, yes, and the victim might have lost consciousness for a brief time, but I do not think she died from the blow. This led me to look for other clues as to the cause of death, and I found several. For one, the deceased had bloodshot eyes, a common sign of asphyxiation. Second, there was bruising around her mouth and nose, again consistent with smothering. Given that, I examined the victim's oral cavity and discovered several distinct fibers."

"Fibers of what?" Kent said.

"A yellow fabric of some sort."

The investigator stroked his chin. "From, say, a pillow?"

"The most common weapon," Abernathy agreed. "I found one

yellow pillow on the sofa in the library that could be a match for the fibers. But the lack of blood on this particular pillow makes it an unlikely culprit given the victim's profuse bleeding. This leads me to believe that the murderer used a similar pillow—and took it with him because of the telltale stains on it."

"From a decorating standpoint, the presence of a second yellow pillow makes sense," Mrs. Kent said. "Pillows oft come in matching pairs; it would be odd to have just one of a design."

"Billings," Kent said, "will you alert your staff to look for the mate to the yellow pillow?"

Their host's nod was reluctant.

"So one hypothesis would be that Monique hit her head, loss consciousness, and came to... only to be smothered by a pillow?" the duchess said meditatively.

"That would be a logical possibility, yes. And there's one more thing." The physician removed a folded handkerchief from his pocket and placed it on Billings' desk. Unwrapping the linen, he removed a thin gold chain, letting it dangle for all to see.

"This was caught inside the bodice of the victim's gown. The chain is broken. It might have happened during the attack, but I can't be sure."

Richard had a sudden hunch. Had Monique been wearing Wick's ring on that chain? If so, the killer might have seen it and recognized the golden opportunity...

Billings rose, his face set in determined lines. "We can't let any of this leak out."

"For the safety of the guests—" Kent began.

"Trust me, my associates can take care of themselves. As for the others,"—Billings waved a brusque hand—"I'll hire on extra footmen for security. Moreover, Magistrate Jones has insisted upon posting his men at the gates. He'll be monitoring everyone going in and out. Now I'll leave the rest to you, Kent—but do it tactfully, understand? Discretion is everything." Billings straightened his waistcoat. "Now, if you'll excuse me, I have guests to attend to."

After the door closed behind him, Kent said with a scowl, "Did he just tell me to solve a murder *tactfully*?"

"I'm afraid so." Mrs. Kent touched his arm. "Never mind him, darling. We need to focus on our strategy."

"Quite right," Strathaven said. "Now that we know how the victim died, we'll have to refine the list of suspects."

"Beginning with Miss Ashe," the duchess said. "Strathaven and I did speak with the maid she mentioned, Mary, who attested to the fact that she helped Miss Ashe to bed. We don't know that Miss Ashe stayed there, of course, but she can be vouched for from one to two in the morning."

"If, as I estimated, Monique's death occurred an hour or two before she was found—thus between one and three in the morning—that gives Miss Ashe at least a partial alibi," Kent muttered. "Given Dr. Abernathy's conclusions, I propose that we draw up a new list of all those who had a connection with the victim. Who might have a motive to kill her."

"Lord Wormleigh ought to be on that list," Violet blurted.

Kent's gaze swung to her. "Why do you say that?"

Her eyes met Richard's briefly; he sent a prayer up that she knew what she was doing.

"Because I, um, heard some ladies gossiping about it last night. At the ball. I don't know who they were since there was a screen between us. But they, um, claimed a servant saw Lord Wormleigh and Monique having words the night she died, *and* Wormleigh was seen outside the library later on that evening."

"Excellent observation skills, dear." Her Grace sounded impressed.

Violet flushed, squirming a little. Richard could tell it made her uncomfortable telling her family a lie. On the other hand, she couldn't very well announce the truth: that she'd overheard Mrs.

Sumner and Price whilst she and Richard had been hiding together beneath the wardrobe.

"Yes, well done, Vi. We'll put Wormleigh at the top of the list." Kent jotted in his notebook.

"Cedric Burns should be on there as well," Richard said, "seeing as he was Monique's colleague."

Kent scribbled. "Any progress on the victim's maid?"

The duchess shook her head. "The sleeping draught that the housekeeper, Mrs. Hopkins, gave Jeanne put the woman out like a light. Jeanne was still asleep this morning. But after this meeting, I'll try to speak to her again."

"I'll go with you. If anyone knows a lady's secrets, it's her maid," Mrs. Kent said.

Fear came as a sudden rush. In the commotion, Richard had forgotten about the maid and what she might know. Wick had said no one knew about his affair with Monique, but he probably hadn't considered the woman's servant. Was Jeanne aware of her mistress' lovers? Would she identify Wick as one of them?

"May I come too?" Violet said quickly. "I met Jeanne before, so perhaps she'd be willing to talk to me."

"Good thinking," her sister said.

Violet looked at him, and the message in her eyes was amazingly clear.

Leave it to me. I'll take care of it.

With no better options, he exhaled, nodding slightly. The truth was that it felt good to have someone at his back. To have someone he could... trust.

"Three interviews gives us a place to start," Kent said. "I've also heard back from my partners, Mr. Lugo and Mr. McLeod. They will be handling the investigation on the London end, questioning Monique's known associates and searching her residence for clues. They expect to report here in three days' time."

Three days. The news further wound the coil in Richard's gut. In London, the investigators might discover evidence of Wick's affair with Monique. They might place him on the list of suspects. An invisible net was closing around Wick.

Looking at Violet, Richard saw his own emotions reflected in her eyes. Concern—and steady determination. The hourglass had been tipped. They had three days' time to find the true killer and prove Wick's innocence.

The group agreed to split up the tasks. The men were to take on Wormleigh and Burns whilst the ladies spoke to Monique's maid. Thea and Tremont had been assigned the duty of chaperoning Primrose and Polly.

Ambrose muttered to Thea and her husband, "Sorry to give the pair of you the most perilous mission of all. Polly won't be a problem, of course—but keep a close eye on my daughter, will you? Of late, Rosie has been attracting trouble the way honey does flies."

"Don't worry about a thing." With a teasing smile in Vi's direction, Thea said, "How much worse could she be than Violet?"

Seeing the twitching lips around her, Vi resisted the impulse to stick her tongue out at her sister. She felt quite proud of her growing maturity.

"Very amusing, Thea," she said loftily and left it at that.

They went off on their assignments. As Violet followed Emma and Marianne to the servant's wing, her anticipation was threaded with worry. What would Jeanne reveal about Monique's past? Did the maid know about her mistress' lovers, including Wick? If she did, how should Violet handle the situation?

Em led the way down the servants' stairs into the kitchen. The large room buzzed with activity, maids and footmen racing to and fro in an orchestrated frenzy. They stopped short at the sight of three upstairs guests in their domain, bowing hastily as Vi and the others walked past.

Vi, for her part, was momentarily distracted from her worries by the scent of baked goods and roasting meat. Her belly rumbled; it had been hours since lunch. She paused and eyed a platter of sandwiches resting on a counter.

"Go ahead and take one, miss." The cook, a jolly bespectacled woman in a pristine apron, nodded at the sandwiches. "I've got plenty."

Violet didn't need to be asked twice. Thanking the good woman, she took one of the triangles and bit into it with relish. Buttery bread, spiced ham, and chutney—heaven. She took another and caught up to the others, munching.

"Goodness, couldn't you wait for supper?" Emma said.

"I'm hungry," Vi protested.

"Tartarus," Marianne said with a faint shake of her head.

A woman dressed in dark bombazine approached them and curtsied. Her tidy appearance and air of command conveyed her status as the top female servant of the household.

"Good afternoon, Your Grace. Ladies. How may I assist you?"

"Hello, Mrs. Hopkins," Emma said. "We're back to check in on Jeanne."

The housekeeper shook her head. "Such a terrible business. One can't blame the poor woman for succumbing to shock. I hope you'll find her in a better state."

Em continued to lead the way into the servant's hall, a long and narrow space dominated by a large trestle table. On one wall hung rows of small metal bells, and Vi spotted the names of the guests written beneath each. Whenever a chime went off, some member of the staff had to abandon their tea or whatever tasks they were doing at the table and dash off.

Violet followed Emma through a warren of hallways and up three flights of stairs until they reached their destination: the garret floor. The cramped corridor had doors on both sides.

Em went to the first door on the right and knocked briskly. "Jeanne? It's the Duchess of Strathaven. I've come to see how you're doing."

No reply.

"Do you think she's asleep?" Marianne said.

"The sleeping draught ought to have worn off by now." Frowning, Em knocked again.

"Try the knob," Vi suggested.

Em did. "It's locked."

"I'll go find Mrs. Hopkins." Marianne was already heading down the hallway.

"Hurry," Emma called after her. To Vi, she said in worried tones, "I have a bad feeling about this."

Vi, too, felt a sinking sensation in her stomach.

Marianne returned with the housekeeper, who produced a key and unlocked the door. When she attempted to push it open, it wouldn't budge.

Vi tried as well, to no avail. "She's barricaded it from the inside."

"We're going to need your strongest footmen, Mrs. Hopkins," Emma said.

Off the housekeeper went again whilst Em and Marianne implored Jeanne to let them in.

Vi had another idea. Going over to the next room, she knocked. When there was no answer, she turned the knob, and, luckily, the door swung open.

Entering the cramped room, she saw at a glance two small cots, one rickety washstand, and—yes!—a dormer window protruding from the sloped ceiling. She went over and pushed up the pane of glass. Peering outside, she saw that the window to Jeanne's room was also open... and it was only about six feet away.

She gauged the slope of the roof with an expert eye: it was nearly horizontal at the edge and easy to traverse.

True, the ground did look rather far away from three stories up, but Vi had completed far more challenging tasks. This would be a piece of cake compared to balancing on a tree limb, for example, or standing on the back of a moving horse. Decision made, she swung her leg over the sill and climbed out. Keeping her body close to the tiles, she began to inch her way over to Jeanne's room.

One foot... two feet... three...

"Good Lord!"

Emma's voice startled her, and she jerked, kicking loose a tile. It tumbled, shattering on the gravel below. Vi kept her balance and her eyes on the goal.

"Gadzooks, don't interrupt me," she said. "I'm trying to concentrate here."

Behind her, she heard Emma's muffled prayer.

...four feet... five...

Her fingers grasped the jamb of Jeanne's window. Holding on, she hoisted herself through the open frame, landing lightly on her feet in the room.

"*Sacré dieu!*" A wild-eyed Jeanne stood backed against a wall. The bed had been pushed up against the door, blocking entry.

Holding out her hands, Vi spoke in the voice that she would use with a spooked horse. "It's all right, Jeanne. There's nothing to be afraid of."

The elderly maid was paler than a ghost, her grey hair loose and tangled over the shoulders of her black dress. "Who are you? What do you want?"

"We've met before—I'm Violet Kent, remember? One of Monique's great admirers. I had the privilege of visiting with her the night before..."

Vi trailed off when she saw moisture well up in the other's

reddened eyes. It occurred to her that this was the first true sign of grief she'd seen from anyone over Monique's death.

Jeanne truly cared about her mistress, she thought with a pang.

"I am so sorry for your loss, Jeanne," she said softly.

Silence quivered between them.

"I... I remember you. My mistress, she was quite taken with you."

"She was?" Vi said, surprised.

"*Oui. Jeanne,* she said to me, *Mademoiselle Kent est charmante et un peu farfelue.*"

Charmante was easy enough to translate. "What does far-fell-loo mean?"

"A little... how do the English say? Madcap."

Vi had been called worse. "Since I just climbed in through your window, I can't argue with that," she said ruefully.

Jeanne's throat rippled above her dark collar. "My mistress would have done the same. She, too, approached the world with boldness and ingenuity. A disregard for useless conventions."

"Boldness and ingenuity," Vi mused, "I like that. It has a nicer ring than impulsive and reckless, at any rate. The truth is I poked my head out the window, and the rest of me just followed."

"My mistress believed that one's impulses are the only true guide—"

"Violet, are you all right?" Em's voice came from the other side of the blockaded door. "Let us in!"

"I'm fine. Give me a minute," Violet called back. Seeing Jeanne tremble again, she said, "That is my sister, Emma. She wants to talk to you about Monique—"

"I won't talk to her—or anyone!" The maid's vehemence made Vi take a step back, as one would from a feral and unpredictable creature. "I'll not allow my mistress' name to be soiled by gossip. She was the last of the noble family of de Brouet, God rest their souls, and I'll not let the memory of their finest daughter be tarnished."

"But we have no wish to harm Madame Monique's reputation," Vi protested. "We only want to see justice done—"

"*Justice.*" Jeanne spat out the word as if it were an epithet. "Do you know how many atrocities have been carried out in the guise of justice? The de Brouets, the family I have served faithfully since the age of twelve, they were delivered so-called justice— dragged from the house of their ancestors, carted like chattel in front of a drunken mob. The last thing they heard was the cheering of those stinking barbarians before the guillotine fell."

Vi's stomach churned at Jeanne's words. Anguish blazed like torches in the maid's eyes.

"Madame Monique escaped from The Terror?" Vi whispered.

"Of course she didn't," Jeanne snapped. "My mistress was only seven-and-twenty, far too young to have lived during the reign of that devil Robespierre. Don't you know anything?"

Violet flushed. Dates had never been her forte. "Er, of course. Sorry."

Jeanne harrumphed. "It was Monique's *maman* and I who escaped, with naught but the clothes on our back. The *comtesse* was forced to sell the last of her family heirlooms for a pittance to pay for our journey across the channel." The maid's rheumy eyes swam with tears again. "We sought refuge and instead found ourselves in a different hell."

Spotting a handkerchief on the dresser, Vi snagged it and handed it over. "What do you mean?"

"Friendless, penniless, what else could she do? What else?" Jeanne murmured, twisting the linen around her fingers.

"What's going on in there?" Even filtered through wood, Emma's voice was insistent.

Seeing the crazed darting of the maid's eyes, Vi guessed the poor thing was a bit let in the upper attics. She needed to calm Jeanne down before the others entered the mix.

"I need another minute," she called.

Jeanne began to speak again. "Monique de Brouet was

conceived in hell, but she survived because she was a fighter." Pride infused the maid's voice, and she spread her arms as if she were about to take flight. "She inherited her mama's beauty and grace, the *élan* of her ancestors, and so she became an *artiste*. Revered by audiences wherever she went."

"She was the greatest acrobat I've ever seen," Vi said.

"The greatest the *world* has ever seen." Jeanne's mood changed with shocking swiftness, and she began to sob. "*Comment cela pourrait-il arriver, ma petite?*"

Cautiously, Vi reached out a hand, patting the other's bony shoulder. "There, there." When the maid didn't pull away, she said, "Why don't you sit a moment?" and maneuvered the weeping woman into a chair.

Then she hurried to the door, pushing the bed away so that Emma and Marianne could enter. The two looked at Jeanne, who was weeping hysterically, too distraught to react to the presence of newcomers.

"How is she?" Em whispered.

Vi widened her eyes and wiggled her fingers by her ears. Her silent way of communicating, *There are bats in the woman's belfry.*

"I have failed her," Jeanne wailed. "Failed the de Brouets."

Emma went over. "Of course you haven't, dear. None of this is your fault."

The maid went on as if she hadn't spoken. "We should have stayed in London. I should have stopped her from coming here. But she wouldn't listen... she never listened..."

"You couldn't have known something like this would happen," Marianne said gently.

Those words seemed to trigger some internal lever in Jeanne. The maid's distress vanished like the floor of the wardrobe. An eerily blank expression took its place.

"You are right." She smoothed out the handkerchief that she'd crumpled. "I couldn't have known. How could I have?"

"So you mustn't blame yourself. Instead, we must focus on the task ahead of us," Em said.

"Task?" Jeanne said.

Em nodded. "I'm afraid we've concluded that your mistress' death was no accident."

Vi braced for Jeanne's reaction, but the other only stared blankly at Em.

"We're trying to identify possible suspects," Em went on. "If you could tell us which of the guests knew Monique, especially those who knew her, er, intimately..."

Please don't say Wick. Violet tensed, readying to cut in.

"I beg your pardon." Jeanne drew herself up, her eyes blazing once more. "Monique de Brouet was no light-skirt. She was a fine lady—the daughter of a *comtesse*."

"Even fine ladies have admirers, don't they?" Em said.

"*Oui.* But my mistress conducted herself with grace and class, in a manner befitting of her ancestors." Jeanne's chin jutted out. "On this, I will never waver."

Whatever the maid knew, she clearly was not about to betray her mistress' secrets. Violet exhaled. She didn't know whether to feel relieved or disappointed.

"What about enemies?" Marianne said. "Did anyone wish your mistress ill?"

Fear seized Jeanne's worn features once more.

"You can tell us," Em coaxed. "We'll keep you safe."

"Safety is an illusion. The darkness always comes," the maid whispered. "The only way to escape it is to flee."

Her eyes shifted like those of a cornered beast. Vi was worried that Jeanne might try to make a run for it... but the maid's expression smoothed once more.

She's truly addled, Vi thought with sympathy.

"There were those who envied my mistress' popularity," Jeanne said. "Josephine Ashe and Cedric Burns, to name two."

"Burns, you say?" Vi knew about Miss Ashe's animosity, but

Burns had seemed like an amiable fellow. "He was at the same table as Monique and I that first night. I didn't notice any tension between the two."

"My mistress would not squabble in the street with that mongrel." Jeanne sniffed. "Burns, however, hounded her in private. Wanting to bask in her reflected glory, he proposed that he and Madame Monique perform together... the nerve, thinking he could partner with my mistress!"

"But he has a partner," Vi said, puzzled. "If he partnered with Monique, what would happen to Miss Ashe?"

"She would be left out in the cold," Jeanne said smugly. "But my mistress had no interest in Burns. No matter how many times he tried to persuade her, she turned him down flat."

"Did Miss Ashe know about his proposal?" Emma said.

"*Je ne sais pas.* But about a month ago, after my mistress turned Burns down for the last time, she went to practice on the tightrope and had a near accident. The rope had begun to fray, you see, and, fortunately, she noticed before it was too late."

Marianne's brows arched. "And you think Mr. Burns or Miss Ashe was somehow involved?"

"The tightrope was new. There was no reason for it to fray." Hostility flamed in Jeanne's eyes. "It was an act of sabotage."

"Sabotage?" Vi whispered. "*Thunderbolts.*"

"We will follow up," Emma said decisively. "Is there anything else you can think of that might be of use in finding your mistress' killer?"

"*Non.* My mistress, she was an angel. What happened to her, she did nothing to deserve." Tears spilled down the maid's cheeks once more. "And now that she is gone, I have but one duty left: to protect and consecrate her memory. To preserve the legacy of Monique de Brouet."

22

Trudging with Kent and Strathaven toward the field where Wormleigh was said to be shooting, Richard told himself to focus. Worrying about the interview presently taking place with Monique's maid wasn't going to accomplish anything. Besides, Violet was there, and he had to trust that she would do her best to manage the situation.

He'd never had someone to share his burdens with before. It made him feel both relieved and uneasy to depend upon another —and a woman, no less. But Violet had proven herself to be loyal and strong in her resolve. God knew he'd butted up against her stubbornness more than once, and as much as that quality had annoyed him, it had also earned his respect.

She was no namby-pamby miss; she meant what she said and did what she set out to do.

Recalling what she'd set out to do beneath the wardrobe made heat surge in his loins. Aye, there were definite benefits to his lass' willfulness. He liked that her passion was a match for his. He liked that they were learning to walk in step. He also liked how her playfulness contrasted with his own somber nature, how she continually surprised him with her antics.

The plain truth was... he liked *her*.

That she doubted his regard struck him as absurd. He'd proposed to her once (and nearly twice). She was the one balking at making things permanent between them. His past rose in his mind, cautioning him to be wary of feminine vacillation. Although he'd shared with Violet the essentials of his past affaires, he hadn't divulged the entirety of his failures. Violet didn't need to be privy to all the humiliating details.

He wasn't eager, for instance, to share the fact that Audrey Keane had tried to make a cuckold of him. That she'd said yes to his offer while she had been pregnant with another man's child. That day, when Richard had gone to tell her that he wanted their engagement made public, he'd come upon her with her secret lover—a soldier whose regiment had recently moved from their village.

Audrey hadn't known if her lover would return for her, and finding herself with child, she'd come up with a contingency plan. She'd strung Richard along, all the while hoping that her true love would come back for her. In a way, Richard didn't blame her for her act of desperation: he blamed himself for being fool enough to believe that he'd swept her off her feet and that she'd actually wanted to marry him.

After all, he'd overheard the recipient of his first proposal, Lucinda Belton, telling her friends what she truly thought of his looks and manner.

No, he decided, there was no earthly reason why Violet should know that the man presently wooing her had been made a bloody fool not once, but twice. A chill snaked through him, and he couldn't stop the thought from forming. What if Violet turned out to be like the others? What if she tired of him? Decided she wanted someone more dashing, exciting...

Like hell that's going to happen.

Then and there he decided there was no time like the present to make his intentions known to her family. Both Violet's brother and brother-in-law were present, and it was best to stake his claim. *Strike while the iron is hot.*

He glanced at the two men walking beside him. He stopped, cleared his throat. "I have a matter to discuss with you both."

"Can't it wait?" Kent's gaze was trained on the figures in the distance. The hunters stood in a line; they were spaced several dozen yards apart, each of them accompanied by a footman bearing a caddy of shooting equipment. "We have to get to Wormleigh."

"I can be quick. The fact of the matter is... I'd like your permission." To quell a sudden feeling of panic, Richard clasped his hands behind his back. "To court Miss Kent."

Kent swiveled. "What did you say?"

"He wants to court Violet." Strathaven didn't look overly surprised.

"That's what I thought he said." Kent's brows knitted. "Why?"

"Er, I beg your pardon?"

"Why do you wish to woo my sister? Forgive me, but from what I understand, you do not hold her in particularly high esteem."

Richard's neck heated beneath his collar. He knew the other was referring to the gossip he'd inadvertently started about Violet all those months ago. In the space of a few short days, his feelings had undergone so radical a change that he could scarcely recall his muddled frame of mind back then. With sudden insight, he realized that his antagonism toward Violet had been directly proportional to his attraction to her. The attraction that he'd tried to resist... and failed.

What an idiot he'd been.

Drawing a breath, he said, "I have offered Miss Kent my sincerest apologies for having spoken carelessly. I cannot excuse my behavior, only say that it was not my intent to give rise to gossip." He paused, searching for the right words. "My regret over my actions has only grown stronger with each moment that I spend in Miss Kent's presence. I misjudged her. I can offer no defense but only assurances that, in the future, I will treat her with the respect and admiration she deserves."

Muscles bunched, he waited for the response.

"Seeing as how she pushed you into a fountain," Strathaven drawled, "I should think you and Violet could call it a draw."

"What?" Kent's gaze shot to the duke. "*Violet* was responsible for that?"

"She confessed all during a sisterly interlude yesterday. Emma told me—she tells me everything," Strathaven said with a hint of satisfaction. "So, you see, Kent, we might actually owe Carlisle thanks for keeping that scandal a secret and protecting our little sister's reputation."

"No thanks necessary. I rather deserved it," Richard muttered.

"Any man who takes a plunge and still comes back for more... well." His Grace's mouth curved. "You have my vote. What about you, Kent?"

The investigator appeared pensive, tension bracketing his mouth. "I will be frank, Carlisle. My middle sister is a unique young woman, not of the usual mold—in fact, she breaks any mold that tries to contain her. Whereas my impression is that you are a traditional sort of man. In a nutshell, my lord, I'm not confident you'll suit."

"I will not lie. I have shared those same concerns," Richard said baldly. "But the fact of the matter is, I am learning that where there's a will, there's a means to compromise. And I am very willing, sir, to work toward bridging any differences that may impede my future happiness with Miss Kent." He decided to lay all his cards down. "I am committed to a future with her; if I had my way, I would be asking for her hand and not merely your permission to woo her. But she wanted more time to further our acquaintance before making any permanent decisions, and I would not gainsay her wishes. So I must satisfy myself today by informing you that my intentions are honorable."

"Pretty words," Strathaven murmured. "Come, Kent, take pity. Look at the poor fellow—I don't think he's spoken so many words at once in his entire life. I can't recall the last time I encountered such earnestness... oh wait, I can. When I first met you."

Kent scowled. "Don't make me regret accepting your suit, Your Grace."

"As if you could have stopped Emma from doing what she wanted."

Impatient with the back and forth, Richard said, "So do I have your permission, Kent?"

After a moment, the investigator muttered, "Aye. If only because you can't be worse than the brother-in-law I already have."

"He means Tremont, of course," Strathaven said, clearly enjoying himself.

Kent scowled. "Now that that is settled, may we recommence with the business at hand?"

"Gladly." With relief, Richard added, "Thank you both."

The three of them identified Wormleigh, and, as they approached him, Richard couldn't help but question the wisdom of interviewing a suspect holding a loaded shotgun. Dressed in hunting tweeds, his belly straining his waistcoat, Wormleigh had his weapon aimed toward the wooded area fifty yards in front of him. A footman stood at the ready with a tall wicker basket of fresh shotguns, a bored-looking tan retriever lounging beside him.

"Lord Wormleigh, may I have a word?" Kent said.

"Quiet, sirrah." Wormleigh didn't turn, kept his focus on the copse up ahead. "The beaters are on the move again."

Richard saw glimpses of the men moving through the dense brush, driving the game out with their sticks and flags. An instant later, a flock of pheasants exploded into flight, their distinctive cries of *kok-kok-kok* muted by the boom of gunfire.

Wormleigh shot. Swore. Grabbed another gun from the footman and shot again.

The birds sailed smoothly on into the horizon.

"Damn and blast." Wormleigh was red-faced. "I could have sworn I hit one."

"Better luck next time," Strathaven drawled.

"We need to speak to you, my lord," Kent said. "Alone, if you please."

Wormleigh waved away the servant, who'd been busily reloading the used guns. Resting its chin on its paws, the retriever yawned and settled down for a nap.

Removing a silver flask from his pocket, Wormleigh said, "Well, what is it?"

"It concerns Madame Monique," Kent said. "I've been tasked with investigating her death, and I'd like to ask you a few questions, if I may."

"I thought Billings said it was an accident. Lord knows I don't have anything to add." Wormleigh took a swig. "I hardly knew the woman."

"Actually, my lord, I'm given to understand that you and the deceased had an argument on the night she died," Kent said.

Wormleigh coughed, spewing droplets of brandy. "Where'd you hear that?"

"Various sources." Kent's expression and tone remained neutral. "One of whom noted that you were also seen later that night by the library. Where the deceased woman was found."

"Are you suggesting that *I* had something to do with...?" The veins on Wormleigh's jowls stood out against his florid complexion. "Sirrah, I ought to call you out."

"It'd be simpler to answer his question." Strathaven cocked a dark eyebrow. "Unless you have something to hide, my lord?"

"I have nothing to hide!"

"Then why don't you answer the man's question?" Richard said evenly.

Wormleigh's eyes darted like that of cornered quarry. Richard saw him take measure of Kent's stalwart posture, the duke's languid menace. Wormleigh's gaze hit Richard, clearly assessing his height and heft... and slid hastily away.

"What I tell you must remain between us," Wormleigh muttered. "Your word as gentlemen."

"I give you my word to be as discreet as possible. If the knowledge you share becomes evidence in the case, however, I cannot guarantee to keep it secret," Kent said.

"Spit it out, Wormleigh," Richard advised. "The longer you draw this out, the more havey-cavey you appear."

"I had nothing to do with the bitch's death," Wormleigh protested.

"But you knew her," Kent said.

Gunfire boomed in the distance, birds squawking.

"We had a brief... acquaintance."

"Define acquaintance," Richard said.

"Bloody hell, Carlisle, must you be indelicate?" Wormleigh found refuge in indignation. "She was my mistress, if you must know. It didn't last long. A matter of months early last year."

"What happened?" Kent said.

Wormleigh took another swig. A long one. "She was a lying whore."

"Explain, please."

"I took a fancy to her after seeing her perform at Astley's. I thought to myself, *a woman who can balance on a tightrope... imagine what she could do in bed.* Those stockings of hers, they don't leave much to the imagination, do they?" When he received only stony stares in reply, Wormleigh grunted and went on. "I made her acquaintance and soon after had what I wanted from her. We had an arrangement, you understand. And since I was paying for her cottage and pin money—and it wasn't cheap, mind you—I believed I was entitled to certain exclusive rights."

Kent's scrutiny didn't waver. "What happened?"

"After maybe two months, I began to suspect that I wasn't the only one in the stables, so to speak. I could never be sure—she was a sly creature—but a man can tell when a filly's been ridden in his absence."

"Do you know who she was seeing?" Strathaven said as Richard's gut iced over.

"When I confronted her, she denied it, called me a jealous fool. I told her I wasn't the least bit jealous—but no man likes a hackneyed mount. She didn't like that, so we had a row, and that was that. She had a temper, that one. Very French," Wormleigh said with a touch of nostalgia.

Kent jotted in his notebook. "How long ago was this?"

"Last February, I believe. Hadn't seen her since then—until this party."

"What was your argument about, then?" Richard said.

Wormleigh shuffled his muddied boots. "I had one too many glasses of wine at supper and got a bit top-heavy. I ran into her in the hallway and sought to, ahem, renew our acquaintance. Don't know why it got her bristles up—I offered to pay for her services. But she got all touchy about it."

"Strange, that," the duke said.

Apparently missing the other's irony, Wormleigh gave a right-eous nod. "Bit high in the instep, if you ask me. As the old adage goes, beggars cannot afford to be choosers. And given that I saw Monique having a cozy *tête-à-tête* with her old friend Garrity after supper, she definitely can't afford to turn down good money. But that was Monique for you: all fire and pride and very little sense."

Richard's nape prickled. "What was the nature of the relation-ship between her and Garrity?"

"It was strictly a monetary affair. She always had need of coin; he's in the business of lending it. Back when I was covering her expenses, I paid off a note she owed to Garrity—and it wasn't bit change, either. As far as I know, the two had been doing business for years."

"Why were you in the library that night?" Richard demanded.

"I never went *into* the library, just walked past." Smirking, Wormleigh said, "On my way to an appointment, you see."

Strathaven's brows lifted. "Appointment?"

"A gentleman goes to enough house parties, he knows to have a bedpartner in reserve if the top choice is unavailable. Monique wasn't the only fish in the sea."

"So you were with someone that night?" Kent said.

"*All* night. What a fine filly she turned out to be. Bit skinny for my taste, but a better ride than I expected, eh?" Wormleigh winked.

"I'll need a name, my lord." Although Kent's features remained impassive, Richard heard the distaste in the investigator's voice.

"Can't give it. She made me promise to keep it a secret." Wormleigh puffed out his chest. "Gave her my word of honor, sirrah."

"She's your alibi," Richard said.

"Josephine Ashe," Wormleigh blurted.

"Right." Kent paused, his notebook still open. "Anything else you'd care to add?"

Wormleigh hesitated. "Come to think of it, there is one thing. When I walked by the library, I heard voices coming from within. I recall the clock chiming; it was just after two."

During the window of time when Monique was killed. Richard tensed.

"Do you know who those voices belonged to?" Kent said sharply.

Wormleigh shook his head. "They were speaking quietly, their voices muffled through the door. It was a man and a woman— lovers, I assumed."

"What made you assume that?" Richard said.

"Who else would be alone in the library at that time of night?" Wormleigh snorted. "And I did catch one word they were saying:

Gretna. Stupid fools were probably plotting to run off together. For love or some equally asinine reason."

"I'll look into it," Kent said. "Thank you, my lord—"

"Hello!"

Richard turned to see Violet ambling toward them. She was a vision of vitality in her blue cloak, the yellow feathers of her bonnet ruffling in the breeze. The duchess followed behind her.

"Good afternoon," Violet said with a pretty curtsy.

"What a pretty picture you make, m'dear." In a blink, Wormleigh transformed into a courtier, bowing over Violet's hand while Richard gritted his teeth. "You are a spot of color amidst this dreary landscape."

"Thank you. Hopefully, I won't tip off the birds."

Wormleigh flashed a smile. "They'll think you are one of them with your lovely feathers."

"Then I hope the hunters won't make a mistake and take a shot at *me*," Violet said.

Wormleigh's smile didn't waver. Richard could practically see the man searching for some flattering reply, and he spoke up to forestall any further flirtation.

"What are you doing here?" he said to her.

"We finished up early. Our chat was uneventful."

Her message was clear: Wick's secret was still safe. Relief swept through Richard.

"I wouldn't exactly call it uneventful," Her Grace muttered. "At least not your part in the business, Violet."

Violet looked uneasy. Before he could ask what her sister meant, she pointed to the copse and said, "Look, the beaters are readying to flush the game again. Are you going to shoot, Lord Wormleigh?"

"Don't think I'll bother, my dear," Wormleigh said grandly. "The guns are defective."

"Really?" Violet glanced at the collection of firearms. "*All* of them?"

For Christ's sake. Having had enough, Richard strode to the caddy. He hoisted out a double-barreled Manton—a damned fine fowling piece—and braced the stock against his shoulder. He maintained a relaxed grip and stance. The retriever perked up, trotting over to him. When the birds burst into the grey sky, Richard took aim and fired. Game plummeted. Tossing the empty gun aside, he grabbed another from the caddy and shot again with the same result.

The retriever leapt into action, bounding joyfully across the field to fetch the fallen birds.

"Double brace," Strathaven declared. "Bravo, Carlisle."

"Thunder and turf, you're a *crack shot*," Violet exclaimed. "Jolly well done!"

The admiration in her eyes made Richard feel taller than a mountain. He counted himself damned lucky that, this time around, he'd found a woman more impressed by shooting skills than drawing room conversation.

He offered her his arm and said gruffly, "Shall we, Miss Kent?"

23

After leaving Wormleigh, the group found privacy beneath the sheltering branches of an oak tree and compared notes on their interviews. Vi let Emma do the talking about Jeanne; she was relieved when her pleading look worked and her sister skimmed over the part involving her escapade out the window, saying merely that Vi's "ingenuity" had gotten them in. When Em was finished, Ambrose related the results of the men's talk with Wormleigh.

Upon hearing of Wormleigh's alibi, Em raised her brows. "Talk about the kettle calling the pot black. To think, Miss Ashe called Monique a harlot for having lovers."

"Sinners are oft those who preach the loudest," Strathaven said.

"And reformed rakes make the best philosophers, I take?" Em teased.

Bending his dark head, the duke whispered something in her ear; whatever he said made roses bloom in her cheeks.

"At any rate, we can strike Miss Ashe off the list," Ambrose said. "She might have been jealous of Monique, but between the maid Mary and Wormleigh, her time is now accounted for."

"We have new suspects to take her place," Richard said grimly. "Garrity and Burns."

Glancing at his pocket watch, Ambrose sighed. "I'll deal with them after I have my daily briefing with Magistrate Jones."

"That bad?" Em said.

"Let's just say that Jones wants justice painted in black and white when the reality oft lies in shades of grey." Beneath the brim of his hat, Ambrose's face was haggard. "Between the magistrate's intolerance of ambiguity and our host's insistence on discretion, it's not easy to carry out an investigation."

"But you'll manage because you're the best investigator in London," Em declared.

As Violet watched her brother stride off, guilt gnawed at her: how long could she keep the secret from him? She exchanged a look with Richard; from his troubled gaze, she knew that he was equally discomfited by their concealment of evidence. Yet they *couldn't* tell Ambrose about Wick's ring now. An uncompromising man like Magistrate Jones would no doubt presume Wick guilty: Wick would be tossed in gaol... or worse.

"Let's get back to the house," Emma said.

The four began the trek back through the waving grasses. Em and Strathaven walked a little ahead, giving Vi and Richard some privacy.

Walking beside her, Richard had a creased brow. "So how, precisely, did you convince Jeanne to let you in?"

Crumbs. "I can be, um, very convincing when I want to be."

"I don't doubt it." His tone was dry. "Care to elaborate on your 'ingenuity'?"

"It was nothing." Deciding it wise to change the subject, Vi said brightly, "We've learned a lot today, haven't we? Two new suspects... and I wonder who Wormleigh overheard in the library —the lovers he mentioned?"

"For all we know, he made that up. The man has more hot air than a flying balloon."

"Yes, I know," she agreed. "Imagine calling a double-barreled Manton defective."

Richard slid her a startled glance. "You know about guns?"

"Enough to know that Lord Wormleigh was the problem, not the fowling piece."

"But how did you learn...?"

"My brother Harry taught me about guns." How she missed her brother, she thought with a pang. She wanted him to meet Richard; she was certain the two would rub along famously.

"Your brother enjoys hunting?"

"Not really. It's the explosion side of things that he's interested in."

"I don't understand."

"Harry's a scientist and the genius of the family," she explained. "He's finishing up at Cambridge, and he'll probably become a professor. Anyway, he's been blowing things up ever since he was a boy, and he used to experiment with flintlocks all the time, trying to get a bigger bang." She grinned, remembering. "When it came to target practice, however, I beat him every time."

"You can *shoot*?"

"Well, yes, although I've never shot at a *moving* object. Just at apples and bottles. Although," she amended in the spirit of honesty, "I did shoot Tabitha once."

Richard stopped in his tracks. "You shot a *woman*?"

"Oh no, Tabitha is Em's cat. And I didn't shoot her with a gun. That time, I was practicing with a slingshot." Seeing his flummoxed expression, she added hastily, "I didn't mean to hit Tabby; it was an accident. She wandered in front of the target at the last moment."

"I... see." His tone said he didn't. "Do you have any other hidden talents I should know about?"

She was tempted to gloss over the truth. Yet another part of her *wanted* him to know her, and how could he, if she wasn't honest with him? If he was going to be disappointed, better now than after they were married, when it would be too late.

Gathering up her courage, she said baldly, "I can ride, shoot, and play cricket. I like swimming and acrobatics. With my trousers on, I can beat most anyone climbing up a tree."

The way he was staring at her made her heart thump nervously. She didn't want to shock or put him off, but she didn't want to hide who she was either. It was one of those instances in which compromise didn't come easily.

"Would you like to do those things with me?" he said.

Now it was her turn to stare. "Pardon?"

"Would you like to ride, shoot, and play other sports with me?" In the sunlight, his eyes had an iridescent gleam. "I could even teach you how to hunt—to shoot at moving objects, if you'd like."

He couldn't be serious.

"Are you funning me?" she said suspiciously.

"Not a bit."

"You'd truly teach me to hunt?"

"Since I'm fairly competent at it, I'd be happy to give you a few pointers."

Fairly competent? She'd never seen anyone handle a double-barreled Manton with such finesse and confidence. Why, to get tips from him, for him to even suggest such a thing...

"How are you at fencing? Archery?" he went on.

She shook her head in wonder. "I haven't done either."

"I have. I could teach you the fundamentals of both."

By... Golly. Her spiraling excitement was almost too much to bear. "You'd do all that? Even though it would be, um, irregular?"

"Who's to say what is regular between a man and his wife?"

His meaning sunk in—and gave her an undeniable thrill. "Are you trying to *bribe* me into marriage, Carlisle?"

"It's Richard, and I'm just trying to sweeten the pot, lass. In fact, when we're married, you could even wear your trousers from time to time—as long as you do so only in my presence."

There was no mistaking the pure male anticipation in his gaze.

Happiness flooded her, made her speechless.

Tucking her hand in the crook of his arm, he steered them toward Em and His Grace, who stood waiting up ahead. "If you marry me, you'll have a lifetime of pleasures to look forward to. Dancing, shooting, riding—we'll do it all. And that's to say nothing of the sporting we'll get up to in the marital bower."

His intimate suggestion made her toes curl in her half-boots.

"Now you're being wicked," she managed.

"Just trying to press any advantage I have." His eyes smiled at her. "By the by, I spoke to your brother and Strathaven."

"Oh." Her heart gave a silly hiccup. "How did it go?"

"They gave me permission. Not that I would have accepted anything else." He tucked her hand more firmly against his arm. "Face it, Violet: sooner or later, you're to be mine."

This time, his determination filled her not with rebelliousness but giddy joy.

———

When the group arrived back at the house, Emma announced that she was going to take a nap. Violet found this strange since her sister never napped, but with no chaperone, she had to bid farewell to Richard. Em and Strathaven went with her to find Polly. The youngest Kent was in her sitting room, having an impromptu tea with Gabby and Rosie.

As soon as Violet was settled, Em left, Strathaven following steadily at her heels.

When the door closed behind them, Gabby said with a frown, "I hope my party isn't wearing out the guests. Everyone is sleepy today."

"Thea and Tremont were chaperoning us earlier, but they went to take a nap too," Polly explained.

Given Vi's recent discovery of physical intimacies, she suspected that her siblings might not be napping—not that she wanted to think about her siblings and the word "intimacies" together in the same sentence. Eww. But she couldn't blame her sisters for wanting private time with their husbands, not when she found herself constantly distracted by thoughts of Richard.

Imagine a lifetime of making love and playing sports, she thought dreamily.

At the same time, marriage wasn't something one ought to rush into pell-mell. Hadn't she promised Emma she'd be more careful? She and Carlisle had had their first kiss only three days ago—although she realized now that she'd been attracted to him far longer. Probably since she pushed him into the fountain. And the intensity of all they'd shared in the past few days made her feel as if they'd known each other for ages. Yet in reality they hadn't...

That was the problem with thinking: like a dog chasing its own tail, she could go round and round forever and never get anywhere.

Too much thinking makes me... hungry.

Her attention veered to the spread of pastries on the coffee table, which were accompanied by pots of preserves and clotted cream. She accepted a cup of fragrant tea from Gabby and happily helped herself to a plate of goodies.

She'd just taken her first mouthful when Rosie demanded, "Tell us everything. And, for heaven's sake, don't spare the good details."

"Yes, I'm dying to know how the investigation is going," Gabby said. "Father never tells me anything."

"Just to be clear, I wasn't referring to the investigation," Rosie said, "but Viscount Carlisle. Everyone's noticed that he's been paying you marked attention, Vi."

"Have the two of you overcome your differences?" Polly said softly.

Violet looked at the trio's eager, wide-eyed expressions and swallowed the bite of cream cake. Gulping tea to wash it down, she said, "As to the investigation, I'm not supposed to say anything. Ambrose made us promise to keep things confidential."

"Papa didn't mean you couldn't tell *family*," Rosie said with a pout.

Ambrose's instructions rang in Violet's head. *The details of the investigation must be kept confidential—and that includes the girls. I don't want their young minds burdened by such dark business. And, for the love of God, say nothing to Rosie—or the entire party will know every last detail of the case by suppertime.*

It was true. When it came to gossip, Rosie was like a bird with shiny objects: she liked to collect and show off her glittering bits of knowledge. And being a popular girl, Rosie was a never-ending source of the latest *on dit*.

Which gave Violet an idea. With Rosie, information flowed both ways. One could learn a lot from the vivacious girl.

"What are the guests saying?" Vi said casually. "About Madame Monique's death, I mean?"

"Oh, it's just the usual mélange of fact, fiction, and speculation," Rosie said airily, "with no way of telling which is which. Although the official story given by Gabby's papa was that Monique's death was an accident, I've heard all *sorts* of rumors."

"Such as?"

The pretty blonde tapped a slender finger against her chin. "Some are saying that Monique's death resulted from her trying a new daredevil trick in the library. Others say she was drinking too much and hit her head. I even heard one version where,"—Rosie's voice lowered to a dramatic whisper—"*she was pushed by a jealous lover.*"

Vi's pulse raced. "Where did you hear that?"

"I don't recall, exactly. It might have been Goggston or Parnell." Rosie frowned. "Or was it one of the other fellows?"

"She's surrounded by so many gentlemen that she can't keep them straight," Gabby said with a droll expression.

"They all seem interchangeable after a while," Rosie agreed saucily. "All the same talk about horses, sporting—and I'm sure when we're not around—*wenching*."

"That's only fair given that we're talking about *them* when they're not around," Vi pointed out reasonably.

Rosie pursed her lips. "But it's not exactly the same, is it? We don't talk about them in the same fashion. Why, I can't even think of a female equivalent for the word 'wenching'."

With a grin, Vi suggested, "*Menching?*"

All the girls laughed, except Polly, whose brows knitted. "I'm sure not all gentleman are interested in that topic. Ambrose isn't, for example."

"Papa is different." Rosie's polished façade slipped, her green eyes soft with girlish adoration. "He's a prince among men."

"Well, I hope there's more than one prince. Because the gentlemen I've met so far are frogs." Gabby popped a jam tartlet into her mouth and chewed.

"As to frogs," Rosie said casually, "have you kissed Carlisle yet, Vi?"

The sneak attack took Violet by surprise. Try as she might, she couldn't stop the telltale heat from rising in her cheeks. Her hands went clammy, her pulse stuttering.

"Oh my goodness, you did!" Rosie shrieked. "You kissed him!"

"Thunderbolts, *lower your voice*," Vi said desperately. "Do you want the entire party to know?"

"So you *do* like him." Polly's aquamarine eyes shone. "I knew it!"

"He has... grown on me," Vi admitted.

"Like moss on a log. How utterly romantic," Rosie said, giggling.

Vi glanced at Gabby, who hadn't said anything, and worry fluttered. Even though the other had repeatedly expressed her lack of interest in Carlisle, would she be all right with *Violet* making a match with him?

Gabby's blue eyes rounded. "Are you certain you like *Carlisle?*"

"I am. I misjudged him, you see. He and I have much more in common than I would have ever guessed, and, beneath his gruff exterior, he's a jolly good chap."

"Then I'm ever so happy for you."

Relief rolled through Vi. "Thank you, Gabby."

"No, thank *you*," the other girl said with an impish smile, "for now Papa can't push me into a future I don't want—er, no offense."

"None taken. I know Carlisle is an acquired taste," Vi said ruefully.

"So will we be your maids of honor?" Rosie chimed in. "I adore weddings. Thea's was ever so much fun. Remember how you caught the bouquet, Violet? Why, you snatched it mid-air—disappointing more than a few unmarried ladies, let me tell you."

"Did *you* want to catch the bouquet, Rosie?" Polly asked before Vi could cut in.

"Of course not, silly. Why would I want to get married when I'm having so much fun? I'd far rather go to someone *else's* wedding—"

"Hold it right there, Rosie," Vi said with panicked emphasis. "You're bringing the cart before the horse. Nothing has been decided yet. So I'd appreciate it if you kept my relationship with Carlisle under wraps."

"Of course," Rosie said innocently. "When have I ever leaked a secret?"

Crumpets, Violet thought. *I'm doomed.*

24

A fter parting ways with Violet, Richard went in search of his brother. He found Wickham having refreshments in the main drawing room, and he was relieved to see the other paying court to Miss Turbett. Her father hovered nearby, watching the proceedings like a hawk.

Richard found a quiet spot in a corner, where he could better observe his brother and the general goings-on. To the casual onlooker, Wick appeared attentive and interested, his golden brown curls leaned close to Miss Turbett's mousy ones. Richard, however, saw the subtle lines of strain on his sibling's face.

In truth, Miss Turbett also looked far from content. Her pale green frock emphasized her pallor, and her lips were pinched. Every now and again, her gaze drifted from Wick to a nearby window with a view of the courtyard and amphitheatre. She looked as if she wanted to be a thousand miles away...

Richard wished that there was another solution to Wick's money troubles. But he couldn't worry about it now. At present he had his hands full dealing with his brother's other looming problem.

"La, Lord Carlisle! Well met!"

He turned in the direction of the simpering tones and wanted to groan as Miss Anne Wrotham approached him in a determined flurry of lace and ribbons. She was accompanied by her grand-mama, Lady Ainsworthy, a dowager countess and famed stickler amongst the *ton*. Richard had a passing acquaintance with the pair —which, for him, was more than sufficient.

The dowager's sour countenance conveyed her displeasure with her present circumstances. Richard had heard that she had deigned to attend the party because her son's estate relied on the support of Billings' bank. Even dowagers had to occasionally sing for their supper. Miss Wrotham, a tall and narrow spinster in her forties, had likely accompanied her grandmama since, by society's standard, she was not only on the shelf, but at the very back of it, and thus had little choice but to descend a rung—or six—if she wanted a match.

"Lord Carlisle," Miss Wrotham said with a breathy, affected lisp, "I was *so* hoping to see you."

Richard didn't like the predatory look in her close-set eyes.

"Why?" he said.

Her harsh laugh grated against his nerves. "La, what a wit you are, my lord. But I am quite certain you understand my meaning. We must stick together, we birds of a more *refined* feather." She cast a contemptuous look around the room.

Richard didn't care for snobs. "I am content with the company, Miss Wrotham."

"Content indeed. How *naughty* of you to tease me, my lord." She rapped her fan against his arm. "But I suppose such familiarities may be permitted since we are old friends."

He'd never cared for empty flirtation. Since he couldn't think of a polite reply, he said nothing. The awkward silence stretched until it was broken by his brother's voice.

"There you are, Carlisle." Wick appeared at his side, saying easily, "I was wondering if I could have a word with you. That is, if you don't mind being deprived of such enchanting company?"

Miss Wrotham preened. "La, Mr. Murray, what a charmer you are."

"Come, Anne, we will leave the gentlemen to their business," the dowager said.

"Do come look for us when you're done!" Miss Wrotham called as her grandmama dragged her away.

"Thanks for the rescue," Richard muttered.

"Least I could do after all you've done for me." Above the complicated folds of his cravat, Wick's face was uncharacteristically somber. "I mean that, Richard. I know how much I am in your debt. For everything."

"Brothers don't speak of debts." As he said the words, however, Richard thought of how Wick had misled Violet about him, and his gut knotted.

"You're a bigger man than I am. A better one too." Wick dragged a hand through his windswept curls, the signet ring gleaming on his hand. "That is why I wasn't truthful to Violet about my debts, you know. I was ashamed of myself. And... envious of you." He exhaled. "Because I'm not as good as you and never will be."

Violet had been right about his brother's motives for lying.

With a sigh, he said, "That's not true, Wick. You have much to recommend you and a bright future ahead. You can change the path you're on, have a fresh start. And you're doing the right thing by courting Miss Turbett."

"Too little too late, but it's better than nothing." Wick's smile was lopsided. "Enough about me. So you and Violet... it's serious?"

He nodded. "All I have to do is convince her to marry me."

"Shouldn't be too difficult. The two of you are a perfect match."

Richard thought so, and he hoped he was beginning to convince her of the fact. Using sports to lure her had been a masterful stroke, if he did say so himself. The truth was that the possibility of spending a lifetime playing with Violet, being with her, filled him with wonder... and embarrassing eagerness.

He reined himself in. He was a grown man, not some greenling. Moreover, he'd come to the conclusion that Violet's insistence that they "like" each other stemmed from her uncertainty about him rather than vice versa. It was obvious *he* liked *her*; hell, he'd said it outright. How much clearer could he be?

Thus, the true trouble, he reasoned, must be that *she* hadn't yet committed her feelings to him. His history reared its ugly head again: securing a lady's devotion had never been his forte. But he told himself that Violet was different, that her uncertainty was understandable given their early antagonism. How many times had she accused him of being stodgy and traditional... a blasted stuffed shirt?

"If only I could get her to see that we're a fit," he muttered.

Hephaestus had managed to accomplish a similar feat. After he'd parted ways with Aphrodite, the humble god had somehow convinced Aglaea, the goddess of vitality, to take him on. But that was mythology; this was real life. How did one go about convincing a beautiful, spirited young woman that one wasn't boring and tedious?

"I assume you've tried the usual strategies of persuasion?" Wick said.

Richard didn't know there were any. "Er, usual strategies?"

"You know. Poetry and poesies, that sort of thing. A trinket to symbolize your affection."

Wilted daffodils blazed in his head. He'd never been good at gifts. Neither Lucinda Belton nor Audrey Keane had been impressed with the trifles he'd presented them with... and reciting poetry?

Out of the question. He had to respect himself in the morning.

Apparently sensing his unease, Wick said hastily, "The gift

itself doesn't matter. With Violet, it's the thought that counts. I'm sure she'll appreciate anything you give her."

The tips of Richard's ears burned as he realized that he hadn't given Violet *any* tokens of his esteem. Their courtship had consisted mostly of arguing and lovemaking. Even he knew that a man ought to go wooing with more than lust in his pocket. But what could he offer her...?

Inspiration struck him like a hammer against an anvil. The certainty of it resounded within him. He knew the *perfect* gift for Violet—and how to deliver it in a suitably romantic fashion.

"Uh oh," Wick said under his breath.

Kent had entered the room and was heading over.

"Time to make myself scarce," Wick muttered. "You'll keep me apprised?"

Richard nodded, and Wick went to find refuge amongst his cronies just as Kent arrived.

"How did the meeting go?" Richard said by way of greeting.

"As expected." Kent's rawboned features looked weary. "On the bright side, the magistrate plans to follow my recommendation and send his men to local stations that sell tickets to Gretna. If Wormleigh was telling the truth about the lovers he overheard, there might be a record in a ledger somewhere of the couple. It's a long shot, but I believe in leaving no stone unturned."

Not for the first time, Richard was impressed by the other man's diligence and clear thinking. He respected Kent, liked the man. Liked all of Violet's family, actually.

"I admire your thoroughness, sir," he said.

"It's part of the job," Kent said. "Where are the others?"

"Miss Kent is with some family members, I believe. Their Graces are taking a nap."

"A nap." Kent's voice had a wistful edge. "Well, I shan't disturb them. By the by, I ran into Billings on the way in. I informed him about Garrity and Burns, and he was adamant that we not approach the former on our own. He's making arrangements for us to have an 'audience' with Garrity tomorrow morning."

"He's that afraid of Garrity?"

"Apparently, the moneylender is a man one doesn't want to offend." Kent sighed. "But it's just as well. I have no desire to cut a swath through Garrity's cutthroats just to talk to him."

"That leaves Burns. Shall we go find him?"

"No need. Speak of the devil." Kent lifted his chin toward the doorway.

Burns had made an entrance. Even as ladies swarmed the blond performer, he had a distracted expression. He craned his neck as if looking for someone... then he spotted Richard and Kent, his gaze widening. Extricating himself from his adoring female horde, he hurried out.

Richard and Kent took off after the juggler. In the hallway, Richard saw Burns' wiry figure disappear into the billiards room. He and Kent exchanged a wordless nod; he strode toward the farther door while the investigator took the closer one. Between the two of them, they would block off the exits to the room.

Richard entered—and Burns nearly ran into him.

"In a rush?" Richard said.

"N-no, my lord." Burns backed away from him. "I was just, er, looking for my partner, Miss Ashe. We have to practice our act —*oof.*"

The juggler had stumbled into Kent, who'd been waiting silently behind him. As most of the male guests were still out shooting, the three of them were the only ones in the room, the scent of cigar smoke and leather heavy in the air. Darting a nervous glance between his captors, Burns retreated to the billiards table occupying the center of the chamber.

Richard and Kent followed, facing Burns across the green baize.

"We'd like to talk to you, sir." Kent's tone was even. "Regarding Monique de Brouet's death."

"I don't know anything about that," Burns said quickly.

"Not too torn up over your colleague's death?" Richard inquired.

The performer flushed beneath his tan. "Course I am. Terrible business. I only meant to say that it came as a shock—a complete surprise."

"How would you characterize your relationship with the deceased?" Kent said.

"It was purely professional." Grabbing an ivory ball, he rolled it around on the table, his movements nimble. "As you know, Monique and I were colleagues at Astley's."

"From what we understand, you wanted to be more than mere colleagues," Richard said.

"Now that's a bleeding lie." Burns' eyes blazed. "I had no personal interest in Monique. My preference is for gently-bred ladies, not strumpets."

"What I meant was that you wanted to be Monique's partner —in an acrobatics act."

The fire left the juggler; he looked ill at ease again. "Nothing came of that. It was just an idea. A way for the both of us to benefit from combining audiences."

"But the benefit would have been mostly yours," Kent said, "as Monique had the greater fame."

"Either way, I asked, she refused. End of story."

Richard quirked a brow. "You harbored no animosity after she turned you down?"

"Look, business is business. Monique was looking after her own interests, and I don't blame her for that." Burns gripped the edge of the table. "I understand how difficult it is to fight one's way to the top—to have ambitions that exceed one's grasp. I might have envied Monique de Brouet, but I also respected her."

"So you had nothing to do with her frayed tightrope?" Kent said.

Burns' laugh surprised Richard. "Let me guess. That maid of hers mentioned it?"

Kent gave a terse nod.

"The old mort's got a screw loose. Thought the world was out to get her and her mistress." The juggler crossed his arms. "Ropes fray; it was naught but an accident. I was definitely not involved."

"One last question." Kent pinned the man with a stare. "Do you know of anyone who wanted Monique dead?"

Burns swallowed. A tremor entered his voice. "No, I do not."

They let the juggler go.

"What do you think?" Kent said.

Richard shook his head. "For an innocent man, Burns seems to have a case of the nerves. But I can't say for certain that I think he did it."

"Agreed. He stays on the list." Kent sighed. "Hopefully we'll have better luck with Garrity in the morning."

25

Later that night, Marianne Kent was reading in bed when her husband came in. She felt a pang of worry at how tired he looked. His handsome face bore lines of tension, and his hair looked as if he'd dragged his hands through it repeatedly.

She put down her book and went to him. "It's been a long day, hasn't it, my darling?"

"It hasn't exactly been the most relaxing of vacations," he said dryly.

She helped him with his jacket, easing the material off his broad shoulders. "How did the meeting with Magistrate Jones go?"

"As expected. He'll be breathing down my neck until the case is solved." Ambrose tugged off his cravat and began unbuttoning his waistcoat. "But he's the least of my worries."

As Marianne watched her husband pull off his shirt, a tingle passed through her. Over a decade of marriage and he still affected her this way. The sight of his whipcord lean torso, the tough planes and ridges of muscle, made her nipples harden beneath her silk robe. Her gaze followed the trail of dark hair that disappeared into his waistband, and her sex quivered.

It had been too long since they'd had intimate time alone. Of late, it seemed that they were always dealing with some domestic catastrophe or another. She'd hoped that the house party would be a vacation of sorts for them—but instead it had turned out to be work. She could see that Ambrose was exhausted, and she didn't want to take advantage of him.

At least, not until he'd had a chance to unwind.

"Why don't you lie down and tell me all about it while I give you a back rub?" she said.

His amber eyes lit up. "That's the best thing I've heard all day."

He removed the rest of his clothing, and, Lord, she couldn't help but wet her lips. Even at rest, his cock hung large and thick between his thighs, his bollocks swaying with visible heft as he walked over to the bed. Pulling back the covers, he sprawled face down onto the mattress.

For a minute, Marianne just enjoyed the view. Heavens, he was beautiful.

She clambered over him, settling her knees on either side of his narrow hips. She placed her hands on his broad shoulders and began to knead the taut muscles.

"God, you don't know how good that feels." His voice was muffled by the mattress.

"Tell me what's on your mind," she murmured.

"Violet, to start. Carlisle asked me for permission to court her today."

Hearing the disgruntled edge in her husband's voice, Marianne said, "And you don't approve?"

"I don't know what to think. One moment they seem like they can't stand one another and the next he wants her to be his wife? It doesn't make any sense."

Poor Ambrose. He did like his logic.

"Love rarely makes sense, darling. Remember how you and I started off?"

He groaned with pleasure as she attacked the knots in his neck. "That was different. There were mitigating circumstances. We each had our secrets to keep—for good reason, at the time."

"Perhaps there's more going on with Violet and Carlisle than we realize."

Given the undercurrents she'd picked up between the two, Marianne suspected there was *a lot* more... but she didn't want to throw fuel on Ambrose's fire. He loved his sisters and, like any big brother, had a tendency to be overprotective.

"That's what I'm afraid of. With Violet, one never knows what is really going on. All these years... and I don't think I truly understand her."

Marianne knew what he meant. Violet's façade of merriment hid a certain skittishness, a reluctance to reveal her true emotions. Even Ambrose, one of the most astute men Marianne knew, had trouble reading his middle sister.

Leaning forward, Marianne pressed her palms into her husband's back. "With Violet, I think you have to let her find her own path... and her own husband. Carlisle may end up being just what she needs.

"You think so?" Relaxation slurred Ambrose's voice. He had his head turned to one side, pillowed by his folded arms.

"He's her opposite. Steady, somber. He'll anchor her when she gets too outrageous, and, in turn, she'll lighten him up when he gets too serious."

"Mmm."

Continuing to massage him, Marianne mused, "And in some ways they're the same. Strong-willed, independent... and both of them enjoy physical activities."

"Mmm."

And speaking of physical activities... Marianne moved off Ambrose, kneeling at his side so that she could work the hard curves of his buttocks, the taut sinew of his thighs and calves.

Soon desire was thrumming impatiently in her blood, and she'd had enough of the foreplay.

Sliding up, she murmured in his ear, "Why don't you massage me now... inside?"

No response.

Frowning, she said, "Ambrose?"

He let out a snore.

He'd... fallen asleep on her?

For a moment, she teetered between exasperation and wifely concern. The latter won out. With a sigh, she drew the covers over his slumbering form, climbed in next to him, and doused the light.

26

That night, Violet had trouble finding sleep. Despite the soothing pitter patter of a light rain that had begun after supper, she found herself tossing restlessly against the pillows. The evening had been a mellow one, with many guests going up to bed early. She hadn't seen Richard and wondered where he'd gone. She'd had a chance to catch up with Wick, however, the two of them chatting briefly in the atrium.

"Am I forgiven, Vi, for lying to you about my debt?" he'd said quietly.

The shame and remorse in her friend's eyes had compressed her chest. She knew why Wick had lied. He'd felt that he couldn't measure up—and she understood the feeling all too well. It wasn't easy comparing oneself to one's clever and capable siblings.

"Of course I forgive you." She gave his hand a quick squeeze. "But it's not my forgiveness you ought to be seeking out."

"I already talked to Carlisle. We made peace."

"I'm glad. He cares about you a great deal, Wick."

"You as well." His knowing gaze made her blush. "So am I to understand that we'll be brother and sister in fact as well as in spirit?"

The return of their old camaraderie made her heart swell and allowed her to disclose her uncertainty. "I don't know, Wick."

"You *do* like him, don't you?"

"Yes... of course. But we're so different."

"Take my advice, and don't let that stop you. God knows he can be a bit blunt and overbearing at times, but you won't meet a finer man." Wick hesitated. "Even if he hasn't had the best of luck with females."

"He told me about his past," she admitted.

"He did? There's a first." Wick sounded surprised. "He must *really* like you."

Hope burgeoned. "Do you think so? Because you know me, Wick, and I can't change who I am." She bit her lip. "Let's face it, I'm a hoyden who forgets proprieties all the time. I'm prone to scrapes, acting without thinking... what if I disappoint him?"

Wick stared at her... and burst out laughing.

"What's so amusing?" she said, stung. It wasn't often that she tried to share her innermost feelings.

"You are. Dear Vi," he said with affection, "don't you understand? Richard is drawn to you *because* you're different from him. He needs your spirit and *joie de vivre*. Otherwise, he'll end up an old stick-in-the-mud. Trust me on this."

Now, moving restlessly amidst the bedsheets, Violet mulled over her friend's words. Could it be true that Richard needed her? He seemed so strong and self-assured. But then she recalled the hints of vulnerability she'd glimpsed in him. How surprised he'd been when she said that she found him attractive. How lonely he'd seemed bearing his family's burdens—and how he'd said she was an ease to him. Her insides melted.

Rap. Rap.

The sound startled her from her thoughts. She sat up, pushing her hair out of her eyes. Was someone at the door?

The double knocks came again... not from her bedroom door, but from... the *balcony*? She jumped out of bed, hurrying over. She parted the drapes, and her eyes widened at the sight: *Richard* was standing outside. Hastily, she yanked open the glass-paned doors. The rain-speckled wind billowed the curtains and whipped against her night rail.

"*Gadzooks,* what are you doing there?" she exclaimed.

"For God's sake, lower your voice, or everyone will know I'm here. Could I explain inside?" he said tersely.

She pulled him into the room. Once she had the doors closed, she turned to look at him. Moisture glazed his stark features, his hair curling against his forehead in wet whorls. He was rumpled and wet from head to toe, his clothes dripping water onto the floor.

She repeated in hushed tones, "What are you doing here?"

"I came to give you something." Looking thoroughly disgruntled, he said, "Do you mind if I dry off in front of the fire first?"

"By Golly, you must be *freezing.* Here, let me help you with your jacket."

Between the two of them, they managed to pry off the sodden garment. After hanging it and his waistcoat to dry on the back of a chair, she went to fetch a towel for him from the washing stand. When she returned, he'd built up the fire in the hearth and was standing on the carpet in front of it, warming his hands.

The firelight cast his features in harsh relief. His damp shirt clung to his broad shoulders, the hard-paved contours of his chest. He'd shucked his destroyed cravat, and the open vee of his collar revealed the strong line of his throat and a glimpse of the hair-dusted muscle below. He'd removed his boots and socks; his soaked trousers molded to his powerful legs like a second skin. The sight of his large bare feet sent a quiver through her.

He was so deliciously primal and gorgeous, the very epitome of what a male ought to be. But what on earth had motivated him to climb her balcony in the middle of the night during a rainstorm? Her heart thumped, a honeyed awareness trickling through her. Wordlessly, she handed him the towel.

He dried himself off with efficient movements. With the towel draped around his neck, he slanted her a look. "Did I wake you?"

"No, I was awake. I'm, um, not a good sleeper." Why did she suddenly feel tongue-tied?

Strained silence descended.

"I hope I didn't startle you," he said abruptly. "This morning, you said we could arrange some time alone together. I took you at your word."

As he spoke, ruddy color rose up his jaw. His shoulders were tense as if he was... nervous?

"I'm glad you came," she blurted.

His lashes flickered. "You are?"

"I, um, didn't get a chance to talk to you this evening. To find out how things went with Burns."

"Oh." His brow furrowed. "In a nutshell, he seemed a havey-cavey sort of fellow, but neither your brother nor I believe he was the killer."

"And Garrity?"

"We're scheduled to talk to him in the morning."

"Oh. That's... good."

Awkward silence stretched once again. Her pulse was racing.

"I brought something for you," Richard said suddenly.

Going to his jacket, he plucked something from its pocket. Returning, he thrust a damp, paper-wrapped package at her as if he couldn't be rid of it quickly enough.

"Um, what is it?" she said.

"Open it, and you'll see." His voice was grim, strangely resigned.

She took the package; it was as long as her forearm and oddly shaped. She unwrapped it with care—and blinked at the revealed objects. One item consisted of two sticks of wood tied together in the shape of a T. The ends of a short cord were connected to the top of the T, the middle section pulled back tautly and hooked onto a wooden latch on the body of the T. Nestled in the paper were also three little arrows, their tips blunted and made of wood.

Recognition dawned.

"Thunderbolts," she breathed. "A miniature *crossbow*. Where did you get such a thing?"

"I used to fashion them for Wick and me when we were boys," he said starkly. "We hid them beneath our desks and drove our tutors mad by shooting at things during our lessons."

She was so filled with emotion that she couldn't speak.

His shoulders hunched. "I thought since you liked to shoot... never mind. It's a stupid thing to give to a lady—"

"I love it!"

She placed the precious gift on a chair and then launched herself at him. In her enthusiasm, she didn't check herself and probably would have felled a lesser man. Richard didn't budge an inch, his arms closing around her like steel bands.

"You do?" His voice was hoarse... hopeful?

Tipping her head back, she told him fervently, "It's the *best* present anyone has given me."

And it was. Not merely because she loved shooting, but because of what the crossbow represented. He *understood* her. Accepted her foibles and eccentricities. He truly liked her after all!

The feeling inside her was too vast to contain. So she shared it with him.

As soon as her lips touched his, desire combusted between them. They sank onto the carpet, tongues and limbs entangled, tearing at each other's clothes. Before she knew it, her night rail was tossed aside, her bare back pressing against the carpet. Hanging over her, he gazed down at her naked body. Her embarrassment dissipated at the undisguised wonder in his eyes.

"By Jove." His voice was as deep as the night. "You're the most beautiful sight I've ever seen."

She trailed her fingers over the granite-hard contours of his chest; in the tussle, she'd managed to get his shirt off. "I was about to say the same thing," she said reverently.

Flecks of ore surfaced in his eyes. "What did I do to deserve you?"

She grinned, about to make a quip, but he lowered his head to her breasts. The hot, wet suction on a taut peak made her spine arch off the carpet. She bit her lip to stifle a moan.

"Your nipples are so pretty," he said huskily. "Sweet and ripe against my tongue. I've dreamed of kissing you here, suckling to my heart's content."

His words inflamed her almost as much as the decadent flicks of his tongue. He licked and sucked, the drugging pulls causing the place between her legs to flutter and dampen.

When his fingers stroked through those needy folds, a groan rumbled from his chest. "You're so wet for me, lass."

Her cheeks flamed. "I... I can't help it."

"Devil and damn, I don't want you to. I want your pussy soaked for me." His eyes grew smoky. "Aye, that's it. Drench me with your dew, sweeting."

She moaned as he pressed deeply, her moors on reality beginning to slip. Then he found that little knot of sensation, rubbing it as his fingers pumped fiercely into her. When he lowered his head, suckling hard at her nipples, she broke free of earthly restraints and shattered into ecstatic pieces.

His chest heaving, Richard stared down into Violet's flushed face. Her eyes were heavy-lidded, sated, her womanly dew slick upon his fingers. Satisfaction flowed through him; at the same time, his cock was an iron ridge in his trousers, throbbing with an acuity that bordered on pain.

The gentlemanly thing to do would be to take his leave. He'd come to give her a present... and now he'd given her two. He couldn't say which was sweeter: her response to the crossbow (a success rather than an unmitigated disaster, thank God) or the tight clench of her pussy around his fingers when she'd found her climax.

His thinking was not helping matters down south. He reminded himself that the point of tonight's excursion was to demonstrate that he meant to woo her with more than lust. So he hadn't exactly proved his thesis... but, then again, she wasn't exactly complaining.

He hid a grin. Bent and kissed her nose. "I'd best be going before we get caught."

Sitting up, he was reaching for his shirt when her hand slapped against his chest. She'd risen, kneeling beside him. "Wait just one minute," she ordered.

He blinked. "Pardon?"

"It's my turn."

"Er, your turn?"

"Fair's fair, Carlisle."

He was about to remind her to call him Richard—but his breath left him in a sharp whoosh. Her fingers were fumbling with the placket of his trousers, the movements an exquisite torture.

But he didn't want her to think that reciprocity was required. "Sweet, your pleasure is enough—"

He bit off a groan as his erection fell into her waiting hands. His randy cock had no scruples whatsoever. It twitched eagerly at her touch, the bulbous head nudging at her palms. With paralyzing pleasure, he watched as her slender fingers petted the thick, veined beast.

"I've been thinking," she said.

"Hmm?" God, he loved her hands. They were meant to frig him.

"You know what you did to me beneath the wardrobe?"

Devil and damn. She couldn't mean...

Swallowing, he said, "Which part, lass?"

"You know... when you kissed me... down there?"

She *did* mean that. Lust roared over him. "When I kissed your pussy, you mean?"

Pink-cheeked, she nodded. "Could I do the same... for you?"

Christ. Fierce arousal gripped him as he struggled for a proper response. His cock, being more forthright, showed its enthusiasm by releasing another droplet of seed. They both gazed at the pearly bead... and then, as if all this were happening in some fevered fantasy of his, she bent her head and licked it off.

Bloody. Fucking. Hell.

Pleasure punched him, reverberating in every sinew, bone, and cell of his being. Her licks were tentative, whisper-soft, and they made him harder and hotter than he'd ever been. This was the sort of thing he'd only paid for, never expected from a lady—and one who he meant to make his viscountess, no less. But watching Violet's little pink tongue lap at his turgid shaft, feeling the indescribable bliss of those velvety lashes, he knew there was no going back.

If she was open to this, hell, who was he to argue? Like he'd said to her, who was to say what was proper or not between them? They would make their own bloody rules.

He planned to teach her all sorts of sports. Why not begin with this? With brimming anticipation, he threaded his fingers through her silken tresses and guided her lips to the head of his cock.

"Take me in your mouth," he said huskily. "Suck me."

Understanding dawned in her eyes. Her lips closed around his crown, and she proceeded to drive him out of his ever-loving mind. She took to fellatio like a fish to water; what she lacked in experience, she made up for in enthusiasm and, *goddamn*, native ability. His fingers tightened against her scalp as she bobbed on his shaft, taking him deeper and deeper. Closer and closer to the point of no return.

Heat frothed in his bollocks, and he knew he was close.

He didn't want to come alone.

In a swift motion, he moved so that he was lying fully on his back, pulling her hips to straddle his head. Her surprised gasp puffed against his erection as he yanked her pussy down onto his waiting mouth. He licked her dripping slit, spearing her tight sheath with his tongue while his fingers diddled her pearl. She went *wild* for him, riding his mouth, cramming his cock into her own as if she meant to swallow him whole.

It was too much. Beyond pleasure. Beyond anything.

"Lass, I'm going to spend," he gasped in warning. "Move aside..."

But she wouldn't be dislodged. Instead, she took him even more eagerly, his eyes rolling back in his head when he butted the silken end of her throat. Hot ecstasy stabbed through his balls. Seed geysered up his shaft, and then he exploded in her mouth. At the same time, her honey squirted against his lips, and he feasted on that rare nectar like a starved man, growling as his climax rocked him to the core.

Afterward, he gathered her in his arms, kissing her reverently. The taste of himself on her lips was intensely erotic... and a little worrisome.

"Violet, was that... all right?" he ventured.

"I'm not sure." She gave him a dreamy smile. "Maybe we should try it again?"

With a relieved chuckle, he scooped her up and carried her to the bed. He tucked her in.

"Don't go," she mumbled. "Stay with me, Richard."

"Time for you to sleep, love."

"I'm not tired." She yawned. "We could... stay up and talk..."

He stroked her cheek. "Rest, lass. We'll talk tomorrow."

Her answer was a soft wisp of a snore.

His lips twitched. Because he'd gotten the last word... finally.

27

At eleven o'clock the next morning, Richard accompanied Kent to Garrity's room. They arrived just as another one of the guests, a respected member of parliament, was leaving. The nobleman kept his eyes averted, mumbling a greeting as he passed.

A pair of burly guards flanked the entrance to the money-lender's suite. The one with a scar on his chin took Kent and Richard's names and told them to wait. He disappeared into the room.

"'Tis easier to get an audience with the king," Richard muttered.

"Aye." Kent took out his notebook, rifling through it idly. "I have a feeling this interview will require stamina. I trust you rested well last night?"

Richard's jaw heated; did the other suspect his nighttime activities? But, no, Kent was scanning his notes, clearly just making small talk.

"Tolerably well, thank you." Richard cleared his throat. "You?"

"Slept like the dead."

The cutthroat returned, waving them in. "Mr. Garrity will see you now."

The spacious suite assigned to the moneylender attested to his power and status. The silk-covered walls, enchanting vista of the surrounding fields, and majestic balcony suggested that this might have been a state bedchamber at one point. Garbed in a burgundy velvet *robe de chambré*, Garrity looked like a king in his high-backed chair by the fire.

He waved them into the adjacent seats.

"Gentlemen," he said pleasantly, "what may I do for you?"

Although Richard had met the other once before—during the tense visit he'd paid to Garrity's office to speak about Wick's debt —the moneylender showed no sign of their having a previous acquaintance. Richard was relieved that the other's famed discretion held up in the present situation. He had no wish to rattle his brother's skeletons in front of Kent.

"Billings has asked me to follow up on the matter of Madame Monique's passing," Kent said.

Garrity's dark brows inched upward. "I thought it was an accident."

"I'm speaking to anyone who had a connection to the deceased. Tying up loose ends," Kent said easily.

"I see. And you wished to speak to me because...?"

"I'm given to understand that you had a longstanding professional relationship with Monique de Brouet."

Garrity steepled his hands. His expression was as smooth as silk. "I don't speak about my professional relationships, Mr. Kent."

"In this instance, I'm sure you can make an exception. Seeing as how your client is dead."

"I make no exceptions. That is how one runs a successful enterprise."

"Another way to run a successful enterprise is to avoid being suspected of murder." Although Kent's voice was calm, his manner conveyed steely resolution.

"So the *accident* has now become murder." Garrity sounded more resigned than surprised. "How... unfortunate. And you think I am somehow involved?"

"I am here to gather facts, sir. I will make no conclusions without them."

Garrity drummed his fingers against the arm of his chair. "Very well, then. I will speak in hypotheticals, and you may draw whatever conclusion you wish. If Monique de Brouet was my client—and had been for a goodly number of years—why would I kill her? One does not slaughter a goose that lays golden eggs."

Richard spoke up quietly. "What if she didn't pay her debts?"

"Anyone who didn't pay their debts, my lord, would not be my client for very long." Garrity's smile was razor-sharp, his meaning even more lethal. "As for my long-term patrons, they are a select bunch. I consider them investments. Like prize crops, they yield bounty time and again, and thus I tend to them, ensure that they continue to produce." He paused. "Indeed, certain exceptional clients become my ambassadors of goodwill, so to speak, spreading word of my services to echelons that might otherwise lay out of my reach. In return, I reward them with a reduction of their loan or even a small commission for any business that they bring to me. A woman such as Madame Monique, with her access to Society, would have been, hypothetically speaking, a valuable asset. Killing her would be cutting off a valuable stream of income —something I assure you I would not do," he said coolly.

Garrity's explanation made sense. While Richard had no doubt the moneylender was as cold-blooded as they came, his instincts told him that Garrity was not a man to turn down a profit for, well, *any* reason. If what Garrity said was true, then not only did he have no motive to kill Monique, but it was in his best interests that the acrobat lived to spread the gospel of his services.

"Is that why you came to the party?" Kent said. "To keep an eye on Madame Monique—your, er, hypothetical investment?"

"My dear sir, at any given party—on any street in London, I daresay—I run into more than a few investments," Garrity drawled. "But the answer to your question is no. Although doing some business has been unavoidable during my stay, my primary objective here is not to gain new clients."

"Then why are you here?" Richard said.

"Pleasure, of course." A calculating gleam entered Garrity's eyes. "Even a man as busy as I am must occasionally make time for diversions."

"Thank you for your time, sir." Kent rose, and Richard followed suit. "I'll be in touch if I have further questions."

Garrity inclined his head. "Let me know if I can be of assistance. Whoever killed Monique de Brouet stole a valuable asset from me." His gaze met Richard's. "It is my policy to ensure that debts are paid."

The subtle threat stayed with Richard even as he returned to the main house with Kent.

"Well, there's another dead end," the investigator said. "This case is full of them. My gut tells me we're missing something... but what?"

Richard ruthlessly shoved aside his guilt. "Any luck in finding the missing yellow pillow?"

Kent shook his head. "The servants were told to keep an eye out, and no one's reported anything. It's possible the killer burned it or hid it somewhere outside the house." After a pause, he added with obvious frustration, "I can only hope my colleagues are having better luck in London."

They parted ways at the house, Kent going off to another meeting with the magistrate. Richard entered the dining room just as the luncheon was starting. Spotting Wick with the Turbetts, Richard headed over; he wanted to give his brother his moral support—and to put a rein on Wick's cronies, Parnell and

Goggs, who were seated at the same table. At half-past noon, the pair of troublemakers already looked well into their cups, and the last thing Richard wanted was for them to offend Wick's future father-in-law.

On the way over, he saw Violet at another table. Their gazes met; she smiled, and damn, if the sight of her sweet, curving lips didn't make his insides hum with lust.

Later, he promised himself.

Greeting everyone at Wick's table, he took the empty seat between Parnell and Turbett. He was halfway through his lobster soufflé, listening to Turbett boast about mercantile exploits, when Parnell said loudly, "Surely there must be a more scintillating topic than your piles of blunt, wot? Ruining my appetite, if you must know."

Bloody hell.

Turbett stiffened. "Your digestive state might be better helped by practicing some abstemiousness, my lord."

Lifting his wine goblet, Parnell took a deliberate gulp. "Better to be plump with grape than shriveled like a prune. Don't you agree, Goggs?"

"Absolutely, Parnell." Goggs slurped from his glass.

Richard set down his fork. "I'm certain there is another subject matter we could all find—"

"Do you smell something, Goggs?" Parnell stuck his long, noble nose in the air.

Goggs' round face creased with confusion. "Er, what, Parnell?"

"I think... yes, I do believe it is the smell of *shop*..."

Turbett threw down his napkin. "I'll not stay and be insulted by a pair of penniless ne'er-do-wells! Come, Amelia, we're going."

He dragged his daughter off.

"Well, thanks a lot," Wick said sarcastically to his friends.

"You *ought* to be thanking us." Parnell took another sip of wine. "We're saving you from a future of disgrace."

Wick spoke before Richard could cut in. "I won't *have* a bloody future if I don't get my vowels back."

You tell them, brother. Richard gave an approving nod.

Parnell rolled his eyes. "Don't be so dramatic, Murray. You don't see Goggs and I panicking, do you? Our debts are at least as big as yours."

"Then perhaps you ought to be heiress hunting as well," Wick retorted.

"Papa will take care of it." Parnell shrugged. "If not, I'll deal with my obligations in the time-tested tradition of gentlemen. We'll flee to the Continent, won't we, Goggs?"

Goggs' eyes darted nervously between his two cronies. "Er, whatever you say, Parnell."

Shaking his head, Wick left the table, and Richard joined him.

"You handled that well," Richard said.

His brother sighed. "Let's go find the Turbetts and smooth things over."

After that task was accomplished, Richard left Wick to search out Violet. Since the inclement weather had kept the guests inside, plentiful indoor entertainment was provided. There was a magic performance in the amphitheatre, some sort of experiment with an electrifying machine in the library, and a game of quoits in the atrium.

Richard found Violet chatting with the Blackwoods in the card room.

"Ah, Carlisle, now that you are here, we have enough for a game of whist," Lady Blackwood declared. "Do say you'll play."

He concurred, and he, Violet, and the Blackwoods located an unoccupied table in the corner. Lady Blackwood declared that it would be the ladies versus the gentlemen, and Violet volunteered to be the dealer.

As she deftly shuffled the cards, she murmured to him, "Any luck this morning?"

He gave a faint shake of his head. "What about you? What were you up to?"

"I was showing Polly and Rosie the crossbow." Her tawny eyes danced. "We practiced shooting at apples, and now both of them want crossbows, too."

"Crossbows?" Lady Blackwood said. "That sounds dangerous."

"It's a miniature one. Made for fun more than doing harm," Violet assured her. "Although it did pack enough of a wallop to knock an apple off the table."

"Wherever did you come by such a thing?"

"It was a present. Carlisle made it for me," Violet said proudly.

"Did he now?" Lady Blackwood gave him an amused look.

Blackwood, the bastard, chuckled. "How very, er, charming of you, Carlisle."

Heat crawled up Richard's jaw. "Are we playing whist or not?"

A grin tucked into Violet's cheeks. There was a merry glint in her eyes as she distributed the cards over the green baize. The game commenced.

After three rounds in which he and Blackwood were summarily slaughtered, Richard began to suspect foul play. He watched Violet shuffle the cards with practiced dexterity, and his gaze narrowed.

"Shall I deal this round?" he said abruptly.

"Oh, I don't mind being the dealer."

Her tones were casual. *Too* casual. He was starting to read the vixen's tells. Of course, being a gentleman, he couldn't accuse her of cheating outright, so he sat back and waited for her to deal.

Again, Violet expertly passed out the cards, each landing precisely before the player.

Richard lifted the edge of his first card. A two of clubs. Lowest of the suit.

To his left, Lady Blackwood made an odd, choking sound when she looked at her card.

"Is everything all right, my dear?" Blackwood's gaze was also narrowed.

"Oh, it's splendid." The marchioness' violet eyes shimmered. "Absolutely splendid."

Richard's second card was another two, of diamonds this time.

When he saw his third card—a two of hearts—he couldn't hold himself back. "Now wait just one minute, you little minx—"

Violet burst into laughter, Lady Blackwood along with her.

Across from him, Blackwood said dryly, "I do believe we've been fleeced, Carlisle."

Lady Blackwood dabbed her eyes with a handkerchief. "It took the two of you long enough to figure it out." She flipped over her cards, showing them the three aces Violet had given her.

"Bloody hell. How did you learn to deal like that? Wait... never mind." Richard shot her an exasperated look. "Your infamous brother Harry, I take?"

"He's a fount of useful information," Violet said cheerfully.

"I'll say. With such skills, the lad could finance his entire education at Cambridge," Blackwood said.

"Harry wouldn't cheat for money." Violet performed an impressive, and rather cheeky, one-handed shuffle. "For him, it's a scientific exercise. And, he says, a way to keep his senses sharp."

Richard raised his brows. "And for you?"

"I do it for *fun*," the little baggage said impudently.

"That is what I adore about you, Miss Kent," Lady Blackwood said, smiling. "You view the world through your own unique lens. One unclouded by mindless convention. It allows you to see opportunities that others miss."

Violet went very still; her lush lashes swept upward.

Frowning, Richard said, "Is something wrong?"

"I hope my words didn't offend, my dear," Lady Blackwood said hastily. "I meant them as the highest compliment."

"Oh no, I'm not offended. You just made me think of something... that's all."

Vi smiled and returned to dealing the cards. Properly this time.

But Richard saw the excited tremble of her hands and wondered what it meant.

After the game, he cornered her by the sideboard, where a cold collation had been laid out. She was busily filling her plate with some of everything. Lord help him, but he even found her appetite adorable.

"What's going on?" he said without preamble.

"I'll tell you—but only if you give me your word to keep it a secret."

Devil and damn. He had a bad feeling about this. "All right."

"Well, this question has been running round and round in my head: what was Monique doing in the library that night?"

"Your guess is as good as mine."

"Mine might be better, actually. You see, ever since I was a girl, I've been trying to emulate Madame Monique. She's been my idol for *ages*, and I've trained myself to act like her, think like her. And it occurred to me that to solve the mystery of her death, we need to retrace her steps and see the world through *her* lens—and I think I'm the one to do it."

"To do what, exactly?"

"I'm going to take a look at Monique's bedchamber tonight."

"The hell you are." Seeing her stiffen, he added swiftly, "Your brother already searched it. He told you to stay out of there."

"And I always do what people tell me to." She rolled her eyes. "My intuition is *telling* me that there are clues in her room, Richard—clues that I'll pick up because I can think like Monique. Even Jeanne, her maid, remarked upon it."

There was no mistaking the stubborn glint in her eyes. In the past, he might have tried to stop her... but he was learning that locking horns with her was futile. It wouldn't win him any points in the courtship arena—*and* she'd go ahead and do what she intended anyway. Only a Bedlamite would attempt the same strategy and expect different results.

Besides, he'd promised her that they would work together. He would just have to find a way to protect her from her own reckless, pell-mell ways. Because if anything happened to her... he felt an acute and foreign spasm in his chest. He would not allow such a possibility. He'd guard his future viscountess, whatever it took.

"Just what are you planning to do?" he said, his voice low.

"After everyone's asleep, I'm going in to see if I can find clues that others may have missed." Her chin lifted, a sure sign of defiance. "And you're not going to stop me."

In a second, he made his decision.

"Quite right," he said. "I'm going with you."

He snagged a piece of ham from her plate and ate it, enjoying her dumbfounded look.

28

R ichard knew he'd made the right decision when, even in the dimly lit hallway, he could see Violet's brilliant smile. It was after two in the morning, and she was waiting for him outside Monique's bedchamber, still dressed in her pink evening gown. The light from her lamp licked the tempting mounds framed by her neckline, highlighting the shadowed crevice between.

"I wasn't sure you would show," she said in a whisper.

"And let you have all the fun? I think not."

"I take back everything I ever said about you being stodgy." Lips curved, she handed him the lamp and reached up to pluck a pair of hairpins from her coiffure. "The door is locked, but I think I can open it with this."

"Seeing as you're a disciple of your brother Harry, I don't doubt your skill. But this might be easier." He removed the master key from his pocket.

"By Golly, where did you get that?"

"I may have borrowed it when I wandered into the butler's pantry by accident." If he was to engage in an adventure, he liked to go prepared.

"You filched it?" She took the key from him as reverently as another miss might accept a jeweler's box. "Jolly well done!"

He stifled a grin at her compliment.

Taking a swift look around the empty hallway, she slid the key in, turning the lock. They went inside and closed the door behind them. Richard didn't think of himself as a fanciful sort, but an eerie stillness shrouded the room. The moonlight seeping in from a gap in the drapery was cold and sterile, adding to the tomb-like ambience.

Violet shivered.

Placing an arm around her shoulders, he said quietly, "Are you certain you want to do this?"

"We're out of leads. I must." In the moonlight, her profile was resolute. "I'll start with the bed and work clockwise. Why don't you go in the opposite direction?"

It was a sound plan, and they set off.

Several minutes passed in which they didn't speak, absorbed in their respective tasks. He heard Violet mutter the occasional *gadzooks* and *crumpets* to herself, which added a certain lightheartedness to an otherwise grim undertaking. As he examined the assorted trifles in a desk drawer, he had a flash of recognition: life with Violet would always be this way, infused with buoyancy and humor no matter what burdens they faced.

And, by Jove, he wanted that future.

"Carlisle, I think I found something!"

Her excited whisper brought him over to where she stood before a bow-fronted wardrobe. The curved doors were open, its innards of silk and lace spilling out. She was on tiptoe, craning her neck this way and that.

She pointed to the high shelf, which was crammed with millinery. "I think I see something there, behind that bonnet, at the very back. But I can't reach it."

Richard removed the impeding headwear. Reaching in, his

hands closed around a heavy rectangular object. He pulled it down.

It was a mahogany box, the lid inlaid with mother-of-pearl.

"It's too big to be a jewelry chest," Violet said eagerly. "I wonder what's inside?"

The bed was closest, so he placed the chest on its surface.

"You do the honors," he told her.

Her features vivid with expectation, she lifted the lid of the box, letting it fall back on its hinges. Nestled in the top tray was a green Chinoiserie silk pouch and what appeared to be a delicate gold chain. She picked up the latter, and sudden heat prickled beneath Richard's collar.

Brow pleating, Violet held up the chain between thumb and index finger. There was a small, bejeweled clamp on each end, and they swung like twin pendulums.

"This is the strangest necklace I've ever seen," she said.

He didn't think it was a necklace. "Er, why don't you put that back..."

She was too busy fiddling with the clamps to listen to him. "Maybe it's broken? This is the *oddest* clasp. The ends don't fit together at all."

"Uh, Violet..."

She tossed the chain onto the bedspread and pulled out the Chinoiserie pouch. "This is heavy. I wonder what's inside."

Before he could stop her, she emptied the contents into her palm.

"Now what do you think these are?" She held up the two golden balls, which rolled together sensuously in her palm.

He swallowed. Twice.

"Oh, *I* know." Her eyes widened.

"You, er, do?"

"It must be for a performance. Juggling or some such thing. Although they'd be dashed difficult to manage given how small they are." She wriggled them around in her hand. "And they have the strangest weight to them..."

"You might want to stop handling those."

"Why? Maybe I could learn to use them as Monique did."

Christ. Try as he might, he couldn't block the image from forming in his mind. He went rock-hard.

"Oh, look. There's another tray beneath this one." Idly jiggling the pleasure balls in one hand, Violet stuck the other in the box. "More circus equipment, perhaps? This one feels oddly shaped..."

She yanked out a jade dildo.

Richard's every nerve caught fire. Lust paralyzed him as he saw her gaze travel over the large carved phallus clasped within her slim fingers, from its bulbous tip down its vein-girdled shaft, all the way to the smooth bulging balls. Recognition dawned across her expressive features—which he might have found comical had he any blood left in his brain. Every last ounce of it had plummeted to his groin, his erection throbbing with agonizing intensity.

Violet let out a gasp, instinctively flinging the dildo away from her. It bounced onto the bed. Unfortunately, she'd forgotten the balls in her other hand and lost her grip on them. They dropped to the floor, hitting the boards with dangerously loud thuds and rolling beneath the bed.

"Gadzooks, I—I have to get those!" Her eyes were panicked.

She dove after them, sweeping her arm beneath the bed, and he had to close his eyes against the unholy temptation of her delicate ankles, her shapely stockinged legs, her pert and wriggling bottom.

"Crumpets, I can't reach them..." She crawled halfway beneath the bed, her skirts bunching up, revealing a flash of her garter, the bare skin just above.

He was concentrating on not unmanning himself when she gave a hushed exclamation.

"Carlisle... I think I found something else!"

Perhaps this was God's way of testing his self-control. "What is it?"

"I accidentally pressed down on one of the floorboards, and it came loose. There's a piece of paper hidden beneath..."

She backed out from under the bed, clutching a folded piece of paper. He helped her to her feet, and they went over to the table with the lamp, spreading the paper on its surface. Together, they peered at the drawing.

He stared at the detailed architectural rendering. "It's a map of the house."

"What was Monique doing with this?" Violet said.

He oriented himself to the various rooms on the map. "Look, that's the library. And something's circled there in red ink."

Violet leaned closer. "I think that's the hearth. What are those two smudged red shapes in the margin next to it? They look like little clouds or something..."

"I don't know. But look here." He traced a blunt fingertip along the red line that started from the hearth and ended...

"That can't be right." A notch formed between her brows. "That line passes through the wall between the library and study, and I don't recall there being a door between the two rooms."

Understanding sliced through him. "There isn't. But I think this map is telling us that there might be another way in."

"You mean... a hidden passageway?" Her eyes were huge. "Oh, Richard, what do you think Monique was doing with this map? What was she planning?"

"There's only one way to find out," he said grimly.

29

A feeling of déjà vu pervaded Violet as she entered the dimly lit library, Richard ahead of her. As he strode off to make sure the room was unoccupied, her gaze was drawn to the bookshelves where they'd found Monique, and her stomach quivered. While she wanted desperately to find the true killer, her anticipation was tempered with disquiet: in retracing Monique's footsteps, what were they going to discover?

Her grip tightened on the map she'd found beneath the acrobat's bed.

Richard returned. "We're alone for now. Let's get started."

They went over to the ancient fireplace. Vi's gaze travelled over the protruding ledge, and she shivered, even though the blood had been scrubbed from the stone. The majestic header swirled with flora and fauna, the plinths supporting the ledge ornately carved with blossoming roses.

Richard was already running his hands over the mantelpiece. "Look for any hidden openings in the nearby walls," he said.

Setting down the map, Vi examined the dark paneled walls to the right and left of the fireplace. She smoothed her palms over the wood moldings and detected no secret entrance. Evidently,

Richard had the same lack of results for he picked up the map again.

"We're missing something," he muttered.

She went to look at the plan with him. Something about the smudged red shapes in the margin continued to niggle at her. Pointing, she said, "What *are* those?"

"They might just be inkblots."

"I don't think so." Squinting, she said, "The ink is smudged, but I see a rounded edge here and another there. It's a drawing. Of a cloud or a..."

"*Flower.*" They said it at the same time, their gazes colliding.

"The roses on the plinth," she breathed.

He went to the plinth on the right side, she to the left. With care, she examined the stone roses: there were three, one facing forward, the other to the sides. She ran her fingers over the cold petals. Nothing special about the center rose... nor the one facing left. As she scrutinized the one facing inward toward the hearth, she noticed a thin fissure, nearly invisible, around one of the petals.

The wear of time... or something else?

"I've nothing on my side." Richard's voice came from behind her. "You?"

She pushed on the petal, tried to jiggle it; it didn't budge. "It's probably nothing, but there's a crack here..."

"Let me have a look."

She moved aside to give him space.

"I see what you mean." He pushed on the petal, and nothing happened. Crouching, he looked at the underside of the flower. "Interesting. There's another crack here, too, around a different petal..."

He studied the flower, then he pushed down on the two petals simultaneously.

Violet's breath held as the stone sections depressed at his

touch. A faint click... and the large panel to the left of the fire-place swung open.

She rushed over. "By Golly, you found it! A hidden corridor."

He raised the lamp. Its flickering illumination revealed a narrow tunnel. "It looks like the corridor goes behind the walls, toward the study."

"Let's find out—" She froze at the sound of laughter outside.

"Christ. Get in the tunnel. Now."

"Wait. The map." She dashed back to snatch the paper, which they'd left by the hearth. She ran back toward the tunnel, Richard pushing her inside and following her, closing the panel shut behind them... and just in time.

She heard the door open to the library, the voices growing louder. The female tones she recognized as Mrs. Sumner's. The male voice... she couldn't be sure, but the cultured accents did not belong to Tobias Price. Apparently, the widow liked variety in her company. A flush heated Violet's skin as conversation turned predictably into another sort of activity.

Richard whispered in her ear, "They're going to be at it for a while. We might as well see if the tunnel is true to the map and takes us to the study."

Collecting herself, Vi nodded. She led the way forward. She was keenly aware of Richard's presence behind her, solid and reassuring.

Turning to him, she said in hushed tones, "How far do you think this passageway goes?"

"I have no idea." He ducked his head to avoid hitting the ceiling, which had dropped even lower. "By Jove," he muttered, "they could have made this a might roomier."

"Obviously whoever built this had little priests in mind. They weren't planning for a man of your size."

"You have a problem with my size, Miss Kent?"

At the gleam in his eyes, warmth stirred in her belly, her awareness of him humming through her veins. The musty air suddenly turned quite humid. She faced forward so he wouldn't see her looking flustered. "Don't go fishing for compliments. We have more important *oof*—"

Her slipper caught on something that clanked, and she pitched forward, the ground coming up at her with terrifying speed. Richard caught her, yanking her back. He held her against his rock-hard physique.

"Have a care, lass," he murmured against her ear.

Her breath rushed in and out of her lungs. "I—I tripped on something."

He raised the lamp, illuminating a dark bag that lay on the ground a few feet away. She retrieved it, her fingers closing around supple leather wrapped around some hard objects. Her mind flew back to the contents of the box she'd found in Monique's room. Although she didn't fully understand the function of those objects—why would anyone want a statue of a man's thingamabob?—she had an inkling that their purpose was salacious.

She thrust the pouch at Richard. "You open it," she blurted.

His mouth twitched. Wordlessly, he exchanged the lamp for the bag and released the drawstring, drawing out the contents. She stared at the thin metal rods he held, each with a uniquely shaped head.

"Lock picks," he said tersely.

His assessment confirmed her own. "Where do you think they came from?"

"My guess is that Monique left them here." His voice was grim. "She got what she wanted and ditched her incriminating tools."

"What was it that she wanted?" Vi said.

He gestured ahead; she saw that they'd reached the end of the corridor, and there was a panel similar to the one they'd entered through in the library.

"We're at the study, so my guess is that she was after some-

thing in there. Something that you would use these,"—his hand
closed on the lock picks—"to access."

Understanding hit her. "You think there's an iron box in the
study?"

"That we'll have to find out from Billings—"

A door suddenly slammed, the walls of the corridor vibrating.
Men's muffled voices came from the other side of the panel.
Violet's heart drummed in her ears.

Richard held her fast, murmuring, "Steady, love."

She couldn't hear what the men were saying, but the cadence
seemed adversarial. She identified the agitated voice as belonging
to Billings; she couldn't make out the owner of the other.

Pocketing the lock picks, Richard took her hand, silently
leading her back toward the library. They hadn't made it all the
way back before she heard moans and grunts that indicated that
the room was still occupied.

"Trapped at both ends." Richard's breath tickled her ear.
"We'll have to wait it out."

She nodded, a shiver of awareness going through her.

He set the lamp down and took her into his arms. Tucking her
cheek against his chest, he stroked her back. "No need to be
afraid, sweetheart. We'll be out of here soon."

Clearly, he misunderstood her reaction. She didn't know if it
was his nearness or their extraordinary adventures this night, but
it wasn't fear she was feeling—it was arousal of a different nature.
And while he no doubt meant his touch to be soothing, it instead
fed the need simmering inside her.

To distract herself, she whispered the first thing that came to
mind. "So those items we found in Monique's box... what were
they for?"

His hand stilled mid-stroke. "I'm not certain that is something
we ought to discuss."

If anything piqued her curiosity, it was something that
shouldn't be talked about.

She tipped her head back. "Why would Monique have a statue of a man's you-know-what?"

"His you-know-what?" Laughter glinted in Richard's eyes.

"You know, his... thingamabob."

He began to shake silently against her.

"What's so funny? You know perfectly well what I'm referring to..."

His wide shoulders were quaking in earnest, to the degree that she worried that he might give them away. So she covered his mouth with her hand. Gasped when he nipped her fingers lightly.

In the next instant, he had her back against the wall, towering over her. It was a tight fit in the tunnel. He filled her vision and senses completely, crowding out everything else.

"Discussion of you-know-whats and thingamabobs aren't going to get us very far. If you want to know what those items are for, then we'll have to improve your vocabulary. Are you up for it, love?"

Mesmerized by his low, husky tone, she nodded.

"Let's start with the gold chain. The one with the jeweled clamps."

Her pulse took off in a sprint when he ran a fingertip along the edge of her low-cut bodice. His finger dipped beneath the pink silk, rubbing against the tip of her right breast. She had to bite back a moan as he stimulated the stiff, throbbing peak.

"One of the clamps would fit here on your lovely nipple, just so"—he pinched the tip lightly, and her eyes widened in surprise —"while the other would attach to its equally lovely twin." He trapped her other nipple between thumb and forefinger, tweaking the pulsing peak. The pleasure, with its slight tingle of pain, melted her center.

"Wouldn't that... hurt?" she said, her cheeks warming.

"Aye, a little. But doesn't it also feel good?"

She couldn't deny that. Could barely breathe for the excitement.

"Imagine a little tug on the chain in between," he murmured, causing her nipples to throb even more forcefully. "Would you enjoy that, lass?"

"I don't know. That's awfully wicked," she managed.

"Aye. But not as wicked as the balls you were playing with."

She wetted her lips. "Wh-what are those for?"

Instead of answering, he took her mouth in a hot, fiercely possessive kiss. Her fingers crushed his cravat as she pulled him closer. She couldn't get enough of his taste, the aggressive thrust of his tongue into her moist cove. When he suddenly withdrew, she moaned in protest.

Panting, pressed against the wall, she stared up into his bluntly masculine features, those heated-iron eyes, and knew the truth: any man she met in the future would be compared to Richard... and found lacking. Because he was all that she'd ever wanted.

And she'd fallen head over slippers in love with him.

"Sweeting," he said, his voice gravelly, "don't you wish to know about the balls?"

Balls? she thought hazily. *What balls?*

In a quick movement, he tossed up her skirts and petticoats, pinning them to her waist with one hand. Her lungs constricted as humid air wafted against her stockinged legs, her bare thighs, kissing her dampened flesh. With his free hand, he took one of hers and brought it there, to that aching apex. She bit her lip, her cheeks burning as he pressed their joined fingers against her sex.

It was so terribly wicked—and so *good*.

"Feel how wet your pussy is," he crooned softly against her ear. "How slick and swollen it has gotten for me. Do you like being petted this way?"

Closing her eyes, she let go of shame, drifting freely into the whirlpool of sensation.

"Yes. Oh yes," she sighed.

The blunt tip of his finger circled her entrance, dipping just inside and no further, teasing her mercilessly. "Now the balls—they'd slip in right here, and you'd feel them inside your cunny, stimulating and arousing you with every move you make."

Thunderbolts. Her eyes popped open. "That's *beyond* wicked."

"Aye." His nostrils flared, and when she tried to withdraw her hand, he trapped it beneath his. Brought their joined fingers to the aching peak of her pussy. "Rub your pearl just like that, lass. Don't stop frigging yourself while I show you the most wicked part."

Most wicked?

Her head was already spinning, her mind inflamed by his naughty words, by how she was shamelessly touching herself at his instruction. The familiar tension was building inside her.

"Don't stop," he murmured and eased his hand away.

Aroused, she obeyed and watched as he undid the fall of his trousers and freed his manhood. The sight of that huge shaft, so thick and long, made her breath hitch. It stood boldly erect, the wide head nudging past the bottom button of his waistcoat. At its base, his bollocks hung like a heavy, ripe plum nestled against a masculine nest of hair.

She couldn't tear her gaze away as he ran his fist slowly from the root of the shaft to the tip and back again. She remembered the potent quiver of his burgeoned flesh within her grasp, the bold, wild taste of him upon her tongue, and another rush of dew slickened her circling fingers.

"Now you'll recall that last item you pulled from the box?"

She couldn't reply, her eyes glued to his jerking movements, the way he wrung a bead of moisture from the engorged dome of his member.

"It's a cock—fashioned from jade. A dildo, it's called." His sensual words heated her ear and her insides. "And a woman uses it for pleasure."

She felt lightheaded—as if she were nothing but a mass of

sensations, all of them raw, real, and exhilarating. Tingles melded together, a swirling, humid vortex beneath her fingers.

"Not that you'll ever have need of a dildo. You'll have the real thing, lass. Imagine my cock inside you. Moving in and out, filling your sweet pussy," he whispered. "How would that feel?"

Her fingers moved on her pearl, quicker and quicker. The answer puffed breathlessly from her lips. "Good. So *good.*"

"Aye, lass." His fist moved like a piston on his cock. His biceps bulged sleekly beneath the arm of his jacket; he touched himself with a ferocity that she would not have dared, and seeing the savage motion, carried out by this proper lord, caused more moisture to trickle between her legs.

"I've touched inside your cunny with my fingers, my tongue. I know how sweet you are, how wet and tight," he rasped. "I can hardly wait to put my cock inside you, lass. To feel you squeezing and milking me harder than a fist."

Her knees wobbled as the vortex whirled faster, her control slipping.

"When you're mine, I'll have you day and night," he growled in her ear. "I'll want to be inside you at every moment, filling you up, loving you—"

It was too much. Her vision wavered as she tumbled over the edge.

He caught her against the wall, his mouth covering hers, swallowing her gasps. At the same time, she felt a scorching wet lash against her thigh. It was followed by another and another, his groans vibrating down her throat, his big body shuddering against her.

Bliss suffused her as they held onto each other, their breaths mingling, hearts pounding as one.

He lifted his head. Despite her lethargic state, the heat in his eyes caused a flutter in her belly.

"Don't keep me waiting any longer," he demanded huskily. "Say you'll marry me, Violet."

She gave the answer in her heart. What else could she do? "I'll marry you, Richard."

Triumph blazed in his eyes. Then he leaned in, murmuring in her ear.

At his question, she had to tamp down a giggle.

"I don't think that any more. In fact," she whispered back, "I'd say you've laid the title of Viscount Killjoy permanently to rest."

☙ 30 ❧

E arly next morning, Richard accompanied Violet to see her brother. Not wanting to add to their sins, they confessed what they'd discovered last night, telling Kent about the map and hidden passageway. Kent didn't appear best pleased by the news that the pair of them had been skulking around unchaperoned in the dead of night; luckily, Mrs. Kent was there to intervene.

"The horses have bolted, darling," she murmured to her husband. "No use slamming the barn door now."

This gave Richard the opportunity to officially ask for Violet's hand. He still couldn't believe that she'd said yes to him, that she was going to be his. And he had their burning passion to thank for it. He was no Casanova by any stretch of the imagination; that inspired bit of naughtiness in the passageway had surprised even him. Yet Violet had that effect on him, unleashing an inner wildness that felt strangely... liberating.

And she was going to be his viscountess. *His.* His insides billowed with warmth as he looked at her beautiful, blushing face. He felt as impatient as a Thoroughbred at the gates—and equally restless. For he couldn't deny that the pleasure of her acceptance was accompanied by a strange apprehension.

What he wanted was within his grasp... but she wasn't his yet. Nothing was set in stone. Promises made could be broken; it wasn't the first time a lady had accepted his offer.

Violet said yes, he told himself. *Leave it at that.*

After a brief discussion with the Kents, they all agreed to keep the engagement under wraps until after the party. There were too many distractions at the moment, the most pressing of which included speaking to their host.

Thus, with the Strathavens in tow, they hunted Billings down in his study.

"We believe we know why Monique was in the library," Kent said without preamble. "And why she was killed."

"Well don't just stand there. Spit it out," the banker said.

"First, I have a question. Do you keep valuables in this chamber?"

From the way Billings' eyes shifted, the answer was clear. "Why?" he said.

"Because we believe Monique might have stolen something from this room."

The banker's lips formed a hyphen. "Impossible. I have a footman guarding the entrance to this room day and night."

"One of the entrances," Kent corrected.

"What do you mean? There is only one door."

"That you know of." Richard spoke up. "Last night, we discovered a hidden passageway between the library and this study. I believe the entrance is behind that panel by the hearth."

"You can't be serious," Billings said incredulously.

Going over to the hearth, which was nearly identical to the one in the library, Richard searched the roses on the plinth. He pushed two of the petals down. There was a clicking noise... and then the panel separated from the wall, revealing the gaping darkness behind.

"Heavens, how exciting," the duchess breathed.

"That's one way to describe it, pet," Strathaven said wryly.

Billings turned paler than a banknote. Without another word, he headed back toward his desk and past it, to the painting of the dead game on the wall. He reached for some hidden mechanism in the frame. The painting swung open, revealing an iron box concealed in the wall.

Removing a key from his pocket, Billings inserted it into the lock.

When the compartment opened, Richard saw a collection of velvet boxes within. With methodical precision, Billings removed each one, piling them upon his desk. He opened the lids: there was a dazzling array of jewelry—necklaces, bracelets, even a diadem. In the morning light, gems glittered in a rainbow of colors, precious metals gleaming.

The banker patted his brow with a folded handkerchief. "Everything's here and accounted for. I purchased these for Gabriella at an auction, outbidding several members of the aristocracy." Satisfaction threaded his voice. "It was mentioned in *The Times*, I believe."

"Yes, I recall the hubbub," Mrs. Kent said. "A stunning array, I must say."

She examined the jewels, Billings hovering beside her as if he expected her to make away with the lot. A muscle ticked in Kent's jaw.

"Well, if everything's here, then perhaps Monique didn't manage to take anything?" Her Grace suggested. "Maybe her lock picking skills weren't up to par."

"I don't think that's the case." Mrs. Kent was perusing a sapphire necklace intently—the one, Richard recalled, that Miss Billings had worn at supper that first night. "Something's amiss here."

"I beg your pardon?" Billings said.

"May I?" Mrs. Kent arched her fair brows.

The banker gave a nod, and she lifted the necklace from its box. Everyone crowded in to have a closer look. The large, faceted blue stones flashed, their depths clear. The web of diamonds that connected them was similarly bright. Richard was no connoisseur of jewels, but, to him, the necklace appeared flawless.

The duchess canted her head. "What's wrong with the necklace? The sapphires have a nice, clear sparkle, don't they?"

"Aye, pet, and that's the problem," the duke replied. To Mrs. Kent, he said, "May I?"

She passed him the necklace, and he turned it this way and that, inspecting it. "No inclusions to the naked eye. The depths are far too clear. The color is straightforward, bland, with little richness."

"So you're saying... it's a fake?" his wife said.

"Yes. Though an excellent copy," he replied. "That is your opinion as well, Mrs. Kent?"

"Indeed," the blonde said. "Quite convincing to the casual observer."

"Thank heavens you're the one who buys my jewelry, Strathaven," the duchess exclaimed. "How I should hate to be taken by cut glass, no matter how prettily made."

His Grace's lips twitched. He chucked his wife under the chin. "I know how you like a bargain, sweeting."

"Now wait just a minute." Billings' voice shook with outrage. "I had these pieces authenticated by a top jeweler. He assured me these pieces, including the necklace, were the genuine articles."

"They are. As was the necklace I saw your daughter wearing at supper that first night," Mrs. Kent replied. "But the necklace before us now is a copy made of glass."

The explanation was clear.

"Monique made a switch, by God." Kent's irises blazed. "This was all part of a premeditated plan. She comes to the party with a map of the house, a replica of the necklace, and means to break into the safe box."

"But something unexpected happens," Mrs. Kent murmured.

"After stealing the necklace, Monique returns to the library, only to encounter the murderer. Is he or she an accomplice in the theft —or is this a meeting of chance?"

"We don't know," her husband replied, "but let's say he or she pushes Monique into the mantel. She hits her head but does not die. So the villain has to finish the job, smothering her with a pillow and dragging her body into the shelves. He or she takes the necklace and leaves."

Frowning, Richard said, "That sounds logical, but what I don't understand is why Monique stole only the necklace. Why didn't she take all the jewelry?"

"Perhaps she was being cautious," Mrs. Kent said. "Replacing one piece with a forgery is one thing; taking the entire collection increases the risk of getting caught exponentially. And let's not overlook the fact that the necklace is the most expensive piece by far."

"How much is it worth?" Violet asked.

"By my estimation, at least nine thousand pounds," the blonde replied.

"Over ten thousand," Billings said in a brittle voice, "according to the appraiser."

Violet let out a low whistle. "By Golly, that *is* a haul, isn't it? But why would Monique risk everything to steal this necklace?"

"From the little Garrity was willing to disclose, she was making her payments to him in a timely fashion," Richard said. "He implied that she was a prime customer, one in good standing. But who knows what other debts she might have had."

"Jeanne, her maid, might know," the duchess suggested. "Now that we have evidence of Monique's plot, we ought to question Jeanne again."

"My thinking precisely." Kent summoned in a footman and gave orders to fetch the maid.

When the door closed again, Billings said cuttingly, "I don't give a damn *why* that French bitch stole from me, I want to know where the bloody necklace is now!"

"I advise patience, sir. The two questions are interrelated; finding the answer to the former may lead us to the latter."

Billings turned red in the face. "In the meantime, I am out *ten thousand pounds.* That is entirely unacceptable, do you hear me?"

"I believe the entire party can hear you," Strathaven drawled. "You were interested in discretion, were you not, Billings?"

It took visible effort for the banker to rein himself in. Clearly, money was the one topic that could rile his emotions.

"Yes, we must be discreet in the search for the thief. Men from the stews,"—Billings straightened his lapels—"they take offense at the slightest provocation."

"If you think cutthroats are touchy, try accusing a dowager of theft," Mrs. Kent said.

"You must not offend anyone," Billings said with finality. "You must find the necklace while maintaining an appearance of decorum."

"Assuming the jewelry is still here," Violet pointed out.

"My gut says that it is." Kent drummed his fingers against the desk. "Working on the assumption that whoever came upon Monique saw a crime of opportunity, he or she was not prepared to take possession of a priceless piece of jewelry. No one has left the estate since we discovered Monique's murder, and the necklace is too valuable to simply send off somewhere—the killer wouldn't risk letting it out of his or her hands. So that leaves the possibility that the necklace is hidden somewhere in the house... or on the estate."

Richard considered the vastness of Traverstoke. "Performing a search will be no small task."

"Indeed," Kent said. "We'll have to start with the most obvious place—the guest chambers—and fan out from there."

"And how do you plan to do this without the guests knowing? Because they must not suspect a thing," Billings insisted.

"We need a diversion," Strathaven said.

"Something that will get everyone off the estate." The duchess tapped a finger against her chin. "A trip to the village, perhaps? An organized activity to draw everyone out."

"How about a fair?" Billings said.

"That would work splendidly," Her Grace said.

The banker gave a curt nod. "Leave that to me. I'll set it up for tomorrow."

"You can set up a fair in one day?" Violet said.

"Money can move mountains, Miss Kent," Billings said crisply. "What's a country fair?"

"A fair's not a bad idea," Strathaven acknowledged, "but we will need someone to accompany the guests and keep an eye on them. The last thing we want is for the culprit to get wind of things and slip away."

"I'll speak to Jones. He can set up a perimeter around the village—yes, *discreetly*." Kent forestalled their host's predictable refrain. "Having a few constables present at the fair, on the pretense of securing goods and preventing pickpockets, will seem like nothing out of the ordinary."

"Then I'd best go make arrangements," the banker said.

When the door closed behind him, Kent raked a hand through his hair. "Bloody hell, I wish I could just search the place and the people and be done with it, discretion be damned."

"Much as I hate to defend Billings, he might have a point. Best to act with stealth when it comes to cutthroats," the duke drawled.

"Aye. Although it will be no small feat to do a thorough search of this place," Kent muttered.

"Could the magistrate lend you some men, darling?" his wife asked.

"Whoever he can spare. Don't forget, he needs to surveil the village."

"The Blackwoods could help," Richard said.

"I'll speak to them. God knows I'll need all the help I can get." Lines deepened around Kent's mouth. "Moreover, we can't all stay here tomorrow; that would rouse suspicion. We'll need to split up, send a few of our team to the village to keep an eye on things." He gave a sigh. "Not to mention on Polly and Primrose."

"I'll go," Violet volunteered. "They'll be plenty of chaperones present, so the rest of you could stay here and help in the search."

"I'll go with you," Richard offered.

Kent narrowed his eyes. The investigator might be weighed down with numerous duties, but evidently he wasn't about to relinquish those of a protective older brother. "I don't think it's a good idea for the two of you to go together," he said stiffly.

"Come, darling, they're practically engaged," his wife murmured. "And there'll be so many others present. I'll ask Lady Ainsworthy to chaperone; she's a stickler for proprieties."

After a moment, Kent relented. "All right. But no more escapades, Violet, do you understand? You must stay with the group and Lady Ainsworthy."

"Of course." Violet's expression was as innocent as an angel's.

The gazes directed toward the ceiling conveyed that she fooled no one.

A knock sounded.

"Must be the maid. Time to get her to disclose her mistress' true motives." In a louder voice, Kent called, "Come in."

The door opened to reveal a young footman. He was alone.

"Where is the maid?" Kent demanded.

"That's just it, sir. I couldn't find her." The footman lifted his liveried shoulders, his expression perplexed. "She wasn't in her room, and all her things are gone."

O nce again, the team split up, this time to investigate Jeanne's disappearance. Ambrose and the men went to talk to the guards at the gates, and Violet accompanied Emma and Marianne to the servants' wing to talk to the staff. Mrs. Hopkins, the housekeeper, had had a tray sent up to Jeanne yesterday morning; the maid who'd delivered it reported that Jeanne had told her to leave it outside the door. That was the last time anyone had heard from the Frenchwoman.

A search of the garret room yielded no clues as to where Jeanne might have gone. She'd taken all her sparse belongings. Save for the empty tray, she might have never been there at all.

Looking around the deserted room, Em gnawed on her lip. "Where did Jeanne go? More importantly, *why* would she leave so precipitously—unless she had something to hide?"

"Surely you don't think *Jeanne* was the one who killed Monique and took the necklace?" To Vi, the notion didn't seem right. "When I spoke to Jeanne, she seemed devoted to Monique, truly distressed over her mistress' death. She's dedicated her life to Monique's family."

"When money is involved, anything is possible," Marianne said quietly. "And we are talking about ten thousand pounds."

"I cannot believe Jeanne would do such a thing," Vi insisted.

"All right, let's focus on where she went for now," Em said. "What would be the best way to leave the house undetected?"

Vi thought about what she'd do. "Climb out through the window?"

"Let me rephrase that: if you were a *typical* person who didn't relish death-defying feats, how would you get of here?" Em amended dryly. "And Jeanne is no spring chicken, mind you."

"I'd take the path of least resistance and leave through the closest door," Marianne said. "If someone asked where I was going, I'd simply make up an excuse."

"Good point. The closest door is this way." Emma's ivory skirts swished as she led the way back down the flights of stairs. Footmen and maids carrying a medley of objects dodged out of their path as they navigated through the narrow hallways into the kitchen, where Emma steered them out a side door.

Stepping outside, Vi saw that they were at the back of the servants' wing, out of view of the main house. Here, workers from the village were busily unloading wagons of supplies onto the graveled drive as their sturdy horses waited, ears and tails flicking. Vi's stomach gave a rumble when one workman yanked the cover off a dairy cart, revealing neat stacks of cloth-wrapped cheese and buckets of fresh milk.

"Are you thinking what I'm thinking?" Em said.

"That we could use some refreshment?" Because Vi was all for a snack.

Amusement glinted in Marianne's emerald eyes. "I think Emma is referring to the fact that we're looking at an easy escape route from the estate."

Her meaning struck Violet. "You mean Jeanne hid in one of the carts?"

"It's a distinct possibility," her sister-in-law replied. "The constables at the gate aren't looking for stowaways. They're just keeping track of the guests."

"Let's go ask the cook what deliveries came around yesterday afternoon," Vi suggested.

"Good thinking," Em said.

Vi thought so—seeing as she was hoping to grow two plants with one seed.

Her hopes came to fruition when the kindly cook not only had information to give, but also provided her with a dish of bread and butter pudding studded with currants. Sitting on a stool at the work table, Vi dug into the treat with gusto as the cook reviewed yesterday's schedule.

"Now let me see," she said, wiping her hands on her apron, "most o' the deliveries came before noon. But the butcher was a bit late, maybe an hour or two after that—had a broken axle on the way, he said. And the greengrocer arrived soon after that, with some fine asparagus and leeks."

"Could you give me their addresses, please?" After recording the information, Em said, "Thank you, Cook. This will aid my brother in the search for the missing woman."

Hopping off the stool, Vi added, "And thank you for the most delicious bread pudding I've ever had."

The cook beamed.

After supper, Richard went to the music room in search of Violet. He spotted her right away, a vibrant bloom in lavender, sitting with Wick and his cronies. Guests as well as professionals were on the program this eve, and at present, Violet's sister, the Marchioness of Tremont, was spellbinding the audience with her rendition of a sonata by Master Beethoven.

Despite her delicate looks, the marchioness had full command of the pianoforte. She wrung power, passion, and tenderness from the keys. Standing at the side of the room, Tremont looked on with unmistakable pride.

When the performance came to an end, the audience erupted into applause. While the marchioness took her well-deserved bow, Richard headed toward Violet.

Making a leg, he indicated the empty seat next to her. "Is this seat taken?"

"Now it is. I saved it for you."

The warmth in her whiskey eyes gave rise to a sweet ache in his chest. It was strange that a thing as small as that gesture—her reserving a place for him—could affect him thus, but it did. He'd never had someone who looked out for him before. Someone to share madcap adventures with and passion beyond anything he'd imagined possible. A true partner.

"Good evening, Carlisle," his brother said from Violet's other side.

Wick appeared his usual dapper self, yet Richard saw the lines of tension around the other's eyes. He wished he could ease Wick's burdens. "How are you?"

"As well as I can be, given the situation," Wick said quietly.

"Don't worry," Violet whispered. "My brother has everything in hand, and Carlisle and I are helping too."

She gave Wick's arm a squeeze. He smiled back at her.

Richard knew her gesture was meant to comfort his sibling, but he found he didn't like it or the warmth of the exchange between the two. Looking at the young, fashionable pair, he felt, for an instant, like an outsider again.

Don't be a jealous fool, he chided himself. *She's your fiancée. She's going to marry you.*

"What *are* you three whispering about?" The drawl came from Parnell, who was sitting behind them with Goggs and some other rakehells. Parnell's aristocratic features were fixed in a mask of ennui. "If it's gossip, do share—the juicier the better to relieve this curst dull evening."

"The juicier the better," Goggs said, chortling. "Good one, Parnell."

"Does the gossip have to do with Madame Monique?" Parnell said.

"Why do you ask?" Richard twisted around to face the other fully.

Parnell's thin brows lifted. "Because rumors are flying. Everyone knows Monique's death wasn't an accident. According to Miss Primrose, her papa is closing in on the murderer as we speak—with your and our own dear Violet's assistance. So what do you have to say to that?"

"That I'll have to have words with Rosie," Violet muttered.

"Come, Vi—Miss Kent," Parnell corrected smoothly after a warning look from Richard. "We're your cronies, and you can trust us. So do tell: *was* it a lover who killed her?"

"It's always the lover in novels," Goggs said with emphasis.

Seeing Violet's desperate look, Richard cut in. "Stop pestering her. This is murder, not some silly game."

"What a killjoy you are, Carlisle." Parnell sniffed. "It's a wonder our Violet wants anything to do with you. A case of Beauty and the Beast, to be sure."

A loud chord crashed through the room—a good thing because it diverted Richard from his intention to rip the lordling's head off. As the music began, Violet placed a hand on his arm.

"Ignore Parnell," she whispered. "He just likes to bait."

With a terse nod, Richard turned to the front where Miss Wrotham was warbling about a lovelorn lass, Miss Turbett accompanying her on the pianoforte. Richard tried not to wince as the former emitted a high trill that scraped like a fork over his eardrums. At the same instant, Miss Turbett hit a discordant chord that threatened to burst said eardrums altogether.

Even the duet from hell, however, couldn't distract Richard from his brooding. Parnell's remark about Beauty and the Beast had resurrected a memory: of overhearing Miss Lucinda Belton talking about him at a ball. Her voice drifted to him now, the way it had from the other side of an Oriental screen...

"*I had to say no, of course,*" *Lucinda said in her distinctive silvery voice,* "*but it was terribly awkward. He'd gone down on bended knee and seemed so* surprised *when I turned him down.*"

"*Did he actually believe that you could love him?*" *Disdain colored another female voice.* "*You're a Diamond of the First Water, Lucy, and he's... well, he's more like a lump of coal.*"

Giggling, Lucinda said, "*His manners are rather... unpolished, aren't they?*"

"*Not to mention his looks,*" *her friend added.*

"*Luckily, in this instance,*" *a male voice drawled,* "*our fair Aphrodite doesn't have to settle for old Hephaestus...*"

"Penny for your thoughts, Carlisle?"

Belatedly, Richard realized that the performance had ended, and Violet was asking him a question. He looked at her pretty, glowing face and hated his own self-doubt. But he couldn't prevent the question from worming into his mind: could Violet love him?

They'd never spoken of that emotion, and, in truth, it wasn't one he took much stock in. Ladies, in his experience, fell in and out of love with alarming regularity. As he recalled, Audrey Keane had once professed harboring that sentiment for him. No, love could not be relied upon. The things that he and Violet shared—passion, liking, and mutual interests—those were what truly mattered... weren't they?

There was no way in hell he could share these jumbled thoughts with Violet. He felt foolish enough having them in the first place. Exposing his humiliating history was out of the question.

"I'm just thinking about tomorrow," he said quietly.

"Me too." Looking around the room, she said in an undertone, "Everyone is carrying on as usual. It's difficult to imagine that somewhere in this room could lurk a murderer."

It was an unsettling observation, enough to dispel his other ruminations.

As Richard surveyed the crowd, he tried to imagine any one of them being responsible for smothering Monique de Brouet and stealing the necklace. His gaze went to Wormleigh standing at the edge of the room, presently flirting with Mrs. Sumner. Nearby, Tobias Price was busy bantering with a matron of his own class. Near the stage, Ashe and Burns were hovering, readying to perform.

Then there was Garrity in the front row. As usual, the other was dressed to the nines, but it was not the moneylender's garb that caught Richard's attention but who he was sitting with.

"I know. I don't like the looks of that either," Violet said, as if reading his mind. "Gabby's far too nice to be entangled with the likes of him."

Miss Billings was staring at Garrity with a rapt expression. Rather like a mouse mesmerized by a snake, Richard thought. The moneylender's words echoed in his head. *Even a man as busy as I am must occasionally make time for diversions.*

He doubted very much that Garrity's interest in Miss Billings was motivated by pleasure alone... unless one counted the man's love of profit. But this wasn't Richard's problem. Billings was also watching his daughter and Garrity, his expression tight.

Ashe and Burns finished to rousing applause.

"I have a hunch that tomorrow is going to bring some surprises," Violet whispered.

Richard shared that portentous feeling: a storm was brewing ahead.

32

The next morning, the guests undertook the journey from Traverstoke to the village in a caravan of horses and carriages. Violet had chosen to ride a spirited dappled grey mare from Billings' stable. Beside her, Richard was mounted on his magnificent Thoroughbred Aiolos, whose sleek muscles rippled beneath his gleaming chestnut coat.

Man and mount were much alike, Vi thought admiringly. Both were noble beasts of strength and grace. Richard looked utterly at home in the saddle, his muscular body moving in synchrony with his powerful steed.

Which reminded her of an idea that had been bobbing around in her head since their last discussion about his stables. With all that had been going on, she'd forgotten to share it with him. Now they had a moment.

"I've been thinking about you and breeding," she said.

"Pardon?" Richard's dark brows shot up.

Realizing how that sounded, she flushed. "Breeding *horses*, I mean."

"Ah." Though his craggy features remained polite, a wicked

bronze spark lightened his eyes. "Too bad. I was hoping you meant something else."

"Stop trying to embarrass me. I'm being serious."

"There's a first. All right, then. What about breeding horses?"

"Why don't you rebuild your stud farm and use the profits to support your estate?"

He looked briefly startled at her question. "Well, it's not as simple as that. Building a breeding program takes time, not to mention a financial investment. And it can take years to achieve success—if one attains it at all. Plenty of gentlemen pursue this as a hobby, sink fortunes into the venture... and wind up with little more than an expensive stable and some pretty horses. Our last monarch being a prime example."

"But *you* wouldn't do that." The idea of Richard being a spend-thrift was laughable.

He canted his head. "You sound rather confident given that you know little about my skill at horse breeding."

"But I know *you*. You're a man who knows what's what. You're methodical, dependable, and clever. For crumpet's sake," she said with a grin, "you secured a skeleton key to break into Monique's room."

Instead of sharing in her humor, he stared at her as if she'd sprouted another head.

"What's the matter?" She patted her riding hat with its smart little amber veil, wondering if it had slipped. "Am I askew?"

"Quite the opposite." He was still staring at her, only now with a heated intensity that made her heart pound. "In fact, you're rather... perfect."

She was speechless. No one had *ever* called her that before.

Seeming to collect himself, he cleared his throat. "As much as I appreciate your vote of confidence, establishing a stud farm is a large risk. One I can't bank the future of the estate on."

"It's only a risk if you don't believe in yourself."

"I do believe in my ability to create a successful breeding

program," he said, "and if it were only me depending on the outcome, then there would be no question of my pursuing it. But it's not just me. My mama, Wick, the tenants—all of them depend upon the health of the estate. They depend upon me to do the right thing."

"Which right thing?"

His brow furrowed. "What do you mean *which* one? As Carlisle, there's one clear duty which I must fulfill."

"Well, you're more than just a viscount, aren't you? You're *you*, too, with dreams of your own. So the way I see it, you have both a duty to others—and to yourself."

As their horses clip-clopped along, Richard's expression remained pensive. "I've never quite thought of it that way before."

"I'm not saying your family isn't important. Yet it seems to me that you spend a great deal of time looking after others and your estate," she said frankly. "What about doing what *you* want to do? Don't you also deserve to pursue your desires?"

"I do, and I'm going to."

"You mean you're going to start up a breeding program again?" she said eagerly.

"I mean I'll be marrying you. There is nothing," he said, "that I desire more."

His quiet ferocity made her breath catch. It was the most he'd spoken of his feelings for her, and pleasure gripped her heart, squeezing exquisitely. Her lips parted, but the only word that came out was a dazed, "Oh."

His lips tipped up at the corners. "As for the horses, I'll think on it."

Despite the tense situation—her thoughts kept wandering to her siblings and how they were faring in their search of the estate—Violet couldn't help but enjoy herself. She loved fairs, the color and excitement. The sunny weather bore hints of summer, drawing out eager hordes.

The village square was crammed with wooden carts and stalls, goods ranging from fresh foodstuffs to jars of jams and honey to local crafts piled high for the visitors' perusals. A fiddler played on the green, the scent of roasting nuts permeating the air. On one side of the square, the owner of the village tavern had set tables and chairs outside so that patrons could enjoy their foaming tankards while taking in the boisterous scene.

For the first hour, Vi strolled around with Richard, although they had to keep their conversation polite with Lady Ainsworthy dogging their every step. Other guests were enjoying the square as well. Vi observed Tobias Price arm in arm with Mrs. Sumner (the two apparently friends again), and Lord Wormleigh was escorting some young miss whose name Vi couldn't recall. A beaming Miss Wrotham accepted an apple that Cedric Burns chose for her from the costermonger's cart.

By the pottery stand, Miss Turbett stood with her papa, looking far less happy. Her expression was pinched, her father's furious as he watched Wick and his cronies make merry at the tavern. At a table adjacent to the raucous rakehells, Gabby sat with her papa and Mr. Garrity. As the redheaded girl chattered away, her parent looked apprehensive and their guest like the cat that had gotten into the cream.

And so the afternoon went.

At one point, Violet wandered off to sample goods with Polly and Primrose. By the time she finished trying all the different flavors of biscuits at a bakery stall, she found she'd lost her companions in the crowd. Lady Ainsworthy was sitting on a bench farther back, waving her fan in an irritable manner. Vi looked longingly toward the part of the village she'd yet to explore: a spire rose enticingly from a churchyard up ahead.

"I know that look. You're off to find trouble." Wick came sauntering up with a tin cup in hand. "If so, may I come?"

She grinned. "I was just going to explore a little."

He handed her the cup. "Here, drink this first. Compliments of the fellows and I." He jerked his thumb toward their chums, who were waving from the tavern.

Vi waved back and gratefully downed the beverage. The cider slid pleasantly down her parched throat, although she grimaced at the bitter aftertaste of the mulling spices. Setting the cup down, she said, "Shall we?"

It was like old times. For the next quarter hour, she and Wick laughed and explored the grounds of the ancient church. Here, the noise of the crowd faded away to birdsong and the chirping of crickets. Surrounded by a wall of sun-bleached stone, the church-yard was littered with crumbling grave markers and overgrown with ivy. The place had a forgotten, almost dreamy feel. Come to think of it, Vi was feeling a little... woozy?

She stumbled, catching herself.

"Are you all right?" Wick came up beside her.

"Nothing. Just the heat, I expect." She *was* warm, she realized. Heat itched strangely beneath her skin, heightening her aware-ness of her clothes, how restrictive they felt.

Concern shone in Wick's eyes. "We'd better get you back."

As he guided her toward the gate, another wave of dizziness surged over her. She pitched forward, would have fallen if Wick hadn't caught her. She sagged against him.

"What's the matter with you, Vi?" He tipped her face up with his gloved hands, the touch of leather sending an odd spark over her nerve endings. He peered at her. "Egad, your cheeks are flushed—"

She swayed forward.

"What in the devil's name is going on here?" a familiar voice growled.

Richard stood in the arched gateway.

33

I n her muddled state, Violet could only stare at Richard's enraged features. His brawny form filled the stone gateway, and he looked foreboding—like the way he had when they first met.

What got stuck in his craw? she thought foggily.

"Bloody unhand her Wickham," he snapped.

"You're not serious, are you, Carlisle? Look at her, she's—"

The next instant, Violet felt herself being yanked away from Wick and dragged to Richard's side. Her senses were already spinning, and the sudden movement didn't help matters. She clung to Richard to stay upright.

"Leave, Wick, before I do something I regret." Richard's voice had a lethal edge.

"I'm not leaving her. She's unwell, you idiot. I was just—"

"Get the hell out."

Vi cringed, Richard's roar pounding at her temples.

"It's all right, Wick," she managed. "I'm fine."

Wick shook his head. "I'm not leaving you with this jealous fool—"

"I'm going to kill you."

Richard's deadly earnestness pierced Vi's haze and gave her enough wherewithal to say, "Please go, Wick. I'll be fine. I want to talk to Richard alone."

"You're sure?" Wick studied her.

She nodded, even though the action made her feel even more buffle-headed.

With a disgusted look at his brother, Wick strode out the gate.

Before Vi could speak, the universe spun crazily. Breathless, she found herself with her back against the stone wall. Richard's hands were planted next to her shoulders, trapping her.

His eyes burned into her. "So has this all been a game to you?"

Game? "What on earth do you mean?"

"You're just like the others. A damned flirt. A trollop."

The burst of anger cleared her head. "Now wait just a deuced minute—"

"Hell, you're even better than them. Better at lying. Better at duping men, seducing them."

"What *are* you talking about? Better than whom?" She was confused—by his anger and her own. And by her throbbing awareness of him, of his large form caging her against the wall. "You can't possibly mean that Wick and I—"

"He was going to kiss you," Richard thundered. "I saw it with my own eyes."

"Don't be silly. I wasn't feeling well..."—she wetted her lips at the flare of his nostrils—"it might have been that cider Wick gave me. It tasted a bit off. Anyway, Wick was just concerned. As any friend would be."

"Aye, I know how *friendly* you can get, so don't take me for a fool. You're not ill—you're bloody aroused. I *know* how you look when you're in the throes. Those flushed cheeks and parted lips, the come-hither heat in your eyes."

His words seemed to tear away some internal blinders. All of a sudden, what she was feeling became clear, the sensations coalescing in a humming rush... of *need*.

Gadzooks. He's... right?

"I d-don't understand." Why would she feel aroused around *Wick*? She didn't desire him.

Richard leaned closer, his expression ravaged. "Don't you? I'd wager my estate that your nipples are hard right now. If I tossed up your skirts, your pussy would be wet and greedy, wouldn't it?"

She stared at him, her breath puffing from her parted lips. *Right again.*

A savage light came into his eyes. He swore, and the next minute his mouth slammed onto hers. The kiss was hard and punishing, but she didn't care because she wanted it. Wanted him. Her arousal blazed, incinerating everything else. Wild for him, she sucked on his tongue, licked inside his mouth, panting for more.

She felt her skirts being shoved up, warm air kissing her thighs. When he touched her pussy, they both groaned. She could feel how wet she was, how her flesh throbbed for his touch.

"Say this is for me, not Wick." His eyes were hungry, tortured. "By God, say it, lass—"

He thrust his fingers into her, and she gasped as the orgasm hit her.

"My, my. This is *quite* the performance, isn't it?"

The female voice perforated Vi's bliss. She twisted to see its source: Mrs. Sumner, standing inside the gate with Lord Wormleigh. Both were watching on with leering expressions.

Richard yanked down Vi's skirts, took a hasty step back.

But it was too late. Mrs. Sumner and Wormleigh had exited, their excitement palpable.

Violet felt the weight of ruination crashing down.

As Richard watched, Lady Ainsworthy's carriage drove off with Violet and the other Kent girls, sending an angry plume of dust into the village square. His mind was in turmoil. What had he been bloody thinking?

The plain truth was that he hadn't been. Seeing Violet in Wick's arms had unleashed a rage unlike any he'd known before. The force of his fury had knocked out all reason, and it still roiled in him... along with prickling agitation.

Wormleigh and Sumner were vicious gossips. They'd wasted no time in hurrying back to the fair to spread lurid tales of discovering Richard and Violet *in flagrante*.

Violet was ruined.

Becoming aware of the keen audience gathered around him on the green, Richard felt his face flame. He wanted to punch his fist through a wall. But that would help nothing, wouldn't stem the damage he'd done to Violet's reputation. By Jove, nothing would. As furious as he was with her betrayal, he was angrier at himself—for hurting her. For allowing himself to hope...

It doesn't matter. You're going to marry her.

At this point, he didn't have a choice. Anguish pierced his anger. Because, despite everything, he still wanted to make her his—

"What the bloody hell have you done?" Wickham shoved his way through the crowd toward Richard. "You stupid sod!"

Richard's fists clenched. "Back off."

Wick glared at him. "Not until I knock some sense into you."

That does it. Red saturated Richard's vision. He threw a punch.

Wick danced out of reach. "Violet's my *friend*—practically my sister."

"You tried to *kiss* her." Richard circled his brother.

"For God's sake, I did not. She was feeling *ill*. I think that cider made her foxed or something."

"So you took advantage of her!" Snarling, Richard issued an uppercut.

Wick dodged at the last moment. "Why would I do that, you imbecile? She's in love with you."

Emotion exploded in Richard. With a roar, he charged his brother, tackling the other onto the ground. His fist connected satisfyingly with Wick's side.

Wick grunted. "Go ahead and pummel me. Doesn't change the fact that Violet loves you."

"Shut the bloody hell up!" Richard pinned his brother, landed a facer.

"Or the fact that you love her back," Wick gasped, "and that scares you witless!"

The words punctured Richard's raw haze. He stilled, his fist poised above Wick's face. "What the devil did you say?"

"You're terrified that she's going to reject you like the others, so you assumed the worst. Because you can't get it through your thick skull that Violet loves you, you didn't give her the benefit of the doubt and instead pushed her away. Which makes you a moron!"

The truth hit Richard like a right hook, the force of it making his head jerk back.

Wick was... right. Every word he'd said—true. Richard had been so afraid of repeating his past that he'd doubted the woman he loved. Doubted that she could love him back. And his fears had led him to act like the worst kind of bastard.

His rage abruptly subsided.

"Bloody hell," he said hoarsely, "I *am* a moron."

"Exactly. Now would you mind getting off of me?" Wick glowered up at him. "We've provided enough free entertainment."

Richard became aware of the murmuring crowd around them. Feeling like the world's biggest fool, he rose... and offered his sibling his hand.

"I owe you an apology," he said gruffly.

Wick touched his swelling jaw and winced. "Save the groveling for Violet. You'll need it."

Richard's throat closed. God... he'd mistrusted her, treated her badly—*ruined* her. Groveling was too good for him; he deserved to be horsewhipped.

With hammering urgency, he said, "I've got to get back to the house. To make things right."

Wick dusted off his jacket, grumbling, "I'll come with you, you great lummox. But only because I want Violet to be my sister. That way, at least I'll have one sibling who isn't insane."

34

The two brothers rode back to Traverstoke as the sun was sinking into the horizon. As dusky light flickered between the passing oaks, Richard's thoughts were a whirling vortex. How was he going to make things right with Violet? If not because of Wick, why had she been so aroused in the churchyard? He still didn't fully understand all that had happened, but he did know that he'd wronged her. He urged Aiolos into a faster gallop.

The sooner he got back, the sooner he could straighten things out. Grovel, if need be.

Nearing the house, Richard saw people clustered outside by the fountain. Amongst them, he spotted Violet with Kent and his wife along with two men he didn't recognize. Nearby, footmen were loading trunks onto a carriage. Richard dismounted, heading straight for Violet, his brother behind him.

As he approached, he saw Violet's flushed face—hell, the tear tracks on her cheeks—and remorse pounded like a fist against his chest. Before he could open his mouth to speak, Lady Ainsworthy pushed her way forward to confront him.

"And there is the defiler himself," the dowager hissed. "Have you no shame, sirrah, showing your face here. My back was turned for a single moment, and you managed to ruin this gel beyond all redemption—"

"Thank you, Lady Ainsworthy, we can take it from here," Kent cut in. "If you would be so kind as to give my family privacy?"

The simmering menace that emanated from Kent gave even the dowager pause. With a huff, she turned and hobbled back toward the house. Once she was gone, Kent said, "Lord Carlisle and Mr. Murray, I'd like you to answer some questions."

The investigator's cool, impersonal tone stirred the hairs on Richard's neck. This wasn't about Violet then? And why did Kent want to question Wick? All of a sudden, the identity of the two strangers struck Richard: hell... *Kent's partners*. The brawny brown-haired fellow was likely Mr. McLeod, the imposing African beside him Mr. Lugo.

Foreboding snaked through Richard. Sensing his brother's trembling tension beside him, he silently willed the other to stay calm. What did the investigators know?

"Mr. Murray, explain your connection with Monique de Brouet, if you please," Kent said.

Devil take it, how had they discovered Wick's relationship with the deceased?

Richard's gaze shot to Violet. She looked as dumbfounded as he felt.

Red splotches appeared on Wick's cheeks. "I—I don't have any connection," he stammered unconvincingly.

"You were not her lover? You did not break things off a mere fortnight before this party, causing problems between the two of you? Monique de Brouet did not threaten to get revenge for the way you treated her?"

"How did you find out...?" Wick's bewildered gaze turned to Violet. "You *swore* you wouldn't tell your brother about my ring. You promised," he choked out.

"Wick, I didn't tell him anything," she said in a trembling voice.

"Ring?" Kent swung to face his sister, his expression thunderous. "What *bloody ring*?"

Seeing the panic in her eyes, Richard intervened swiftly.

"It's not her fault. It is mine," he said. "We found Madame de Brouet's body exactly as we described, but we neglected to mention that... Wickham's signet ring was in her hand. I knew my brother had nothing to do with it—he wasn't even at the house during the time she was killed—but I feared that such evidence would be falsely incriminating. To protect Wick, I decided to conceal the fact of the ring. Miss Kent had nothing to do with that decision whatsoever."

"Richard," Violet whispered, "you know that's not true—"

"*Stay out of this, Violet.*" Hellfire blazed in Kent's gaze.

She bit her lip and fell silent.

Turning to Richard, the investigator snarled, "I ought to have you dragged in front of the magistrate along with your brother. You've aided and abetted a murder suspect, and you've involved my sister in this mess!"

"The m-magistrate?" Wick's chin quivered. "He knows about me?"

"Yes, I told him," Kent snapped. "It's my duty to aid in the apprehension of criminals."

Fear tangled inside Richard, but he kept his composure. "Wickham is no criminal. He didn't kill Monique de Brouet," he said with quiet vehemence. "It is true that they were once lovers, and she kept that ring as a memento of their affair. But you'll recall that Dr. Abernathy found that broken chain? Well, whoever killed her must have seen her wearing the ring on the chain, tore it off, and put it in her hand to frame Wick—"

"And did they also place the murder weapon in your brother's room?" The rejoinder came from the brown-haired McLeod whose arms were crossed over the wide girth of his chest. "Because you ken we found that too."

Frost spread over Richard's insides. "What murder weapon?"

"The missing pillow. The yellow fabric matches the fibers found by Abernathy on the victim, and the pillow is stained with blood," Kent stated. "An hour ago, we found this pillow stuffed beneath your brother's bed."

Richard's heart thudded in his ears.

"I-I don't know anything about that damned pillow," Wick stammered. "I didn't put it there!"

"Then Lugo and McLeod arrived from London. With this." Kent withdrew a leather bound journal. "After searching Monique de Brouet's home, they found her diary, which gives a detailed account of her relationship with Wickham Murray. With this, she could have blackmailed your brother, put a dint in his plans to marry a respectable young heiress to pay off his debts." As if reading Richard's thoughts, Kent said in a steely voice, "Yes, I know about your arrangement with Turbett. He's been less than discreet about his willingness to buy himself a son-in-law from a noble family."

Richard was paralyzed by helplessness, unable to think or do anything to protect his brother.

"And now," Kent said with quiet lethality, "we discover that your brother's ring was found on the dead woman's body, *and* you concealed this fact from the authorities. Do you realize how guilty this all looks?"

"No," Wick whispered, backing away. "*No.*"

Before Richard could stop him, Wick sprinted for his horse, panic imbuing him with uncanny speed. He mounted, spurring his horse, racing down the drive. Dimly aware of the investigators' shouts, Richard ran for his own horse, intending to halt his brother's desperate flight which would only make matters worse—

His boot wasn't even in the stirrup when a fleet of constables rode up, blocking Wick's escape route. They circled him, a black carriage pulling up behind them.

Magistrate Jones stepped out from the equipage, his black coat swirling.

"Wickham Murray," the magistrate said in sepulchral tones, "I hereby place you under arrest for the murder of Monique de Brouet."

Richard surged forward; Lugo and McLeod held him back.

"Calm yourself." Lugo spoke for the first time, his accented baritone resonating with warning. "There's nothing you can do for him now."

"He's my *brother*. And he didn't do any of it," Richard shouted.

He struggled against the men's hold, but between the pair of them, they held him fast. He could only watch as Wick was dragged from his horse, irons clamped on his wrists. One of the constables shoved Wick into the carriage.

"Wick," he shouted at his brother's disappearing back, "don't panic. Just hold on. I'll find the true killer, clear your name..."

The carriage drove off with the convoy of constables.

When the dust cleared, Lugo and McLeod released him. Panting, Richard battled hopelessness and despair. He looked for Violet—only to see that she'd been loaded into a waiting carriage with the other Kent girls, the door closing.

"Violet! Wait—"

He sprinted toward the moving conveyance only to have Kent and his partners block his path.

"From here on in, stay away from my sister," Kent said in tones that brooked no refusal. "Go near her, and you and I will be meeting at dawn."

Richard's chest constricted. "But I love her—"

"I don't give a damn. You're a liar and a scoundrel, and I won't have you near her."

As Kent stalked away, flanked by his partners, Richard couldn't argue—because the man was right. He was a scoundrel. He'd failed his brother and Violet. Standing alone once again, he watched the carriage disappear into the darkening night, carrying his dreams along with it.

35

I nside the carriage, Violet slumped against the squabs. Her mind swirled with worry over Wick and Richard, and her own disgrace was like an uninvited guest in the cabin, muting conversation and camaraderie. Rosie, sitting on the opposite bench with Marianne, was devoid of chatter for once, staring out into the passing darkness, and beside Vi, Polly fiddled listlessly with the strings of her reticule.

Vi could stand the oppressive silence no longer.

"Why do we have to leave?" she burst out. "I need to be at the estate—to help Wick. Why won't Ambrose give me a chance to explain things?"

"Do not blame your brother," Marianne said sharply. "He's trying to minimize the scandal you've caused. The whole party is abuzz with how Carlisle has ruined you, and the longer the two of you are under the same roof, the bigger this disaster is going to get. Even with Emma and Thea staying to control the damage, there's no telling if you'll have any reputation left after this."

"Right now, my reputation is the least of my worries—"

"If you don't think of yourself, think of Ambrose." Her sister-in-law expelled a breath. "Do not test your brother, Violet. If you force his hand, he *will* call Carlisle out."

Horror and shame collided in Vi. By Golly, she'd made a hash of things. The truth was that, even if Ambrose was willing to listen, she didn't know *how* she could explain her scandalous behavior.

Although she'd always been a creature ruled by impulses, her sudden arousal had taken her entirely by surprise, a storm without any warning. One moment she'd been angry at Richard's unfounded accusations... and the next they were kissing... and more.

Even now, a bewildering hum of lust lingered in her—which made no sense given the enormity of the disaster that had befallen those she loved. Her throat cinched. Wick had been dragged away in chains, his future hanging precariously in the balance. Richard had been left alone to deal with the mess, and, if her present exile was any indication, Ambrose might try to separate her and Richard for good.

"It's not Richard's fault," she said desperately. "I was a full participant."

"To what are you referring to, precisely? The concealing of evidence,"—Marianne's brows arched— "or your public ruination?"

"Um, both?" Vi said in a small voice. "He took responsibility because he's a man of honor, but I wanted to protect Wick as much as he did—"

"And so you lied to your brother. Through your actions, you not only betrayed Ambrose's trust, but you put his professional integrity and reputation at risk." Her sister-in-law's face tautened with disapproval. "If word ever got out that a member of his own family sabotaged a murder enquiry, how do you think that would make him look?"

There goes the idiot sister again, making a mull of things... Only it wasn't some prank this time, some silly scrape. She'd caused a true and utter catastrophe.

Hanging her head, Violet whispered, "I'm sorry. I was only trying to do the right thing. I never intended to deceive Ambrose for as long as I did. At first, I just wanted to find out the truth from Wick before going to Ambrose with the ring... but then Magistrate Jones entered the picture, and I knew he wouldn't be the type to listen to Wick's explanations, not when the evidence seemed so damning. And I knew if I told Ambrose about Wick's ring, he'd feel duty-bound to tell Jones—and I didn't want to put him in a bad position. So, in a way, I was trying to protect Ambrose too," she finished miserably.

"Oh, Violet, your brother is perfectly capable of making the right decisions." Some of the chill left Marianne's voice. "Now you must trust him to do the right thing."

"Wick didn't kill Monique. I *know* he didn't—not only because he's my friend but because he wasn't even at the house. He was out drinking and passed out in the woodcutter's cottage. Why, he didn't even know Monique had died until Richard and I told him the next evening. Please," Vi pleaded, "you've got to convince Ambrose to keep looking for the true murderer. Or an innocent man is going to hang."

A notch formed between Marianne's brows. "Ambrose is the best investigator in all of London. You must trust his judgement."

"I do. I know now that I made a grievous mistake in not trusting him from the start," Vi said earnestly. "But I can't change what I did, and once Ambrose calms down, considers all the evidence and clues, he'll know that Wick isn't the criminal. And he'd hate himself if he played any part in the wrong man being convicted—"

"Say no more." Sighing, Marianne said, "We'll be staying overnight at the nearest inn, and I'll write him a note then."

"Oh, thank you—"

"Thank me by not causing any more trouble this trip, all right?"

With his head in his hands, Richard sat on his bed, trying to sort out his jumbled thoughts.

What should I do next? How can I help Wick? Win Violet back?

The sounds of chatter and bustling came from the hallway. Gossip was running rampant with news of Violet's ruination and Wick's arrest for murder. With the case closed, many of the guests were making preparations for departure the next morning. Apparently, they'd had enough of the house party from hell.

Fear churned in Richard's gut, and he dug his fingers into his scalp, wanting the bite of pain to clear his mind. For once in his life, he had no way to fix the situation—no way to help his own kin. The only one who might be able to clear Wick's name was Kent. But that bridge had been burned to ashes.

A knock made Richard raise his head. He didn't know who would be paying a visit. At the moment, he was persona non grata: despoiler of an innocent and brother of a murder suspect.

"Come in," he said.

It was the Blackwoods. Richard rose as they entered, closing the door behind them.

"How are you faring, old boy?" Blackwood said.

Richard didn't realize how much he'd needed to see a friendly face until that moment.

"I've been better," he said quietly.

"We know everything. And we're here to help," Lady Blackwood declared.

"Thank you, my lady." Humbled, he said, "That means more than you could know."

"We were talking to Kent just now. He has his doubts about your brother's guilt. As a matter of fact, he's sent his partners to investigate some other possibilities." Blackwood's words ignited a spark of hope. "But he felt duty-bound to inform Jones about the ring and the pillow and, well, the magistrate took matters from there."

"I understand that Kent only did his duty. It was my mistake for hiding evidence in the first place." Hunching his shoulders, Richard said gruffly, "I respect the man for doing what is right despite what his personal feelings must be."

"Make no mistake, Carlisle, you are not his favorite person at the moment," the marchioness said dryly. "The concealing of evidence aside, what possessed you to take such a risk with Violet's reputation this afternoon?"

Other than the fact that I'm an ass?

He dragged a hand through his hair. "I mistook an innocent moment between her and my brother for a ... a tryst. I was angry and snapped at her."

"You forced yourself on Violet?" The marchioness' voice was sharp as a blade.

"*No.* No, it wasn't like that." Flushing, he tried to explain the baffling events. "My behavior was abominable, but she was... willing."

More than willing, in truth. Violet had been incredibly, unbelievably aroused. And she'd been that way *before* his arrival. He recalled how she'd looked when he came upon her and Wick: her cheeks flushed and eyes glassy, her bosom heaving. Seeing her thus had fed his jealous rage, catapulting him to the wrong conclusion. But if she and Wick hadn't been up to something, then what had caused her to be that way...?

"Why would she be willing if you were maligning her?" Lady Blackwood demanded.

Good bloody question. What had Violet said? *I wasn't feeling well... might have been that cider Wick gave me... tasted a bit off.* Richard frowned; Wick had mentioned something about the cider, too. *Might have made her foxed,* he'd said.

One cup of cider? And Violet hadn't been acting foxed, exactly, more like she'd been...

The answer slammed into Richard's brain.

"Drugged," he said.

"Pardon?" Blackwood said.

"I think Violet might have been drugged. With one of those infernal powders that heighten the senses..."

Frowning, Blackwood said, "An aphrodisiac, you mean?"

"Aye." It would explain Violet's symptoms, her odd behavior. Why she'd been so randy...

"She was flushed? A bit groggy? Her eyes dilated and glassy?" Lady Blackwood said.

For a lady, Richard thought the marchioness had rather worldly knowledge.

"Aye, and she said she'd drank some cider that tasted strange," he said.

"Who gave her the cider?" Blackwood said.

"Wick—but he wouldn't drug Violet," Richard said quickly.

"Then who did it? And why?" Lady Blackwood's violet eyes were narrowed.

Richard's gut told him that Violet's drugging was no coincidence. "I think it may be related to the murder and the theft of the necklace," he said slowly. "First, someone frames my brother, and now Violet, who has been making headway in the investigation, gets ruined. Discredited."

"Distraction and diversion are two of the best strategies for obscuring the truth," Lady Blackwood agreed. "The question is who committed these vile deeds?"

Again, it occurred to Richard that Lady Blackwood's shrewdness was odd for a gently-bred female. He glanced at Blackwood, who didn't look surprised by his wife's acuity. In fact, the other looked proud—and not a little besotted.

The way I feel about my lass.

Fire reignited in Richard.

"I'll start with Wick's cronies," he said. "They were with him at the tavern. They might know who came in contact with the cider."

"You do that, and we'll go explain things to Kent," Blackwood said. "Get him on board."

Richard was heading to the door. "Thank you, my friends. I need all the help I can get."

After going through the public rooms and seeing no sign of Parnell or Goggs, Richard went to the rakehells' bedchambers. He didn't find Parnell but cornered Goggs in his room. Goggs looked flustered, his thin brown hair disheveled; from the heap of clothes and open valise on the bed, it appeared he was attempting to pack.

"Thought I'd get a start on things. Everyone's leaving on the morrow now that..." Goggs' pudgy cheeks reddened. "I'm, er, sorry about Wick. I can't believe he would... that is, if there's anything I can do..."

"Today at the fair, I saw you with Wick," Richard said without preamble. "At the tavern."

"Me and some of the fellows, yes. We were having a few rounds." Goggs wetted his lips. "To pass the curst dull time, you know."

"When Wick left to speak with Violet, he took a cup of cider with him. Do you recall?"

Goggs blinked. "I, um, think so."

"Who came in contact with that cup?"

"In contact? Don't follow, old boy."

"Do you know who was in possession of that cup? At any time."

The other's forehead wrinkled. "Why does it matter?"

Richard was losing his patience. "Just answer the bloody

question."

After a second, Goggs said, "Well, Wick had it."

Damn and blast. I'm getting nowhere—

"But I think it was Parnell who bought it. Yes, I remember now," Goggs said slowly. "He thought Violet might be thirsty and suggested Wick bring it over to her."

Parnell. Richard wouldn't put drugging—or murder and theft —past the bastard.

"Where is Parnell now?" he demanded.

"He, er, decided to spend the night in the village."

Seeing Goggs shift uncomfortably, Richard said, "Spit it out."

"If you must know, he was in the mood for some bedsport. Said he fancied sampling the local fare."

Bloody hell. Back to the village then.

As Richard turned to go, Goggs said, "By the by—I'm sorry about what, er, happened with Violet." He studied his muddy boots. "She's a good sort, would have liked to say my goodbyes before she was packed off to London."

Richard jerked his chin in acknowledgement and hurried off.

36

I t took Richard three hours to track down Parnell. After carousing all night at the fair, the bastard had apparently taken off with some local rakehells to a neighboring village. There, he continued his rabble-rousing at the public house before going home with one of his newfound friends and a barmaid with a salacious reputation.

Richard now approached the address he'd been given by the proprietor of the public house. Raising his fist, he banged on the door until a groaning voice emerged from inside.

"Bloody hell, I'm coming. Stop that infernal racket—"

The door opened to reveal a puffy-eyed fellow, his blond hair standing up in disordered tufts. He wore a stained dressing gown that he'd clearly just thrown on.

He glared blearily at Richard. "Who the devil are you?"

"I'm here for Parnell."

"Don't know any Parnell, so you'd better toddle off—"

Richard inserted his boot to prevent the door from closing. He gave the wooden barrier a shove, causing the other to stumble back and out of his way. He strode into the small cottage, grabbing a taper off a side table to light the way. There were only two bedchambers, and he found Parnell in the second one.

The bastard was naked in bed with a voluptuous brunette—the barmaid, no doubt. Both were snoring. Next to her was a third pillow with an indentation still upon it.

Richard set down the lamp and shook Parnell's shoulder. "Get up, you bastard."

Parnell smacked his lips, his eyes still shut.

The blond man came marching in. "This is my house, and you're trespassing—"

Richard swatted the other out of his way and went to the washing stand. Finding the ewer full, he returned and dumped the contents over Parnell.

Parnell jolted upright, swearing. "Wh-what the devil?"

The barmaid turned onto her other side, still snoring.

"Did you give Violet the poison?" Richard growled.

Clearly still three sheets to the wind, Parnell stared at him with bloodshot eyes.

"Carlisle? That you?" he said, slurring. "What in blazes are you doing here?"

"Did you give Violet the poison?" Grabbing hold of the other's shoulders, Richard gave a forceful shake.

"Poison? What poison?" Parnell groaned. "For the love of God, stop that manhandling, or I'll cast my accounts."

Richard pinned the other against the headboard. "I'll snap your bloody head off if you don't confess the truth. Goggs told me anyway. You were the one who bought Violet the cider."

"I didn't buy her anything," Parnell protested. "Old bacon-brains mixed things up as usual. He was the one who bought Violet the drink."

Richard's insides went cold. "You're lying. You drugged her."

"Drugged? What are you... *oh*." Unholy glee lit Parnell's eyes. "Is that why the two of you were caught making the beast with two backs in broad daylight?"

"So it *was* you." Richard slammed the other's head against the wood.

"Ouch! Stop that. I wouldn't stoop to using the stuff—do I look like I need to?" Parnell gestured to his bedpartners. "I ain't desperate like Goggs."

Richard froze. "Goggs?"

"How d'you think he gets all those tavern wenches to sleep with him? He thinks it's his little secret,"—the lordling smirked—"but I figured it out ages ago. Why on earth would he drug Violet, I wonder?"

Pulse racing, Richard grabbed clothes off a nearby chair and tossed them at Parnell. "Get dressed. We're leaving *now*."

Richard arrived back at the estate an hour before dawn. The journey would have been quicker had Parnell not needed to retch twice on the way back. He dragged the pale-faced bastard up the steps into the main atrium. Despite the early hour, Kent was there, conferring with McLeod.

Richard hesitated. Had the Blackwoods succeeded in smoothing the way with the investigator?

Kent's keen gaze shot to Richard. "We found the lovers."

"Pardon?" Richard didn't follow.

"The lovers Wormleigh overheard in the library—turns out he was telling the truth about them. MacLeod here accomplished what three of the magistrate's men couldn't. He tracked down the purchase of a pair of tickets to Gretna to a station two villages away. The tickets were sold a week ago to a Mr. and Mrs. Cedric Burns."

"They were supposed to leave the morning that the de Brouet woman was killed. According to the ledger, the couple didn't show for their journey," McLeod said. "The tickets went unused."

"At first Burns refused to say anything," Kent went on, "but somehow Amelia Turbett got wind that we were interrogating him, and she rushed to her lover's rescue."

Richard's head jerked. "Miss Turbett, you say?"

Kent nodded. "Apparently she and Burns have been carrying on in secret for months. She told us everything. How Monique overheard her and Burns in the library. Threatened to blackmail them. One thing led to another, and Miss Turbett pushed Monique into the fireplace. An accident, she claimed. She and Burns thought she'd killed Monique so they panicked, called off their elopement plans, and tried to wait things out."

Richard's head spun. "They have the necklace?"

"Burns claims he knows nothing about stolen jewelry," Kent said. "We searched all of his and Miss Turbett's belongings and found nothing."

"Our theory is that someone else came upon Monique in the library," McLeod added. "Saw the necklace and stole it, smothering Monique in the process."

"We need to question Goggs," Richard said sharply.

Kent frowned. "Goggston? Why—"

Richard gave a rapid-fire summary of what he'd discovered about the drugged cider.

"What is more, Goggs is swimming in debts," he said in grim tones. "Parnell confirmed that both he and Goggs have been dodging moneylenders for the past year. Parnell has his papa to fall back on, but he says Goggs' father cut him off months ago. Goggs is in desperate straits."

"So he had motive to steal the necklace—to take it from Monique by any means necessary." Cursing, Kent said, "Let's go get him."

Leaving Parnell in McLeod's custody, Richard and Kent took off running to Goggston's chamber. When Richard's knock went unanswered, he took a step back and kicked the door open. He rushed inside, Kent at his heels; the empty room with its unmade bed confirmed his fear. After a quick search that revealed no clues as to Goggs' plans, they went to the stables. Goggs had left behind his own mount, taking one of Billings' carriages instead.

"Goggston won't get far," Kent said. "He has no more than a few hours' lead on us. I'll send men along all the main roads—"

"Why do you think he took a carriage?" Richard said tersely. "He'd make far better time on horseback."

"What are you getting at?"

"He knows we're onto him—that's why he lied to me and cast blame on Parnell. He knows he's only bought himself a little time and can't outrun us." Goggs' words hammered at his brain. *Would have liked to say my goodbyes before she was packed off to London.* "And he also knows where Violet is headed."

"Bloody hell." Kent paled. "The bastard's gone after her. For insurance."

37

P *fftt.* The wooden arrow hit the apple, the impact pushing it over the edge of the table. It hit the floor with a soft thud. A direct hit.

Sighing, Violet put down her crossbow and went to fetch the fallen fruit. Since sleep had eluded her, she was trying to distract herself with target practice. Unfortunately, the crossbow reminded her of Richard and all the uncertainties in their future.

How were they going to save Wick? Would Ambrose ever forgive them for hiding evidence? And why had Richard acted so angrily—so unreasonably—in the churchyard? Was there something he hadn't told her about his past? Because she had an inkling that his failed courtships might have had something to do with his reaction...

Placing the apple back on the table, she took another shot, driving it over the edge once more.

"For heaven's sake, don't you *ever* sleep?"

Rosie's grumbling voice, which emerged from the bedchamber adjoining the sitting room, broke Violet's reverie. She was sharing a suite with Rosie and Polly.

"Sorry," she said in a small voice. "I was trying not to make too much noise."

A sound like "grrr" came in reply.

Not wanting to disturb her roommates further, Violet decided to take her target practice outside. The watery light of dawn was already slipping through the curtains; it was early enough that no one would take note of her. She wrangled on a front-lacing corset and her simplest dress, throwing her blue cloak on top. Lastly, she tucked her crossbow and sticks into a knitting bag and slipped from the room.

Given the hour, the corridors of the inn were deserted, and she made it past the dozing clerk at the reception without waking him. Outside, she inhaled deeply; the invigorating, greenery-scented air reminded her of Chudleigh Crest. Feeling marginally better, she headed toward the courtyard. She turned the corner... and stopped short. A familiar figure was adjusting something on the outside of a mud-splattered carriage.

"Goggs?" she said, startled. "Is that you?"

He spun around. His chubby face had a sheen of sweat. "Violet! Lord, you gave me a scare."

"I'm sorry. I didn't mean to." She ambled up to him. "What are you doing here?"

His eyes darted around the environs. He tugged on his waistcoat, which had ridden up on his belly. She noticed that his hands and the garment were streaked with dirt.

"I came to find you," he said.

"Me? What for?"

"Carlisle—he sent me. He has a plan, you see, to free Wick. And he needs your help."

Excitement shot through her. Richard had sent for her... and he had a plan to save Wick!

"What does he want me to do?" she said eagerly.

Goggs unlatched the carriage door, held it open. "Get in. I'll explain on the drive back."

She went to the door, tossed her knitting bag inside. As she was about to climb in, a thought stopped her. *You can't just leave without telling the others, you pea wit.*

Turning, she said, "Wait, I have to tell Marianne first—"

"There's no time. We have to leave. Now."

"But my family will worry." Something in Goggs' expression gave her pause. "Why... why didn't Richard come himself?"

"You ask too many questions."

Goggs' face had lost its amicable mask, a hard and foreign glint in his eyes. He looked like... a stranger. Sudden fear welled inside her. Before she could gather the breath to scream, something crashed into the side of her head. Through the exploding pain, she felt herself being shoved into the carriage and then she knew no more.

Richard was the first to arrive at the Red Lion. The inn was the first on the road to London, the obvious place to stay given Mrs. Kent and the girls' late departure last evening. Goggston would look here first. Pulse racing, Richard tossed Aiolos' reins to a waiting stable hand just as Kent and McLeod thundered in on horseback. The three of them entered the inn. After a quick exchange with the innkeeper, they headed for Mrs. Kent's suite.

She opened the door on the third knock, still tying the belt of her silk wrapper.

"You're all right." Relief threaded Kent's voice. "Where are the girls?"

"In the suite next door." Frowning, she said, "What is going on, Ambrose?"

Kent was already headed to the next room. He banged on the door.

After the fourth knock, Richard said impatiently, "Move aside."

"I can kick down a bloody door," Kent snapped.

Just as the investigator reared back to do so, the door opened.

"Papa?" a sleepy-eyed Primrose Kent said. "Why on earth are you pounding like that?"

"Thank God. You're safe." Kent exhaled as a drowsy-looking Polly Kent appeared behind the other girl. "And Violet's in there with you?"

"Actually... she isn't."

At Primrose's reply, Richard's gut turned to ice.

"Where is she?" he said roughly.

Primrose frowned. "I don't know exactly. When I woke up just now, she was gone. Earlier she couldn't sleep and was keeping everyone awake with that dashed crossbow of hers. Maybe she went outside to practice?"

Panic roared through Richard. "She went outside? *Alone?*"

"I-I'm not certain of it," Primrose said, her voice quivering. "It wasn't like I told her to go—"

"Concentrate, Rosie," Kent cut in. "What time did Violet leave the room?"

"Maybe... an hour ago? I don't know." The girl's bottom lip trembled. "I was half-asleep, Papa."

Unable to wait a moment longer, Richard turned and strode to the nearest exit. He heard Kent saying behind him, "Keep the girls with you, Marianne, and lock the door. Strathaven will be arriving shortly to escort you all back to Traverstoke."

Outside, Richard jogged along the perimeter of the inn, McLeod going in the opposite direction. They met at the side of the building. McLeod crouched, staring at markings in the dirt.

Peering over the other's shoulder, Richard said grimly, "Footprints?"

"Two sets. One larger, one smaller, the latter leading from the hotel. And look here, see how they're smudged?"

"A struggle." Richard's heart kicked against his ribs.

"There's fresh carriage tracks, too." McLeod pointed to the

markings as Kent joined them. "Wheels are wide, a heavy conveyance. Wouldn't go faster than five miles per hour, I'd guess."

Kent followed the tracks to the end of the drive. "Looks like they're headed to London."

"We can catch up to them," McLeod said.

Richard sprinted to his mount. Grabbing the reins from the stable hand, he leapt into the saddle.

"Go, Aiolos," he urged. "We've got to get to Violet."

The Thoroughbred whinnied, tossed its mane in understanding.

They took off, dust churning in their wake.

38

Violet opened her eyes... and let out a groan as pain stabbed through her temple. By Golly, her head hurt like the devil. And why was the world bumping up and down? Come to think of it, where on earth *was* she? She made out velvet squabs, dirty windows, swaying straps...

It returned to her in a flash: *Goggs.*

He'd hit her on the head—and shoved her inside the carriage. Goggs, whom she'd believed was a friend, had *kidnapped* her! Why would he do such a thing? Stunned, she could think of only one explanation: he was the villain. He'd killed Monique, stolen the necklace. Now he was making his escape, and he'd taken Violet as a hostage.

The *bounder.*

Indignation cleared her head, gave her strength. Grabbing hold of a passenger strap, she leveraged herself up to sitting position. One of the wheels hit a rock, and her head whirled, but she took a breath and tried to focus.

Think, Violet. Figure out a way to get out of here.

She reached for the door handle. It was jammed, wouldn't budge. *Crumpets.* She looked to the windows. Goggston had smeared them with mud, presumably so that no one could see her inside. What a time for him to turn out to be clever!

Running her hands along the frames of the largest windows, she discovered that they, too, were locked shut from the outside. *Drat.*

Without much hope, she tried the small, narrow window next to the main one—and excitement surged in her when it budged. She pushed harder and was rewarded by a blast of cool wind against her cheek. The window was too tiny for her to climb out of, but she could poke her head out to assess her situation.

She could see Goggs' profile on the driver's perch, and just the sight of him made anger quicken inside her. Focused on the rock-strewn road, he didn't notice her. Surveying the passing fields and woods, she didn't see any farmhouses, any people who might hear her if she cried for help.

Pulling her head back inside, she considered her options. She could wait, hope for a passing carriage and shout for assistance then... but who knew when the next carriage would come along? Or if the people inside would even hear her?

Besides, she hated waiting.

Which meant she needed another plan. Something to break the main window perhaps? She looked around the cabin for a tool to use... and her gaze snagged on the leather handles lying next to her feet. *Her knitting bag.*

Leaning over, she lifted it with reverent hands. She'd tossed the bag in before Goggs had shoved her into the conveyance. He'd clearly forgotten about it—or maybe he hadn't even given it a thought. After all, what danger could a lady's accoutrement possibly pose?

Pulling out her miniature crossbow, she grinned. Some men gave jewels, other poesies and books of poetry. But it was the rare man who gave the perfect gift.

God love you, Richard... and I love you, too.

She counted out her ammunition: three arrows. Given the

blunted ends, they wouldn't significantly injure Goggs, but they would definitely distract him. Maybe he'd get irritated enough to pull the carriage to the side of the road and try to take the crossbow from her. At least then she'd have an opportunity to escape.

Her strategy in place, she loaded the first arrow. She firmed her grip on her weapon, and, leaning out the window at an angle, managed to align her shot with Goggs' head. She pressed the trigger.

"Ow!" he yelled. "What the bloody hell...?"

With one hand, he swiped at his cheek. She saw with satisfaction the thin line of blood trickling toward his jaw. His bewildered gaze landed on her, narrowing at the sight of her weapon.

"You stop that, you plaguey chit, or you'll be sorry!"

"Let me go, or there'll be more where that came from!" she shouted back.

"Don't you threaten me, you little bitch—"

Vi ducked inside and reloaded. Assumed her position at the window again. *Pfftt.*

This time she broke the skin by his ear.

"I'll kill you if I have to!" Mad desperation glinted in his eyes. "Just like that French bitch, do you hear me? She laughed at me, taunted me when I tried to take the necklace from her—and now she's *dead*. Have a care, or I'll do to you what I did to her!"

Vi reloaded a third time. She aimed and fired. At that same instant, Goggs turned toward her, still shouting obscenities... and the arrow hit him straight in the *eye*.

Oops.

He let out a scream of pain. Both hands went to cover his bloody eye, leaving none on the reins.

"Gadzooks," she breathed.

That was her last thought before the carriage hit a rock and careened out of control.

Richard's heart seized when he saw the carriage lying on its side just up ahead. Its team had broken free, the horses specks in the distance. He brought Aiolos to a halt, jumped down, and raced to the carriage.

The door facing up was open.

"Violet!" he shouted, leaning in.

Empty. No sign of her.

He raised his head, scanned the surrounding fields—and saw them. Violet dashing through the knee-high grasses... being *chased* by Goggs. His momentary relief at seeing her alive and in one piece was replaced by a rush of pure rage.

In an instant, he was on Aiolos, riding toward them. Behind him, he heard his name being called, but he rode on with only one purpose in mind. *Protect my lass.*

Dirt flew as Aiolos' hooves cut through the field, Richard closing in on his target. Registering his approach, Goggs spun around. Richard got one look at the other's startled expression before he launched himself off his saddle and tackled the bastard.

They landed with a bone-jarring thud. Gaining the upper position, Richard rained blows down on his foe. He landed a resounding facer.

"Confess your sins, you conniving bounder," he snarled.

Goggs raised his arms, trying ineffectually to defend himself. "Stop. Please. I admit it was me—Monique, the necklace, everything!"

"Then this is for my brother." Richard plowed his fist into the other's jaw. "For betraying your *friend*."

"Wick has it all. Looks and ladies." Tears streamed from Goggs' eyes. "It's not fair!"

Richard's next punch made bone crack against his knuckles. "And this is for Violet. For drugging her, kidnapping her, and chasing her across a bloody field!"

Goggs gave a feeble moan, and his head fell to one side.

Richard was yanked backward. He fought against Kent and McLeod's hold.

"Calm yourself, Carlisle." Kent's tone was firm. "The last thing we need is another murder on our hands. Goggs is down for the count."

"I don't give a damn," Richard growled through a haze of bloodlust. "I'm going to tear him from limb to limb."

"Not that I disagree with the sentiment," McLeod muttered, "but you ken you have an audience?" The Scot jerked his chin to the right.

All of a sudden, Richard became aware of Violet... standing there in front of him like a dream. The one he feared he'd lost forever. An undertow of emotion swept through him as he hungrily took in the sight of her dirt-streaked face and tumbled locks.

"Lass," he said through ragged breaths. "Are you... all right?"

"I'm fine," she said tremulously. "I hit him with the crossbow, Richard! Got him in the *eye* and made him lose control of the carriage. When it tipped over, the door flew open, and I was able to make a run for it. The bounder started to chase me—but you got here in time."

Richard's lungs strained, his inner pendulum veering madly between relief and chaos.

Because now that the danger was over, his treatment of Violet rose like a spectre to haunt him. Could she forgive him for the way he'd acted? For doubting her and accusing her so unjustly?

Remorse and self-recrimination twisted inside him. Aware that Kent and McLeod were busy dealing with Goggs, he knew there was no time like the present to address his wrongdoing.

Pushing the words through his tight throat, he said, "Can you ever forgive me, lass? In the churchyard, I was a bastard to you. I know I don't deserve another chance but I—"

She launched herself at him, and he acted reflexively, his arms closing fiercely around her. Hope trickled through him. She was letting him hold her. That... that had to be a good sign, right?

"Why did you get so angry?" Her voice was muffled against his waistcoat. "Was it because of the ladies in your past?"

She'd figured it out. No surprise there. His lass was quick-witted.

"I didn't tell you everything," he said gruffly. "How the first one turned me down because she thought I wasn't handsome and charming enough for her. How the other duped me... planned to make me a cuckold. She was already pregnant with her lover's child and was only going to marry me if he didn't return. Luckily for all of us, he did, and she eloped with him."

"Butter and jam." Vi leaned back, her eyes wide. "Why didn't you tell me all this before?"

Swallowing, he said, "I didn't want you to think that you were getting a bad bargain. You're so beautiful and full of life—you could have anyone. And I'm... I'm..."

"You're the man I love," she burst out. "The strongest, fiercest, and most irresistible fellow I've ever met! Everything I could want."

Her words pelted him like sunshine. He absorbed their vital warmth. They dissolved the shadows of his past and made him blink in wonder at the brightness of his future.

Heart drumming, he said, "So you... forgive me?"

"Yes, of course." She gnawed on her lip. "The truth is I *was* acting, um, strangely. But I swear it had naught to do with Wick. I don't know what came over me—"

"You were drugged, lass," he said quickly. "Goggs put a powder in your cider that caused that reaction. He hoped to create a distraction, to throw us off his scent."

Her eyes widened. Then she shot an indignant look at the unconscious villain. "Thunder and turf, I should have taken his other eye out, too!"

"God, I adore you, do you know that?" Richard cupped her

jaw reverently with both hands, his voice trembling with the intensity of his feelings. "My brave, loyal, and terrifyingly resourceful lass. You are the rarest flower, Violet Kent, and I love you with everything that I am, now and forever. Will you marry me?"

Her eyes glimmered. "I already said I would."

"Say it again. I want to hear you say that you'll be mine."

"I'll be yours," she whispered. "Forever."

Unable to tear his gaze away from her, he said without turning, "Any objections, Kent?"

"Far be it for me to interfere," came the dry rejoinder.

His heart full, Richard gazed at his bride-to-be. "We're going to be so happy, lass."

"I know." Mischief joined the love in her eyes. "Now aren't you going to kiss me?"

"Brazen little minx, aren't you?"

She grinned. "You like that about me."

Since she was absolutely right, he saw no reason to contradict her. So instead he kissed her, she kissed him back, and the world faded to the blaze of love and passion...

Until Kent coughed and McLeod said loudly, "I see two words in your future, Carlisle: *special license*."

39

B ack at Traverstoke the next afternoon, feeling much more
the thing after a good night's rest, Violet gathered with her
family and friends in a private sitting room. Magistrate Jones and
Billings were also present. Ambrose had just concluded his explanation of yesterday's events.

"So, in the end, what began as an accident became a crime of
opportunity." The magistrate sat at the head of the circle in a
high-backed chair, his expression severe. "Miss Turbett pushed
Monique de Brouet, unintentionally injuring her. When Goggston
came upon the unconscious woman, he found the necklace on her
and tried to take it. But she came to, resisted, and he smothered
her."

"That is the gist of it, sir," Ambrose said. "It turns out that
Goggston was being hounded by the cutthroats from whom he
borrowed money. In trying to keep in step with his friends, he'd
landed himself in desperate straits. When the necklace presented
itself to him, he saw it as the solution to all his problems."

"Who would have thought Goggs capable of such evil?" Em
murmured to Violet.

Goggston's voice rang in Vi's head. *She laughed at me, taunted me when I tried to take the necklace from her—and now she's dead. Have a care, or I'll do to you what I did to her...*

At the time, Vi had been too focused on getting free to be frightened. But now an icy rivulet trickled down her spine. How wrong she'd been about Goggs. On the outside, he'd seemed amicable and innocuous yet on the inside...

She felt a hand on her shoulder; turning her head, she looked up at Richard, who was standing behind her chair. The understanding in his eyes anchored her. As ever, his presence was solid and reassuring.

"So how did he plan to get away with the crime?" Magistrate Jones asked.

"I don't think he had much of a plan, sir, but he did manage some inspired deviousness. When he saw Mr. Murray's signet on the chain around Monique's neck, he hit upon the idea of framing Mr. Murray by placing the ring in the victim's hand. Then he went and buried the sapphire necklace and the blood-stained pillow in the woods for safekeeping. As the days went on and no mention was made of Mr. Murray's involvement, he began to fear that his ruse hadn't worked."

Violet exchanged a guilty glance with Richard, and he spoke up.

"I would like to offer my apology again, sirs, for impeding the investigation," he said in grave tones. "I was trying to protect my brother, but instead I paved the road to hell."

"Having started down that road myself once or twice," Ambrose said dryly, "I know how tempting it can be."

Knowing this was her brother's way of saying bygones were bygones, relief poured through Violet. She wanted her family to adore Richard as much as she did.

"Back to Goggston," Ambrose went on, "he panicked that we were closing in, and he began to strike out. The day of the village fair, he planted the pillow in Mr. Murray's room. And then he drugged Violet, hoping to discredit her and Carlisle, whom he'd feared had caught his scent." Ambrose paused. "He got careless with that last move, and when Carlisle questioned him about the poisoned drink, he knew it was only a matter of time before he was found out. So he bought himself time by blaming Parnell and made a last bid for escape—kidnapping Violet to use as a bargaining chip."

"Very thorough, Mr. Kent," the magistrate said with approval.

"What I still don't understand," Billings put in, "is how Monique de Brouet arranged for such a clever switch. Now that I have the real necklace back in my possession,"—the banker's nod to Ambrose passed for gratitude—"the resemblance between it and the fake copy is extraordinary."

"The answer to that question was provided by Jeanne, the victim's maid, who Mr. Lugo tracked down and my sisters interviewed this morning. I shall leave it to them to share their findings," Ambrose said.

All eyes turned to Violet and Emma.

"You start, dear," the latter said with an encouraging nod.

Taking a breath, Violet began. "Jeanne told us that the necklace was, in fact, a family heirloom of the de Brouets. Monique's mama had had to pawn her favorite piece of jewelry to pay for their escape from The Terror. Growing up, Monique had heard much about the necklace and possessed a small portrait of her mother wearing the piece. When the necklace went up for auction several months ago, Monique recognized it straight away. She wanted to get back what she felt was hers: the legacy that had been robbed from her. According to Jeanne, Monique didn't think of it as stealing."

"Not stealing indeed," Billings muttered. "I paid for that jewelry fair and square. I have the receipt to prove it—which makes de Brouet no better than a common pickpocket!"

Beside him, Gabby wore a pained expression. "But, Father, if her family lost the heirloom due to such horrific circumstances—"

"Money paid equals ownership," the banker said sharply. "That necklace belongs to me."

Gabby bit her lip and fell silent.

Violet rushed to fill the awkward silence. "Jeanne says she tried to dissuade her mistress from the plan, but Monique became obsessed with reclaiming what she saw as her birthright. When she received an invitation to perform here, she saw it as a stroke of Fate. She had a fake copy of the necklace made, using her mama's portrait as a guide. She researched the house, obtained a map of its inner workings, and made her plan."

"Which went awry when she ran into Miss Turbett and Mr. Burns in the library," Emma added. "Those were Monique's fatal flaws: she was an opportunist and too reckless by far. She thought she could profit from discovering the lovers' elopement plans. Instead, she drove Miss Turbett to act rashly... which led her to lose everything."

"And this maid, Jeanne, why did she run?" the magistrate asked.

"She saw it as her sacred duty to protect the de Brouet name. She feared that if she stayed the truth would be coerced from her," Violet explained. "She didn't want to taint Monique's name —for the world to see the last of the de Brouets as a common thief. So she fled to preserve her mistress' honor." Vi paused, adding truthfully, "And she's also a bit batty."

"Poor thing was frightened half to death," Em said. "Jeanne may have survived The Terror, but it left its mark. And now she has no place to go. No position or pension after all those years of faithful service."

Strathaven narrowed his eyes at his duchess. "Why are you looking at me like that?"

"Because you're the most generous of husbands," Em said brightly.

"Bloody hell." He sighed. "Am I also now the employer of one batty old maid?"

"Did I mention you're clever as well as generous?"

The magistrate rose. "I believe I have all the information I require to close the case. The true villain is in custody, and the necklace has been returned to its rightful owner. The only matter left to attend to is the release of Mr. Murray, which I shall arrange for forthwith."

Vi shared a relieved smile with Richard.

Billings escorted the magistrate out.

When the door closed, Ambrose said, "All's well that ends well, I suppose. Mr. Murray is free and Goggston behind bars. And, as it turns out, Miss Turbett will have her happy ending."

"She will?" Violet said.

"Given her involvement—albeit unintentional—in Monique's death, Miss Turbett is ruined. She'll never live down the scandal. Since he wants grandchildren, Turbett decided that Burns is a better choice than none at all. Once the investigation is closed, Miss Turbett and Burns are headed to Gretna."

Richard exhaled, and Vi understood his reaction immediately.

"Oh no. Wick's debt to Garrity," she blurted.

"Mr. Murray's debt is to *Garrity*?" Ambrose said sharply.

Vi wanted to kick herself. "Um, I..."

"It's all right, lass," Richard said. "Your brother already knows about Wick's debt. He just didn't know to whom the money was owed." Rubbing his neck, he said, "I'll think of some other way to help Wick..."

"Why don't you just speak to Mr. Garrity?" Gabby said curiously.

Looking ill at ease, Richard said, "It's, er, not that simple, Miss Billings."

"Why not?" Gabby's blue eyes were puzzled. "Mr. Garrity is ever so kind and understanding. I'm sure if you'd just explain the situation..."

"Garrity is one of the most dangerous and ruthless men in all of London," Ambrose said flatly.

The shock on Gabby's face confirmed Vi's suspicion: the girl had formed a *tendre* for the moneylender.

Color suffused Gabby's cheeks. "I'm certain that isn't true, Mr. Kent."

"I'm afraid it is, my dear," Emma said gently.

"Well, I don't believe it." Gabby rose, her chin lifted. "If you'll excuse me, I have a few errands to attend to."

She left the room.

"Should I go after her?" Vi said worriedly. "Try to talk some sense into her?"

"You can try. We all can." Em sighed. "But that doesn't mean she's going to listen."

———

Closing the door to the suite that evening, Ambrose called for his wife.

Her voice drifted through the doorway of the adjoining room. "Just finishing up. I'll be right with you."

Sprawling on a divan, he declared, "This is the most exhausting party I've ever attended."

"You say that every time, darling," she called back.

"This time, I mean it." He shrugged out of his jacket and unknotted his cravat. "How many parties involve solving a murder, returning stolen goods, *and* planning a wedding for one's sister?"

"You're happy for Violet. And you like Carlisle. Admit it."

Marianne knew him too well. The fact was he did like Carlisle, whom he judged a reliable and honorable sort of man. One couldn't fault a fellow for trying to protect his kin, after all.

More importantly, there was the way Violet had blossomed under Carlisle's influence: overnight, Ambrose's middle sister had matured, her girlish exuberance transforming into the glowing confidence of a young woman in love. Ambrose could scarce credit the changes in the little madcap.

Carlisle, for his part, wasn't one to wear his emotions on his sleeve, but there was no mistaking the deep and abiding emotion in the Scot's eyes whenever he looked at his bride-to-be. As if he couldn't believe his good fortune.

Smiling, Ambrose leaned his head back and slung an arm over his eyes. Yawning, he said, "You're right, of course. I'm glad Vi will be settling down with a decent chap. But I can't say I'll be sorry to leave this place tomorrow."

"Tomorrow will come soon enough." Marianne's voice entered the room. "In the meantime..."

He removed his arm, looked up. All vestiges of fatigue vanished, replaced by hot, belly-clawing hunger. The front of his trousers instantly tented.

For his wife was standing in front of him—and she wasn't wearing a stitch.

"The party's not over yet, darling," she said with a sultry smile.

She lifted one knee onto the divan, then the other, straddling his lap.

Then she proceeded to affirm yet again that he was, indeed, the luckiest bastard alive.

40

TEN DAYS LATER

Filled with triumph, Richard swept his new wife into his arms. With the skirts of her lemon yellow travelling dress billowing over his arm, he carried her over the threshold. Compliments of the Tremonts, their bridal bower was the finest suite at Mivart's, a grand London hotel. The lavish room was done up in shades of ivory and gold and boasted separate sitting and bathing rooms attached to the main boudoir.

"This suite is the *utmost*, isn't it?" Violet said gleefully.

Captivated by her glowing eyes, he said huskily, "Aye. The utmost."

Setting her gently down on her feet, he watched with amusement as she tossed off her bonnet and gloves and scampered through the rooms like a curious kitten. Her explorations were shared with him via her adorably scattered commentary.

"... oh look, they've left us a bottle of champagne... by Golly, you ought to see the bathing tub, it's enormous... butter and jam, the bed is the largest I've *ever* seen..."

Her last comment got his attention. Grabbing the bottle of

champagne and two flutes, he went into the bedchamber... and stopped short at the sight of Violet on her back on the cream-colored counterpane. Her arms and legs were stretched out as if she were lying on a bed of snow, making a snow angel. She was grinning up at the canopy.

Joy punctured his chest. Standing in the doorway watching his wife at play, he vowed to protect her youthful exuberance for as long as he lived. Then she leaned up on her elbows, and the flirtatious warmth in her tawny eyes turned his thoughts from her adorable qualities to her womanly ones. Her lithe form and gorgeous face made his blood thrum, beckoning him like a fever dream.

But he didn't want to rush things. This was their wedding night; he wanted to make it special for her. And if the fact that she was a virgin made him just the slightest bit uneasy, he reasoned that it was only natural. For tonight was to be a first for him as well: he'd never taken a lady's innocence before.

Popping the cork of the champagne (and trying to push a related image out of his mind), he poured two flutes of the bubbly golden liquid and brought them over to the bed. He handed Violet one and sat next to her on the mattress.

He tapped his glass to hers. "Cheers, lass."

"Cheers." Her eyes out-sparkled the champagne.

For a few moments, they drank in companionable silence.

"Did you enjoy the wedding?" he said.

As McLeod had predicted, they'd wed by special license, the small ceremony taking place at the Strathavens' townhouse. It hadn't been a big to-do; they'd only invited her family, Wick, and a few close friends to share in the special occasion. Since all Richard had wanted was to make Violet his, he was well satisfied with the wedding. But was she similarly so?

"It was first-rate," she said happily. "Everything from the ceremony to luncheon to the tossing of the bouquet."

"Tell me the truth: were you aiming for Miss Billings?" he asked.

"It was the least that I could do." Violet's eyes grew shadowed. "But I'm worried about her... and Wick, too."

Richard shared her concerns. Three days ago, Wick had brought news that he'd negotiated a new arrangement with Garrity: he would be *working* off his debt to the usurer. He'd refused to elaborate further, and to Richard's protests he'd replied firmly, "For once in my life, I'm going to take responsibility for my actions. I have a chance to start afresh, and I'm taking it. I hope you'll support me, brother."

What could Richard say to that? His younger brother was finally growing up. He had to trust Wick to find his own way.

As for Miss Billings...

"Do you really think that she persuaded Garrity to give Wick a job?" he said.

Because as surprised as he was at Wick's newfound maturity, he was even more surprised that Garrity had agreed to new terms. The moneylender wasn't known for having changes of heart—if indeed the man even possessed that particular organ.

"I don't know. Gabby's being a clam about it." Vi nibbled on her lip. "And when Gabby doesn't talk, then one truly has cause for worry."

Richard got rid of their glasses and pulled her into his lap. "We'll be there for Wick and Miss Billings if they need us," he said simply. "In the interim, we'll have to trust that they will find their own happiness. As we have."

"Yes." The shadows lifted; she smiled at him. "What did you think of Harry?"

Richard had got on with Harry Kent immediately. The lad knew a thing or two about sports... even if he tended to view everything through the lens of science. During the wedding luncheon, Harry had expounded upon the importance of considering force, acceleration, and momentum in improving one's punch in the boxing ring. It had been fascinating, a conversation unlike any Richard had had before.

"I like Harry. And your entire family." Richard cleared his throat. "They are very generous."

In truth, their generosity had astonished and humbled him. The dowry put together by her family had been far more than he'd anticipated, enough for him to get his estate truly back on its feet. What was more, Strathaven had offered to stake Richard's breeding program for a share of future profits.

Richard wasn't used to getting help. As much as he appreciated it, he also felt... uncomfortable.

"It's not charity, you know." As ever, Violet was able to read his thoughts. "Think of it as an investment. My family knows, as I do, that you're going to make a smashing success of things."

God, her faith in him... he'd never known anything sweeter.

"What did I do to deserve you?" he marveled.

She looped her arms around his neck. "You didn't let a trifle like a dip in a fountain dissuade you from courting me?"

"Minx."

Unable to resist any longer, he kissed her. The simmering hunger between them boiled over, their lips and tongues melding, their mouths feasting. She tasted of crisp champagne and warm woman, a mix that made him feel drunk with desire. Before he knew it, his hands were tearing furiously at her garments, and hers were just as eager upon his.

When there was nothing between them, he lay her down and gazed at her. She was his Aglaea: the embodiment of grace and sensual vitality. Her glossy tresses framed her vivid face, a blush spreading like a sunset over her flawless skin. Her breasts surged temptingly, the tips stiff and needy. As her slender limbs moved restlessly against the counterpane, he glimpsed the sheen of dew on her pussy and swallowed.

Her charms... too innumerable to count.

"You're so beautiful," he murmured.

"I was about to say the same thing."

His chest burgeoned at the admiration in her gaze.

"I could look at you day and night," he returned.

"Gadzooks, you're not actually planning on doing that, are you?" Her eyes widened. "You know how much I hate waiting."

Her unmaidenly response made him laugh. "Far be it for me to make a lady wait, then."

He palmed one firm breast, his thumb skating across the rosy tip, and her bottom lip caught beneath her teeth. He swooped down to suckle her sweet tits, lured back and forth between the lovely swells. He took his time, laving her nipples, licking and teasing them until they were glistening and swollen and she was panting his name.

Only then did he move lower, trailing kisses down the smooth valley between her ribs. She squirmed and giggled when his tongue dipped into her belly button. Settling himself between her thighs, he pushed them farther apart. He inhaled the scent of her arousal, his erection jerking against his thigh.

Her legs twitched bashfully against his palms.

"Spread wider for me," he coaxed. "That's it, love, show me your pussy. No reason to hide such a pretty part of you, is there?" He petted her silky curls, then reverently parted her folds. "By Jove, you're drenched for me."

"Richard, you're driving me mad," she gasped. "*Do* something."

"Do you have anything particular in mind?"

Her hips lifted in a silent plea, and his mouth watered.

"God, yes," he said thickly.

Violet cried out as the relentless sensual assault of Richard's mouth brought her to a third peak. His kiss had been so hot, the wicked words he'd muttered even hotter. "Christ, I love licking your pussy. Tonguing your pearl. Come for me, give me more of your sweet cream..."

Since she'd done so—thrice—she judged they were ready to move onto other things. She wasn't afraid of what was to come. She wanted it. Wanted to be as close to the man she loved as possible.

"Richard," she said.

He raised his head. His strong jaw glistened with her juices, and his eyes were glazed.

"Come to me," she whispered.

His gaze flared, and then he surged up her body, taking her mouth in a sinfully erotic kiss. She felt the heavy thrust of his cock against her belly and shivered with anticipation.

"Are you frightened, love?" he murmured.

His loving concern undid her even more.

She cupped his jaw with both hands. "No, Richard. I want to be yours. Now."

"You are, Violet." He leveraged himself over her, and her hands latched onto the powerfully flexing muscles of his shoulders. When he notched his cock to her opening, moistening the blunt tip in her slick folds, they both moaned. "By God, you are."

He entered her slowly, and she felt herself stretching around him, tightness giving way to an exhilarating sensation of fullness. No pain... only wholeness. Oneness. He was so snugly wedged that she fancied she could feel each vein and ridge of his shaft, each delicious pulse. When he butted against some exquisite spot inside, she jolted.

"Am I hurting you?" He froze, his chest and neck taut with tension.

"No, no, keep going..."

He slid in deeper and deeper, and, inch by inch, he filled her body and her heart to overflowing. When he was fully seated inside her, she saw him looking intently at their joined bodies. His gaze lifted to hers, and the sheen in those scorched-earth eyes halted her breath.

In a gravelly voice, he said, "You're mine, Violet. As I am yours. Forever."

A vow. As deep and elemental as his presence inside her.

"Forever," she whispered. "I love you, Richard."

"I love you, lass."

He leaned down to kiss her and, at the same time, began to move. Slow, steady thrusts that awakened her to a new and intriguing pleasure. Her body moved instinctively to explore this new delight, her hips finding a rhythm to match his. All the while, their eyes remained open, their gazes connected, nothing hidden. This bold sharing intensified each movement of their heaving bodies.

The pace of his loving increased, his cock drilling deeper and deeper. Soon her hips were rocking from the force of his thrusts, and, to hold on, she wrapped her legs around his lean waist. The new position made each lunge of his iron-hard shaft graze her throbbing peak, and she moaned, tipping her pelvis back further, wanting more of that sweet friction. Suddenly, a dam burst inside her, convulsions rippling from her core, stronger than any she'd felt before.

"Lass, you're loving me so well," he groaned. "Can't stop, I'm going to spend so hard for you..."

A shudder passed through his large frame, his face contorting. He gave one last desperate surge, plunging so deep that he nudged her womb. A harsh groan tore from his chest as he detonated inside her, flooding her with pulse after pulse of his hot essence. Even after he was done, he continued thrusting slowly into their mingled warmth as if he couldn't get enough.

Staring up into her husband's sated face, she realized that she'd never felt so connected to another. So safe and loved. And they had a lifetime of this ahead of them...

He kissed her forehead tenderly. "What are you thinking, my love?"

Grinning, she told him the truth. "That I just found my new favorite sport."

His laughter filled the room and her heart.

EPILOGUE

"Last one back to the stables is a rotten egg," Violet declared. Richard grinned... because it was just the sort of thing his viscountess *would* say.

"I'll give you a head start." He tightened the reins as Aiolos stamped his hooves in eager anticipation. Ach, he knew just how the stallion felt. Since his marriage, he'd discovered the surfeit of delights that each and every day could bring—all because of Violet.

Wonder and pride expanded his chest.

The love of his life rolled her eyes. "As if I *need* a head start. I'm going to win this fair and square. On the count of three, ready? One... two... three!"

She took off like a shot. Riding as one with Moonlight, the silver grey Arabian mare he'd given her, she galloped through the heather and swaying grasses toward the newly renovated stables in the distance. She was riding astride, in the pair of trousers he'd had specially designed for her to wear during their romps together. He gave his lady as much advantage as he dared—not enough to let her suspect that he'd done so—before he gave his mount the signal. "Go, boy!"

Aiolos needed no further urging.

Exhilaration fired Richard's blood as he followed close on his beloved's trail. Somewhere along the way her bonnet flew off, but she seemed to take no notice, her thick, glossy braid flowing free in the hot summer air. He saw her sneak a glance back at him; that move cost her. Aiolos sprang forward, his longer stride beginning to eat up the difference between him and the dainty, fleet-footed mare.

But Violet, as Richard knew full well, was not the kind of woman to yield (except when he was making love to her and, by God, that was sweet). Sure enough, her elegant spine curved over the saddle, her slim, trousered legs tightening on her mare's sides.

Lucky, lucky mare.

Recalling how Violet had ridden *him* before breakfast made Richard lose a few precious seconds, but he snapped his attention back to the race as they neared the stables, Vi less than a length ahead. He could see the finish line—the entryway to the stable's courtyard—and the stone water trough sparkling just beyond.

Bending forward, he said, "Let's show the girls what's what, shall we, old boy?"

Aiolos made a noise that sounded like a laugh. The Thoroughbred burst into full speed, hooves thundering, spraying the air with clumps of gravel and grass. They crossed the finish line a heartbeat before their fierce competitors.

Richard dismounted as Tom, the stable hand, came jogging over. Tossing the gap-toothed lad the reins, he strode over to Violet. She put her hand in his, jumping down in a graceful motion.

"By Golly, that was brilliant!" Her cheeks were pink, her tawny eyes lit with good humor. "Admit it: Moonlight and I almost had the two of you."

"It was close," Richard agreed.

Aiolos huffed as if in protest, but when Tom brought Moonlight closer, the stallion adopted a more gentlemanly posture. He allowed the delicate mare to have the first drink from the round stone trough at the center of the courtyard before he took his fill. Then he stood beside her, nickering softly while she fluttered long eyelashes up at him.

"Methinks love is in the air," Vi said, grinning.

And who was Richard to interfere with love?

Turning to the stable hand, he said, "Give them a long cooling down, Tom—out to the orchard. The apples are in, and the horses deserve a treat."

"Yes, m'lord." Whistling cheerfully, Tom led the way, the horses swishing their tails in unison as they followed.

Once alone, Richard turned meaningfully to his viscountess. "Now as to the matter of the forfeit..."

"Forfeit?" Her brow pleated; she had a dusty streak across her adorable nose. "I don't recall there being any forfeit—"

Her words ended in a shriek because he'd swept her off her booted feet. In three steps, he reached the trough... and released her gently. She made a shallow splash. The water wasn't deep— about the same depth as that long ago fountain, actually.

"Gadzooks!" Appearing stunned, she gawked up at him from where she sat, knees splayed, shallow waves rippling around her. "What was that for?"

"Guess."

Her beautiful eyes narrowed. "Revenge?"

His smile deepened. Devil and damn, he enjoyed playing with her. In the months since their marriage, they'd worked together to improve their estate, and, with Violet at his side, it hadn't been drudgery. With her, labor was mingled with laughter and light-heartedness.

Every day held surprises. Fun.

"Well, you win." She looked down at herself and wrinkled her nose. "Crumpets, my jacket is soaked. I'd better save it from further damage or my maid will have my head."

Deftly, she unbuttoned the garment, a feminine version of a

man's riding jacket. She passed it over to him, and he took it absently, entranced by the sight before him. Beneath the jacket she wore a white linen blouse, which the soaking had rendered nearly transparent. In the bright sunlight, he could see the outline of her pink and delectably puckered nipples...

"Be a good chap and help me up, will you?"

He leaned over automatically, extending his hand, swallowing as he saw how the wet trousers clung to his wife's incomparable legs—

Her hand gripped his firmly, and too late he knew he'd been had. The next instant, he was pitching forward into the trough. His bride's merry laughter accompanied the giant splash.

Scowling, he pushed wet hair out of his eyes. "Think you're funny, do you?"

"Hilarious," she got out between chuckles.

Her joy was so infectious, so damned delicious, that he leaned over and kissed her.

One thing led to another, and she gasped, "Richard, not here. We're going to drown!"

Good point. Water sluiced off of him as he rose, taking Violet with him. He made for the nearest point of privacy. The scent of fresh hay, leather, and horses greeted them as he strode purposefully down the aisle of stalls, the half-dozen occupants twitching their ears curiously as he passed. He entered the empty stall at the end, kicked the door closed behind him, and deposited Vi on the bed of clean straw.

He tugged off his sopping boots and made short work of the rest of his clothes. Already, he was fully aroused, his erection bobbing heavily as he stalked toward his wayward spouse.

"You're still dressed," he observed mildly.

She was biting her lip, fighting laughter. "Really, Richard, this is beyond outrageous. You don't have to prove anything. I'll be the first to vouch that you're no stick-in-the—*oohhh*..."

Exactly. Yes.

Within minutes, he had her naked (a not to be overlooked benefit of allowing one's wife to dress in trousers) and panting beneath him. He licked his way over every inch of her. She returned the favor, driving him half out of his mind.

When he judged her ready, he flipped her onto her hands and knees. Clamping his hands on her slim hips, he entered her in a swift thrust that had them both moaning. They'd discovered that this was one of her favorite positions—yet another way in which she was perfect for him. Through a haze of lust, he watched her pussy spread around the thick, veined meat of his cock, taking him to the balls. Enveloped by her snug, wet heat, he knew he wasn't for long.

Sliding one hand under her, he found her little nubbin. He rubbed it, pressing it against the plunging steel of his rod. Panting, she arched her back, grinding her bottom into his thrusts. He gritted his teeth as his bollocks slapped her dewy lips, harder and harder, pleasure reverberating down his spine.

When he felt the first rippling clench of her release, he hauled her up by the hips, lifting her knees off the ground. He held her aloft, slamming his cock into her spasming sheath in rhythm to her breathless cries. Fire sizzled up his shaft, and he threw back his head, shouting out as he ejaculated. As he poured the hot load of his essence into his wife's generous keeping.

With a satisfied groan, he flopped onto his back, pulling her atop him. He tucked her head against his chest. Time slipped by unheeded as their heartbeats slowed in languid unison.

Finally, he said with reluctance, "We'd better get dressed before anyone sees us."

"In a moment." She lifted her head to look at him. "There's something I have to tell you first."

For a man who'd never been able to read women, it never ceased to amaze him how clear her thoughts were to him. From the shy yet eager expression in her eyes, he knew what she was about to say. His heartbeat began to race again.

His throat tight, he said, "Are you... we...?"

She smiled. "There'll be a new Murray sometime next spring."

Unable to find words, he kissed her instead. Emotion brimmed between them. When they parted, they were both breathless.

"Are you feeling well? Is there anything I can do—*by Jove.*" The realization made him jerk upright. "I just dumped my pregnant wife into a trough... made love to her in a *stable.*"

"I know. Wasn't it tip-top?"

He had no resistance against her flirtatious grin. Against the love and devotion in her eyes, a mirror of his own feelings. Cupping her precious face in his palms, he demanded, "Do you know how much I adore you?"

"I have a pretty good idea, but you can show me again if you want." Her glowing smile lit his world. "There's always the new gazebo to break in."

He laughed. Because life with Violet was an adventure... and always would be.

ABOUT THE AUTHOR

USA Today & International Bestselling Author Grace Callaway writes hot and heart-melting historical romance filled with mystery and adventure. Her debut novel was a Romance Writers of America® Golden Heart® Finalist and a #1 National Regency Bestseller, and her subsequent novels have topped national and international bestselling lists. She is the winner of the Daphne du Maurier Award for Excellence in Mystery and Suspense, the Maggie Award for Excellence in Historical Romance, the Golden Leaf, and the Passionate Plume Award. She holds a doctorate in clinical psychology from the University of Michigan and lives with her family in a valley close to the sea. When she's not writing, she enjoys dancing, exploring the great outdoors with her rescue pup, and going on adapted adventures with her special son.

Stay connected with Grace!

Newsletter: gracecallaway.com/newsletter

Reader Group:
facebook.com/groups/gracecallawaybookclub/

f facebook.com/GraceCallawayBooks

BB bookbub.com/authors/grace-callaway

o instagram.com/gracecallawaybooks

a amazon.com/author/gracecallaway

ACKNOWLEDGMENTS

For my readers who asked for Violet's story... this one's for you. I hope you had as much fun reading it as I had channeling my inner hoyden!

For my writing tribe who keeps me sane: Tina, you're the best partner-in-crime a gal could ask for. Diane, thanks for all your brilliant editorial feedback. Sandy, hugs for answering my panicked messages and sharing your expertise on all things equine.

For the creative geniuses behind my brand: Erin Dameron-Hill, Period Images, and Atomic Cherry Design, thank you for making my books and website so absolutely gorgeous.

For my family who burned the midnight oil with me on this one. For Candace, best beta reader and sister. For Brian, whose edits made me laugh and go, "Damn, that's good." You're the best, baby. And for Brendan, our little hero.